Midwinter

Nate let out his breath. The encroaching frost was gone, but the air remained chill and dry, tasting of old leaves and fire. "Evie—"

"That gives me two months," I said, and started across the plaza. The circle scuffed underfoot; any trace of blood was long gone, as was the mark on my throat.

Inside, though, my brain was screaming *midwinter! Midwinter! I'm not ready to be torn apart by the Gabriel Hounds.*

I'm not ready to die.

Praise for Margaret Ronald's first Evie Scelan novel,

SPIRAL HUNT

"I loved, loved, loved this book. . . . Fantastic, moving, thrilling—deeply thoughtful—and beautifully crafted."

New York Times bestselling author
Marjorie M. Liu

"[A] fun adventure, a promising start to a new series."

Locus

By Margaret Ronald

The Evie Scelan Novels

SPIRAL HUNT
WILD HUNT
SOUL HUNT

MARGARET
RONALD

SOUL HUNT

HARPER Voyager
An Imprint of HarperCollins*Publishers*

This is a work of fiction. Names, characters, places, and incidents are products of the author's imagination or are used fictitiously and are not to be construed as real. Any resemblance to actual events, locales, organizations, or persons, living or dead, is entirely coincidental.

HARPER Voyager
An Imprint of HarperCollins*Publishers*
10 East 53rd Street
New York, New York 10022-5299

Cover art by Don Sipley
ISBN 978-0-06-166243-0
www.harpervoyagerbooks.com

First Harper Voyager paperback printing: January 2011

Harper Voyager and) is a trademark of HCP LLC.

Printed in the U.S.A.

10 9 8 7 6 5 4 3 2 1

For my parents, who let me get as many books as I could carry from the library

SOUL HUNT

One

There aren't too many days when I wish I had never heard of the undercurrent, but Halloween's close to the top of the list, right after Marathon Monday and just before the date of the seer enclave's damn holiday picnic.

Halloween traffic for a bicycle courier is usually not much different from your basic day-to-day Boston mess: taxis, buses, SUVs resolutely ignoring the narrow nature of city streets, and an awful lot of cyclist-shaped blind spots. But there's enough of the undercurrent awake and in motion on Halloween that it's a perpetual distraction, and this year was no different. In the past, I'd had either a clubbing binge with Rena or Sarah's Samhain party to look forward to; this year, Sarah was so busy with managing her "community watch" that she'd had no time for the party, and Rena, well, Rena and I weren't speaking. On top of that, I had my own plans, which were not something to look forward to either.

All of this meant that on this particular Halloween, instead of threading my way back to Mercury Courier for another job on my beat-up loaner bike (the replacement ever since a curse-riddled jackass had turned my old bike into aluminum salad), I needed to stop for a moment's rest. Not that it helped much; even the salt tang of the harbor couldn't quite cut through the day's murk. I locked up my bike by the Boston Aquarium, made my way through a screaming gaggle of kids on their way to see the seals, and damn near collapsed out on the end of the dock.

Slumping against a piling, I closed my eyes. The air smelled of dead fish and kelp—the famous sea breeze that some people find so refreshing—and, below that, the many scents that my talent could distinguish, the ones that didn't quite exist in a rational sense. Burnt ginger, clinging to a woman in a business suit stumbling over the uneven paving stones; mud and cheap newsprint, following an entire tour group as they hurried to catch up with their umbrella-wielding guide; damp cats and cinnamon, hovering over the entrance to a building as if it were waiting for someone. Every scent had its meaning, though I could only understand them by association, and every scent laid a trail for someone like me—someone like the Hound—to follow.

Even in my worse moments, and there had been a lot of those lately, I could still focus on those scents, the pattern that they laid over the world, the sense they made. I sighed and blew on my hands, trying to make them feel a little less like they'd been immersed in ice water.

"Scelan," a woman's voice called somewhere below me. I ignored it, trying to hold on to the pattern a little longer. The scents sharpened, and a tang of fireworks crept through them. I opened my eyes, briefly cringing at the sunlight. No obvious, immediate source, though someone nearby was working magic. That scent is distinctive enough that it'll pull me out of anything else.

"Scelan! Hound! Are you even awake?"

I scanned the docks, then glanced down to see a figure in a heavy parka sitting in a motorboat just at the edge of the dock. The person pushed back her hood to reveal ash-blonde hair streaked with gray and a lined but carefully made-up face. "Tessie?" I said. "What are you doing off your boat?"

"Technically I'm not off it," she said, thumping the hull. "Are you free, girl? Something's wrong up the Mystic, and I might need your nose."

I hesitated—I was free, at least until Tania from Mercury Courier called to find out why I hadn't checked in yet. But there are things you don't do in the undercurrent, and one of those is favors for an unspecified return. It leaves the scales unbalanced—and a favor is a dangerous thing to owe. "You sure you need me?"

Tessie pointed, and I followed her gesture to see a thin line of smoke rising past the buildings. "I'll pay your standard rate, contract and everything," she called. "Just hurry up and come along."

"Coming," I said, and scrambled down the ladder into the boat. Tessie fired up the motor, and we skidded off across the harbor, skirting the yachts and boats drawn up along the shore for the season.

"I didn't catch it till just now either," she yelled over the roar of the motor. "It might be nothing, but my nets were tangled this morning, and I found two broken hooks in them—"

"In English, please," I called back. "I don't speak oracular."

"Could be nothing. Could be bad." She shrugged.

That was the problem with magic that let you get a look at the future. Most of the time it was so opaque as to be almost useless. Of the diviners I knew, Tessie made the most sense, and that wasn't saying much.

But how had I missed the scent of smoke? I'd even been actively using my talent a moment ago, and this much smoke should have caught my attention immediately. Granted, I'd been having off days these last few weeks, and today was no exception, but I was the Hound, dammit. I should have noticed.

I touched the knot of scar tissue at my throat, where a little horn-shaped mark deformed the notch in my collarbone. These days, I was more than just one Hound, if you wanted to look at it that way. "Tessie," I said, scooting forward and immediately regretting it as we hit the wake of a returning tugboat. "What do you need me for?"

She frowned and pulled up the hood of her parka, even though it couldn't have been nearly as cold for her as it was for me in my courier gear. "Depends on what we find. Mostly I just want someone on hand in case I have trouble."

Tessie's one of the fixtures of the magical undercurrent of Boston, though like everyone who made it through the years of the Fiana, she prefers to keep a low profile. (I'm the poster child for why doing otherwise is a bad idea.) As long as I'd known her, she'd never set foot on land, although the docks, the boats, and pretty much anything along the water's edge were hers to look after. Although I didn't entirely trust her—most magic is founded on stealing pieces of other people's souls and using them to subvert the laws of nature, so anyone in the undercurrent might regard you as a renewable resource—she rarely gave anyone any trouble. Come to think of it, this was the most agitated I'd seen her.

"Just keep your eyes open," she said finally as we coasted below the Tobin Bridge into the mouth of the Mystic River. "If something looks really wrong—holy shit."

That was an understatement. A small ship, maybe a yacht—from the looks of it more suited to the high-class marinas we'd just left—had been moored at the end of a commercial dock, next to several fishing boats. Heavy black smoke obscured the entire back end, orange glints sparking along the dock to the other boats. As we approached, a flapping, burning cable smacked across onto the closest fishing boat, leaving a trail of flame that rapidly expanded. "This is what you meant by bad?" I called, fumbling for my phone.

Tessie shook her head thoughtfully, though her

hand on the tiller didn't slacken. "Not quite. I thought . . . no."

A blare of sirens echoed across the water, and the sullen glow of the fire was joined by flashing red and white lights. Someone must have called it in before it really got going. I started to relax my grip on my phone, but stopped as a fresh gust of wind carried both smoke and scent across the water to us. Smoke, the char of things that were not intended to burn, and under it an acrid tang that I knew well: sweat and fear. "Someone's in there!"

Tessie bared her teeth, then shook her head. "There'll be more in a moment. Hound, can you steer?"

"What? No—not well anyway—"

"Then I'll let you off." She did something to the engine, and we skidded across the tops of the waves, right up to the side of the fishing boat. "You take care of any people, and I'll start a patterning to hold off anything else in the fire. And keep your senses open—tell me what you scent!"

I stood and caught at the ladder hanging off the end of the fishing boat, then had to lock my arms around a rung as my head swam. It wasn't seasickness, or even a head rush, but it also wasn't unfamiliar; I'd been having bad grayouts for a few weeks now. It was, however, poorly timed. Before I could call to Tessie, she'd steered to the side of the burning yacht, caught hold of the hull, and scrambled up, parka billowing behind her. For a woman so much older than me, she was surprisingly nimble.

I shook my head until the fog retreated a little, then hooked my arm around the next rung and hauled myself up, smearing salt and greasy residue all down my front. It didn't smell so much like fish as of predigested fish, and if I hadn't been nauseated before, this would have done it.

Somewhere here, though, amid the sparking fire—too much for me to put out, now, and the sirens were already coming close enough—someone was very scared. I turned my back on the fire and tried to catch that scent a second time, concentrating on the pattern, the pattern that had eluded me before and that *I should have noticed, dammit, even before Tessie found me—*

There. Not the stink of fear, strangely enough, but a clearly human scent, just ahead of me. I ran to the little door leading into the main part of the boat and slammed my shoulder against it.

Of course, it wasn't locked. I fell into the room, almost sprawling against the far wall. Someone shrieked so close to my ear I jerked away.

Blinking, I realized that whatever the fear had been, it probably hadn't come from here. A skinny teenage boy with his shirt off jumped away from a bunk with an even skinnier teenage girl on it. "Jesus!" the boy yelled, scrabbling for his clothes. "Jesus, who the hell are you—"

Good to know someone had even worse timing when it came to romance than I did. "There's a fire," I said, and pointed to the hatch. A few tendrils of smoke drifted across the light, proving my point. "Get your clothes and get out."

With the self-preservation instinct common to all teenagers, the kid backed off and glared at me instead. "This boat's private property, lady."

"Shut up, Devin," the girl said, yanking her shirt over her head. "How bad's the fire? My dad's gonna kill me if anything happens—"

"Not bad yet. But you want to get out of here, now." I closed my eyes and tried to concentrate again. Devin and his slightly more sensible girlfriend ("Shut the fuck up, Devin, and get your coat," she told him without even a backward glance) might be a lot of things, but they weren't the source of the fear-stink I'd caught. *Not here*, I thought, searching for the source of it, that familiar tang, *but close, close . . .*

The scar at my collarbone shifted like a trapped

snake under my skin, and my eyes snapped open. *You are hunting*, a voice like the cold breath of winter whispered in the back of my mind, and a chorus of murmurs followed it, like the shifting noises of a crowded kennel.

"I'm trying to," I muttered back. Devin's girl, having shooed him most of the way up the stairs, turned back to give me a wary look. I ignored her—but the Gabriel Hounds, the Whistlers, the Gabble Retchets whose mark I carried in my bone and whose Horn I had once called, they didn't. At the back of my mind, where the distinction between my own thoughts and those of this spectral pack blurred, I-or-one-of-them briefly wondered what her flesh would taste like torn from bone, what a chase she could lead us.

The Hounds were not a part of me and my heritage, nothing to do with my talent save a shared name. Well, and a canine echo in my past; an ancestor of mine way back had spent most of his life as a hound, and passed on some of his talents to a few of his descendants. But he hadn't, to my knowledge, had anything to do with the Gabriel Hounds. That was all my doing; they were a burden I'd taken up after claiming the Horn of the Wild Hunt from a walking dead man. At the time, I'd thought that I had no choice but to claim it; these days, I was less sure.

Moments like this just brought that regret home. "*No*," I said, and Devin's girl, maybe hearing an echo of the Gabble Retchets in my voice, fled. "No, I just need to find whoever it was that was scared."

You mean other than yourself? The Hound's amusement was almost manifest: a doggy grin, made much less friendly by the sheer amount of teeth in that mouth. But it withdrew, though I could feel it and the rest of that chaos-pack watching, awake and aware now.

It didn't matter, I told myself, even as a new wave of dizziness washed over me. I lurched to the stairs, hung on to a railing for a moment while the world shifted in and out of focus, and dragged myself up into smoke. Devin and his girl were gone, though I could still hear her yelling, and from the relief in her voice I guessed they were on the docks. Good. But someone else, someone scared, someone whose fear was like anise to the Hounds . . .

When I'm hunting, properly hunting, the world dwindles down to that one scent, and I can focus solely on it. This wasn't like that. It was as if the smell of smoke, omnipresent now and thick with melted plastic and oil, washed out everything else, save that one harsh burr of dread—

I turned to face the burning yacht. The boat I stood on might be saved, but that one would be a loss—and just then, someone emerged from the hatch that mirrored the one I stood at.

It wasn't Tessie; that much I could tell right off. For one thing, Tessie kept her hair cut short, not back in a thick gray ponytail; for another—and more important—Tessie had never had a beard that impressive. The man was bent double, probably tall to begin with but stooped under the burden he carried slung over both shoulders. I scrambled to the edge of the fishing boat, staring. He was carrying a man.

Worse, I knew that man. A sting of damp woodchuck and ash touched my nose, somehow aligned on the same thread of fear that I'd followed, and that was a smell I'd know anywhere: Deke, the pyromancer of the Common, the man who could see anything in a candle flame. The graybeard yelled something to him, but Deke hung limply over his shoulder. "Deke!" I called, but just then a gust of smoke hit me smack in the face, and the smell alone was enough to send me reeling.

The graybeard, one foot on the far rail of the yacht, glanced back at me. His eyes narrowed. "Stay back, girl!" he shouted. "She's going down."

I coughed black muck over my sleeve and tried to follow, but he crouched, still with Deke over his shoulders, and leaped off the yacht, landing on the next boat over, sending it rocking like a rowboat in a gale. Deke's scent (still alive, I could tell that much) and the scent of fear receded with him.

Well, now you know how the fire started, a dry, cynical voice said in the back of my mind. I snorted, then stopped. Where was Tessie? I risked a glance at the pier, where two fire trucks were already unspooling their hoses. No sign of her. As for scent—

I shook my head and spat again. Nothing. Even the smell of smoke was muted, subsumed by the taste of ice water in the back of my throat. "Shit," I muttered, and gauged the distance between the fishing boat and the yacht. It couldn't be that far; the yacht was snuggled up between the two boats to either side, and that man had made the jump with Deke on his back—

No one has ever accused me of good judgment. I ran for the edge and jumped, landing on a coil of smoldering rope. My ankle turned, and I went sprawling, smothering the fire under my leg. (Not the best firefighting technique, I'll say that right now.) Here the fire wasn't so bad, but Tessie wasn't up top. She had to be somewhere below, in the hold where the smoke would be worse—

I didn't let myself think. Instead I slid down the steps the graybeard had come up, trying to scent for Tessie—or anything, anything beyond the encroaching feeling in my own gut.

This is bad. A canine murmur settled around me, and for a moment I didn't just feel the shifting of the Horn under my skin, I saw the Gabble Retchets, the hounds of the Wild Hunt flickering in and out of existence, their shapes never quite congruent with real space. *We knew you were foolish, that you could make bad bargains, but not that you would throw yourself into the fire so.*

"Like you care," I said, pushing aside crates and charred boxes to reach the door.

We do care, another Hound said, brushing against

me as it paced past a fresh flame. *You carry the Horn. We do not want it turned to ash.*

"Yeah, well, I'm not happy about carrying it either. You'll get it back soon enough." I was sweating under my courier gear, and the smoke—God, the smoke was going to kill me soon, and if it was bad for me, then how bad did Tessie have it? I turned in place, trying to scent her, or at the very least figure out where she'd come in with regards to where I was now. "For now I just need to find her."

We could hunt her for you.

That turned the air cold, or maybe it was just the sweat on my skin freezing. "What?"

We could hunt her. Sound the Horn, call us forth, and we will hunt her for you. The closest Hound, the one currently in the shape of a great ashen thing with bloodied ears, grinned up at me. *It is what we are made for. Like you.*

That was not a comparison I cared to hear, now or later, but it didn't change the pressure at my throat. I didn't have to reach up to recognize that the scar had shifted, become a horn on a strap of leather slung round my shoulder, its weight light but insistent. I swallowed. "If I sent you to hunt her, you'd tear her throat out."

The Hound grinned wider. *Maybe not.*

Another snapped at the flames behind me. *You have already sounded the Horn once, incurring the Hunter's wrath. What is it to do so again?*

"More than I'm willing to do," I snapped, and pushed past them, my hands encountering nothing but cool air and shadow as they swept through. Even that, though, was enough to both chill and preserve me. I kicked a sack out of the way to find another ladder leading down into the hold. "Listen, I'm no more happy with this than you are, okay?"

The Hounds paused, fading. *Whatever gave you the impression that we were unhappy with you?* one asked, its head cocked to the side.

And that right there was another thing I didn't want to think about. Besides, there was Tessie, standing in the middle of a low-ceilinged, open room. This one was empty, stripped to the bare metal of the hull, and Tessie stood frozen in the middle of it, oblivious to the smoke curling around her head. I crouched and ran to her. "Tessie!"

"It's not here," she said vaguely, staring off into the smoke. "I'd thought—"

"Tessie, this boat's going up, and you need to—dammit." I caught her arm and pulled her down, so that her head was no longer wreathed in smoke.

She blinked at me, the whites of her eyes gone yellow and watery. "Don't," she whispered, though I doubted she was actually addressing me. "They might be out there—if we stay still, they won't see us—"

"If we stay still we are going to end up well done. Or maybe brined, depending on whether this boat sinks first. Come *on!*"

She shuddered, staggered, then leaned heavily on me. It was enough of an assent; I pulled her arm over my shoulders and practically dragged her to the ladder. The Hounds were gone—well, technically, they were still with me, but at least they had the tact to remain silent—and the next room was thick with smoke. But cool daylight shone through the way I'd come in, and I dragged Tessie toward the upper ladder.

We'd gotten maybe two steps from the top of the ladder before the first blast of water from the firehoses hit the decks, and with it came a last billow of smoke and oil scent. The stink of dead fireworks hit me like a cosh to the back of the head, and I stumbled out into light, losing my grip on Tessie and collapsing straight into the puddled water on deck.

Two

I came out of it propped up against what felt like a piling and with the feeling that something was missing. It didn't help that the first thing that met my eyes seemed to be a two-headed, human-sized cat talking to a blue rock. I squinted, tried to shake my head, then winced as my brain banged against the inside of my skull. Someone had put a dry blanket over my shoulders, and I pulled it up one-handed, rubbing it over my head until my hair stood up in spikes. That was one advantage to having short hair these days; with the braid I'd lost a few months back, I'd have been cold for hours.

"Of course she was here," a woman's voice said, high and clipped and with that edge that meant her patience was about to run out. Sarah. "I'd asked her to keep an eye out for any sort of trouble like this—Evie's always out and about, so it makes sense to have her on point and alert. I don't know why you see this as a problem." Sarah, lying her ass off.

I dragged the blanket off my head and into my lap and rubbed my eyes until they decided to function. The two-headed cat-thing was still there, but it was now revealed as Sarah, wearing a bright green coat and a cat-mask, the latter pushed up over her face so that it was out of her way. She must have come straight from her shop, the Goddess Garden, without bothering to ditch her Halloween gear.

How had she known to get out here so fast? I hadn't called, and Tessie certainly wouldn't have bothered.

Tessie. I pushed aside the blanket and got to my feet, digging my fingers into the piling to keep myself steady. I was on the dock, facing the water now, and from here I could tell two things: one, that yacht couldn't have been legally moored so close to those two boats, and two, that wouldn't matter anymore because there wasn't much of a yacht left. The fiberglass hull was cracked and charred, the deck no more than blackened boards, and the—whatever you call that little steering part near the front, over the hatch where I'd gone in for Tessie—was a melted lump of slag. Smoke still rose off the wreckage in damp black wisps, forlorn as the severed, ashy rigging, and a couple of firefighters stood on the dock, arguing over whether to go on board or not.

I didn't see Tessie immediately, but there was an ambulance not so far away. If I'd made it off the boat, then she must have too, right? I closed my eyes and tried to get a sense of the trail, since that at least would tell me which way she'd gone, then stopped.

I couldn't scent anything.

A chill coiled in my chest. No. No, I couldn't have lost my talent, it was the only thing that I knew I could rely on, it was the one thing that made me who I was. I swallowed down my panic and concentrated, hoping that I'd just been mistaken.

After a moment—a moment like groping blindly through an unfamiliar room for a light switch that might not even be there—I realized that I wasn't quite lost. But the scents that I was so used to following, the patterns that I as Hound could discern, were distant, as if behind a thick blanket of fog. Tessie's mantle of diesel fuel and makeup hung in the air, but to get a hold on it, I had to concentrate hard, shutting out everything else. Even the smoke, which was still so omnipresent that my clothes stank of it, was muffled.

I shuddered and opened my eyes. The grayouts, I was getting used to; the bad mornings where it was difficult to even decide to get out of bed, I could handle. But this—my talent, the one constant I'd always depended on, fading just like everything else—this, I couldn't stand.

"And furthermore," Sarah said behind me, "I think it's unconscionable that you're giving such a hard time to someone who under any other circumstances would be considered a hero. Is it official policy to interrogate anyone who drags a friend out of a fire?"

"That is not what we're doing, ma'am," another woman said, and my stomach turned over. I knew that voice. "And I think maybe you ought to let her speak for herself."

Crap. Not that I'd had any real chance of getting out of this anyway, but still . . . I turned around, leaning back against the piling again so that I was partly sitting on it. Sarah turned, pushing the cat mask a little further up her forehead, and the woman she was talking to—the one I'd misidentified as a blue rock, with perhaps some justification, tilted up her chin as she looked at me.

Lieutenant—or whatever rank she now held—Rena Santesteban of the BPD. Just the last person I wanted to see, and I suspected I was the same for her.

Sarah and Rena were, for a while, the closest things I had to friends, and a good example of why the periphery of the undercurrent is so unpredictable. You wouldn't think to link the two of them together in any other circumstances, but both have brushed up against the nasties of the Boston undercurrent often enough that they know to stay out of the depths, and both of them have, on occasion, expressed impatience with me. And just at the moment, they wore remarkably similar expressions.

That's where any connection ended, though. Sarah dealt in fringy stuff, the edges of the undercurrent that were so powerless you couldn't even move a handkerchief with them, and the New Age elements that even New Agers don't buy. But beneath that façade of fuzzy-headed optimism was a diamond-hard core of bullheaded idealism, with sprinkles on top.

Case in point: faced with the fragmenting chaos that was the undercurrent without the Fiana in charge, Sarah's approach had been to try to create a community watch, something for magicians and small-timers to be a part of so that they wouldn't always have to watch their backs. In theory a good idea, in practice less so, and in reality about as easy as yoking ferrets to pull a sled. Sarah knew better than to dabble in the scary parts of magic—and she'd been scared away from the truly numinous aspects of it, a fact that I still shared some blame for—but she still believed that we could, in time, all pull together.

Rena had gone the other way. Which was part of why we weren't on good terms at the moment. "Miss Scelan," she said, turning over a page in her notebook. "Can you tell me what happened here?"

"Where's Tessie?"

"She's all right," Sarah said. "Smoke inhalation, but the EMTs said she'll be okay. They've taken her to Mass General. Which is where you ought to be right now—"

"I'm fine," I said at the same time Rena said, "That can wait." She shot me a narrow look and waited. "I'm fine," I said again, very aware of just how not-fine I really was. "Tessie lives on the harbor, and she noticed the fire starting. I was nearby, so she picked me up for help. That's about all there is to it."

"Evie, you don't have to say anything," Sarah began, putting herself between me and Rena. "I can have Alison here in ten minutes, and she'll tell you that there's no legal requirement for you to talk to the cops right now."

I shook my head. "Alison's an environmental lawyer, Sarah. I don't think it's the same thing."

Sarah shrugged. "Doesn't stop her from offering her opinion on everything else." She got a faraway, goofy look in her eyes. Say whatever else you like about

Sarah, the woman's a romantic of the beyond-hopeless variety when it comes to her girlfriend.

Rena cleared her throat, still waiting. I put my hands on Sarah's shoulders and carefully pushed her out of the way. "Sarah, go away. I can handle this. Go—I don't know, go see what they're up to." I pointed to the far side of the street, where a few familiar faces—men I knew from the shallower parts of the undercurrent—were clustered, watching the husk of the yacht. Maybe Tessie hadn't been the only one to have caught on to the uncanniness of this fire.

Except that as far as I could tell, the only thing wrong was that it had happened at all. And you could say that for any number of fires across Boston on any given day.

The dreamy look dropped from Sarah's face, and her black brows drew together. "Fine," she said. "Fine. I'll be over here, and then—" She didn't quite look over her shoulder at Rena, but it was close. "Then I want to hear about this, okay?"

I nodded, trying to look honest and reassuring. From Sarah's sour expression, it didn't work. She retreated, leaving me on the dock with Rena.

You know that feeling you get when you run into an old ex? And for whatever reason—it's too soon, you're still dating his best friend, the breakup involved his stealing your stereo—you know there's no way to have any kind of civil conversation. Yeah. Take that and wring the romance out of it, then add a good dose of female friendship—and if you've made it through junior high you know how potentially poisonous that can be—and you've got a pretty good idea of how glad I was to see Rena. We'd been good friends, to the point that I'd cried on her shoulder after breakups and she'd thrown up in my bathroom after too much clubbing. But she'd cut off ties with me after the whole mess involving the Horn, mainly because I'd been so damned closemouthed that I'd ruined her case and, depending on how you looked at it, gotten her partner badly hurt.

The thing was, Rena had been completely justified in cutting those ties. I'd hidden too much, and I hadn't thought about the consequences for anyone but myself. And of all the times to run into her again—

"So since when have you been playing harbor patrol?" I asked.

"What is your relationship with 'Tessie'?" she asked without looking up.

"Business contact. I've done some informal work for her over the years, usually just research. Seriously, Rena, what brings you out here? You're usually not in this part of the city. I didn't even think you were in this precinct."

Rena turned the page over without looking up. Sarah might hide behind her status as an outsider, as someone who dealt with the undercurrent but didn't let it touch her, but she had nothing on the armor Rena put on when she was in full-cop mode. No wonder I'd registered her as a blue rock when I was so out of it.

"Do you know the owners of this boat?" Rena continued.

"No. At least I don't think so; the only person I know who owns a boat is Tessie, and this wasn't hers." I hesitated a moment, remembering Deke and the big guy who'd carried him out. Deke was, unfortunately, trouble. The man liked fire; he was a pyromancer, after all, and he could see things in flames that I sometimes didn't even see in real life. But he stuck to stuff like newspapers, branches, maybe a couple of open grills if he was lucky. Not a whole damn boat.

And besides, if he'd been the one to set the fire, I thought, he wouldn't have smelled so damn scared. Deke wasn't scared around fire, the same way I wasn't scared of big dogs (quasi-immortal chaos-beings aside). If I could just find his scent again, take time to sort out the impressions before the boat sank completely and the nullifying sea devoured it . . . if my talent hadn't deserted me completely now . . .

I've never been a good liar, and Rena is very, very good at reading silences. She glanced up at me, her mouth a hard thin line. "You don't think so?"

I opened my mouth to answer, and tasted ice water and ferns in the back of my throat. A cold coil twisted down from my stomach, and the first sparks began to flicker at the edges of my vision. Great. "No," I said. "Jesus, Rena, you know me. Do I look like the kind of person who hobnobs with boat owners? I think you need some kind of . . . of permit for that. Or maybe a McMansion somewhere."

The corner of her mouth twitched up, but Rena wasn't about to let herself smile. "Why did you board the Mirabelle first?"

"Mirabelle?" I glanced over my shoulder at the fishing boat next to the dead yacht. My vision kept graying out; never quite fading, but color going out of the world one second and returning the next. It was like trying to watch a film projected on water. "You mean the green one? There were people on it. Tessie dropped me off there, then got on—boarded—the burning one to see if she could help."

"Seems a strange thing to do, if she didn't know the owners."

"Yeah, well, that's Tessie for you. She wanted to check it out." This was all starting to piss me off, and since that little thread of anger was about all I had that reached through the fog, I held on to it tight. "You know," I added, lowering my voice. "*Bruja* shit. That sort of thing."

The tip snapped off Rena's pencil. "You can take that *bruja* shit," she whispered, the last two words—her usual terms for what I had to deal with on a regular basis—coming out with a poisonous sibilance, "and you can drop it right back in the harbor where it came from."

"Then I guess I got nothing more to say to you. Because if you don't want to hear about any of the undercurrent, then there's only so much I can explain."

As if to prove my point, the gray sparkles started up again. Great. I was going to pass out onto my old friend, and I'd be lucky if I just ended up in the drunk tank for it.

"Evie—"

"No." I shrugged my jacket back into place, hoping that motion wouldn't throw off my balance even more, and turned as if to go. "Either you're sticking to your guns, in which case I can't tell you any more, or you want to know everything, in which case it's gonna be a shitload of magic, okay? Make up your mind, because until then I'm gonna stick to my side and not bother you with anything that isn't your business."

Whether it was the momentary anger or just my body deciding that it was done messing with me, color and sense began to filter back into the world as I turned away. Rena cleared her throat. "It is my business," she said quietly. "When it becomes this—" and I didn't have to look to know she was gesturing to the smoldering hulk in the harbor, "—it is my business."

That was true, as far as it went. But I didn't have the energy to convince her that you couldn't separate magic from business. I didn't think Deke had started the fire, but I'd do some checking up on my own, and if it turned out differently, I'd come back to Rena. Until then, she could whistle for me. "You know where to find me," I said over my shoulder. "If you decide you can handle some of the weird shit, then come on over."

On the far side of the street, the muttered discussion between two men in cheap suits had turned into an actual argument. Both were shadowcatchers, the bottom-feeders of the undercurrent, trading in loci that wouldn't power any kind of magic beyond a twinkle. Sarah, as always, had stepped into the middle of the fray, trying to calm everyone down. "That's not the problem right now," she said as I reached her side. "Until we know what happened—and I'd like to stress that we don't know that anything unusual happened—then there's no reason to go making a fuss."

"Fuss? Fuss? What is this fuss?" the skinnier man snapped. "No, what I am saying is that if the community watch cannot be bothered to, hah, *watch* for this sort of aetheric disharmony, then what good is it?"

"Don't start with the ether stuff again," muttered his compatriot.

That at least was enough of a distraction. The skinny one was someone I knew, vaguely; he called himself the Elect of the Order of the Revealed Golden Veil of Isis-Sophia, or something like that with a couple extra titles tacked on. He was pretty harmless, an academic adept, of the kind that brush up against real magic once or twice in their lives and immediately dive headfirst into the esoteric cruft of centuries. On the rare occasion that an academic adept wanders into something huge, the result tends to be unpredictable, and by that I mean anything from blowing up someone's house to releasing ugly things into the steam tunnels under Boston College. I was pretty sure the Jesuits had taken in the last guy to do that, and after I'd helped with the cleanup, one of the chaplains there had given me an official, if quiet, commendation. (I'd also come away from the cleanup with a knife scar in my left buttock that I preferred not to think about.) This sort of person was what the undercurrent now consisted of, since the big guys on top had been taken down. The Elect, Tessie, Deke . . . the small fry.

I touched Sarah's shoulder, grimaced as the cat mask turned toward me, and moved so I could see her face. "All set. Listen, I—"

"You're sure?" She caught my forearms, searching my face. "Evie, what happened?"

"Pretty much what I told the cops. Tessie knew there was a problem, came to pick me up, and I had to go into the boat to get her out. I'm still not sure what the problem was—" something to do with Deke, undoubtedly "—but I can check it out with her later on. Listen, did Nate get in touch with you about Katie?"

"Katie?" She looked away, first at her hands, then at the two small-timers. "You mean—"

"For tonight," I said. Nate's little sister was nine years old, and she'd become very attached to Sarah and Alison. And me, though that didn't speak well to her tastes. "And did you get the list I asked you for?"

"Oh yeah. That was no problem." Sarah dropped my arms and started rummaging through the little crocheted purse she carried (how she kept more than a set of keys in there was beyond me, but then again I preferred to lug around my Mercury Courier bag). "No, tonight's fine. Alison will be over around nine. I pled religious holiday to reschedule the watch meeting, but there's enough overlap between groups that I actually have to attend a Samhain ceremony or I'll get called out on it."

"Sarah, your Samhain rituals usually include a big party and someone throwing up in the back room."

"Yeah, makes me sorry I couldn't plan one this year. I guess I'll have to go through with the whole meditative observances." She grinned at me. "Like your plans are much better. What, you finally wanted some quality alone time with Mathy McBonyButt?"

"Please tell me you don't call him that around Katie." I was an only child, but one thing I knew about sibling dynamics was that you never, ever gave a younger sister a new name to call her brother.

"Only around you, girl." She finally produced a paper folded up into a tight square, a bright green flyer wrapped around it. "I also printed off the schedule for the watch meetings—we could really use you there, you know. The other page lists all the names I could find. But this is folklore, so there's a lot of redundancy—I mean, Wodan isn't always the same as Odin isn't the same as Wutendes, not in these circumstances."

"So long as the names are all here." I took the paper and unfolded it. She'd listed the leaders of the Wild Hunt, from all the different traditions where that legend reasserted itself. Maybe fifty or a hundred names, most with epithets like "blood-handed" or "vengeance" or "corpse-god." Nice guys. "Thanks," I said, and tucked the paper into my breast pocket. My fingers brushed the knot of scar tissue at my throat, unnaturally cool, and I felt the Hounds stir.

"Welcome," Sarah said. "But I thought your research into the Wild Hunt was done, Evie. Didn't that all end a little while back?"

At the back of my mind, one of the Gabriel Hounds let loose a low chuckle, like the sound an ogre might make when devouring an exceptionally tasty baby. "Not really," I said, a little too loudly. "Soon, though. I'll let you know what happens."

Sarah gave me a strange look. "You do that," she said, but just then one of the shadowcatchers—not the Elect, but the other—took a swing at his fellow. "Whoa, whoa, whoa!" she yelled, interposing herself between them. "What the hell, guys?"

I glanced over my shoulder. Rena was still at the dock, interviewing Devin and his girlfriend, but her partner Foster had noticed the commotion and was headed our way. The cool October light picked out a livid pink scar, brilliant against his dark skin, that ran down his cheek, narrowly missing his eye. I felt the Hounds shift again. That wound—as well as a number of others that I couldn't see but knew were there—was the result of an echo of these Hounds attacking Foster, and a major reason why I didn't blame Rena for hating me.

For just a second, I tasted blood in my mouth—not real blood, but the memory of it, and the Hounds' quiet approval. I gagged, clamped my teeth together, and backed away, bumping into Sarah. "See you later," I managed, and hurried away from the pier, trying not to run but really, really wanting to get out of there. Because maybe if I did, I'd stop salivating at the thought of human flesh.

Three

The afternoon had already turned toward evening by the time I got back to my bike, and either trick-or-treating was running late this year or I'd made good time, because I damn near ran over about twelve different clusters of kids on my way into Allston. They knew to look out for cars, but one person on a bike? Not so much. Not even the flashing lights clipped to every available surface got their attention.

Scent didn't help me so much when I navigated, so I was somewhat able to ignore the lack of it, concentrating instead on the costumes and the traffic. Halloween for me as a kid had always been one big blur of candy and plastic costumes, at least until I hit twelve and it switched over to egging cars and worse. I'd done enough on Halloween nights not to be nostalgic about it.

And tonight—I resisted the urge to touch the scar at my throat—would just add to that.

The lights in Nate's apartment were dark, so he and Katie were probably still out getting the year's worth of processed sugar product. Which was good, because I wasn't doing so well—the sparks at the edge of my vision had returned, heralding another grayout—and I really didn't want them to see this. I locked my bike to the railing, then made it up the porch stairs before sagging against the wall.

I slid down until my butt hit the boards, hands pressed against the back of my neck. I took a deep breath, then another, trying to focus on Nate's battered old running shoes. Didn't work; the world kept going in and out of focus and—worse—in and out of color.

It hadn't been this bad in a while. The taste of ice water and ferns clotted up in the back of my throat, and I scrunched my eyes tight shut, reminding myself that I wasn't underwater, I could still breathe. After a moment, the cold shivers passed, and I tilted my head back till it bonked against the siding of Nate's apartment building. Made it through another day.

There was probably some psychological term for whatever was happening to me. It wasn't quite PTSD, because I hadn't been through enough for that to really happen, right? Besides, for that I'd be flashing back to whatever trauma I'd encountered—my run-in with the hounds of the Wild Hunt, maybe, or the shoot-out under Fenway—not feeling as if I were underwater. Not remembering what should have been a triumph.

No, more likely I'd worked myself too hard, done too much, and now I was just worn down. Courier work lessened a bit at this time of year, not quite to the trickle it would be during the holidays, but enough that I usually had some breathing space in October. I'd even hoped that the Sox might help me out of it, but while this year they'd made it into the playoffs, they'd then shot themselves in the foot, reloaded, and shot the other foot. Metaphorically speaking. So baseball season was effectively over, unless I wanted to pick one of the two West Coast sun-boys for a consolation cheer. Most years I did that just so I could scope out who'd be up for trade, but somehow this year I just didn't have the heart for it.

Could be worse, I told myself sternly. I could be

in Tessie's shoes, in a hospital with God knows what wrong with me, or like Foster, mauled and recovering. *So stop fucking whining, Evie.*

I nodded, as if answering myself, then took a deep breath and tried to believe it. At the edge of my senses, the smell of cheap chocolate and dry leaves settled in, a purely real smell with nothing of the undercurrent about it, the kind of scent that anyone with a working nose could detect. And, along with it, warm polished wood with a tang of something wilder, and electric blue like a static shock writ large in the way that children's scents were brighter and more forthright than adults'.

My eyes snapped open. That wasn't a normal scent, that was one my talent detected, and it—

"Evie?" What felt like a gauze-wrapped cannonball hit me in the stomach, and I nearly fell over, the air going out of my lungs in a whoosh. "Evie, I knew it was you! Look, Mr. Houck down the street was giving out whole Hershey bars!"

Something pink and twinkly hit me in the nose, and I sneezed. "Hi, Katie."

"Hi! Nate told me you'd be over for Halloween, and guess what Alison said she'd come over too only then I'm going over to watch movies with her and look, a whole Hershey bar!" Katie Hunter—nine years old, small for her age and dressed as a pink fairy princess—sat back on her heels and held up the item in question, beaming. "Do you like my costume?"

"It's, uh, it's very sparkly." I'd never gone in for pink. Except for fifth grade, which does not count, and a jury of my peers will back me up on that.

She grinned, exposing a gap where she'd recently lost another tooth, then regarded me critically. "You're not in costume."

"Was I supposed to be?"

"Nate is." She pointed at the man coming up the stairs onto the porch, dressed in a lab coat and goggles. They made him look more than a little ridiculous, which I supposed was the point, but underneath the coat he wore the same fraying shirt and jeans that I'd gotten very used to. Most of Nate's clothes were like that; he was one of those guys who look like they've been put together from spare parts, all knees and elbows, stretched out like a scarecrow who'd spent time on the rack.

Although, I admitted, he did seem to be inhabiting his skin a little more easily these days. That was probably the one good thing that could be said for the curse his father smacked him with. And call it a flaw in my standards, but I rather liked how he moved, all gangling and graceless. I grinned at him, and the last of the grayout faded from my bones.

"He was supposed to be a wizard," Katie stage-whispered to me. "To go with my costume. But he forgot and he had to get something at the last minute." She turned and gave him a look that I swear she must have learned from Sarah, the see-what-inferior-materials-I-must-work-with look. "So instead he's an evil scientist who's kidnapping fairies and turning them into trolls."

"Trolls, huh."

"All in the name of science," Nate said, and held out his hand. I took it and let him pull me up to stand beside him. His fingers were warm against mine, and even though that flicker of scent—his real scent, the one I would know him by anywhere—had faded from my perceptions, somehow it didn't matter so much.

I pretended to look him up and down critically. "You don't get too many mad mathematicians, do you? More mad chemists or physicists."

"That's what my advisor says. But once my dissertation is done, I'll show those fools who called me mad. Mad, I tell you!" He attempted an evil laugh, which faded into a chuckle as he mussed his little sister's hair. "Besides, tonight I'm whatever Katie tells me to be."

Katie pushed his hand away, and Nate turned to face me fully. "Are you okay? When we came up the street, you looked like you were barely moving—I didn't even know it was you."

Damn. "I'm all right," I said. "Had a rough day."

Nate, however, wasn't the kind to be easily deflected by something that noncommittal. "You smell like smoke."

"I do? I mean, still? Crud. I thought that would have gone away."

A thin line appeared between Nate's brows. "You didn't . . . Evie, how often do I smell something that you don't?"

This was not a conversation I wanted to be having just yet. "You mean when you're like this?" I asked, looking him up and down. With any luck, the reference to his curse—and the shape it forced on him—would be enough of a distraction.

He stilled a moment, perhaps startled that I was so openly talking about his other shape, but his lips curled up in a slow, secret smile. "Even when I'm . . . not myself," he said. "You're the much better hunter."

He put his hand on my shoulder, and I stepped closer, leaning into him. Katie made a face that was mostly for form's sake as Nate put his arms around me. "Let's hope I never have to prove that again," I said, and reached up to kiss him.

It didn't quite feel natural yet—relationships and I haven't had a very good history—but something about being closer to him made the world come together a little more. He tasted like coffee—not good, plain unadulterated coffee, the kind I like, but the weird stuff with flavors and too much sugar and probably frothed milk of some kind. Even if I couldn't stand the sorts of things he drank, I liked how they made him taste. I smiled against his lips, then stepped back. "Alison's coming over later tonight, yes?"

"At nine!" Katie hurried up to the door and hopped there, waiting for Nate to unlock it. "We're gonna watch movies all night."

Nate shook his head and went to let us in. "If Child

Protective Services ever finds out I'm letting you do this on a school night, I'm going to be in so much trouble."

"But you're not worried about that," Katie pointed out. "Because otherwise you wouldn't be joking." Nate glanced at her, a frown touching his brow. "Besides, they won't find out."

The last words came out with a peculiar finality, and this time it was my turn to give Katie a hard look. Some kids were more perceptive than was good for them; in Katie's case, this was compounded by a hefty dose of the Sight. So far, she'd had it under control, but now and then she came out with pronouncements that shouldn't have come from a nine-year-old. It was troubling, as was the fact that she'd already brushed up against more of the undercurrent than was good for her.

Still, for the most part she was a normal kid, as proved by the thump as she rattled up the stairs, still chirping about movies and Hershey bars and pixies. "I got the list," I said to Nate, quietly enough that she wouldn't hear. "I'm going to go through with it tonight."

"You're sure?" He reached out and touched two fingers to the scar at my collarbone.

"Nate, earlier today I was drooling over their remembered taste of human blood. I can't deal with having them with me any more. And—" I swallowed, very aware of how the Hounds listened. "And I'm getting too used to it."

He looked skeptical at that, but stepped back anyway. "Then go on up. We've got a few hours to kill; you might as well have dinner with us."

The next few hours were mostly taken up with getting Katie to eat something that wasn't pure sugar. I ate as much of her Halloween loot as she'd let me have just to get it away from her, which just left me more jittery than before. Nate handled it all with weary ease. He'd know, after all; he'd been through this many times.

His mother's death had landed him *in loco parentis* for a much younger sister, and he'd wrenched his life into a new pattern so that he could watch over Katie as she deserved. That was part of the reason for the early gray in his hair and the hollows under his eyes. It was only in the last couple of months that he'd started to find some balance, and half of that was because at least one night a week I watched over Katie while he prowled through what little wilderness was available in Boston. And if there had been a few more coyote sightings, if the feral cat population was both down and scared, well, those were acceptable side effects.

It'd be flattering me to say that I was the cause, but I'd certainly helped matters along. Or, to look at it from another point of view, I'd made things worse by dragging him into contact with the undercurrent. Maybe the actual curse hadn't come from there, but he'd been more susceptible because of me, and that was even before he'd been thrown into a quarry, before I'd had to beg for his life back.

Bad bargain, the Hounds had said about that, and I touched the lump at my throat again. The same subconscious murmur responded, and I shivered.

Eventually, Nate settled down next to me, jolting me out of my thoughts. "Alison's here," he said, touching my knee with two fingers. "She'll watch Katie while we're gone."

I leaned back against him. It wasn't particularly comfortable; Nate hadn't been designed for comfort. But he was warm, and the back of my head fitted nicely against his shoulder. "Are you sure about this?" I asked.

"You asked me that already."

"I know. I just . . . it'd make more sense for you to stay here, rather than run off with me for an evening."

His mouth crooked in something that wasn't quite a smile. "Not everything makes sense. I learned that a while ago, and with you I'm starting to actually understand it."

He had a point. But I had to try. "You know I can do this on my own."

His hand stilled on my knee. "I know," he said. "And if you ask, I'll stay here."

For just a moment, I was irrationally angry that he'd given me the choice; this was a lot easier when someone else did the deciding. But the choices, and the consequences, were up to me. "Come with me," I said, and pushed away from him. His eyes crinkled up at the edges, and he took my hand.

Sarah's girlfriend Alison, a slender black woman with a runner's physique and prematurely graying hair, was on the stairs with Katie, arguing over what movies to watch. She made an odd sort of fairy godmother for Katie, though no less than Sarah and I did, I supposed. But the longer she stayed up with Katie watching squeaky-voiced heroines defeat ultimate evil, the less time Katie would have to tinker with magic.

"Sarah says hi," she said between Katie's assertions about Halloween and how awesome it had been and how three pirate-costumed fourth-graders had gotten into a fight right in the lunchroom. "She claims she'll be meditating, but I suspect she'll just take the chance to get some uninterrupted sleep."

"Thanks," Nate said, sliding his jacket on. There were patches on both elbows and an unidentifiable stain on the back, probably remnants of the jacket's former life. "I know you had a lot of work to take care of."

"Still do. But damned if I'm doing it tonight. Sorry, kiddo." She scruffed Katie's hair, and Katie hugged her back. "Get going, you two. This town closes up around two o'clock."

"That's what we're counting on," I said.

City Hall Plaza isn't a pretty space even on the best of days, and tonight it was pretty damn bleak. Unrelieved stretches of concrete, the looming block of brutalist architecture in the background, and, if I listened or stretched my senses, the faint sounds of the local pubs still holding out till last call.

"Why here?" Nate asked as I locked my bike to one of the racks by the road. "It seems a little weird to do it right out in the middle of everything."

"Because this is a goddamned desert at night," I said, smacking the lock into place and walking out into the plaza. "And I don't know of any other places where we can count on few people showing up. Not on Halloween."

"Maybe a school? Office building?"

"You're kidding, right?" I glanced over my shoulder at him. "Remember high school? Two years running I snuck into the science labs and set shit on fire. No, this will do *because* it's out in the open." And tonight, tonight I wanted this out where it wasn't hidden. So much magic went on furtively, in the interstices, that I wanted to draw a distinction between that and what I did.

Because I wasn't a magician. As much as I'd been a part of the undercurrent, as much as I depended on it and used it and craved the hunt that my talent gave me—or had given me—I'd always kept that distinction in place. It wasn't much, and it sure as hell hadn't kept the taint of the undercurrent from me, but it was enough. A magician would have kept the Hounds to hand, would have reveled in the kind of power they provided; a magician would have warded her home and summoned entities to do her work at the first sign of the grayouts.

A magician wouldn't have bothered to return the Horn of the Wild Hunt.

I glanced around as we descended into the plaza at Government Center. Empty plaza, check, a few stragglers heading home, check . . . okay, not quite empty. Even though it was cold enough that my fingers were starting to go numb, a few people had staked out a spot right by the plaza. "Okay," I said, looking back the way we'd come. "So it wasn't such a good plan. Let's see, the Common's out, but if we wait maybe an hour we should be all right—"

Nate didn't hear me. When I turned back, he was already headed toward the little group, shoulders hunched down into his ill-fitting jacket. I cursed and followed, skipping a little to catch up.

Trouble is, the man's got longer legs than I do, and he's surprisingly quick when he wants to be. Which meant that I got there a little after he did, just as he was asking if they wouldn't mind moving on, just so he could clear out the space before tonight. Most of them looked like office workers, maybe spilling out from a party of their own, come to bitch about their bosses and pass around a bottle of something. Not too far from what I used to do with a few friends back before I went on the wagon, except without the ties and with Mad Dog instead of whatever pretty white wine was currently sending up a fresh tang through the frost. Anyway, they looked like they didn't quite buy Nate's story of needing to check the area before a concert tomorrow, but most of them looked as cold as I was, so they weren't arguing.

All except for one, a doughy guy in shirtsleeves and a wide purple tie with Mickey Mouse printed on the end in a pose that was probably meant to be ironic. I didn't need my talent to smell the booze coming off him, and for whatever reason—maybe he knew that this was technically illegal—he wasn't having any of it. "Bullshit," he said as I reached them. "There's no concert here tomorrow. You're fulla shit."

"Vinny, please," one of the women muttered. "I'm cold."

"Doesn't matter," I said, catching up to Nate. "Look, it's a nice night, there's a bar right there where you can get a decent drink—"

Nate, though, still wasn't listening. "Do you have a problem with it?" he said, shrugging his shoulders back just a little.

"No. No, I got a problem with *you*." Vinny jabbed a finger at Nate, then at me, then back at Nate, as if trying to count us and failing.

"Then you're welcome to take it up with me," Nate said, still in that same quiet, cool voice. I glanced at him out of the corner of my eye. If I concentrated, I could just make out his scent, gone cold and strange.

Vinny hesitated—contrary to some beliefs, drunks do have self-preservation instincts; they're just not very strong and usually pointed in the wrong direction—and squared his shoulders. "Yeah, maybe I will. Whaddaya gonna do, huh?"

"Vinny, *please*," one of his friends said, but the others hung back, maybe used to this by now, maybe too drunk themselves to bother.

Nate didn't move. Instead, he shifted just slightly, so that his feet were squared against the ground, and he crouched just a little. Somehow this didn't do anything to mask his height; if anything, the man loomed more, his lack of bulk suddenly less of a handicap and more a sign of starvation, of hunger.

The headlights of a passing car washed over his face and away, and I saw the flash of teeth as his lips pulled back. To Vinny and his friends, it probably looked like a smile.

It wasn't. And I knew that posture. I'd seen it before, used by a different man to the same effect. Nate's father had been very good at intimidating just by calling on a few shifts in his physique—the result of what he called a "bearshirt" curse, a legacy of the berserkers of the old North, who fought just as well using teeth and claws as with any weapon they carried. He'd rarely needed to change all the way, not when a little did so much.

He'd passed on that same curse to Nate, when he needed to be rid of it. Nate had, I'd thought, adjusted to it. But there was a difference between adjusting to it and enjoying it. And if I'd been able to scent him, I knew I'd sense that undercurrent of wildness, his curse not so far beneath his skin as it ought to be.

I stepped between them, one hand on Nate's chest, the other extended to Vinny, two twenties in it. "Forty bucks says there's a better beer selection at the Black

Rose down the street. Okay?" Even through the jacket, I could feel a shiver run through Nate at my touch.

Vinny blinked at me, then looked past me at Nate. Whatever he saw there made him blanch, just for a second. "I'll remember this, pal," he grunted, taking the money.

"I won't," Nate said, and Vinny turned red, but whatever he'd seen was still enough to spook him, and the money gave him cover for retreating. He muttered something more and waved off his friend as she started to hand him his jacket.

I let out a long breath, the vapor disappearing into the diamond-hard air. Only then did I glance back at Nate. His smile had faded, but that strange tension was still in his bones. "I had it under control," he said.

"Bullshit. Yeah, you could have won that fight. We both know that. You probably could have left him dead on the sidewalk. But that's not what's called for right now." My hands dropped to my side. I was suddenly cold in an entirely mundane way, one that had nothing to do with grayouts or the Hunt or anything else. "I mean, Jesus, Nate. I already lost you once, I don't want to lose you to an assault charge too."

He blinked, and a little of the man I knew returned to his eyes. "You're right. Sorry. That was—I'm just a little worried about what we're doing tonight. I mean, you and I both have fought these things, remember?"

Yes, we had, if anyone human (or curse-ridden, or Hound) could be said to have fought the Gabriel Hounds. And it had almost killed him. Two months back, in the last hot spell of the summer and the dying end of August, Nate had run to an old stone quarry in the first throes of his father's curse, and I'd tracked him there. That had been one of the better conclusions to a hunt, even with the guardian spirit of the now water-filled quarry trying to beguile us both.

And then I'd faced down the Wild Hunt on the banks of that same quarry. Nate had been with me—he'd been the original prey for the Hunt, in fact—and in the fray he'd fallen from the cliff. I still didn't know how badly he'd been hurt, because the spirit of the quarry had caught him. And I, bedraggled, wounded, and furious, had demanded it give him back.

It had. But it had claimed to do so as part of a bargain. And I didn't know what it had taken from me in return.

A flicker of a thought surfaced at the back of my mind, and I stepped on it, ignoring the twinge low in my gut. I *didn't know*. Couldn't.

Bad bargain, the Gabriel Hounds had said at the time, though I'd bargained nothing away. Nothing.

As if summoned by my memory of them, the Hounds stirred, first at the back of my mind, then as flickers around us, no more than shadows in the mingled moon and streetlight. *It was a bad bargain*, one said, pressing against me as it paced like a huge cat. *Bad enough that we fear for you, as you carry us.*

Nate drew a sharp breath, and one of the Hounds grinned at him, a flash of teeth that was there and gone before either of us could properly focus on it. "Evie—"

"Yes," I said. "They're here." Who was I to argue with Nate about the possibility of attacking someone? I had these hounds at my command; I could probably tear apart a regiment. The thought made me ill and—worse—hungry. "And you won't have to worry about me anymore," I added, addressing them. "We're putting an end to this now."

I unfolded the paper Sarah had given me, read it over, then motioned Nate closer. "Okay. Here's what we do. Take this—" I handed him a stick of plain sidewalk chalk, nothing fancy about it, "—and draw a circle around us. Doesn't have to be perfect, just has to encompass the two of us."

Nate complied. The chalk skipped and snagged over the bricks, making an uneven circle. "It's not complete," he said, poking at one of the breaks where the space between bricks hadn't taken chalk.

"That's not a problem. Not for us." Though it

would be, if we were doing this by the usual, careful rules. "It's just to outline the space." I tucked the list under my arm and unclasped my utility knife, then looked from one hand to the other, considering.

Nate rose to his feet. "Is that for what I think?"

"Yep." Both arms were still healing from the wounds they'd received a couple of months ago: one was a long slash that I'd inflicted myself in order to draw the Hounds to me, the other a jagged wound that had been the result of drawing the Hounds to me. Neither one had been serious, but they'd only just gotten to the point where steering my bike didn't hurt anymore. I didn't really want to reinjure either arm. "Okay. Here are the rules." I set the point of my pocketknife against the scar at my throat, gritted my teeth, and pressed down. The scar shifted—for a moment I had the weird feeling of something under my skin trying to get away from the steel; not a comfortable feeling, let me tell you—and parted with a faint sting, like a trapped wasp.

The Hounds, silent beside us, sighed gently at the scent of blood, a sound like the wind through a gibbet.

I smudged my finger against my throat, nodded at the blood—black in the streetlight—then bent to smear it on the brick just outside the circle. "Don't say your name, even if asked. You can say mine, but no one else's. In fact, it's better if you don't speak at all. Don't shed any of your own blood. And don't step outside the circle."

Nate glanced at the smeary pink chalk. "It doesn't look like much."

"It's not." Another smudge of blood, across from the first. North, south, east, west. Or close enough. So far, no trace of magic, only blood and chalk and the piss-and-cement smell of Government Center. And that was hoping I'd be able to identify any change when it happened . . . "But it's better than nothing."

He nodded slowly. "I'd thought that magic would be a bit more . . . well, elaborate."

"It usually is." I straightened up, wiped the blood off my knife with a spare tissue, then pressed that against the cut until it stopped bleeding. "For the same reason that OSHA regulations are elaborate." Nate gave me a baffled look. "Safety. Security. Most magicians aren't just going out and calling on any entity they can find; they have a specific goal in mind, and specific protections, and multiple ways out if something goes wrong." Magic 101, the basics of it.

"This just seems . . . I don't know. Too easy."

"It's only easy," I said, "because I have this." And I tapped the scar of the Horn again. "Like calls to like; the Horn will call to the hunters. And the rest of it's easy because I'm not going to hide myself." I glanced at him, thought about the danger I was exposing him to, the danger I'd already put him in, the trust he put in me. "If I'm going to give this back properly, I have to do it with my real name, my real soul on the line. I owe them that much respect."

And I owed myself that respect. Call it a stubborn streak, but I would not do this as a magician. I would do it as Genevieve Scelan.

Nate nodded, then put his arms around me for a moment. I rested against him, then stepped away and unfolded the list.

The invocation was almost clownishly simple: blood, incantation, then a list of names. But that was what was dangerous about this: I recognized only a few of them, but some of these names were ones that called directly to the spirits involved, rather than dancing around with euphemism and flattery as most invocations did. This was dangerous precisely because it was simple: there was no room for safety in this kind of invocation, no careful hedging about of protection for the summoner. Maybe it was because forbidding any one entity, for whatever reason, would diminish the power of the summoning.

The Horn of the Wild Hunt was something that didn't exist. There was no unified Hunt, no single

Hunter. But a woman named Abigail Huston, with the help of her perfidious son, had used that very lack to conjure up something new: a central reflection of all other hunts, an axis where there had been none, a focus for the energies of all Hunts. The Hounds it called up weren't the Seven Whistlers or Wuotis Heer or the hosts of Herlethingus; they were all of them, and more, and unnameable ones as well. To return the Horn, I had to call up all of these Hunters, all of those who led the Wild Hunt, and I couldn't do so with any barrier between me and them.

"Hecate," I said, and it was not my imagination that made the minimal moonlight above shudder slightly. "Herle. Black Matilda. Red Edric. Come and hear me. Wodan. Comte Arnau. Perchta. Come and hear me."

Name after name, names that I knew and names that I didn't and names for which Sarah had scribbled a helpful phonetic guide just above. I kept my eyes on the paper, trying not to miss a name. "Evie," Nate said.

I held up my free hand, still spotted with blood. "Herne. Diana. Gwyn. Come and hear me." The air went heavy and thick, like a lead blanket had dropped over us. And at the back of it—

"Evie!"

—at the back of it, slow and heavy like a fuse burning, the scent of magic.

I could have cried for the return of scent—even this minimal touch of my usual senses was like the first few glimmers of light after imprisonment. Instead, the last name still ringing in my mouth, I looked up. Nate pointed across the plaza. "Looks like Vinny's back for more."

Crap. I turned to see a man in shirtsleeves and a loosened tie—but this man was shorter than Vinny had been, and thinner. He wore a Phantom of the Opera mask, gleaming white under the lights, and the eyeholes of the mask remained dark as he turned to face us. "Okay. Don't leave the circle, but let me do the talking. If we're lucky he'll just take a piss and move on—"

I stopped. Beyond the man, at the next cross street, a woman in a black bustier over a shiny cheap polyester dress emerged. She wore a red sequined mask that didn't quite match the rest of her clothes, and she too was facing us. Another flicker of movement caught my eye: someone walking toward us without breaking stride or slowing, dressed in the blue button-down shirt that was the unofficial uniform of men in the financial district, with a full-face rubber mask of JFK.

"Oh, shit," I muttered.

"You mentioned getting attention," Nate murmured, and I turned to look where he pointed: more people in costume, including a little kid in foil armor with the visor down, descending the stairs from the T entrance. "I think we've got it."

"If it helps," I managed, "you can think of them as conduits. Manifestations, rather than the real thing. If the real thing were here—well, the world couldn't take that."

Nate came to stand beside me. "It doesn't help," he said after a moment.

"No, not really." More figures followed, one by one, left and right. Maybe fifty, I thought, then rejected it; maybe a hundred people, all in costume. Were they illusions wearing the faces of others, or real people, ridden by whatever entity had chosen them for this? I glanced at the rank of children who'd moved to the front, some in those plastic smock-costumes that were the last resort of tired parents, and shivered. I hoped it wasn't the latter; this was the sort of magic that should not come close to children.

I crumpled Sarah's list of names against my leg. The last few stragglers—a ninja, a guy in a hockey mask, and a woman in what could only be described as a Little Red Riding Crop costume—joined the silent, waiting assembly. It should have been ridiculous, but that intent hush pushed it over into the uncanny.

"I am Genevieve Scelan," I announced. "Called Hound. I have something of yours."

"Hound," said one of them, a man in a dinner suit with a brilliant green mask, and the others took up the word. "Hounds." Their eyes focused on me, and abruptly the pressure increased, till my vision darkened—or maybe that was just their attention darkening the world. The attention of the dark half of the year, of the stub of midwinter, the nights drawing in and the cries in the heavens, old chaos woken from a sleep of centuries. I staggered and fell to one knee, and at the back of my throat, I tasted ice again. *Not now*, I thought, trying to catch my breath.

"No!" Nate pushed me away from the edge. His shoulders heaved, and I caught a trace of his scent changing, altering along the lines of his curse.

Oh, that wouldn't be good right now. You don't put prey in front of hunters. Nor do you put a rival in front of them. I caught at Nate's hand, willing it to stay human, willing him to stay who he was. "I'm okay," I whispered. "Don't—I'll be okay."

He glanced at me, and for a moment it was his curse looking back, unwilling to hear me. But Nate was, or had been, very good at controlling himself before this all started. He nodded to me, and his hand closed around mine.

Bit by slow bit, I recovered some ground. I was Evie, I reminded myself. I was the Hound. I had seen gods, had even helped to kill the mortal prison of one. I had summoned up the dead of an entire cemetery. I had outrun the pack these entities commanded, the pack that now milled around in my head. I had chased my prey through the underground and over water—

I got my feet under me, gripped Nate's hand more tightly, and pulled myself upright.

—and *that* had been just in the last few months.

"As you say," I acknowledged, panting a little. "Hound, in the flesh. I have something to return to you."

The dozens of masked faces watched me, expressionless. "Return," they said at last.

I hesitated. Here was where I hadn't quite thought things through. I had thought that the hunters, all or some of them, would just take the damned Horn away from me. There were enough powerful entities before me that they should have been able to do so.

One of the children in the front—this one in a bunny suit, as if the riding entity had tried to make it as uncanny as possible—spoke. "You must give it," he said, and though the voice was that of a child, the undertone was a woman's, old and cracked. "You have won it fairly in battle. Even crippled and halved as you are, I cannot take it from you."

The part of me that has never, never liked bowing to anyone did the mental equivalent of jumping up and down with both middle fingers raised. *Ha, so there's something a human can do that you can't! Up yours, ineffable divinity!* The rest of me was starting to panic. What was I supposed to do?

I touched the knot of scar tissue. How did I give up something that had become part of me? And did I even want to? The thought shuddered through me like lightning coming to ground. I mean, yes, I had spent the day nauseated by the Hounds' taste for blood, and they were not a safe thing for a human to have. But over the last few weeks, there had been days when the only thing I was sure of was the chorus of the Hounds in my head, their everpresent breath of winter. And today, I'd lost my sense of smell. Even now, even after that first breath of fireworks, I could feel that impression fading. The Hounds were monsters, creatures that were so far from humanity that words like "monster" didn't even apply, but they could hunt. By giving them up, I might be giving up the only chance I had to hunt again.

I let go of Nate's hand. No. I couldn't let myself think like that. Gagging, I forced myself to remember the taste of Foster's blood (the Hounds sighed in remembered appreciation) and stepped to the edge of the circle. An image flashed into my head, a memory of the night by the quarry when I had bargained something away in exchange for Nate's life, when the Wild Hunt had passed from Patrick Huston to me. Huston had kept the horn sealed away in his own long-dead flesh, infecting the Gabriel Hounds with a kind of mortality, which was the only reason I'd been able to stand against them at all. I remembered him putting his hand to his throat, tearing the flesh there . . .

I touched my own throat. Cold blood made the skin slippery, but I could feel something . . . "This is probably going to get gross."

Nate's grip on my arm tightened, but a puff of breath crystallized over my shoulder: a laugh, and very much the laugh of a man struck by his father's berserker curse. "Gross I can handle."

"Good." I stroked the scar one last time, finding the notch I'd made, then dug into the skin, my broken and ragged nails making first divots and then crescents of pain. I did my best not to scream—I don't think you're allowed to scream when you're the one doing the hurting—and tore the scar free, a patch of ragged flesh coming with it. I started to gag—which hurt worse—then stopped, raising my hand. I held only a plain, bone white horn the length of my hand, its dark leather baldric hanging over my knuckles. The pain in my throat deadened, as if someone had slapped Novocain on it, and when I raised my head I felt the flex of raw skin there. New skin—like what you get before a blister has fully healed, the sensitive, thin skin of a burn.

Nate's hand on my arm was so tight it hurt. I tilted back my head, showing him the patch of new skin, and a little bit of color returned to his face. He slowly let go of my arm. The air seemed to shiver, and the Gabriel Hounds, echoes only in shadow, sat curled at my feet, tensed as if awaiting only a nod to go streaking after their prey.

You don't have to give it back, one of them said, jaw dropping open to reveal teeth the color of old blood.

Another stirred, pressing up against my legs. *You can keep it a while longer. It won't make a difference, in the end.*

We like *you*, said a third, and the look it gave me might have been called puppy-dog eyes if it had been on anything smaller than a tiger and not so capable of crushing my skull in its jaws. *You gave us your blood. You make a good Hound. We are honored to be carried by you.*

"Thanks," I said. "It's an honor to know you think so." I glanced out at the assembled masked horde. "But that's not going to make a difference, is it? If they ask you to tear out my throat, you'll do it."

With glee. The answer came quickly, without hesitation or shame. *But we would sing your name after your death, and your blood would be a taste we carried into the end of days.*

"Well, that's comforting. I suppose." They said that you didn't truly die until everyone who remembered you was dead. Did it count if what they remembered was how good you tasted?

You don't have to give it up, the first insisted again.

"I know," I murmured. Even though I feared them, I knew them for kin, along that strange alignment that made me a Hound like them. And they were right.

I needed to hunt. But I wouldn't use them for it. Even if it meant I would be hunting blind from now on.

I tossed the Horn out across the plaza. It curved over their heads, then hung at the apex of the arc, unmoving. For a moment the air around it seemed glassy, like a reflection, and then with a sound like glass breaking and a scent of burnt mercury so powerful it broke through my fog, the Horn shattered.

Nate looked away with a curse, blinking fast, and I caught my breath, unwilling to acknowledge even to myself how much I wanted to snatch it back. Not least because I was now certain I was alone in my head.

When I opened my eyes again, the Hounds were gone, and the assembled revelers were stirring, some even muttering to each other. "This has been used," a man in a hockey mask said, his voice shifting from chorus to chord and back, like a soundtrack coming out of synchronization. "You dared to use this."

"I did," I said, meeting his empty gaze. "And I did so without permission or leave."

"She did it for me," Nate broke in. "On my account."

The mask shifted to face him, and his words cut off in a hiss of indrawn breath. I knew what he was feeling now: the pressure of attention from a couple of hundred entities, some of whom were dead, some who were still vital, all in natural conflict and artificial concord in this one moment. "It doesn't matter why I did it," I said, feeling the shudders run through him. "It was my decision alone."

"Only because you were trying to help me," Nate managed, a note of exasperation still clear under the strain. He shook himself, a gesture that didn't quite match with his human bones, and stood with his feet braced. "She had to do it."

One of the children—a boy in a pirate's costume, with a big jeweled eyepatch pasted onto the mask—cocked his head to the side. "You," he murmured, as if amused. "Little wolf, little madman. You will not go ignored."

"Dammit," I muttered, but I held on to him, propping him up as much as giving comfort. "You just can't stay out of it, can you?"

He shook his head, and I didn't have to look at him to know he was grinning, baring his teeth in a grimace that was as much defiance as amusement.

The assembled horde regarded me again. "No one may call on our hunt without our leave," a woman in a cat mask said.

"And you called on all of us," said a man in what looked like Japanese formal armor.

"And we have your name," added a third—this one a bronze-skinned man bare to the waist, wearing a feather mask more suited to Mardi Gras. "All of us have a claim on you now, Hound. Crippled and halved as you are, we still have that claim, and we intend to call it due."

I nodded, but inside my stomach froze up. This wasn't just a matter of offending one spirit. I'd offended all of them, even the ones who hadn't deigned to send a representative, and now every one of them had a lien on my soul.

Another breeze drifted over us, yanking on my hair like an importunate toddler. "Midwinter," they said in concord, and that single word seemed to resonate through the ground, crystallizing the air around it. "We will come for you at midwinter. You will be our prey."

I caught my breath, stung by it even though I'd known something like this must have been coming. Nate moved closer to me, his natural warmth stolen away by the promise of winter that surrounded us. "You mean—" he began.

"If I can escape you," I said hesitantly, trying to feel out the edges of this sentence.

The ones closest to me turned their heads to the side, and for a moment I had the sense of the Gabriel Hounds arrayed around me again, only this time we were on opposite sides. "You do not understand," said the closest, a man in top hat, tails, and a Mexican wrestler's mask. "You will be prey. We will hunt. So it is, now and forever, till the end."

"You mean you'll kill her," Nate said.

The boy pirate shook his head. "No. We will always hunt her. That is how we hunt. That is what it is to usurp our power. She will be our prey as long as the Hunt lasts." He looked at me again, the eyepatch glittering, then, as one, the gathered crowd turned their backs on us.

A wind swept across the plaza, tasting of frost and exorcising the heaviness of their attention. One by one, the crowd dispersed, some of the figures slowing as they reached the edges of the plaza and the anima that had ridden them here dissipated.

Midwinter.

Nate let out his breath in an exhalation that no longer turned into ice on the air. The encroaching frost was gone, but the air remained chill and dry, tasting of old leaves and fire. "Evie—"

"That gives me two months," I said, and started across the plaza. The circle scuffed underfoot; any trace of blood was long gone, as was the mark on my throat. Inside, though, my brain was screaming *midwinter! Midwinter! That's less than two months—I'm not ready to be torn apart by the Gabriel Hounds, I'm not ready to die—if I'd known, if I'd known I never would have—*

No. I would have. And I had known. The Hounds had as much as warned me.

Nate ran to catch up with me. "Two months isn't enough, Evie."

"Yeah." I paused at the edge of the plaza, listening for sound to creep back into the world. "I kind of wish I'd gone trick-or-treating with you now."

"Jesus." He touched my arm, and I started to push him away—I couldn't break down here, not out in the open, please—but just then the taste of ferns and ice surged up in the back of my throat, and with it came the gray edges encroaching on my vision. I tried to brace myself and lurched against Nate instead, then stayed there a moment, sick with the cold in my gut.

I guess this was proof that the Horn hadn't been causing these grayouts. Damn. And I'd just lost not only my last chance at a hunt, but my chance at a future beyond midwinter.

"I—" I said, then, as my mouth filled with cold water, spat to the side. "Not now, okay? I can't—can't deal with this now."

His lips brushed my hair. "Not now," he agreed, but his arms were still tight around me, as if he feared I'd run the second I had a chance.

Four

So what do you do when you know you've got two months before a grisly end? Sleep, apparently. Nate brought me back to my office, and I fell onto the futon-couch without bothering to unfold it into an actual bed. "No you don't," he said, put me in the chair behind my desk, and folded it out himself. By the time I realized that I probably ought to be helping him with the bedclothes, he'd already finished and was helping me back up.

Sleep fell like lead wool around me, so heavy that I didn't even run in my dreams as usual. I surfaced briefly when Nate's cell phone alarm went off in the morning and he uncurled himself to get it, leaving a great cold empty spot all along my back. Usually I was the first one up—I had to be, with my schedule for Mercury Courier the way it was—but today the world ended right where my cocoon of blankets did. I heard the shower turn on, then sank back into shifting dreams of cold water over my head.

When I woke again, Nate was fully dressed—*damn, missed him naked*, some automatic response in the back of my head muttered—and by the side of the bed. "I have to go," he said, touching my face. "Are you going to be all right?"

I blinked until he finally came into focus. There

were so many things I could say to that—*yes, for now*, or maybe *I just got a sentence of eternal punishment, why wouldn't I be all right*, or even just telling him not to worry. But I couldn't even muster the will to be snarky about it. "Yeh," I mumbled. "Mmkay. See you."

His brows drew together, that little worried line between them becoming deeper. "Evie."

"Mmfine. Go on. 'll take care of this." I tucked my head further under the covers. "Mmfine."

His hand stayed warm against my cheek for a moment more, but even though he was no longer quite as beholden to his schedule as he once had been, there were times when he had to go. And now was one. "Come by any time," he said, and pressed something into my hand. He was gone by the time I uncurled my hand to find what he'd slipped into it: a pair of keys on a curl of wire.

It was probably a sign of how long it had been since I was in any sort of stable relationship that it took me so long to figure out what he'd given me, because my first thought was something along the lines of *goddammit, now I gotta get to his place before his workday ends, or else he'll be locked out*. Once I realized, I turned red and dropped the keys onto my bedside table, a grin pulling at my lips. Okay. Okay, maybe I could manage this.

My own alarm rang about ten minutes after he left, and when it went off, I slapped it away and just rolled over. Getting up took an effort of will, and once I was up it still took me five minutes to decide that yes, I wanted to shower and get dressed. Not even the unseasonably warm weather—something that normally would have been a blessing for a courier, this time of year—could make things better.

By the time I was upright, dressed, and had decided that yes, I probably ought to eat as well, I'd missed my shift at Mercury. I started to call Tania, stopped, then dialed her assistant, who's very good at organizing but whose response to customer service or any kind of courier dealings is to pass it on up the food chain. Tania would give me hell; her assistant would take a message and pass it up to Tania. Who would then give me two hells when I next saw her, but bothering about that just now felt outright impossible.

Instead, I wrangled my bike outside, stared blankly at the street for a few minutes wondering if this was really where I wanted to be, then started out for Mass General.

Tessie looked better and sounded worse than I'd expected. They'd moved her out of the ICU, but there were still an alarming number of machines hooked up to her, and a mask hanging over her face that she kept pushing away to talk to me. "Of course I had it worse," she said, her voice a gargling rasp rather than its usual husky alto. "I was down there in the hold for, I don't know, ten minutes? And that's where the worst of the smoke was. You got maybe a breath of it; I had my lungs full."

She held the mask up again and took a deep breath. Even without my talent, the air here smelled frighteningly sterile, with that strange blank scent that compressed oxygen sometimes has. That was some mercy in how my talent had dimmed; the scents of hospitals are usually enough to raise my hackles and draw forth a lot of unpleasant memories. Now the fog was almost a blessing.

Tessie took my expression for needless worry, and she waved a hand, strangely naked without its usual complement of jewelry. "Don't let this thing fool you. It's not the smoke inhalation that's the problem; it's that I haven't been to a doctor in ages and now they can't wait to get their needles in me." She sighed theatrically, but it turned into a cough.

"Why didn't you get out?" I said, pulling over the one chair in the ward. It wasn't a private room; a teenager with an IV and a handheld game was in the other bed, but he had his headphones turned up so loud I could hear the little tinkly music of the game he was playing.

Tessie paused, then gave me a coy little smile and tugged on the tubes hooking her up to the monitors. "It's a bit hard to get free of these, and after all, it's been ages since I had so many men interested in me—"

"No, I mean out of the boat. You were just standing there when I got in, and you couldn't have gone far. And there didn't seem to be anything else in the room with you." My nose hadn't been quite useless at that point, even with the smoke.

Her gaze dropped to her lap, and she smoothed out the blankets. "Tell me you won't let this get out."

I nodded to the jacked-in teenager. "And neither will he."

"This is so embarrassing . . . I was too scared."

"Of the fire?"

Tessie shook her head. "No. Definitely not that, although given this—" she raised the mask and inhaled again, "—I probably should have been. It was just . . . look, do you ever have nightmares where you're being watched, and if you move even a little it'll see you fully and you won't be able to get away?"

I stared at her. She'd turned pale and nervous, her hands plucking at the blankets as if wanting to pull them up over her head. "Not quite," I said after a moment. My nightmares, when I remembered them, had usually been of a much different sort. "But I think I have some idea what you mean. Like a deer in the headlights, right?"

"Yes. No," she added after a second, raising her index finger as if to point out the flaws. "Deer are hypnotized. This was . . . oh, I don't know. More like a rabbit. Or being in the dark and knowing there's a cliff somewhere, and the only sure ground is what's under your feet. I probably would have stayed down there till we hit the bottom of the harbor if you hadn't come for me." She exhaled. "I owe you, Hound."

I shifted uncomfortably. I didn't much like the idea of keeping a debt around after I was gone. "Only for the standard contract. I'll add a couple hundred hazard pay. So was it something on the boat that had you scared, or someone? Can you remember?"

"I am remembering, Hound, and I've told you what I know. It wasn't anything that happened, it was just a, a feeling. And as for whether it was what drew me there—" She shrugged, looking wilted. "I don't know, and now that I've spent a night on land I can't really call on my usual nets to tell me. I'm sorry I'm not more help."

I glanced up at that. Tessie gave me a sad smile, and even without my talent I finally caught a little of the change in her. Some magicians relied solely on loci; some relied on careful ritual, and then there were those who circumscribed their own lives and made alliances based on those prohibitions. By staying away from water for the night, Tessie had lost her power. It might come back—the same way her lungs would recover, one breath at a time—but it was a lot less likely.

That changed some things. Not just the balance of power in Boston—Tessie would now be lower in the hierarchy, one more in need of the protection Sarah's community watch offered—but, more immediately, what I could tell her. I'd been worried that Tessie might react badly, but if she was powerless . . . "Do you know Deke Croft?"

"The hobo pyro? I know of him; I don't bother with going inland to see him."

"He was on the boat too. Him and this old guy with a beard. Did you see either of them?"

Tessie shook her head. "No. I didn't have time to see anyone. But . . ." Her brow furrowed. "You understand this is all a bit blurry, but I don't think that was an oracular fire. I don't think he set it."

"You can tell the difference?"

"I could. Not so much now. Can't you?"

With my talent muffled? Not a chance. I smiled

and shrugged. "Whatever scared you got to him too, I think. Would it still be in Boston?"

She turned to gaze out the window, at the gray landscape. The faint squeal of T trains slowing down on the tracks echoed from the Longfellow Bridge, and the kid by the window cranked up his volume to compensate. "I don't know. It might have been just one time, released by that fire; it could have been a ward. Into the harbor . . . that was the only sense I got. It was gone, into the water." She closed her eyes, then pulled herself together and straightened her spine, the dreamy, fragmented part of her falling away as if sliced. "And I'm sure I don't have to tell you that if it went into the ocean, it's no matter. Nothing can magic the sea." Her lips curled up in a smile that made her appear maybe ten years older. "I've based my life on that."

And now that was gone. On impulse, I reached over and took her hand. Tessie, startled, grabbed back, tight enough that my bones squeaked. "And you'll go back to it again. The sea's the sea; it won't change."

"Not more than it already does, at least." She gave a surprisingly deep laugh and let go.

I made it to the door, then paused. "Do you want me to check in on your boat? I don't know much in the ways of wardcraft, but I could maybe lock it up or something."

"Oh, bless you, no. A, um, friend of mine is taking care of it. He came to see me this morning. Such a *lovely* man," she added with an eyebrow waggle that could only be called wicked. "Maryam up on the hill put me in touch with him a little while back."

"Wait. Maryam, with the—"

"Yes, the rocks. She's not there all the time; even us grand dames have lives too. Anyway, you don't need to worry about my home. I'll be there soon enough, anyway."

A nurse poked her head inside, frowned at the teenager, then turned to face Tessie. "Mr. Troyes? It's time for your blood stick."

I glanced at her, unsure I'd heard right. Tessie sighed. "That's another reason I'm not so happy about being here; they're such sticklers for what's on my ID, rather than my real name. All right, you candy-striped harpy, let's find a vein for you to pillage." She gave me an exasperated look as the nurse replaced her mask and scolded her for not keeping it on at all times.

I headed down the hall and to the lobby. Whatever had scared Tessie . . . the graybeard? He hadn't seemed all that scary, all things considered, but if he was a magician . . .

If my talent had been functioning properly, I'd have gone to find Deke in a heartbeat, first to see whether he was all right and second to figure out why he'd been there. But as it was, I might concentrate for a half hour and come up with nothing.

And did I have enough time left that I could squander it on a fruitless search?

That particularly morbid thought followed me as I got into the elevator next to an orderly in blue scrubs and two girls comparing casts. It didn't help that we emerged into the middle of a shouting match on the ground floor.

"Shouting match" is probably the wrong term to use, all things considered. After all, it implies that there's at least some give and take, that both parties are shouting equally. This was pretty much one-sided, and if it hadn't been for the first words I caught as I got off the elevator—something involving "locus" and "theft"—I would have walked right by.

Well, that's not strictly true. I could tell when magic was being worked, even if it wasn't quite in my senses.

The parties involved were a pair at the far end of the lobby, and they looked like something out of a bad improv skit. One was a middle-aged woman with her hair up in a perm that had gone limp some time ago, earrings so heavy they skimmed her shoulders, and a black velvet jacket over a white blouse and gypsy skirt. The other—the man she was berating—was a small

Indian man in a threadbare three-piece suit, holding his bowler hat between his hands as if it might shield him from her. They could have been any arguing couple—okay, any arguing strangely dressed couple—except that no one was looking at them. No one even came up close to them. As I walked from the elevator to the front desk, the two girls in casts headed straight for them, then veered around in a perfect arc, not even looking as their steps shifted.

Had I had my talent in full strength, I'd have scented the fireworks-and-rain trace of magic, undoubtedly from an aversion ward of some kind. As it was, though, only the faintest tang of gunpowder made it through the fog, and every time I looked at them my eyes started to water.

I thought seriously about just turning around, but this was a hospital, for God's sake. There were limits.

The two didn't even look up as I approached, so secure were they in their ward. "Hey!" I said, and grabbed the man by his sleeve and the woman by the back of her coat. "What the hell do you think you're doing?"

The man gave a squeak, then looked up at me, eyes wide. I knew him: Byron Chatterji, one of the adepts that I'd even consider calling ethical. The man didn't use any loci, or at least none that were based on bits of other people's souls. He worked on a principle called "severance and return," which, in his case, involved a complicated still out in an abandoned railway car in Medford. There was a lot of mumbo jumbo and mystical terminology for what he did, but what it came down to was that you really, really didn't want to accept if he offered you a drink from his hip flask.

The thing was, he was the last person I'd have expected to do something as stupid as putting up a ward in a hospital. Which left the woman, who twisted around in my grip to focus a spiteful glare on me. "What business is it of yours?" she snapped, her earrings swinging around like little scythe pendulums.

"It's the business of anyone who's affected by that damn ward." *And can notice it*, I added mentally, then paused. "Hang on, don't I know you? Patricia Wheelwright, yes?" I'd done maybe one job for her, back when I was starting out, and since then the only thing I could remember about her was that Sarah really didn't like her, for some reason.

Wheelwright tugged her jacket free of my hand and brushed it off as if I'd left crumbs. "The name is Sosostris," she returned ponderously. "What's the matter, Hound? Let a few victories go to your head and you forget everyone's profession?"

Oh yes. That was why; Sarah had ranted to me for an hour about how Wheelwright had claimed that professional name ("and I bet you she's never even read Eliot!" had been the gist of it, which honestly didn't mean much to me). And the other reason was clear: Wheelwright was a scam artist, even lower than the likes of Chatterji. It's a historied racket; you convince a mark that they've been cursed, then milk them for all they're worth while "dispelling" the "curse."

And these were the people that Sarah was trying to unite into some coherent organization. Good luck with that.

"I know yours well enough," I said. "And you, Chatterji, what are you doing here? Both of you, for that matter. You know better than to waste yourselves hiding some plain bickering like this!"

Wheelwright sniffed, but Chatterji just polished his bowler hat on his sleeve and smiled. "We—I have come in hopes of seeing Miss Troyes, yes? I had heard she was injured, and came to pay my regards."

"Pay regards, my ass," Wheelwright sneered. "You wanted to get your hands on her loci."

"While I will admit to a certain concern in that regard, I must point out that that is a regrettable falsehood." Chatterji's smile widened—it did that when he was embarrassed—and he bowed slightly to Wheelwright. "At least it is when applied to *my* circumstances."

"Are you accusing me of theft?" Wheelwright demanded.

"Not in the least—" Chatterji began, in that tone that meant a long argument over semantics was about to follow.

I cut him off, raising my hand between them. Chatterji actually flinched. "Which of you set the ward?"

At that, Chatterji looked down at his feet. "It wasn't his fault," Wheelwright muttered. "He didn't want our quarrel to bother anyone."

"Then don't have the damn quarrel to begin with! Jesus, this is a hospital, not some back alley—you don't throw magic around like that!"

"You do when it is necessary," Chatterji maintained, but he didn't look up.

"Anyway, if that moistened bint from her houseboat is here, it's a wonder there aren't more of us around." Wheelwright jerked her head toward the front desk. "Only they're not being cooperative. They tell me there's no Miss Troyes here, and since Sonny Jim stopped by, I figured he must have pulled a fast one on their records—"

"I protest," Chatterji responded, again meekly. The man was made of meek.

"She's not here," I said. If these two headed up to see Tessie, they'd drive her crazy in no time. "They moved her to Mount Auburn."

Chatterji nodded and seemed ready to walk off, but Wheelwright's eyes narrowed. "Then what are you doing here, Hound?"

"Blood test," I lied equably. "Had to pick up my results. No, you don't get to know what they were. Now dispel this damn thing and get out of here."

Wheelwright glared at me, working her lower lip between her teeth. Chatterji, however, straightened and whispered in her ear. I caught the words "Bright Brothers" and "just herself" and even if Wheelwright still looked skeptical, she nodded after a moment. "Fine. But you just watch yourself if you come down my way. I don't like being bullied."

"And I don't like bullying," I said as she took a length of rowan wood about the size of a lipstick case from her purse and twiddled it between her fingers. "So we're well matched."

Chatterji, meanwhile, had taken a long pull from his vile hip flask, then flicked a few droplets from it in the four directions, dispelling his part of the ward. He mistook my look of revulsion—again, I was glad my talent wasn't picking up the scent of the flask—for reproof and gave me an apologetic shrug. "It seemed necessary. For precautions. You understand?"

"Not really," I said, but I followed them out. Precautions were wards in your home, not tossed down to hide an argument. Something was seriously wonky with the world if this sort of thing was becoming routine. Or perhaps something was just wrong with Chatterji and Wheelwright. I waited until they disappeared around the corner, then bent to unlock my bike.

Maybe it was an aftereffect of that burst of anger, maybe it was the result of being nearby when Wheelwright and Chatterji dispelled their respective wards, but this time, I caught the scent before I saw the person. A thin trace of damp woodchuck and burnt-out matchsticks wove past me, and it was probably a sign of how bad it had gotten for me that I didn't recognize it until I'd stood up again. "Deke?" I whispered, and turned around, the helmet in my hand whacking against the bike rack so hard it rebounded into my leg.

No fires. No immediate sign of him—but there, coming out of one of the EMT bays on foot was a hulking figure in a leather bomber jacket dwarfing a little skittish shadow at his side. "Deke!" I yelled.

The shadow spun like a cornered cat, but the minute he saw me his face lit up, and he started yanking on his friend's arm. The big guy turned, and a chill trickled down my back as I recognized the gray-bearded man who'd carried Deke out of the fire. Deke grinned—a wider grin than I'd ever seen on his face—and waved like a deranged marionette. "Hound! See, I told you I'd find her, this is the one I was telling you—"

I tucked my helmet under my arm and approached, still not quite sure what to make of the other man. You know how there are some people that seem like they're made for certain situations? The guy with the Santa Claus beard, or the thin-lipped woman who just needs a nun's habit and a ruler? This guy was a little like that. He had a clipped, gray-going-to-white beard and a long white ponytail. Drop him into the middle of a Renaissance festival and you'd never see him again, or put a yellow rain slicker and hat on him and you'd expect there to be fish for sale nearby. He looked a little older than Deke, but in much better shape, though given Deke's shape that wasn't difficult. And his eyes—very bright blue, like the sky above us—were as hard and keen as awls.

Though I couldn't rely on my nose as fully as I was used to, I didn't sense any reason for concern: the man smelled of salt and tar, with maybe a touch of granite worn by waves, and more important, Deke seemed at ease around him. Whatever had spooked him so, it no longer affected him. "Hey, Deke," I said. "You all right?"

"What? Oh, I'm fine, I'm fine."

"He got a bit of smoke in his lungs," the big guy said. "We were just getting him checked out."

"Yeah, Tessie got it too. She was in the boat," I added to Deke's look of incomprehension. "Got her out, but she'll be in the hospital for a bit longer."

Deke's face fell. "Tessie? Oh, no. No, I didn't know that."

The big guy hadn't quite stepped between me and Deke, but something about his posture made him look like a bodyguard sensing a threat. "You're the girl I saw on the fishing boat," he said. "You saw me carrying Cam out of there."

"Cam?"

" 's me." Deke thumped his chest. " 's my name. Roger knows it. We knew each other in high school."

Oh yes. Deke's full name was Decameron Croft, the legacy of parents who were classics professors at some little college on the Coast, parents who'd disowned him a long time back. I wasn't sure I blamed them, knowing how much crap Deke could get into if left alone.

Deke, oblivious to my train of thought, punched Roger in the arm, and Roger, a brief, fond smile breaking out under his beard, punched back, sending Deke staggering a couple of paces. "We go way back," Deke said happily, then paused. "I'm sorry Tessie got hurt."

"She'll be all right. But what were you even doing out there, Deke? I mean, I know you like fire, but that —"

Roger held up one scarred, slablike hand. "That's my friend's business, and you'll just have to—"

"No, no, it's okay! This is Scelan, the one I told you about. Hound, the finder, remember? She could help you!" Deke turned that happy smile on me and back to Roger. Guy looked like a puppy on Christmas—okay, a bedraggled, mud-rolled puppy that had fallen on its head one too many times, but still that innocently enthusiastic. It wasn't something I was used to seeing from Deke, but it was certainly a step up from the paranoia I'd encountered so far today.

Roger's brow creased. "Maybe. I don't know, Cam, okay? And now's probably not the time to talk about it. I gotta get moving or she'll be pissed."

"Then when would be a good time?" I asked, stepping back a little, arms crossed. If I could get something out of Deke, I might be able to figure out if what scared Tessie was still around to be reckoned with. And a job . . . well. We'd see.

"Tomorrow?" Deke said. "Or—or the day after? Anytime. Anytime is good."

I glanced at Roger. "For you too?"

He sighed and ran a hand over his face. Yes, I'd seen that look before, on the face of anyone who had to deal with the undercurrent on a regular basis but who preferred to stay out of it themselves. He caught my recognition, and the corners of his eyes crinkled up; not quite a smile, but enough to say *adepts, huh?* to someone who knew what was going on.

Yeah, maybe I liked him. At least I could respect him for saving Deke.

"If you're Scelan, then I owe you thanks for keeping Cam safe this long." He thumped his friend on the shoulder again, and Deke grinned up at him. "But yeah, come find us anytime. I'm not going anywhere for a while. Not least," he added with a wry glance at me, "because that was my boat."

Five

In hindsight, I should have headed home, or gone in to Mercury Courier and begged Tania's forgiveness, or even gotten in touch with Rena to smooth over what had happened. Anything to keep hold of that elusive clarity. Instead, I lost a few hours, biking down to the locks by Lechmere and watching the fresh water meet the sea.

You ever been so tired that actually thinking takes effort? So drained that it's either a choice between moving and thinking, and by a certain point the distinction becomes moot? Yeah. That was kind of what it was like, but with no goddamn reason. I'd slept—God, it sometimes seemed like I'd been sleeping forever with no benefit to show from it—and I'd had everything else in order. So why the grayouts, why the lethargy, why the damnable fog that kept me from hunting?

At this rate, I might even be glad to meet the Hounds when they came for me at midwinter.

I shoved that thought away. I had a long way to go before I hit that point.

Besides, even if the undercurrent was having another upset, at least one person in it was doing all right. It helped to know that Deke had someone looking out for him. You needed that, in the undercurrent.

Especially for seers and pyromancers and the like; they'd have trouble knowing which way to move if you didn't point them in the right direction.

The thought jostled something else loose, and I checked my phone. Yes, I had just about enough time to get there.

Schools these days are a bit more paranoid about who they let walk off with their kids. Not that I blame them; Katie herself had run into trouble with someone who'd falsified records to make it look like he was an accepted guardian. I'd gotten her out of that, which was only fair since it had been my fault she was even there to begin with, but falsifying records might have been the easier way to go based on how much information I had to turn over before it was okay for me to pick her up from school. It wasn't something I did often, but my schedule was better for it than Nate's, most days, and while Katie was usually fine on her own, I knew she liked having someone to meet her.

So I pulled what little volition I had together to bike down to Allston and stand outside Katie's school with a permission slip that said it was okay for me to be there. There were worse places to be on a day like this; the bright blue of yesterday's October had faded into sullen gray, one month clocking over into the next.

A lingering scent of oil smoke hung in the air, turning the usual dry-leaves tang of fall into something richer and heavier. I could just catch the nuances of it if I concentrated hard. Leaves burning, maybe. I focused on that as the bell rang and the doors slammed open, using it to keep me grounded as the first wave of kids swarmed out of the building.

Katie wasn't among them, nor was she in any of the little groups that walked out, talking among themselves (or, in one case, making robot noises). I waited till the roar died down a bit, then sighed and walked onto the school grounds.

Out onto the playground, past the gravel and the blacktop . . . good God, this brought back unwelcome memories. I hadn't thought images about the number of fights I'd gotten into in grade school, but just the scent of asphalt could bring that back in a heartbeat.

Strangely appropriate, too. I hadn't even rounded the corner when I heard an outraged shriek followed by, "Take it back! Take it back!"

A cluster of three little girls stood by the swings, and as I approached, the one in a red-and-black coat launched herself at the one in pink, knocking her to the ground. Something bright and shiny went flying and landed with a clang against the swings, spilling water over the sand.

"Knock it off!" I yelled, running over to them.

The third girl shrank back into the bushes, hands curled tight in the sleeves of her duffel coat. I yanked the girl in red and black off the one in pink—then stopped as scent and sight intersected. Katie stared up at me, eyes wide, and when I moved closer she cringed away as if expecting me to hit her too. "Katie," I said, then stopped.

"Make her take it back," the girl I had by the shoulder sobbed. "She said my mom and dad are gonna split up, and it's not true—"

I let go of her and glanced where the shiny thing had fallen. Sure enough, it was a little silver plate, maybe the only real silver thing Nate owned. Katie went red and, instead of getting up, curled so that she was hugging her knees. "You said that?" I asked softly.

Katie didn't meet my eyes. "Carla hit her first," the third girl said suddenly, maybe hoping to get out of trouble if she switched loyalties. The girl in red and black glared at her. "Well, you did."

"Then don't do it again." I glanced at Carla, whose lower lip was still sticking out and trembling. "It's not going to happen. No one can see the future. Remember that." I pointed back toward the gates. "Go on home."

They retreated, arguing as they went. I waited till they'd gone, then picked up the silver dish. At least I'd had the decency to hide my shit when my mom caught me smoking up in my room. "Katie, you know better than this."

Katie, still waiting for the next blow, looked up at me through her fringe of fluffy brown hair. She had the same eyes as her much older brother, wide and gray and guileless. "What do you mean?"

I spat in the center of the silver plate and drew a circle, then wiped it away. It wasn't much of a banishment, more what adepts did as a form of housecleaning, but it would mute any echoes coming off the act of scrying. "Katie, what the hell did you think you were doing?"

"Nothing, now." She got to her feet, wiping her nose.

"You scryed just for the sake of hurting her?"

"No! I mean, I didn't know—" She bit her lip, hands curling into little fists. "She hit me first!"

"I bet she did. But that doesn't mean you can fight back like this." I sighed. "Katie, you shouldn't even know how to do this. You're too—goddammit, you just shouldn't." Age didn't enter into it; dabbling in the undercurrent tended to result in someone getting swept under, and Katie was too good a kid for that to happen.

She mumbled something, still not looking at me.

"What was that?" Christ, I was starting to sound like my mother—well, not *my* mother, who'd been very silent on the subject of the undercurrent and practically begged me to do the same. But somebody's mother.

"I said, Sarah taught me."

"Sarah taught you."

"Yeah." She glanced up at me, her jaw tightening in what I was starting to recognize as a sign that she wasn't about to give ground. "She said I needed a focus, so I could at least direct what I was seeing and not have it go all over the place. She said Danielle from the seer enclave told her since they couldn't start teaching me—"

"Sarah taught you," I repeated. Okay, there was some reason behind it, since Katie's case of the Sight was the kind that could eventually prove a problem—ask any seer who's stepped off the curb while seeing two weeks into the future. And the enclave had refused to tutor her, officially because they were full up but unofficially because being a seer didn't make you a decent human being, and there were a few residents of the enclave who were better off away from small children.

But none of that meant anything if Katie was using magic so cavalierly. And Sarah was up to her eyeballs in the undercurrent these days, so her judgment wasn't the best. "That covers how you did it. Mind telling me why?"

Katie opened her mouth, then closed it and stared down at the ground. "She was gonna hit me anyway," she muttered. "She doesn't like me—and it's worse because I told her her witch costume was all wrong. She said she was a Salem witch, and her costume had all these little twinkly red bits at the bottom, like flames, you know? Only the Salem witches didn't get burned. They got *pressed*."

There was a peculiar satisfaction in that last word that might have been amusing in other circumstances. "And that's why you used your Sight."

Katie shrank a little. I sighed, tucked the dish into my bag, and knelt beside her. "I wanted to get her back," Katie whispered. "She—I thought if I did that, she'd stop bothering me."

"You didn't think to talk to Nate? Or your teacher? Or me?"

Katie shook her head. No, I guess she wouldn't have. I hadn't, at her age. Not that that had turned out well for me, either, which was why I remembered not just the smell of blacktop but the taste of it. Only this was more serious than elementary-school bullies, and the worst that could happen was a lot more than a broken nose behind the basketball court. Katie might have her three fairy godmothers, but if the lesson she got from us was that magic was okay to wave around like this, then something had gone seriously wrong.

If she had someone watching over her, it might be better. Someone to walk her through the rough spots, show her not just the ropes of using magic but when not to use it, how to stay out of it, how to keep a part of yourself separate so that no matter how weird things got, you were more than a shadowcatcher on the corner scraping for bits of people's souls. More than the Elect of the Revealed Golden Hoo-ha, whatever his name had once been. More than Deke, or Wheelwright, or Tessie.

And I wouldn't be around to help her. The thought crashed in on me like an iceberg against a hull. I didn't have years to teach her what I knew; I had two months. Less than that. And then I'd be—well, "dead" wasn't quite the word for it. Eternally hunted. Absent.

"Okay, kid," I said finally, and got to my feet. "Field trip time."

"But I'm supposed to be going to Sarah's—"

"I'll call her. There's someone I want you to meet." I held out my hand. "Coming?"

She looked up at me. "You won't tell Nate?"

"Don't know yet."

That got her. Katie trudged to my side, dragging her feet as only a little kid can.

The thought of Nate made me touch the silver dish through my bag. Katie had some reason for what she did; she believed it was because her Sight had failed that bad things had happened to her brother. Because she hadn't seen it, she reasoned, she hadn't kept Nate's father from cursing him, or stopped the Hunt from coming after him. I knew better; the first was his father's fault and no other's, and the second was my own damn fault.

But I'd gotten him back. I rubbed at my stomach, where a chill like a block of frozen lake water settled and refused to dissipate. That was the important thing.

I had to focus on the important things these days.

We crossed over the old train yards on a footbridge painted with a brilliant blue eye. "Okay, Katie. The first thing you have to understand is that most magic doesn't work the way you and I use it. That's blood-magic, a hereditary thing." I wasn't entirely sure of the genetics, but "inborn" was close enough. "What most people do is use pieces of a person's soul, severed off and turned into a . . . a kind of battery. Those are called loci, and they're nasty."

My voice must have wavered or something on that last word, because she gave me a skeptical look. "How do you take away part of someone's soul?"

"Shadows. Blood. Sometimes it's the same as a contract, sometimes it's by usurping the natural order of things, sometimes it's different. I knew someone who claimed to be able to siphon enough out of photographs . . . there are a lot of ways. The point is that when that's the basis for magic, it causes problems." And because most magicians were selfish people with all the altruism of a feral cat, they were usually pieces of other people's souls.

Maybe a locus had belonged to a kid who'd taken a piece of candy from the nice but weird guy down the block and given up a piece of her soul in return; maybe someone who'd crossed a shadowcatcher's net; maybe someone who'd even traded it voluntarily, not knowing the downsides. And there were downsides; you healed from a soulwound eventually, but the days before you healed were rough. You could kill someone that way, at least in theory, and most magicians were careful not to, since the loci would then lose their power. But a person left without color vision, or willpower, or just broken—magicians didn't care about that, as long as their loci continued to be usable.

"Even you?" Katie asked.

I shook my head. "No. Not me."

"Sarah?"

I hesitated there. No, Sarah didn't use loci; she

stuck to the kind of minor stuff that drew on either goodwill or ritual, working within the natural laws rather than subverting them. But if Sarah was teaching Katie, I wasn't sure how much I wanted to encourage her. "That's a different matter. But the woman I'm taking you to meet doesn't use loci either."

We made our way across the rail yard and up into the neighborhoods that were a spark nicer than Katie's. I stopped in front of a little house on a scrap of land, surrounded on either side by triple-deckers like the one Katie and Nate lived in. "We're here."

Katie blinked, and I could see her taking in the dilapidated but not ramshackle nature of the house, the weeds straggling over the rocky lawn and the fence whitewashed to a defiant glow, as if this one bulwark might hold off any of the encroaching decay. "It doesn't look so bad," she said.

"It's not." I knocked on the fence, then opened the gate and let the two of us in just as the front door opened. A young woman in a heavy parka, her brown hair streaming back from her face, tucked a pair of flattened tote bags under her arm. "Afternoon," I called.

She jumped, clutching the bags to her chest, and turned to look at us. "Afternoon," she answered, then paused. "Aren't you—"

"Scelan." I'd visited a few times, mostly back in the spring. Summer was less of a problem for Maryam; I made a mental note to come back in a few weeks and check on her. "I'm sorry, I should have called ahead of time. Is Maryam in?"

The girl hesitated, glancing behind her at the locked door. "She's out back," she said. "She's been there since noon. Could you—would you keep an eye on her? I don't expect any trouble, but I don't like leaving her alone. I'll be back in fifteen minutes, I swear."

"Happy to." I stepped away from the gate and motioned for Katie to make room. "Take your time."

"Thanks." The girl scurried past us and headed

down the way we'd come, her stride lengthening as she walked.

Katie watched her go. "Who's she?"

"Maryam's niece. Or perhaps a cousin; I can't remember. She takes care of Maryam." And she'd just left her aunt-or-cousin in the care of people she barely knew. I wasn't sure how much I blamed her; long contact with someone so steeped in the undercurrent could do that to a person. "Maryam's lucky to have her around," I added, walking around the side of the house, toward the scrap of backyard.

"Why—" Katie stopped as we rounded the corner.

"This is why." I let go of her hand and crouched next to a raised garden bed full of rounded gray stones. A middle-aged woman lay on the stones, arms out to the side as if embracing them, and though her face was turned to the side to give her room to breathe, the stones she lay on pressed hard into her face. She looked like a corpse—pale, unmoving, even the rise and fall of her chest slowed to a fraction of usual breath. I touched her sleeve, then her hand: warm, then cold. How she kept warm in all this was something I'd never learned.

Katie hadn't moved from the corner, hands drawn up before her as if to ward off the sight. "What's she doing?"

"Well." I stood, dusted my hands off, and leaned against the back porch. "Maryam is a . . . well, the closest term is geomancer, and that's still inaccurate. She doesn't divine anything using stone, but the source and focus of her magic is the earth. Slow power, but strong, and certainly she's had time to master it. She is the most powerful adept in the city." Even when the Fiana had ruled the undercurrent of Boston, that had been the truth. I assumed that what kept her safe then was the same thing that kept her safe now: the stone magic she worked had no practical applications, and Maryam had no interest in practical applications to begin with.

"But what is she doing? She doesn't—does she have to do it like this?"

I shrugged. "It's a closed book to me, kid. I don't know stone magic. I had her try to explain it to me once, and it all went right over my head. She believes this is the right way; isn't that enough?" I sank my hands into my pockets. "As for what she's doing, ever heard of the Bloody Bluff fault line?"

Katie shook her head, unable to look away from Maryam, prone and pleading with the stone below her.

"It doesn't get as much press as the San Andreas, but it's right below us. Runs along Boston, near Lexington. Maryam claims she's holding it together, transferring some of its energy to other places, so that we don't get a nine-point earthquake running down the Freedom Trail."

Katie's eyes widened, and she bent and put one hand flat on the ground as if testing to see how stable it was. "Has it worked?"

"Don't know. There hasn't been an earthquake here in a while, though, and I've heard we're overdue for one." I leaned back. "So you tell me. Is she an incredibly powerful adept, using her talent in the most altruistic way possible, devoting her life to preventing a catastrophe, or is she a crazy woman who talks to rocks?"

Katie shook her head. "That's mean, Evie."

"That's the undercurrent. And the answer is: both. This is what you have to understand about magic, Katie." I closed my eyes and inhaled: damp November air, warming just a little, rotting wood from the shed across the way. Nothing more. I leaned further back against the porch, trying to ignore the sudden dizziness that shook over me. "You can have the best of intentions," I went on, "the best of support networks—remember how I said Maryam was lucky to have her niece?—and all the skill in the world, and it doesn't prevent you from becoming this." I opened my eyes, watching my breath fog in the air. "Have a seat, kid. We'll be here a while." Katie gave me a scared look—scared of what, I wasn't sure—and I shrugged. "I said we'd keep an eye on her."

So we did. Katie sat on the steps to the back door, her knees drawn up and her arms locked around them, gazing at Maryam with the same worried, thoughtful gaze. At least I'd got her thinking. It started to rain after a little while, a thin drizzle that was more of a mist than actual rain, and I shed my coat to drape it over Maryam. She stirred as I did so, a treble clatter of pebbles alerting us as her right hand closed, then opened again. She sighed, seemed to press herself even more closely into the stones, then brought her hands out in front of her and pushed herself up to her knees. "Oh," she said, brushing a few stray pebbles from her face. "That was a nasty one."

"Handled it well, though." I waved, mostly to let her know we were here. Maryam's eyesight wasn't so good.

She blinked a few times, then caught at my coat as it started to slip from her shoulders. "Genevieve," she said slowly, a smile gradually lighting her face. "Oh yes, I handled it. Managed to redirect most of the pressure into northern Greenland, but I can't say that it'll hold for too long." She edged backward, off the bed of gravel, and rocked to her feet, wincing as each muscle protested. "Either they're getting worse, or I'm getting older."

"Could be both," I said, coming forward to help her with the coat. Katie leaped up and tagged along beside me, practically holding on to my sleeve.

"Could be." She accepted my help, sliding one skinny arm and then the other into the sleeves, then blinked. "This isn't mine . . . Did Natalie forget to leave my jacket out again?"

"She's at the store." I offered my arm.

Maryam took it and leaned on me, stretching her legs, making sure she could walk. "Then she should have left it—ah." She opened the storm door, but instead of going inside, took a heavy wool coat from a peg just inside the door. "Can't stay out long, not if I want to get some sleep," she said, shrugging out of my coat and into hers. "Natalie's been nagging me to spend the nights inside these days. I tried explaining things to her, but, well." She settled down on the stoop and patted the space beside her. "Have a seat, Genevieve. I haven't seen you in ages."

"I was talking to Tessie this morning, and she mentioned you." Which was probably why I'd thought of taking Katie here in the first place.

Maryam raised a hand to her mouth to cover a smile, a strangely girlish gesture for a woman in her late fifties. "Oh, yes. Tessie and the gentleman. I'm so glad that worked out."

It had? The thought of Tessie and Maryam sharing girl-talk over some new man was amusing in a libido-shriveling way.

Katie, perhaps impatient at this grown-up diversion, held out her hand. "It's very nice to meet you, Miz Maryam."

Maryam started, then clasped Katie's hand with both of hers. "And nice to meet you as well, young lady. Who is this, Genevieve? Your daughter?"

"No," I said quickly, and Katie gave me a funny look. "She's a friend of mine. I thought I'd show her around a bit."

"Around? Hm. Hm, yes. Would you like tea? I could ask Natalie—no, you said she was out."

Maryam always offered me tea when I visited, and after the first few times I'd learned to say no. She wouldn't have the chance to make it, anyway. "I'll pass on tea, Maryam, thanks. Besides, we can't stay for too long. How are you doing these days?"

"Oh, fine, fine. There was a brief flare-up in the upper mantle last week, but nothing I couldn't handle. The trick of it is managing the magnetism at the same time as you leave the ley-lines where they were." She glanced over her shoulder at me. "You don't ever want to touch those. I learned that early on, when I was just starting out. Scrambled a few, and, well, let's just say that there's a reason the exits at Newton Corner are always a mess. And you? I'd heard you were up to big things lately. Brought down the Bright Brotherhood, I hear."

I managed a smile. Trust Maryam to be several months behind. Or maybe it took something that big to make her take any kind of notice. "It wasn't just me."

"Good, good." Maryam sank her hands into the deep pockets of her overcoat, then frowned and extracted a small thermos. "Ha! Knew I'd prepared. Genevieve's friend," she added, unscrewing the top of the thermos, "do you know the secret to good hot cocoa?"

Katie shook her head.

"You melt a whole chocolate bar into it." She winked at Katie, who grinned back, then poured a splash of lukewarm cocoa into the cup. "Now. Are you a magician?"

"Yes," Katie said just as I said "No." Maryam's eyes crinkled up at the corners, and Katie glared at me. "No, she's not," I said.

"Good." Maryam nodded. "Good. Because you're still growing, girl. You need to have a good sense of self before you begin any sort of work, otherwise your Self becomes the Work. Do you understand?" Katie nodded hesitantly. "Good. Now, Hermes Trismegistus' laws of the microcosm are all well and good, but if you start treating them like the sum of all knowledge, then you'll run into trouble. Don't you agree, Genevieve?" She took a sip and passed the cup.

"Oh, trouble, yes," I agreed. The cocoa was so thick it barely poured, but it tasted a bit stale—whenever she'd prepared it, I doubted it had been this morning. I passed it to Katie anyway. She took a long drink, getting chocolate on her nose, then leaned across me and presented it to Maryam with both hands.

Maryam took the cup gravely and nodded, as if Katie had just passed some test. "Trismegistus was fine for his times, but we know so much more now. And it's not just the microbiology of the body that matters in the sense of the Work, it's—" She stopped, cocoa halfway to her lips.

"Maryam?" I reached out just in time to catch the cup as she let go. Warm cocoa splashed out over my hand and onto the step.

Maryam stood up, her eyes going unfocused. "Flare of some kind . . ." she muttered. "Lynn volcanics acting up again."

Without another word, she dropped the thermos—Katie scooped it up before more than a second splash could spill—and flung herself onto the bed of stones. Pebbles sprayed out around her as she hit the rocks, and her hands flexed, as if she wanted to dig herself deeper. The muscles of her back and neck tensed, and she let out a slow exhalation like a moan, the breath seeping out of her. After a moment her breathing slowed, her hands ceased grasping at nothing, and the tense lines of her back eased. She was as she had been when we arrived.

Katie edged to the side of the gravel box. "What was she—"

"Plate tectonics don't stop for cocoa breaks." I took the thermos from her, shook out the last of the dregs, and screwed the top back into place. "And she's strongly attuned to any changes. This is probably the longest conversation I've had with her." I set the thermos next to her, so she'd see it when she got up, and went back to the screen door. "Or maybe she just has a broken synapse somewhere."

"Don't say that."

"Why not?" I opened the door and took down a couple of scarves from the second peg, then returned to Maryam's side. "I respect Maryam," I said, tucking the scarves over the old geomancer's exposed hands. "I like her too. That's not usual in the undercurrent, because most adepts will backstab you—or, if not, just generally be unpleasant. But even though Maryam's a good person, she's not reliable for anything that isn't a mile beneath the earth's crust."

The drizzle had started up again, damping Maryam's hair down into a gray matted mass, like sodden felt. Katie's hand crept into mine, and I squeezed it gently. A rustling came from behind me, and I turned to see Natalie come around the side of the house, lugging several grocery bags. Her face fell as she saw Maryam. "She's still like that?"

"She got up for a bit," I said. "She'll be all right."

"Oh. Good." Natalie gazed at her charge for a long moment, then sighed and set the bags down. "Thank you for keeping an eye on her."

Katie went up to her. "Could you thank her for the hot cocoa, when she gets up?" She had a smudge of chocolate on her upper lip, I noticed. Natalie nodded absently and went to the side of the gravel bed, where she took a big porch umbrella and started setting it in place above Maryam.

We left without saying more, and the drizzle solidified into something colder and nastier. I tugged Katie's hood up over her head. "This is the thing about magic, Katie. It's like saltwater. It corrodes. You might think it's just a handy shortcut or something to pass the time, but so much of magic is built on getting out of something you shouldn't that it turns your sense of karma inside out. And the magic itself . . . the natural end of it is never pretty."

"Maybe—" Katie hurried ahead of me so that she could turn and face me. "Maybe it wasn't always like that."

"Maybe. But it's that way now." She gave me an exasperated look, those gray Hunter eyes far too piercing. "Look, you want to theorize about a Golden Age, be my guest. But we're not in it. Magic stopped being the province of the numinous some time ago, and now it's with the opportunists. You invite magic into your life, and this is what you're inviting as well. Deke, Maryam, Chatterji—all of them are best-case scenarios. It never turns out well, Katie. It never turns out well."

Katie swallowed and looked down at the sidewalk. We walked back in silence to the Goddess Garden, Sarah's little shop.

I sometimes wonder why someone who knows almost as much about the sillier aspects of the undercurrent as I do runs a store that specializes in said silliness. Even the pagans that I've met agree that most of the wares in the store verge on the ridiculous, and that's quite a feat considering that pagans in general hate to agree on anything. The contents of the store aren't, by any objective measure, much worse than what you'd get in a tacky New Age store in the mall, but something about them just pushes the whole thing over into a weird ironic self-awareness. That, in itself, accounted for some of Sarah's younger customers, the same way that kitsch has its own enthusiasts.

But even so, Sarah knows the undercurrent, she keeps contacts with the few adepts who can handle human interaction, and she knows her way around loci and basic invocations, to the point that she stays away from them. Therefore she ought to know better than to stock crap like *The Divine Bull: How Mithras Influences Wall Street* or *Freya's Futhark Friends*.

I suspect that's a major reason why she keeps it the way it is. It's a statement on her part, a way of saying *Yes, I know that there's this deep undercurrent full of esoteric meaning, and I reject it.* When I first encountered the store, not long after Sarah had moved to Boston full of enterprising spirit, I'd assumed it was a front, that she was hiding behind a completely obvious mask in order to run her business with the undercurrent unhindered. That led to a few misunderstandings that were a lot funnier in hindsight—I had a rash from her poison-ivy trick for months—and, eventually, to our current relationship. (It's very hard to get through an evening stuck in the middle of Jamaica Plain covered in mud and thistles and not come out of it either fast friends or mortal enemies, and luckily for me Sarah had chosen the former.) And for all the work she does in the undercurrent, I was pretty sure that it was the cheap crap that kept the store afloat.

"Welcome to the Garden," droned one of Sarah's interchangeable assistants when I opened the door, ducking around the orange-and-black streamers that festooned the entire front section of the store. This one was a guy—apparently the latest Black T-Shirt Girl hadn't worked out—and I was surprised he could see me through the greasy bangs that hung over his eyes. "Blessings on you and would you care to try our new line of Karma Kosmetics?"

"No," I said. Sarah's orange thug of a cat Mulligatawny jumped down from his perch on a Laughing Buddha's head and stalked up to me. We exchanged glares, and Mulligatawny immediately turned his back on me and began washing himself. Yeah, I felt the same way about him. Katie, of course, hunkered down next to him and offered her hand, which Mulligatawny sniffed but didn't deign to lick. "We need to talk to Sarah."

"Miss Wassermann is busy right now—"

"Bullshit. It's Wednesday, and she never leaves before eight on Wednesdays. If she's not up front, she's in the back. And we—" I gestured to include Katie, who shrank away from my hand as if I held a weapon, "—need to have a talk with her."

The kid gave me a long look, then made a show of taking the phone from under the counter. "What did you say your name was?"

"Genevieve. Genevieve Scelan."

The last name got him, and he set the phone back down, not even pretending to call. "Oh. She mentioned you."

"Did she say to keep me away?"

"No, she said if I got in your way she wouldn't pay for the dental work."

At that I had to smile. "Then let her know we're here, all right?"

He ducked through the heavy velvet drapes that had replaced the door to the back room a little while ago (probably not long after a well-meaning jackass had held me at gunpoint in that very space, and I suspected because of that) and yelled something. After a moment I heard a theatrical sigh, and Sarah entered, smoothing down the flutters of her skirt as the velvet caught at them. "Evie, you're a marvel. The second I tell myself you're not coming and I really ought to get that inventory done, you show up. I don't know whether I should bitch you out for keeping me from work or thank you for saving me from the dullest part of the day."

I didn't answer just yet. For a fraction of a second—nothing more than a blip—the patterns in the air became clearer, the scents coming into focus as if a lens had passed in front of them. Incense and green growing things and a pinprick scent like the center of a compass—the impression I'd always had of the Goddess Garden, returning in reality rather than memory. But no sooner had I registered and understood the scent than it was gone again, and with it the rest of my talent.

Goddammit. Losing it entirely might be better than this constant shifting back and forth. I felt like a dog on a leash, yanked in too many directions and away from the important stuff.

Katie wordlessly left Mulligatawny for Sarah, who went all misty-eyed and hugged her tight. "Hey there, small cute. How's my girl?"

"Good," Katie lied, muffled up against Sarah's mighty bosom.

"She was scrying in the playground," I said thickly, leaning a little on the counter to disguise how out of balance I felt. There weren't any gray sparkles, not yet, but the ice-water feeling had lodged nicely in the pit of my stomach.

Sarah stared, first at me, then at her. "Really?"

Katie drew back a step and nodded, staring at the floor.

Sarah put a hand on her shoulder, patting it absently. "How about you go on back and get me a Coke from the cooler, okay? And one for Evie and Duncan, all right?" The kid at the register—Duncan, apparently—started to protest, but he was smart enough to recognize a distraction when it was given. He retreated as well, even pulling out a pair of headphones to show just how little he was part of this conversation.

Sarah was silent a moment, hands smoothing her skirts. "Believe what you like of me," she said finally, "but I did not teach her to use any puddle in a playground. That's just asking for trouble."

"Technically, she wasn't using a puddle," I admitted. "She'd brought a silver plate from home. I didn't realize you'd gotten as far as metallurgical magic."

Sarah's hands paused on one box (TeenyVamp Anti-Sunlight Kits! the side read). "I hadn't," she said slowly. "I mean, she might have overheard me talking about it, but she'd have to make the connections and then put them into practice . . . She's a smart kid."

"That's the problem. She's too smart, and she doesn't yet know what will bite her."

"Kind of like someone else I know," Sarah shot back. "What are you, her mom?"

"I'm *nobody's* mother," I snapped, louder and harsher than I meant to. Sarah's head jerked up, and her eyes narrowed. "I mean, it's none of your business what I am to her. Okay? What matters is that nobody, nobody should be teaching these things to a child."

"She needs to know them," Sarah said. "She can't walk through it blind."

"And how is it going to help, huh? Sarah, you know the undercurrent. You know what it is, and what it does to people. It's poison, even if all your community-watch stuff has wrapped it in fluff. Please tell me you haven't forgotten that."

"I haven't." She set the kits on a high shelf and turned to face me, eyes narrowed. "But I haven't forgotten that you don't treat it with kid gloves, either. For crying out loud, Evie, you're the one who went around giving your real name to magicians and barging your way through the undercurrent like a, a Doberman in a nursery. And now you're scared? *You*?"

"I'm not—" I heard how high my voice sounded and stopped myself. "It's got nothing to do with being scared."

"No, scared doesn't even begin to cover it," she snapped. "For the love of all, what is *wrong* with you, Evie? You seemed okay for a while, you were finally getting some from your skinny-butt guy, you'd faced down worse things than I liked to think about, but then it just . . . you just drained away. It's like you're a bad recording of yourself." She paused, as if hearing her words for the first time, and the lines on her brow began to shift, from anger to something else.

When had this turned into something about me? *Why* had this turned into something about me? "Katie's the important thing," I insisted, and the ice in my gut spread, sinking lower. "You can't teach her magic like that without teaching her the downsides too. And, Jesus, Sarah, there are so many downsides it's hard to find a way up."

She wasn't listening anymore. Instead she'd ducked back behind the counter and was rummaging through the shelves, picking up the imperfect crystals that she sold as Soul Lenses (twenty cents a pop at the local gem store, less if you have time and a rock tumbler). "Hang on," she muttered, banging her head on the inside of the case, "hang on."

"No. No hanging on, Sarah. You need to stop these lessons now. For Katie's sake. For my—" I stopped. I could ask her, as a last wish, and she'd probably do it. But that would mean telling her about the Hunt, and about midwinter. My mouth filled with water that tasted of ferns, and I swallowed it down, nearly choking. "Stop teaching her. Please."

"But you were wrong," Katie said quietly, and both of us turned to look at her. She stood in the doorway, a velvet drape sagging over her head, three hobbit-sized Cokes in her arms. "You've worked with magic for years. You invited it into your home. It's part of you."

"Don't go any farther with this, Katie," I said.

She shook her head. "You know it doesn't have to be like that—like they were. You aren't crazy. You're not living in a drain. You have us, you have me, you have my brother—"

I had all those things, and most of my sanity to boot. So she had a point. I'd lived with my own blood-magic for thirty-odd years and used it openly for more than ten, and if there was any close parallel to her own Sight, then my talent came close. I was the best rebuttal she had.

And I was going to die in less than two months. Because of what I'd done in the undercurrent.

"You don't know everything, kid," I said, and turned away. Sarah caught my sleeve, and I jerked it free. "Don't teach her any more, Sarah," I said. "Have some goddamn pity."

Six

The sun was barely down by the time I got home, but for all the energy I had left it might as well have been midnight.

In some ways, I thought as I hung up my helmet, stripped rain from my jacket (dumping it into the little fountain by my desk, which burped and sizzled but didn't burble to life as it usually did), and shook the last of the cold water from my hands, the last few weeks of slow time had been all right. It was a step better than running myself ragged, as I'd been doing in the weeks beforehand, and even if the undercurrent contracts had dwindled, the mainstream stuff was still coming in at its slow, dependable trickle. Some days I didn't even feel up to handling that much, but I'd dragged myself out of bed anyway and gone off to Mercury Courier or off to the suburbs again.

I took a dry towel from the wardrobe and rubbed it over my head until my hair stood out in all directions. Maybe one problem fed into the other, though. Maybe I'd been so tired because there'd been so little work, or I'd gotten little work because I'd been too listless to search for more . . . either way, these last few weeks had been rough. And that wasn't even counting the Sox. Goddamn.

I poured myself a glass of water from the tap,

glanced at the heap of paperwork on the desk—end-of-the-month bills, end–of-the-month invoices that mostly came back with excuses, research that needed to be done so I wouldn't get caught off guard again, all the things that I just hadn't had the heart for lately.

I wrapped the damp towel over my shoulders and curled up on the unmade futon. Rain and more rain . . . water and more water . . . I took a sip from my glass and grimaced. The water from the tap tasted downright foul, like something had died in it, and the smell wasn't much better. Boston city utilities were clearly acting in their usual stellar fashion.

There were a dozen things I needed to do, half a dozen that I probably ought to get to, and I had energy for maybe three of them. I burrowed deeper into the towel, closing my eyes. Everything seemed so out of focus these days, as if I were perpetually seeing things through a film of something, like opening your eyes under water.

No. Not under water. I shuddered and sank deeper, but it didn't do any good. The image of water over my eyes stayed, and my arms were too heavy to push it away. The smell of foul water, ice water, the taste of ferns and a cold stone in the pit of my stomach . . .

No.

Something nuzzled up against my hip, a cool but living bulk, and something else joined it along my shoulders. I opened my eyes to see a flicker of frost, fur so thick it was barely fur anymore, a flank that breathed as a red-eared head settled in next to me. One cold, depthless eye stared into my own. *This isn't good,* the Gabriel Hound murmured.

"Like you give a damn," I muttered in return, but I didn't move. That on its own was a bad sign; if my flight reflexes weren't kicking in by now, then the wiring in my brain had seriously short-circuited. I tugged one arm free and draped it over the closest Hound, the scar on my forearm where I'd fed it exposed to the orange light of sodium streetlights. "So long as I'm there at midwinter, what do you care how I feel?"

Oh, you will be there at midwinter. Not even death could keep us from you. It licked its chops, almost meditatively. I shuddered, but pressing back only brought me closer to another Hound, and a second long muzzle nestled into the hollow between my hip and ribs. *But what good is a hunt when there is only half of the prey? When the prey is weakened? The one who freed and fed us deserves to go out in better form.*

We do care, said the one currently squashing my liver. *We are not our masters. And we prefer a hunt to a slaughter.*

"Nice to know," I said drowsily. Strangely enough, it did help, in the same way that fresh water might help a prisoner.

Then take comfort here, and heal. For yourself as well as us. Their bodies were cold around me, not like Nate's warmth, but there was something similar to be drawn from the contact. *Sleep, and remember hunting. Come back, and remember hunting.*

One shifted near my feet, and I felt a faint nip, like a needle stabbed and withdrawn so fast it was gone before the pain arrived. *We are terror and chaos, but we are not what cloaks the city. And we do not like it. Nor do we like the patterns that are rising to pull you in—the old women your future is thick with, the old woman of the past, they worry us.* It exhaled, and for a second the lights dimmed, became like sunlight filtered through smoke. *Darkness in its proper place and time. Ware the old gray women.*

"I'll keep it in mind," I said, and—I have no excuse for this other than I was dead tired and not in my right mind—reached down and scruffed the Gabriel Hound's ears as if it were a puppy. It froze, and though the connection between us was severed, I could sense both amusement and worry in its posture. But sleep took me, and dreams of hunts that I would no longer follow.

In the morning I was still a mess, and that's not counting the persistent doggy scent that would not come out of my hair. I showered and made my way down to Mercury Courier, still in the same fog.

There was a word for this, I thought as Tania yelled at me. Well, she didn't yell, exactly. Tania doesn't yell. Tania explains very seriously and at length why she is disappointed in you and what options she will need to pursue as a result, with frequent references to your track record and how uncharacteristic this is for you. But the cumulative effect is worse than getting yelled at. Normally I could defend myself, pointing to the amount of work I'd put in for Mercury Courier over the last few months and why I was the most reliable of their couriers. But this morning, with the gray wash over everything like dirty water slopped over the world by a careless laundress, I couldn't even remember to nod in the right places.

Tania waved her hand in front of my face, and I realized she'd been waiting for an answer for some time. "Um," I said. "Sorry. It won't happen again."

"Genevieve, honey, that is not what I—" She paused, giving me a long look, then to my surprise took my hand and led me to one of the few chairs in her office that wasn't piled high with papers. "Honey, I don't know what's been wrong with you lately, but it is starting to worry me."

I sat down, blinking until the world came back into focus. "There's nothing wrong with me."

She squeezed my hand so hard it hurt, the pain sparking like a beacon's spotlight. "Girl, I have one brother who's been in the closet since God made him, one who's dealing out of his apartment, and two sisters who are both bipolar. And every single one of them can tell me that and have me closer to believing it. So do not bullshit me, Genevieve, because I do not have the patience for bullshit."

I met her eyes—big and dark, with yellowed whites from too many years with whatever condition meant she needed those coke-bottle glasses to see a computer screen. "I don't know," I said finally. "I don't know what it is. It's not—" I stopped. It wasn't the sentence from the Hunt, though damned if I could say why. It was something else, I realized. The grayouts were only a symptom of it.

"Don't tell me what it's not. Tell me you're getting help for it."

"I—"

I stopped, staring at the plate-glass window that separated her office from the main functions of Mercury Courier. Tania had long ago started treating it as a message board, and pages with important notes written forward and backward lined so much of the glass that you couldn't even see much through it. But what I could see through it wasn't nearly as important as what was reflected in it: Tania's back, her desk, the mounds of paper . . . and where I was, barely a shadow.

Mirrors will show a lot of things. But mirrors are also very good at lying. For truth, you want a reflection that isn't cast off silver, that comes from water or ice or good polished steel. Or, in a pinch, glass that's forgotten it's glass.

"I'll go to someone," I said slowly, and shifted in place. The little engraved mirror for Business of the Month above the door showed a flicker, but not much else. "I'll go today. I didn't—Tania, I didn't quite realize that it was a problem."

Her lips twisted. "That's always the case."

"No, I mean—" Christ, I'd even said as much to Katie yesterday. How did most magicians work? By getting loci. How did they get loci? By stealing pieces of people's souls.

And what happened to the people whose souls had been stolen?

Tania, perhaps seeing what I did even if she'd mistaken it for something else, patted my hand, then returned to her desk, unearthed a time sheet, and handed it to me. "Genevieve, if I needed all Mercury's boys to be on an even keel the whole time, I'd have no employees left. But that doesn't mean I don't mind when you go off the rails. So get yourself cleaned up—I don't care what you have to do for it, just do—and try to remember that you can rely on someone else."

"I will." I'd have to, to break this.

There's a difference, however, between knowing that something is wrong and being able to do something about it. Doubly so when the problem is all in your head—and by that I don't mean that it's not real. I've seen magics work that had effects only in someone's head—some *geisa*, for example, did nothing but make their targets obsess over one particular task, and some hauntings only took place in people's nightmares. You want to tell me the bloodshed that came out of those magics wasn't real?

Somehow I made it to the Common after my shift. The evenings were earlier now, and the first few streetlights had begun to come on as I arrived at Park Street. A few of the downtown retailers had jumped the gun and were swapping out pumpkins with Santas, and the remnants of some rally were draining away from the street in front of the State House. I ignored them in favor of the Common itself. Solid ground, the center of the city, the place where I should have felt most at home.

And I did, in a way. I hooked up my bike to a convenient rack, glanced at a couple of the newer bikes with envy, and walked on. A big fountain stood at this part of the Common, one that had been dry for years, and around it lingered a few clusters of people: college kids waiting for one last friend to join them, tourists squinting at a map of the city, homeless men arguing with each other. I sank down onto the rim of it, fumbling for my phone. Sarah, I had to call Sarah—she had some idea of what was wrong with me, or at least I could explain it to her once I'd apologized—

"Hey! See, I told you, I saw she'd be here, look!"

The rasp of a voice was one I knew, though I'd rarely heard it this cheerful. Deke wasn't cheerful as a rule; seers rarely are. I raised my head—the color had drained from the world again, really not good—and focused on the little figure vaulting the fence from the grass, and the big man behind him.

Deke scurried up to me. "Hound? Hound, I got a job for you. A good one, too. I can pay, or Roger can pay, and so can his partner. What was it you said, you can tell her what she lost? More?"

"Can't do it," I started to say, but Deke wasn't listening.

A shadow fell over me, no cooler than the air but somehow stiller. "I don't think she's in much shape to help us, Cam," Roger rumbled.

"She can too—she can find anything, right, Hound? I told you, we have a real treasure here in Boston, we're not just the scatterdust we were—"

"I believe you. But look at her. Really look." Roger knelt down next to me and put two fingers under my chin. I instinctively winced away from him, and he nodded. "How long has it been?"

I started to tell him to fuck off, that it was none of his business and that besides I didn't know what he was talking about, but just then I looked down at his other hand. He was scratching an arc into the dirt at the base of the fountain, a segment of a circle marked with lines and shapes and letters in several scripts. If I was recognizing it right, it was part of a Gebelin circle. I'd seen one too many adepts attempt small-time summonings with a similar circle, outfitted to the nines, and then lose all their loci and power without even getting any real answers. But this circle was different; the lettering around it was in different scripts—Cyrillic, Greek, something that looked like Urdu, and a rounded, simple hand that should have been English but kept sliding away from my eyes.

Roger hadn't just learned to draw a Gebelin circle, he'd improved on it. "You're an adept," I said.

"That what they're calling it? Yeah, all right. How long?"

I thought back to the last time I'd tasted ice water and stone that hadn't come from nowhere, to the abandoned and filled-in stone quarry and its nascent spirit. To the spirit that had caught Nate, even if only for a moment, and given him back to me. For a price. "A little over two months."

"And you're still walking? Damn." He stood up and murmured quietly to Deke for a moment. "Okay, let's get this straight. I am doing this out of sheer curiosity, and you are under no obligation because of it. Got it?"

I raised my head. "Doing what?"

Deke scampered off to the edge of this little plaza and eyed the trash cans as if judging them. Roger, meanwhile, scuffed the heel of his boot over the Gebelin arc and redrew it with the toe, only a segment this time and turned inside out. "Well, you don't have many options, do you? You've sustained a soulwound as bad as anyone who stayed too long near a shadowcatcher's net. Normally I'd say rah-rah, let's go back and get it, dive in guns blazing, but you're in no shape to do that. And the other ways of breaking it involve staying nine days and nights surrounded by iron, and you don't have time to do that."

No. No, I didn't. I got to my feet and glanced back at Deke, who was busily dragging another trash can to the edge of the plaza. "Soulwounds heal," I managed. "You recover from them eventually."

"Yours isn't healing. Whatever got its hooks into you hasn't drawn them back out." He paused as he drew another segment on the far side, eyeing me with furrowed brow. (Which made it a little difficult to take him seriously; he looked like a long white caterpillar had settled in above his eyes.) "Makes me wonder if it took something else . . . no, you'd be in worse shape."

"Hard to imagine that," I muttered. "But look—you can't do this, here, out in the middle of everywhere—"

"Rather we hid it away somewhere?" Roger grinned at me, and I remembered with chagrin a very similar conversation I'd had out here with a member of the Fiana, a man who'd been trying to draw me into his net. Only that time, I'd been the one unafraid of working out in the open. "No, like I said, this is just an experiment. And the experiment in question," he added as Deke nodded to him, "is how long it takes to get arrested. *Now.*"

Deke dropped a match into the first trash can, and sodden as it must have been after yesterday, it still caught fire. The segment of a circle Roger had drawn flickered, and though I could have easily written it off as an optical illusion from the fire, I knew better. *Get out*, I thought, *get out, you know better than to let someone encircle you even if they mean well—*

But at that moment two things happened: a dull, cramping pain sank into my stomach, and the first traces of fireworks scent touched my nose. Somewhere, the quarry still had hold of me, but I had my talent—I was my talent, I could make it through.

Deke lit another can, and across the Common I heard a shout from a cop. We didn't have much time. Nearby, the few people who'd remained in the circle of trash cans were looking around as well, some blinking as if they'd just heard a wake-up call, some patting their pockets as if they'd lost something. A severance circle, I realized, and smiled; Roger didn't do things by half measures.

Which was a good thing, because this cramp wasn't going away. I sat back down, hard, on the lip of the fountain, and curled up tight, arms wrapped around my belly as if holding myself together. The taste of ice water filled my mouth, and I swallowed it back down, refusing to vomit.

The quarry spirit had taken part of me, I finally acknowledged. It had taken part of my soul, my reflection, my sight—and it had kept taking. That was what had caused the grayouts, the fog over my talent, the lethargy. I made myself let go, got to my feet, and tipped my head back. More fire, now, ringing me in four points, and if the cops hadn't shown up yet then they sure as hell would in a moment.

For just a second I heard a cry, a high wail that was no more than possibility. I drew a deep, shuddering breath, tipped my head back—

—and yelled a stream of curses at the sky.

Roger guffawed, and I thought I heard Deke yelp, but those were lost in the snap of something parting, some strain finally broken, some thick invisible membrane breaking around me. And with it came a rush of scent, the patterns of the world reestablishing themselves.

Yes, I thought, and closed my eyes, reveling in the sense of—not wholeness; even with my imperfect understanding of the world I could tell that something had been severed—but sufficiency. I might be injured, but I was no longer fettered—and most important of all, I was myself again.

I opened my eyes and to my surprise, the first person to meet them wasn't Deke or Roger (who, I now knew from scent, were standing to my left just outside the circle), but one of the historical tour guides who shepherd packs of visitors around the Common: a small black woman in period dress, her white skirts glimmering in the streetlights, her hair up under a bonnet. She gave me a small, tight nod as if she approved of my choice of profanity. I grinned at her, then turned to Roger. "Thank you."

"Ah, that's much better. I much prefer talking with people who are all here." He glanced at the sky, then at his watch, and frowned. "Even if it's cost me a little time. Come on, Cam, I gotta get back or she'll have my hide."

"Wait." I stepped down from the fountain, marveling at how easy it was to walk again, how clear everything seemed once more. "What can I do to thank you?"

"Thank me? For what? No, no, you just got caught up in an experiment. No debt on either side." Deke grabbed his sleeve and whispered urgently, but Roger shook his head. "No need to bother her with that. Talk to you later, Hound."

Deke, crestfallen, waved at me but followed along in his friend's wake. I stretched, reveling in how good everything felt, then glanced back for the tour guide. She was gone, of course.

By the time I let myself into Nate's place, Katie was already asleep (or at least her light was out; if she was like me, she'd have learned to read with a flashlight under the covers) and Nate was on the couch with a new stack of midterms in front of him. "Hey," he said, looking up. "You all right?"

"Yes." I smiled and settled in next to him. "Yes, I am. For the first time in a long while."

"Good. That's good." He put an arm around me absently. "Aunt Venice called; she wanted to know if you could track something down for her."

"No discounts for your family," I said, trying to make sense of the papers in front of him. Higher math was not my specialty, even at those points where it intersected magic. Especially not those.

"And Sarah called. She wanted to make sure you were okay."

"Crap. I pissed her off. And Katie. I should apologize . . . I'll do it in the morning." I leaned against his shoulder, but the tension in his muscles had nothing to do with the phone calls. "What's wrong?"

Abruptly Nate dropped his pen and pulled me close, so close I damn near had trouble drawing breath. I squawked, but the way he held on to me wasn't so much possessive as desperate, as if I were a lifejacket in a storm. "You can't go," he said into my shoulder. "At midwinter. You can't go."

"I don't want to," I said, and reached up to touch his hair, early gray and brown sliding through my fingers. "I'll figure something out—I'm sure I can, somehow. But I have to do this on my own. Nate, you can't save me from this."

He was silent a moment, then loosened his hold and sat back, though he still didn't quite meet my eyes. "I nearly attacked someone today. I . . . I was thinking about you, about the Hunt, about how damn powerless I am, and suddenly this argument I was having with one of the other TAs just seemed so fucking stupid in comparison. I nearly—" He touched his cheek, then his lips, as if reassuring himself that they were still in the right place. "It's the first time it's happened like that. And I thought, what if you're not there? You keep me in check, Evie. I know where my limits are, with you. If you're gone—"

I put my hand up, stopping him, then cupped it around his cheek. "You're only just now noticing? It's a curse, after all. It's not meant to make you a productive member of society."

He exhaled, a short, bitter breath that was somewhere between a laugh and self-inflicted contempt. "I'll trust your word on it. I have trouble trusting my own . . ." He looked back at me. "They have noticed," he said. "Not . . . not anything explicit, but my students, my advisor, the other TAs . . . they know something's different. And they're a little scared of me. Whenever it gets close I can feel the pressure in the back of my head, and I think they see it too. They back down."

I shrugged. "Must be nice."

"No. They look at me . . . they look at me the way people looked at my father."

I nodded at that. His father had tried the same intimidation on me, only there was too much of the hound in me to react the way he'd wanted. "Nate, trust me on this. You're not your curse."

"I trust you," he said, softly enough that I didn't quite think I'd imagined it. "But I want it gone."

"Then we'll find a way to get rid of it before I go." I

stopped, realizing what I'd said. Nate's eyes met mine, and to keep from talking more I kissed him quick. "There are ways," I said. "Your father got rid of it, after all—there's the wolfskin he hit you with—"

"Long gone, I'm afraid. He took it back."

"Well, there are other ways. Maybe nothing so simple as a usual cursebreaking, but there are fissures, places where it's not as strong. We'll find a way. Okay? Trust me."

"I do trust you," he whispered, and sighed against me. "More than I can say."

I rested against his shoulder a moment. "So what were you arguing about?"

"What? Oh . . . the TA. Possibility theory. It's a little difficult to explain; it's the counterintuitive parts of higher maths, which is why it was a problem."

I thought about what the quarry spirit had done, and how it could have done that to me. There were some things I knew about magic, and permission, and purposefully misinterpreting words, but still . . . "Yeah," I said, chasing that from my mind for now. "Possibility is a bitch. Fortunately, so am I."

"Not to me," Nate said, and kissed my cheek. Well, he'd meant to kiss my cheek; I turned just in time to catch his lips against mine, and from there things got interesting, enough that I was reminded anew how it felt to keep his wild side in check.

That night, tangled up against Nate and pleasantly sore all over, I dreamed of the Hunt again. They were very happy, very happy indeed.

Because now I'd taste a whole lot better when they came to tear me apart.

Not the most encouraging dream.

Seven

Tania gave me a measuring look when I got in the next morning, but she sent me to Somerville and Medford without a question, then out to East Boston and Charlestown. Any past November, I'd be begging Tania for a double shift on an unseasonably warm day like this one so I could sock away some extra cash. Mercury Courier doesn't close down during the winter, but the shifts are slower and harder, and I'd gotten stuck short of money in February before, when the heaps of dirty gray snow made everything just that much worse.

I spent most of the morning going back and forth between towns on either the far side of the river or the far side of the harbor, and just for some extra fun, over the railroad tracks. Want to dislocate a biker's shoulder? Send her over the tracks repeatedly. If it doesn't do that, then it'll sure as hell turn her forearms to mush. The damn things are worse than potholes.

I did most of my work for Mercury in a thoughtful haze, going from place to place without quite registering where I was headed or what I carried. Boston traffic's useful for that—you can concentrate solely on what's in front of you, and that'll be enough to occupy most of your thoughts and then some.

In fact, I even had enough presence of mind to

search for the book for Nate's Aunt Venice. It was a little unusual—normally I'd want the signed contract in hand before I started work, even for someone who wasn't in the undercurrent—but I had the excuse, I had the means, and my God, I could hunt again. That was enough of a reason, as far as I was concerned.

Unfortunately, from finding the scent of that particular book (sand and dust and a peculiar greasy green quality that I was learning to associate with old glue) to finding the pages that were missing took all of forty-eight minutes. Not even enough to run over my lunch break. I spent another ten minutes in front of what I'd found—a senior art exhibit at Boston University, where the pages had been collaged up and turned into

History Devours Itself 4: What We Have (Is) Known

and tried to fight down the vague disappointment in my stomach. I had so little time left, and it had been so long since I'd had a truly satisfying hunt . . .

It was probably that, more than any sense of obligation, that made me seek out Deke. And it was definitely that need to hunt that made me use my talent to track him down rather than just calling him on my cell. (Deke didn't like phones, but he'd started to carry one just in case—to call the cops, he explained, though I couldn't imagine what problems he'd have that a cop could help with.)

I found him down by the waterfront, on the footbridge across Fort Point Channel. I locked up my bike by the courthouse and started across, whistling through my teeth, waving once he saw me.

They'd done their best to spiff up this part of the city—luxury hotels, new construction, a fragment of a park—but fragments of the old waterfront remained. Namely, one big house out in the middle of the channel itself, on decaying pilings like dead man's fingers. Since the pedestrian bridge at the mouth of the channel had been a swinging bridge once upon a time, the house had probably controlled the mechanism that opened the bridge to let ships through. But time had passed, and the only boats that sailed this way now were small enough that they could go right under the bridge, and the house over the water sat and sagged, so isolated that only one graffiti tag marked its side.

Deke, however, seemed to be regarding it like a homeowner deciding on new landscaping. "Nice place," I said as I reached his side.

"It's okay," he said. "Better than the drains."

I glanced at him. "You're living out here now? I thought you hated the water."

He shrugged. "Easier to see Roger this way. 'Sides, I don't hate it so much, just what—" He stopped, and the faint smile dropped from his face. A shudder coursed through him, and for a second I caught a stink of fear rising off of him, so acrid and sharp I wondered that the bundled-up families passing on the far side of the bridge couldn't scent it as well. That was the same fear I'd smelled on the burning yacht, before Roger carried him off. Deke shook himself and pulled himself together with an almost audible clunk. "I manage," he finished. "Talking of Roger, there's something I want to ask. He won't, he's too suspicious of anyone he doesn't know, but there's something he wants found—"

"I know," I said. "I guessed. That's why I'm here."

Deke's face lit up. On the heels of that sudden fright, his undiluted excitement seemed a bit strange, but also a relief, given that I was hoping for a job. "Really? Oh, Hound, I'm so glad—he's needed help for a while, and now I can help him out, I'm so glad—"

I held up one hand. "It depends on what he's looking for, okay? Where is he?"

Deke pointed.

I looked. "The courthouse?"

"No—no. Out in the harbor. See, he was late last

night, because we were helping you. He's not supposed to be away from the water at night. She doesn't like it."

"She?" I glanced again at the courthouse—no, at the harbor beyond it. "Tessie? She said someone was looking after her boat."

"No! No, not Tessie. Not Tessie at all." He hesitated. "I'm really sorry about her. Is she okay?"

"Last I heard." And I hadn't gone back to check on her, more's the pity. Stupid of me. "So who's 'she'?"

"She's his ally. Sort of. It's . . . look, I can take you to him, okay? He can't be on the mainland, not for another few days, because he wasn't in sight of water when the sun went down. But I can take you to the island. And bring you back. Promise."

"I don't know, Deke—"

"He said she can help you. When we were talking, he said about the hold on you. On your life. Roger said she can help."

I froze. For a moment the air felt heavier, the sun (what there was of it, this late in the day) more piercing, even the rough planks under my feet seemed to communicate their presence up through my bike cleats. The touch of wind on my skin felt more real, more alive than it had in weeks, and it would be gone so soon—

If there was even a chance, didn't I have a responsibility to find out?

"Okay," I said. "Let's go."

Deke gave a happy whoop and, before I could do anything, clambered over the wire fence that separated us from the outside of the bridge. He motioned for me to follow, and I did.

I glanced at the other pedestrians—not many, not with night coming on earlier—and scrambled over, expecting at any moment to hear a yell from some security guard. Nothing, not even when I landed on the far side next to a No Trespassing sign. *Rena would kick my ass if she could see this*, I thought.

Below the bridge, in the underpinnings of steel and concrete that held it in place, was a narrow wooden walkway—the close end of the one that led to the little house in the middle of the channel. A tiny boat, the kind that aspired to be a Zodiac but had given up on those aspirations some time ago, floated just under the bridge. "I'll take you to him," Deke said, and settled expectantly in the boat, one hand on the motor.

We slid out from under the bridge, following the curve of the marina. Deke chattered away about Roger and the time he'd saved Deke from some bully or another back in high school . . . or maybe it was two different stories, I couldn't tell. Only half listening to Deke, I watched the city recede behind us.

Technically, the islands are still part of Boston, as is the harbor itself, but . . . it's different, being out on the water. I wasn't sure I liked it. We swept past the docks on either side of the harbor, past the barren wasteland of office buildings and parking lots on the waterfront, past Castle Island and the other remnants of Southie that I still carried with me. The great white eggs of the water treatment plant on Deer Island, at first so small and ridiculous, loomed up into huge structures just as their smell—rotten eggs and sewage wasn't the half of it—loomed up as well. Just in time for the first big waves too. I held on to the edge of the boat and tried not to barf.

Across the water, through the shoals of the islands . . . One island had DO NOT APPROACH signs up on every beach, with a big biohazard sign next to the largest and WARNING ASBESTOS beneath that, though how asbestos got out here was beyond me. Another was no more than a little circular wall, seemingly there for the sole purpose of holding the beacon that warned us away. Deke made a gesture over his shoulder at it, as if warding it off.

We arrived at the far side of a long, flat island large enough to have a few hills on it and an imposing gray stone building beyond those hills. The air smelled of salt and dead fish, with that peculiar scraped, gritty scent of beaches in this part of New England, and the cheery little refreshment shack at the end of the dock had long since been boarded up for the winter, making it just as inhospitable as the stone walls behind it. Whatever that other building was, it took up most of the island.

Roger met us at the dock, a big fuzzy hat pulled cockeyed over his head so that he looked like some bizarre Canadian pirate caricature. "Cam!" he roared, and hauled Deke out of the boat with one hand. "Great timing. I've got fish on the grill. And who's—" He stopped. "Huh. So you came out, after all. Cam, I told you not to go bothering her."

"She came looking for me!" Deke hauled a box out of the back of the boat (I realized I'd been sitting on it most of the way) and tucked it under his arm. "She can help, Roger, I know she can."

"If you say so." He gave me a long look, then thumped Cam on the shoulder. "Go on; fire's already started. Hound—you mind if I call you that?"

"Better than 'bitch,'" I said.

A slow smile crept up Roger's face, drawing brows and whiskers together in a wrinkly gray mass. "So it is. Well, Hound, welcome to Georges Island. Home, for now."

"You're living out here?" I asked, climbing out of the boat.

"It's not so bad. So long as the rangers don't notice me, and I got ways to make sure they don't. Besides," he gestured to the big stone building that eclipsed the far side of the island, "there's plenty of room in the old fort. Not like anyone's using it these days."

"And from what Deke told me, staying on the mainland isn't an option."

Roger chuckled, following me off the dock and onto the gravel path. "Not if I don't want to pay for it, like I'm doing now. My boat was better, but after what happened, well." He shrugged.

"What did happen?"

"Not sure. One minute Cam and I are talking in the galley, he's catching me up on all the local gossip—I can't believe the Sox actually won since I last left town, can you?"

"Didn't help them this year," I said, more bitterly than I'd meant.

"Well, you win some, you lose some. Anyway, one minute we're shooting the shit, the next the room's full of smoke and the hold's on fire. Cam takes one look at the flames, screams, and falls down, and it's all I can do to get him out of there." He gazed out to sea, and I didn't have to know directions to know he was looking out to where the yacht had gone down. "I'll miss her. That was a fine little ship, with a good history, and she served me well."

I glanced ahead. Deke was well ahead of us, and probably out of earshot, but I still lowered my voice. "I hate to ask, but Deke is, well, known to be something of a pyro in these parts."

"He was with me the entire time," Roger said, still staring out to sea, then turned to face me, his eyes cold and hard as ice. "And I'll thank you never to insult my friend to my face again."

I looked down at my feet. "Sorry."

"I should think so." He quickened his stride, following Deke around the curve of the path. "Oy, Cam! Leave the fish, okay?"

One side of the island turned out to be a little park, with picnic tables and playing fields and greenery that was only now turning brown. True to his nature, Deke was at the grill already, oblivious to the rest of the world. Roger had a pair of fish wrapped up in foil and on the coals, and he and Deke talked a bit in low voices. Well, Roger talked; Deke seemed happy to be silent, so long as there was fire.

Me, I kept walking, past the gates to the fort and the stone above them reading FORT WARREN 1850. At the edge of the field, the gray stone walls rose up in a forbidding barrier. I went up to the walls and laid a hand on them: cold stone, smelling of grease and tar and the quenched scent of dead gunpowder. That last made me pause—the scent of magic is something like gunpowder, like fireworks set off during a storm—but this was a purely material scent. Someone had stockpiled armaments here, a long time ago, and they'd never had cause to use them.

I closed my eyes and inhaled, shivering against the constant wind off the harbor. Stone and salt, cold and damp, the patterns of tourists not just from today but from the whole summer, fragments of kids who'd scrambled over these walls during the summer . . . and below them, the patterns of long use from years before, so deeply etched into the place that they might as well have happened only a few weeks back. Mildew and old piss and the back-of-the-tongue cardboard scent of very stale bread—not real scents, but traces ground into this place, impressions of the people who'd lived here, who'd been prisoned and prisoning, guarded and guards. You could make this a tourist site, have guides in costume and concerts on the Fourth of July, but there was something about this place that still felt gray and melancholy.

Roger's salt-and-granite scent approached, echoed by the crunch of footsteps on gravel, and when I opened my eyes he held out a beer. "Thanks for coming out."

"Welcome. But no thanks," I added. "Swore off some time ago."

He shrugged. "More for an old sailor, then." He leaned back against the wall, watching Deke.

There was something about him that made you believe you were in on the joke too. I didn't much like charisma, and I've always hated charm, but Roger had something else about him that didn't fall easily into either category. Which made me wonder what he was doing with Deke. "So what is it you need found?"

He opened the beer and hunkered down against the

wall, taking a long sip. "You know," he said, "time was I thought Cam was nuts too. Nice, but, you know, nuts. Then I joined up and . . . well. Being out on the sea does different things to different men. I've known some Marines who got religion and some who became flat-out atheists, and both from the same thing happening to them. Me, I just kept my eyes open, and . . . you learn a few things that way."

I thought about what I knew of the sea and magic. You can't magic the ocean; it's too wide and too varied, and the water in it flows from too many different streams for you to name and bind it. Kind of like the Wild Hunt, come to think of it. But that didn't mean there weren't powers out there, ones that I didn't know the first thing about dealing with.

"So about then I start thinking that you know, maybe there's something to what Cam was always talking about way back when." He gave a long sigh, then creaked to his feet. "And then there's how I got into it, but that's another story."

"I believe it," I said fervently, and followed him back to the grill. Deke had found several dry sticks—don't ask me where; there wasn't much cover on this side of the island—and stuck their ends in the coals, like a blacksmith with his irons.

"Then what I say will make more sense to you than it would to most other people. I'm not like Cam here." This he punctuated with another slap on Deke's back, and Deke punched his friend in the arm weakly. "I don't have the spark for it. Most I've ever seen was a man on my crew a little while back who had a touch of the Evil Eye. Worked in our favor, then. But I don't have that advantage. And I'm just a grunt, when it comes down to it. Just a simple sailor man." He winked at me.

"Sure," I said. "And I'm just a biker girl."

"No shit? I always wanted me a Harley." I opened my mouth to say that that wasn't what I meant, then let it pass. "Not that I could use one much, things being what they are—" he gestured to the surrounding ocean as if that explained it, which I suppose it did in a way. "Anyway. What I did for you back on the mainland is probably the extent of the book learning I've got. Never had the patience for it, never got my hands on a copy of the Unbound, never could stand any of the dipshit discount Crowleys drawing their circles and chanting their mantras." I thought of the Elect or Chatterji. Yeah, I'd lack patience in that situation as well. "So I took the other option: I made allies."

Allies. I'd once heard magic could be split into three categories, blood-magic, like Deke's and Katie's sight and my own talent; ritual magic, like the Elect and Sarah's work and the majority of adepts; and spirit magic, which depended on entities that ranged from gods to mauled ghosts. The categories weren't perfect; they blended back and forth with worrying regularity (case in point: the Fiana had been ritual magicians, but they'd used spirits—chained, betrayed spirits kept in vessels of flesh—as their source of power), but they would do for a quick glance. And of the three, I considered spirit magic the least reliable, because if you didn't have the upper hand at all times, you were essentially dependent on the goodwill of something inhuman. I touched the shiny patch of new skin at my throat, where the Horn had rested. "And that's why you're stuck out here," I said.

Roger shot a narrow glance at me. "Yeah. Yeah, it is. Not the worst of the bargains I've made by a long shot—and don't think I'm going to tell you the rest—but it does have some problems. Like now, for example."

He handed one of the sticks to Deke, who reverently accepted the fire and began turning it back and forth, searching with haunted eyes. "I've currently got an ally," he said, nudging the foil-wrapped packets out of the coals and giving them a poke. "And she's got a bit of a problem. If she didn't, I'd be back in Malacca right now, but that's neither here nor there . . .

anyway, she's injured. Old wound, but one that's been draining her for some time."

"Sounds like you should have chosen a better ally."

"Hey, I don't turn down offers. Besides, usually she's fine, just needs to recharge now and then. That's why I make it up to Boston on a regular basis; that's where she got hurt, and where she feels better. Like being close to what was stolen helps her, a bit. Only this time we had that trouble in the harbor, and now I don't have a ship. But Cam tells me that not only is Boston no longer *terra non grata*, but that you might be able to fix things for my ally. Like permanently." He snorted, then carefully extracted both packets and slapped them on the picnic table. The wood charred and smoked, but didn't catch. "Cam! Fries are up."

"Thanks," Deke muttered, and jammed the unburnt ends of the sticks in the ground, so that they continued to smolder, like poor attempts at tiki torches.

Roger prised open the foil with thick, bent fingernails. "I only made enough for two, but you're welcome to a bite. Better than the noodles Cam brought up; I don't know what I'll do with those."

"Don't knock the ramen." I usually ended up living on the stuff in March and April, when my courier budget finally ran out. "But no. Thanks."

Roger gave me a sideways glance. "Smart. You don't like incurring debts of any kind . . . very smart. All right, here's one thing I'll swear right now, on my mother's dear gone soul, and on the waters of Oceanus the mighty. Neither I nor my allies will do harm to you or yours."

That was . . . well, easier than I'd expected. And now for the tough part. "And what do I get in return for my work?"

"Dina can tell you." He finished off his fish with a couple of bites, then licked his fingers. "Cam, watch the fire, would you? I'm going to take her into the fort."

Deke nodded, still looking from fire to fish and back.

"You're a cautious woman," Roger said as he led me back along the path to the dock. "So I should warn you about this now: Dina's a little scary."

"Scary?"

"Oh, she's harmless. Especially now. But she doesn't like to be seen, and she's . . . well. Best to let you find out for yourself; I can see you won't believe what I tell you." He led me to the huge gate in the stone wall that we'd passed on the way over, and gestured within. "Fort Warren. Not that it's much of a fort; it was more of a prison back in the Civil War, and they did some stuff with it in World War Two, but that's about it. Still, good enough for a place to crash."

It was enough of a fort for me: huge stone walls encompassed a wide expanse of green lawn, streaked with trails from the tourists who wandered over it in summertime. Beyond the walls, waves crashed on the stones, their impacts muffled only slightly. "She's here?"

"Sort of. Listen."

I did. The sounds here were mostly wind, punctuated by the slow, mournful note of a beacon out in the harbor and the clang of buoys. But . . . there. One moment present, the next caught by the wind and reduced to only a memory, the thin sound of a flute wound up from the fort, a hollow, aimless reel like that of a lost Pied Piper. Every other note dissipated on the wind, but it was there. "That's her?"

"That's her." He led me to the thick far wall, which was notched with doors and gaps, some of them set with lights, some not. "Barracks were this way, once. And when it was a prison, the mess hall. But there's not much here now."

He pointed to the ceiling—no electric lights on this entrance, as opposed to the one a few yards down—and a warning sign saying that people who ventured into the fort did so at their own risk. "You got a light?" I said.

"She doesn't like it." He grinned. "I'll be right beside you," he said, and stepped into the darkness. I hesitated, cursed, and followed.

The flute hesitated briefly, as if the player had heard me, but continued. I edged forward, one hand on the wall, opening my eyes wide as if that might help bring in more light. The dimness of the unlit corridor faded further into total blackness, and my hand slid off the wall into nothingness.

I did have a light on my keychain, the little red lights that certain pocketknives have in the place of the tweezers everyone loses in the first two months. But it hadn't worked in a while—not since I'd used it to guide my steps up to the top of the tower in Mount Auburn Cemetery, come to think of it. Maybe the stress of the later encounters had broken the bulb. It didn't matter; what was important now was that I had no way of seeing who I was supposed to be meeting.

I shouldn't need to, though. Closing my eyes—the difference was negligible—I turned to the right, reaching out to trail my fingers against a wall that receded out of reach within the first few steps. The scent here was of damp leaves and dust, cobwebs that had never been rained on but nevertheless had the same clumped, sticky feeling just from the pervasive dampness. The flute echoed in here, and I suddenly realized I was in a much larger room than I'd expected.

I took a deep breath, trying to figure out where I was, what this room might have been. The scuffed salt-stone scent was still there, just muted beneath the layers of decay and neglect, and Roger's salt and sweat was still present, a few feet ahead of me. And beyond that . . .

My eyes snapped open, even though there was nothing to see. Beyond those scents was another, akin to the scents outside but somehow magnified, as if seen through a lens of bloody water. Seawater. Black sand. Even, somehow, the scent of splintered wood. And a dull, corroded scent that I knew at once, even if it was as immaterial as the ghost scent that so marked this fort, even if it was only a psychic scent rather than a real one. It was a signifier only, not a trace of reality, but it still made my spine tingle all the way down to my tailbone.

Whoever was playing that flute smelled of corpses, long dead and rotted. "Roger—"

"It's okay," he rumbled somewhere ahead of me. He didn't have any trouble finding his way, at least. "I promise."

The reel hadn't changed since I stepped into the dark. I waited while the flute player continued, winding through the last few phrases as if fumbling its way through a labyrinth (far too apt an analogy for the moment, but it stayed with me), and, when the last note died and its echoes strangled on themselves, Roger clapped.

"Thank you," said a woman's voice. She wasn't close, perhaps at the other end of this wide room, but her voice was clear and unaccented. She sounded old, not cracked or anything like that, but without the tics and swiftness of a younger woman's speech.

"Hello," I said.

"You're here," the woman said. "I'm so tired," she added, and I realized she wasn't talking to me.

"I know, Dina," Roger said. "It'll be all right. I've brought someone who can find it."

"Find it." She took a deep breath, and I heard a slight scuffling around, like . . . rats . . . or, no, like someone finding a case and putting an instrument away. Right? "You . . . you are a mother, yes?"

"What? No! No, I'm not."

"But—" She hesitated, her scent somehow static even as I could hear her moving. "I see. You have severed that."

"I don't know what you're talking about—" My voice went high, and I clamped my mouth shut to keep from embarrassing myself further.

"You lost something, didn't you?"

I saw in memory—as if it were projected on the blackness before me—Nate falling from the cliff above the quarry, blown back by an explosion, his body fading.

"You bargained something away."

What will you give me in return for him? the spirit of the quarry had asked, cradling Nate against the column of falling water that was its body. And then a wall of water, striking me, passing through me, leaving only the taste of dead leaves and ice in the back of my throat and a cold, coiling presence in my gut.

"I didn't bargain," I said through dry lips. "I didn't offer anything to it. It just said it accepted and gave him back. And how do you know all this, anyway?"

"How do you know where the scent leads? How do you know how to raise your eyes to the sun?" There was a faint rustling: petticoats, I thought briefly, then revised that to leaves, or papers, or something that made more sense in here. "We both have our inborn talents. This is one of mine. Think back. It asked what you would give it, and you cried out . . ." She slowed, as if reviewing the scene in her head. "You called it . . ."

A cold, gnawing feeling rose up in my stomach—no, not my stomach but lower, like a cramp that wouldn't fade. "I called it a son of a bitch."

Dina was silent, but it was the silence of a teacher, waiting for a student to draw some connection. Beside me, Roger drew breath sharply.

For a moment I didn't understand. For another moment after that, I didn't want to. Then, "Oh, no. No. That can't—"

"Can't it?"

"That makes no sense," I said, and my voice came out as more a plea than a statement. I cleared my throat. "No sense at all. There'd have to be so many factors that worked just right—I'd have had to, to catch it right away, and I'd have noticed—"

"It's what you're afraid of," Dina said.

"It makes no sense," I said again, more weakly. It did—just in an undercurrent fashion. Son of a bitch. And I was the Hound, the queen bitch. A spirit could purposefully misinterpret that, turn it against me, claim the possibility—there didn't even need to be a reality, and the blood I'd shed a week after that night indicated there had not been—of a child and make that its link to me. And then, month by month, the quarry spirit would have stolen more of my life, in the same way that a growing fetus draws on its mother's strength.

My stomach lurched. I was suddenly very glad I hadn't taken Roger's offer of the fish.

"Nothing makes sense," Dina snapped, her voice suddenly parting into three, like a unified voice splitting into a chord. "Nothing," she repeated, again the tired woman I'd heard before. "But I could do something about it."

That got my attention. What kind of idiot does "something" about it in these circumstances? "No," I said. "That's over and done with. Besides, none of this is going to make me trust you any more. If I'm going to find this—this thing for you—"

"It's a sunstone, about the size of a Ping-Pong ball," Roger said quietly, the timbre of his voice changing as he turned back to face me. "Polarized feldspar; it'll show light through when held in the right direction. Useful for determining your position even on a cloudy day. Which was why, I believe, the Vikings prized them. Good for navigation." Though I couldn't see him, I had the sense that he was smiling.

"I've been without it so long." She drew another breath, and though it was a quiet, unassuming sound, something about it still sawed against my bones. "Please. If you bring it back, I can give you back what was stolen—or, no, there is more. I can keep the Hunt from coming for you."

I caught my breath. "You can do that?"

"I can. At the height of my power, I can. If I have the sunstone, I can."

I closed my eyes. In the past, I'd made bad bargains, negotiated with people who didn't have my best interests or even their own best interests at heart. But most of the time, when that had happened, it was because I'd been ignorant or overconfident. The worst scrapes I'd gotten into were mostly because I was convinced I could help someone. This wasn't the same thing at all.

Someone had once said of me that I'd taken on a *geis*, an obligation, that I couldn't turn down anyone who was genuinely in need. I couldn't cling to that now. If I took this on, it would be a free choice on my part, and I'd have to suffer the consequences.

And this was a devil's bargain. All I had to do to know that was trust my nose.

"I want your word," I said, forcing the words out through lips like iron, "that you won't hurt me or mine if I do this. My friends, my loved ones." At least I could keep the fallout from touching them. "You won't lay a hand on them, you won't work to hurt them—nothing."

Roger chuckled. "Suspicious, aren't you?"

"I'm standing in a pitch-black room with a magician and a creature that can read my worst fears. I think a little suspicion is called for."

"I will swear," Dina said. "No harm to you or yours, and you bring me back the sunstone. By the gods of the earth and the sky and the harsh depths of the sea, I swear."

"Okay," I said. My skin had gone from cool to chilled, and I wrapped my arms around myself to keep from shivering. "I'll do it, then. Where do I find it?"

The rustling started up again, drawing nearer and lighter, like skirts over stone but not nearly so heavy. "I can give you a token, something with which to find the thief."

Her offhand confidence in me was less inspiring and more creepy. I stepped back, the heel of my sneaker scraping against the wall I'd followed into this room.

"Hold out your left hand." Something nudged against my fingers a few times, as if she couldn't quite see how to place it in my hand. Perhaps she was as blind as I. A thin bundle wrapped in stiff cloth pressed against my palm; something like two broken pencils. "That should lead you to the thief," Dina said, and while her voice still sounded distant, the breath of her words stirred my hair. "Good luck."

"Luck has nothing to do with it," I said, and tucked the bundle into my jacket pocket.

She smiled—I couldn't see it, but there's a peculiar exhalation that comes with a certain kind of smile, and right then I could hear that puff of breath. "Don't worry. Soon you'll know."

My breath caught again, and I sidled back, wanting to get away but unwilling to turn my back on her. My fingers brushed the wall, and I felt my way back, lichen and slime and weird iron hooks and latches dragging along my palm, until finally I turned the corner to see what little light remained at the end of the hall. Roger followed beside me, silent as a shadow.

The last glow of daylight had faded, and I quickened my pace. "I'm so sorry, Hound," Roger said quietly. "If I'd known—"

"Shut up," I said, and kept walking.

Eight

Deke knew enough not to talk to me on the way back, though he paused as we tied up (at a real dock, not the weird little thing under the bridge) and turned to face me. "I told him you were good, Hound," he said. "I know you'll find it."

"Thanks," I said listlessly.

"Roger's a good man," he added, uncoiling a rope and throwing a loop over one of the posts on the dock that had a RESERVED sign on it. "Always visits when he comes by for his friend to . . . to recharge. This time I thought, you're free now, the city's free, maybe you can help him. So he doesn't have to keep coming back here."

I didn't answer, just climbed up onto the dock. The ocean sloshed underfoot, and I had to shift from one foot to the other to keep my balance.

"And maybe if you can help him, then he can help me. That's right, isn't it, Hound?"

I slung my messenger bag into place and glanced back at him. "Why—what do you need help with, Deke?"

He huddled in the end of the boat, tipping it so that it lurched in the waves. Even in a craft that small, he seemed smaller, and the warm gold light from the waterfront didn't help that. "I see things, sometimes, in the fire . . . sometimes they don't go away. That's why I've made preparations. I'd want to go out like a Viking, me. I'd go properly."

There's a limit to how much I can be around adepts in a day before my brain starts to skip a groove, and I'd hit that limit a while back. "Okay, then. You take care, all right?"

He nodded and cast off again, headed to whatever pitiful shelter he'd made in that horrible old house by the bridge. I turned away, running my fingers through my hair as if to shake the last of the salt spray from it, and climbed up onto the marina.

The chill in the air didn't seem to mean anything to the beautiful people of Boston; some charity had organized a jazz concert out on the waterfront, and the whole marina glittered with it. I passed by men in suits with martinis in hand and women in cocktail dresses and seriously inadequate shawls, all talking and laughing about things that probably meant a lot, outside the undercurrent. Only the waiters paid any attention to me in my beat-up jacket and scruffy biker gear, and they only did so to stay well away from me. Which was a pity, because for a moment I had the urge to snatch one of the glasses off their trays and forget what I'd just learned for a while.

I shook my head. That wasn't the answer, not with everything else I had right now. The quarry spirit was severed, I was whole again, and now I had a chance at living past midwinter. It wouldn't even be the first time I'd helped an entity of dubious morality. No one could call the Morrigan a good goddess, and yet I'd brought her back to wholeness. (And killed her again, but we could pass over that for now.)

I drew out the bundle of cloth, the token Dina had given me to find her thief, and examined it under the lights. Oilcloth, or something like it: soft, coarse cloth that had been soaked in some waxy substance for so long it didn't feel quite like cloth anymore, although it wasn't unpleasant against my skin.

My first impression of broken pencils hadn't been far off, I thought as I unwrapped it; this looked like a very old, shriveled, oversized clothespin. Two shriveled, blackened sticks of uneven length stuck out of a slightly thicker lump about the same length. One side of it was ragged and more shriveled than the rest, and the whole thing stank of age and salt.

It wasn't until I turned it over and saw the fingernails at the ends of the two sticks that I realized what I was holding.

I yelped, dropped the bundle, and then fumbled as it fell to keep it from skittering across the pier into the harbor. My fingers snagged on the oilcloth so that the mutilated hand ended up snuggled against my chest, like some zombie trying to cop a feel. I gagged and peeled it away, looking at it in the bright light. Now that I knew what it was, I could see the details more clearly: this was half of someone's hand, mummified by age and desiccation. Whatever wound had torn away these fingers and section of palm, it had long shriveled up, peeling back at the edges to reveal bone turned brown from exposure to air and salt. The whole thing had shrunk a little; impossible to say now whether this had come from a man or a woman.

If this was Dina's "token," it was a wonder the sunstone had ever been stolen. I looked around to see if anyone had noticed me juggling body parts. Nothing, but I kept on walking anyway, following the water. If I remembered right, there was a little stub of a rose garden, just planted on the greenway now that the Central Artery was gone. I closed my hand over the fingers and headed in that direction. If I had to do my search using such a grisly token, I could at least do so from a point of protection.

There's a magic to certain open spaces, and one that I've never quite understood. It's not a natural magic in the sense of a spirit or a genius loci or the pattern of ley-lines, nor the consecrated space of a chapel or a gravel garden. But something to do with how the place is kept and maintained—or even how it was built in the first place—tends to accrete its own magic. It's similar to how Fenway Park has its own field about it, the result of generations of people pinning their hopes and their moods on what happened on that scrap of green. What it means in practical terms is that, simply, certain places have different affinities.

Boston Common, for all its role as a park, was best for travel or for starting journeys. There was a scrap of a playground in South Boston that, because of the care and the time and the emotions invested in it, had an affinity for change; you spent time there, and you came out wanting to alter your life in some way, usually for the good. And there was a tiny chapel on the waterfront, deconsecrated now and converted into some kind of utility station, that comforted people whose loved ones were away. That one, though, I knew only by hearsay, since most of my loved ones hadn't moved away; they'd just died on me.

For a number of reasons like the ones I've mentioned, rose gardens are safe havens. I wouldn't trust one to hide me from active pursuit, or even from a passive scrying, but something about the act of placing the roses, encompassing a small space with them, creates a bulwark against ill influences. In terms of protection, it's probably on a par with a ditch, compared to, say, the six-foot walls and spiky bits that a proper ward provides. But it's enough for me, most of the time.

Safely in the roses—a few of them still clinging to summer, thick with brilliant pink blossoms that practically glowed in this light—I unwrapped the fingers again and, grimacing, raised them to my face, seeking the scent that I could follow to Dina's sunstone. Salt. Tar. No rot; just the dry, leathery smell of old skin and an undernote of bone that made my lips pull back from my teeth. All scents of a thing, of the disembodied fingers on their own, of this lump of mummified flesh. No trace of the person they'd belonged to.

I drew my knees up so that I was curled into a ball next to the roses, sitting with my back against one bush and my toes just brushing the edge of the path. With any luck I wasn't all that visible; I didn't know how long it would be before a police officer came by to inform me that I couldn't sleep here, and right now I didn't really want to deal with the cops. I laid the grisly scrap on my knees and regarded it, then took a deep breath and closed my eyes.

I'd done something like this before, sinking into a full trance to read the scent around me in an attempt to glean information that either was too faint or too fleeting to follow without heavy concentration. But then I'd been searching the broad spectrum of scents for one in particular, like a satellite scanning the streets of a city for one specific person. This was diving into one scent, one pattern, trying to find the original defining characteristic.

Deeper, down so that no scent beyond this one in front of me even penetrated my consciousness, deeper still . . . My ears began to feel as if I were trying to sneeze with both my nose and mouth shut. Salt and preservation and, faintly, the first echo of blood and rot . . .

There. I almost missed it, since it was so like what I'd been ignoring till now. Fish and tar and salt, but of a different quality than the salt that was part of the thing's dead scent. This had a tang to it, like meat kept in brine, or olives . . . the hand had belonged to a sailor, or someone associated with the sea. Which made sense if I thought about it, since going back a few hundred years, most people had some kind of association with Boston's shipping, hadn't they?

The conscious thought started to pull me back up out of the well, nonverbal thought receding from me as if I'd accidentally caught hold of a passing buoy and now was being dragged up to the surface. And with it came something else: the sizzle of gunpowder, long wetted but not quite useless. Old magic, waking up.

My eyes snapped open, and for a moment the world shivered before me, the greenway's lights becoming the dull glow of lanterns, the greasy glow of burning whale oil sliding across water . . . no. No, it was the greenway again, though the light jazz down the waterfront had faded. The rosebud that had brushed my forehead when I began now curled away from me, as if it had had time to grow and decided I was not a safe place.

I was inclined to agree. The fireworks scent of magic was gone, but it had been unmistakable, even if old and slow. Like stepping into a rusted bear trap . . . okay, no, I didn't much like that metaphor. Like finding a letter to yourself from decades before you were born.

I realized I'd clasped the mummified fingers between my hands and pressed them close against my neck, so that their freakishly smooth surface (like old leather stretched over twigs, and oh God it was warm now from my own body heat) rested against the skin of my throat like a lover's caress. I fumbled them away, then groaned as my muscles tried to seize up. Didn't monks do this sort of thing? How did they manage to sit for hours and still get up afterward?

I edged out of the rose garden, creaking a little. I might have the scent, but tracing it through this—it was like following a groove in the sidewalk, blindly, using only your feet. And the trail itself didn't even make any sense. Think of the paths you walk during a week: to your home, to the grocery, to work, to visit friends, the routes you take or don't, the grooves worn by your passage over time. Usually that's what I find: the paths laid down by someone over the course of time. But this one wasn't like that; even taking into account the years, it felt incomplete. Like one wrong note or a single broken stone in a handful of pebbles, drawing attention because of its imperfection. Or half of a puzzle piece . . .

The incompleteness of the scent seemed matched,

somehow, by the visual echo that refused to leave. Every time I turned my head, the lights and activity of the waterfront retreated into shade, a forest of masts stark against a dull gold sky. When they were present, the scent felt almost complete—almost, but still broken, missing some vital part. It wasn't disruptive, just a sort of very strong visual déjà vu. It didn't feel wrong, though—I didn't get the sense I was in danger. Instead I just felt watched. As if someone was alert now.

Well, these days I was more alert than I had been. Besides, I was the Hound, I had the scent, and I needed this stone if I wanted to live past midwinter.

I followed my nose out across the greenway into the nest of bars and shops that made up Quincy Market. No sign of Vinny and his friends this time, thank God, but every now and then the few people I passed seemed to slip into conversations that didn't make sense in this century, words that were echoes rather than real time.

There were ways to set up wards so that only a person fulfilling certain characteristics would trigger them—say, a blood relative on a Tuesday, for example. But most were so complicated and so useless that adepts didn't bother. And "ward" was really the wrong word; it was closer to the original definition of a *geis*: a prohibition or decree meant for one person in certain circumstances. Should this happen, you must do thus. That sort of thing. Such patterns were old in terms of use, but they weren't something I expected to run into in Boston. (At least now that the Fiana were down.)

Stranger still, the visual echo vanished as soon as I left Quincy Market. I looked back as soon as I realized it was gone, then checked my steps.

Through the twisty streets to a package store—what most non-Bostonians would call a liquor store—on Haymarket. I paused a moment just outside the door, trying to guess the building's age. It didn't seem old enough to have been around back then, but it was worth a try.

The bell chimed as I entered, and a skinny kid at the front counter looked up. "We're closing in ten minutes, lady," he said. "Make it quick."

"Sure," I said, and slipped between the aisles. I hadn't been in one of these places in years. At the back of the store was a spiral staircase leading down and a handwritten sign on pink posterboard: VISIT OUR WINE CELLARS—TASTINGS TUESDAY NIGHTS. I glanced over my shoulder, but the kid at the counter was ringing up three bottles of vodka for a little old lady in black.

The stairs led down to a cramped cellar about a third the size of the building above. I didn't know much about wine, but this looked like a perfect place for it: cool, a little damp, the brickwork exposed and smelling faintly of soot. And—if I ignored the coolness and the trails of recent customers and the muted, indistinguishable scent of the wine quiescent in its bottles—the scent of tar and salt and adrenaline was present as well. Dina's thief had come this way, once, and the brickwork looked almost old enough for it.

I ran my fingers over the wall at the base of the stairs, trying to get a sense of which way the thief had gone. Down here, it was clearer than it had been, as if the passage of time meant less underground, or as if this were closer to the source. Or, to take the simplest answer, because fewer people made it down here. South, I decided, turning and edging around a rack of bottles. He'd come this way from the harbor and gone almost straight south. Only given the cowpaths of Boston streets, going straight in any direction for long was damn near impossible—

I stopped. The far end of the cellar was sunk a little further into the wall, in the shape of an arch. Above, the bricks followed that arch, continuing it into the ceiling and spreading out, but the rest of the ceiling was newer, as were the close walls. Whatever passage had been down here was long bricked over, and the current owner had put his best wines in front of it.

I started taking down bottles, putting them to the side, trying to find a way to get to the brick itself. I wasn't hoping for a secret entrance—okay, maybe some part of me that had watched too much Scooby-Doo was hoping for it—but in some way I was hoping for at least one more clue. Maybe the thief had stashed the sunstone here, maybe there'd be something more . . .

The clerk's footsteps creaked overhead, and he called down the stairs. "Lady? We're closing. Lady? Goddammit."

I dragged the half-empty rack to the side, enough for me to see the complete lack of secret passages or hidey-holes, and slammed my fist against the brick. Nothing. I could feel the trail pass into the stone and beyond. It must have been laid before this passage was closed off, but that didn't help much now, did it?

It didn't matter. I'd look up records for this place, find out who owned it, maybe work out a way to dig . . . there had to be some way to get through.

Something twisted against my chest, and I scratched at it absently before realizing that it wasn't my biker gear fraying at the seams. Instead the inner pocket of my jacket twitched and jumped against my skin, like a trapped frog.

I stifled a yelp and clamped my hand over the jacket. The fingers twitched faintly, like a dying fish, and I damn near flung the things into the corner of the room. Instead, gritting my teeth, I withdrew them and held up the weakly shivering bundle.

The ceiling creaked again: the kid, coming downstairs this time. I reached up and put both hands, one still holding the fingers, against the brick—

The fingers flexed in mine, like someone trying to clasp my hand, and the ceiling overhead vanished, replaced by a brick arch, dank and slimy with condensation. I caught my breath, then gasped a second time as the total lack of scent hit me. I couldn't smell anything, not even myself.

The tunnel was no longer bricked up. Instead slick, oily water half filled it, stretching out ahead and behind me. A strange, brassy light filtered through grates overhead, not daylight or even a close approximation of it but something else, like light seen through smoked glass. But past it, down at the far end of the tunnel, there was a single flickering flame: a lantern, held aloft by someone standing on a rickety dock amid crates and barrels painted a dull black.

Smuggler's haven, I realized. This was still Boston, but long ago, when patriots and opportunists had good cause for sneaking cargo in under King George's nose. This would have been underground, and it might have stayed the same since then.

I squinted at the person holding the light. She wasn't the thief, of that I was sure. For one, her hands—one on the lantern, the other clenched in her dress—were intact. For another, this small, grim, brown-skinned woman was not the sailor I had scented; she was a landswoman. Her clothes—well, you see Colonial re-enactors and tour guides all over Boston, particularly during summer, and while their styles are all accurate, there's a certain vibrancy that comes from using modern fabrics and modern sewing techniques. This woman looked faded, belonging to another era, but her dress was still scrupulously clean, the kind of clean that I knew from my mother: too proud to look poor.

She was the same woman I'd seen on the Common, I realized, when Roger and Deke broke the quarry spirit's hold on me. Only here she wasn't out of place; here she was in her element, and she stood with a calm control belied only by her tight grip on the lantern.

"Meda!" A man's voice, somewhere behind me, and for a moment I mistook it for the package store clerk. I turned to see a little boat, floundering down the tunnel. One oar was jammed in the stern; the other had been put to poor use by the man in the boat, who seemed to be using it as a canoe paddle. His left hand was tucked tight under his right arm, and though I couldn't see his face the grubby sheen of his jacket seemed darker and shinier right there. *Blood*, I thought, and held tight to the dead fingers. "Meda, are you there?"

"I am, and don't shout. The master will hear." Her voice was strangely accented—the cadence of the past, perhaps, or something else—and it did not echo, unlike the man's.

"Old Grouchy can hear and dance a jig for all I care. I have it, Meda, I have it. I am sorry, it was not enough, I was not enough, but I have it and there'll be no more at Nix's Mate—"

Meda stiffened and lowered the lantern. She glanced up at the grating, then straight at me. She had the look in those eyes that I'd only seen in very strong magicians. There's something about it that marks you—Maryam had it, Roger had a flicker of it, all the members of the Fiana shared in it—and this woman could have faced down any of them. And though I couldn't explain how, I thought she knew me.

"Aye," she said. "No more." And she raised her other hand in a gesture I didn't know, as if to cast sand across the water.

I started to step forward, and my nose mashed up against the bricks, hard enough that tears sprang to my eyes. The vision or whatever it was vanished, and the fingers were again dead flesh in my hand. "Fuck," I mumbled, stuffing them back in my pocket, then stopped.

The scent was gone. Not ended, not out of range, but gone. Even the pitiful traces I'd followed this far no longer existed, as if they'd been swept up by a tidy housemaid. "God dammit all to hell—"

"Lady, I told you—" The stairs creaked, and I

turned around too late. The kid stared at me, then at the scattered bottles, then back at me. "Jesus! Jesus Christ, what is going on?"

"It's all right," I said. "I just had to, to find something."

"What?"

"See, I wanted to look at the wall, only it wasn't there—" God, my head was starting to pound, not just from the bonk on my nose but from the incomplete hunt, the pressure of that lost scent an ache both physical and mental.

"At the wall." He nodded slowly, holding his hands out at his sides as if to show that he was unarmed.

"No, really—" I snorted and rubbed at my nose; I'd skinned it. That probably wasn't helping my case. "It was important. Say, do you know when this building was built?"

His eyes widened. "Okay. Okay, lady, we're closing now," he added, speaking carefully and slowly, "so unless you want to look at the wall some more—"

"Thanks, no. I um. I can pay for what I've done," I added, trying to find my wallet.

His eyebrows went up even further, and he took a step back, closer to the stairs. "That's, that's okay. Whatever you've done is between you and God, okay?"

Ah, crap. There was no way I was going to get out of this conversation looking sane, was I? I edged toward the stairs. "That's not—"

My cell phone chimed weakly with an errant signal bouncing down from above. I jumped; the kid jumped about a foot higher and ended up in the corner holding a bottle of chardonnay like a really ineffective shield. "I'll take this outside," I said brightly, and ran up the stairs, face flaming. On the way out, I dropped what cash I had in my wallet on the counter; at least that might make up for the extra work.

The number wasn't one I knew. I caught the ring just before it swapped over to voice mail. "Scelan."

"Evie?" The voice was Sarah's, speaking over what sounded like a crowd of people.

"Sarah! Jesus, I'm sorry—I'm so sorry, I meant to get in touch earlier—"

"Evie, I need help," she said, practically shouting over the sound of the crowd. "I'm at the watch meeting in Dorchester, and we need a neutral voice here—"

Someone—a man's voice, high and hysterical—interrupted her, and I heard Sarah cover the phone to speak back to him—then a wet thump, and a cry.

"Sarah? Sarah!" I stared at the phone, but the connection was lost. *Goddammit.*

Nine

The trouble with being a biker in Boston is that while it'll get you through traffic more quickly than a car—which is why Mercury specializes in downtown work—it's still a lot slower overall. Especially if you happen to leave your bike in another neighborhood entirely.

According to the schedule Sarah had given me, the ersatz "community watch" had been meeting on the Triplets' turf this time. The Triplets didn't quite run a protection racket. They'd put down roots in the community, but they didn't really care too much about what went on in it, so long as they knew who was currently on top. They only dealt with organizations—gangs, families, parishioners—and they'd curse anyone for a fee. Not all the curses worked, which they freely admitted, and I'd heard Sarah speculate that the degree to which they did work depended on how much the Triplets valued the target and client both. But enough were effective that they brought in sufficient cash to own bits of other local businesses, thus making a legitimate living. (Which is more than can be said for most magicians.) Between that and a tacit agreement with some of the local Babalorishas, they had a quasi-symbiotic role with the neighborhood. They'd even been one of the first to acquiesce to Sarah's community watch.

They also didn't like to come out in public. Which made arranging meetings on neutral territory difficult. If something had gone sour there—

I cut off the thought and ran a red light, careening into a little alley off the main drag. The street was pretty run down, with grates and locks over every storefront and the crumbling look that happens when neither the current owner nor the previous had any money to spare for upkeep. A Vietnamese grocery took up one corner of this skinny block, a car-repair shop took up the other, and in between—

Well. In between was a crowd. Looking over their heads as I approached, I could see a little of the problem: the middle window of the upper story had been smashed in, and while I didn't scent any magic immediately, a stifled, flat smell hung over the block, as if someone had tried but failed to complete an invocation. More important, there was already an ambulance on the far corner.

I locked up my bike and tucked my helmet under my arm. Someone at the edge of the crowd glanced back, then did a double-take and nudged the guy next to him. Great. "What the hell happened here?" I asked before they could get away.

They just gave me a wary look, but one of the guys with them was a lot more talkative. "You would not believe it—one moment we're just sitting out front, minding our own business, then this crazy white guy in like a purple bathrobe ran up the road, pushed past us, and ran in yelling. Next thing we know he's hitting people, saying they wrecked his place, and then he must have like thrown a chair or something because the window broke."

"That's good glass too," said the girl next to him. "Not supposed to break easy. And I didn't see no chair."

"What, so he like, broke it with his mind?"

"I didn't say that," the girl insisted, even as the two who'd first noticed me looked at each other. "Only that I didn't see no chair."

"Thanks," I said, and slid past them. Crazy guy in a purple bathrobe? Well, I knew plenty of crazy guys, but not their off-duty dress. Broken glass littered the sidewalk, and not just from the second-story window. The ground floor was a restaurant: GRILLED MEATS AND PICKLE, named by someone with a greater desire for honesty than for appealing marketing. And it, too, had a smashed window—broken right below the stenciled graffiti above the frame: three *3*s, positioned so that they formed a triangle. "Goddammit," I muttered.

"Hound," a deep voice said behind me. I turned to see a tall black man in a red hooded coat standing at the edge of the crowd. "You took a long time."

"Had a long way to come," I said, racking my brain for his name. Haroun, that was it. Current liaison for the Triplets, though who knew how long that'd last. Others had been discarded for getting too full of themselves, promising what couldn't be delivered, or skimming too much. And by "discarded" I mean that the former liaisons hadn't been seen in Boston again. I used to know one man who claimed they were sold for parts, but that never seemed quite plausible. "What happened? Where's Sarah?"

"Sarah?" His lips curled. "You should be worried more about your other friend. The one who came here yelling."

Other friend? Who? "All I know is I got a call from Sarah—"

"He came in here," Haroun said, easily talking over me as if I were an unruly student and he the professor, "interrupted our discussions, and accused us of conspiring against him. And then he hit Younger in the face."

"Oh, shit." It's not a good idea to hit a magician, and I'm saying that as someone who's done so in the past. With enthusiasm. The trouble isn't that it gets you hurt right away, it's that there tend to be consequences. Particularly if you're attacking one of the

Triplets. "Is Younger all right?" Haroun nodded. "And the other guy?"

He made a gesture like flicking dust from his sleeve. "You're sure you don't know him?"

"She knew him."

I turned to see Sarah, wrapped up in a brilliant pink coat and holding an icepack to her face. "Sarah! God, are you okay? Did he hurt you—"

She took the pack away, revealing a bruise the color of raw steak all across her cheekbone. I made an inarticulate noise, but she didn't seem to notice, staring at me hard instead. "Haroun, can you bring a light closer, or maybe one of those glass . . ." He handed her a shard of glass, silvered on one side, possibly from a mirror inside the restaurant. "Thank you." Sarah held it up, angling it between us, and muttered something as she examined my reflection. "You're all right," she said wonderingly. "I'd thought—"

"You thought right." I took the glass from her hand—after the number of cuts she'd sustained there in the past, you'd think she'd be more careful—and closed my fingers over hers. "I'm okay now. There was a severing."

"Severing? But then you're not okay, you're just not getting worse." She turned my hand over, held it out in front of the light from the store, and glanced at my shadow, as if expecting it to be faded. Well, after a few days more of the quarry spirit drawing on me, it would have been. "A severing doesn't bring you back to yourself, it just stops whatever's leeching off you—and how did you let something do that in the first place?"

"I'm fine. Really. Now, how did you manage to get that shiner?"

Sarah sighed and glanced at Haroun as if for confirmation. He drew breath to answer, but just then a new commotion started, this time at the front door. A wail of utter misery echoed from the door, followed by its maker—and two cops, one at each elbow. "My home," cried a sad little man in, yes, a purple bathrobe, though now that I saw it I could recognize it as the kind of "ritual garment" that some of the stranger adepts wore: purple silk with characters embroidered on the edges, now stained with food and grease and worse. Definitely worse, I thought, taking a sniff. "My home, all my books, my loci, my *pomegranates*—"

I took a step forward, even though I knew I couldn't do anything. He turned as I did so, spotted me, and flinched away, into one of his escorts, who grumbled and pushed him upright again. "Hang on," I said. "Wasn't he at the docks when that boat caught fire? The Elect, or someone like that."

"Yes," Sarah said, replacing the icepack on her eye. "He was the one who called me to let me know something was going on. Saw you pull Tessie out." She sighed and balled up her other hand in the folds of her coat. "She's out of the hospital, by the way."

"Good," I said absently. The little man in purple seemed a threat about on the level of damp paper towels, but the police still bundled him into the car and drove off. "But if he was helping you then, why—"

Sarah rubbed her unhurt eye, and for the first time I could tell how much this was draining her. The little squabbles may have been no more than she expected when she first got into this, but enough of those will sap your strength. "Someone trashed his place. I didn't catch everything he said, but it sounded like an invocation of some kind."

Haroun cleared his throat. "An Hourglass Pinch, supplemented by a souring. It is a common curse, if you want to destroy a man's possessions. He thought the Triplets were to blame." Whatever changed on my face, it was enough to tick him off. "No, Hound. They were not. No more than Wassermann here was helping them."

"Sounds like he needed a scapegoat, then. Your bad luck it was you."

Haroun's lip curled. "Luck," he said. "You tell me now you believe in luck? You are in the wrong business, Hound."

I thought of Dina, of the bad bargains I'd made. "That's very likely."

Haroun's brows rose at that, and for a moment I thought he might even be softening a little. Sarah shook her head. "Look, wrong business or not, can you keep an eye on things here? Haroun and I—if we've got a chance of keeping a lid on this, we need to get down to the station."

"You're kidding." Put me in charge of anything? How the hell was I supposed to keep magicians from fighting, put them all in time out?

"Right now we've got a few too many scavengers about," Sarah added, tipping her head toward the crowd. "The Triplets' wards will hold, since they're in retreat right now, but I need you to do damage control. The last thing we need is—" She stopped, leaning forward. "What happened to your nose?"

I rubbed at the skinned spot. It still hurt. "Long story."

"You haven't gotten in a fight again, have—? Never mind. Will you stay, just for a bit?"

"Sarah, I don't know—"

"People listen to you. They'll give you a chance." She glanced over her shoulder and edged closer. "But only one chance, so don't screw it up."

"Yes, thank you for that vote of confidence." I switched my helmet to my other hand and ran my fingers through my hair. It was stiff from salt spray and greasy from the day's sweat. "Okay. I'll run interference for you."

She nodded. "Great. Haroun, we'll take my car if that's all right with you."

I could have warned him against the car; it was a beat-up beige hatchback that had probably last had a tune-up in the Cretaceous, but Haroun nodded, made a gesture to the storefront, and followed. He was good at this, I thought, as they got in and drove off. I hoped the Triplets would keep him on for a while; people with sense were always in short supply in the undercurrent.

And right now I had to face some of the consequences of that. I turned to face the crowd and smiled brightly, and a few of the onlookers—the ones who'd just come to see the show, or who lived nearby and wanted to know what was up—smiled back. Unfortunately, that didn't include the shadowcatchers who'd stopped by, and it certainly didn't stop one particular voice in the back. "—the nerve, the absolute nerve to tell him to go away! And this after all that had happened—I don't even see what the problem was, all he did was slap the boy, it wasn't even that hard—"

I made my way through the last of the crowd and put my hand on the speaker's shoulder. "Madame Sosostris," I said, showing all my teeth in something that wasn't quite a smile. "So good to see you out and about."

Wheelwright turned white at the name—maybe hiding your real name is good for magicians, but for a charlatan it doesn't help to have your stage name associated with outbursts like that—and choked on her next few words. I turned the glare on the people around her, but it faded as I recognized some of them: Kassia, a woman who worked pretty much the same racket as Wheelwright but under the Triplets' protection; a guy in a green mechanic's coverall, and Byron Chatterji, flipping his bowler hat between his hands as if he were about to pull a rabbit from it. "Got here a little late, didn't you, Hound?" Wheelwright managed, choking up her grip on the huge purse she carried.

"Too late to see what happened."

"What happened? A ghetto spat, that's what happened, and it's not nearly as important as you're making it out to be." Wheelwright turned and shook a ringed finger in my face. "Do you know, I had two balloons full of pigs' blood—pigs', mind you—thrown at my windows this morning. And I had a full schedule too—do you know how long that took me to wash off?"

"I wouldn't have thought your clients would notice," Kassia said sweetly.

Wheelwright turned to her. "You—" I closed my hand a little more tightly on her shoulder. "Go to hell," she said through gritted teeth.

"My still," Chatterji said lightly. The words dropped into the argument like fine china on a stone floor. I turned to look at him, and he smiled nervously. "Someone has smashed my still. It will take months to rebuild, and I have not loci for more than five weeks."

"Why do you even *need* a still?" Wheelwright snapped.

"Ah, see, that is a very interesting question," Chatterji responded, perking right up at the chance for a lecture. "You see, there is the principle of severance and return—"

"The point is," Kassia said, spreading her hands, "something is going wrong, and it is going wrong over the city. In years past, so I am told, one group bore the brunt of it, but that brotherhood is done with." She made a genteel gesture in my direction, of either thanks or warning, and I inclined my head in response to both. "Now there is this community watch, and either it is ineffective or it has turned malicious."

"There's no call for that," I said, letting go of Wheelwright. "Sarah is working with the Triplets to find out what moved the Elect to do this."

Kassia turned and spat. "You sound like the police. How can we trust you?"

I started to answer, try to come up with some of my credentials, but stopped as I realized that I didn't have anything concrete to give her. This was the undercurrent; someone could work for you for twenty years and still betray you. Trust was a scarce commodity.

Or at least that was the undercurrent as it had been. Not as Sarah wanted to make it. Not as I'd envisioned it, once.

"You don't," I said. "So you can ignore me, and go on building your own alliances in hope that they'll protect you, or you can give this a chance and maybe get something better out of it by the end."

Kassia gazed at me, eyes narrowed, then nodded once. "Or I can do both. You will forgive me, but I think I would prefer that."

Wheelwright had latched on to Chatterji, taking his arm like a dowager with a gigolo. "It sounds fascinating," she cooed. "How is the principle worked?"

From the look on his face, it seemed that Chatterji rarely got a willing audience for his favorite subject. "Oh, you see, it's a very simple principle of severance and return. By removing a part of oneself, or letting it pass from you in the natural course—I of course use the diluted humors of one's own body, since the kidneys are the seat of the passions and thus the perfect last point of divergence—you then spend time without it, creating a severance, so to speak—"

The man in the mechanic's coverall edged closer to me. "He's not talking about what I think, is he?" he murmured.

"Yes, he is—" I rubbed at my eyes "—if you think that he's talking about drinking his own pee."

Chatterji, with the luck of the talked about, caught my last few words. "That's a very simplistic way to think about the principle," he admonished, wagging his finger at me. "All it takes is severing a part of oneself, healing, and then regaining that part after time away. It makes sense, if one thinks of the soul as a contiguous object, as an echo of the greater Sophia—"

The mechanic shook his head. "It's a load of crap! Or, sorry, a bucket of piss."

Wheelwright shot him a nasty glare. "There's no need to be bitchy because you're jealous."

Ah, Christ. "That's enough of that—" I started, just as a second police car drove up. The woman in the driver's seat got out and looked right at me, and her eyes narrowed.

Damn. Rena.

I turned a little, pretending that I hadn't seen her. What the hell was she doing here? Her precinct wasn't even near Dorchester, was it? And she hadn't gotten transferred . . . come to think of it, I wouldn't have heard if she had been transferred . . . but no, she'd been up at the docks a few days ago. Was there a connection between that fire and this?

My head started to pound, and I realized there was at least one connection: me.

"Enough," I said again, moving between the mechanic and Chatterji. "Call it a difference of opinion, okay? Let it go before I bust both your heads." The mechanic glared at me but relented, and Chatterji, who'd moved into his usual deer-in-the-headlights stance, relaxed enough to remove Wheelwright's hand from his arm. "Now, let's all just make our way out of here, okay? It's too cold and too late to argue."

Kassia nodded at that, but Wheelwright had turned away, toward the cops. "Finally. Maybe we can get some sense out of this." She marched right up to Rena's partner, Foster, and planted herself in front of him before he had a chance to even look at the scene. "I saw the whole thing," she declared, and right away I knew it was a lie. "The poor man was out of his mind. Obviously insane. Obviously incapable of understanding what he was doing."

"I see," Foster said smoothly. He glanced at the crowd—now that cops were here, they were slipping away like bad dreams in the morning—then nodded to Rena. "You want this?"

"I'll take it," she said without taking her eyes from me. "You do what you do best." Foster had come up from forensics, I remembered; he was better with the concrete evidence. Which, unfortunately, left me with Rena. Wheelwright was going on about how awful it was that some poor deluded man could have done such a thing, it couldn't really be his fault, could it?

Kassia, meanwhile, had slipped away with the rest

of the crowd, and the mechanic was trying to do the same. And just then Chatterji did one thing for which, harmless little man or not, I could have strangled him. "Miss Scelan here can tell you what happened," he said brightly, and made a little ingratiating bow to Rena.

Overwrought courtesy wasn't working on her. Right now she was as stony as the walls of Fort Warren. You could have frozen the air from the look she gave me. "Yes," she said, turning over another page in her notebook. "Tell me what happened."

I glared at Chatterji, who gave me an encouraging smile and a thumbs-up, and sighed. "Okay," I said. "First thing you need to know is that I wasn't actually here."

Rena wrote a line and waited.

"The people you really want to talk to are Sarah Wassermann and Haroun Lahyani. They should already be giving statements. I'm just here because they called me in to cover for them."

"Cover for them." She glanced at me. "In what way?"

Shit. "Make sure no fights broke out after they left, that sort of thing. The, the guy who got hit was a magician. Is a magician. So's the one who did it, only he's not very good."

She kept writing. "Uh-huh." It'd been years since Rena didn't believe me when it came to the undercurrent—the amount of magic she'd run into made that difficult—but it surprised me how much her disbelief, feigned or real, stung. "And he used magic?"

"No, he used his hand. And maybe a rock, for the windows. I don't know."

"Was this before you hurt your nose?" She gestured with the tip of her pen.

I sighed. "This was earlier. I told you, I wasn't here."

"Uh-huh. And I should be talking to you why, then?"

"Because—" I glanced back at Wheelwright and Chatterji, who had clumped together again. "Because

I know about this sort of shit, Rena, and you'll get a more understandable story from me than you will from anyone else."

Her lips twisted, and right away I knew I'd made a mistake. "Somehow I doubt that," she murmured. "Listen, Evie. When I said I wanted out of this kind of *bruja* shit, I didn't mean for more of it to follow me home, okay? Do you know how many things like this—" she gestured vaguely at the broken windows, "—have happened lately? And how many of them have something to do with your woo-woo friends?"

"I—" I didn't know. At least two, from Chatterji's and Wheelwright's remarks, but the undercurrent's a secretive place. If something bad happens to an adept, his or her first reaction is to cover it up to hide any perceived weakness. So if word of more than a few had gotten out, that meant there were many, many more out there. "I've been kind of out of it," I said lamely.

Rena flipped back through her notes. "Vandalism. Vandalism. Arson. Assault with a non-deadly weapon—that'd be a bladder full of bean flour, in this case, and if you know the reasoning behind that I'd appreciate your not telling me. More arson. And vandalism. And that's just this week. This is what your—magicians—are getting up to lately, is it, Evie?" She didn't even look up from her notes as she said it.

I almost snapped right back at her—*they're not* my *magicians, dammit*—but thought better of it. And besides, they were. Not in the sense that I could tell them what to do, but in the sense that I had some kind of responsibility for them. "Everyone's been paranoid lately," I said quietly, and Rena's pen paused. "I'm not entirely sure what's causing it. Kass—some people think it's cyclical, but I think it might be some kind of, of external factor."

"Fluoridated water, no doubt."

"Jesus, Rena, will you take this seriously?" I swayed a little. Rena glanced at me, wariness giving way to concern. "You ask me to explain, but I can't because it's all crazy talk to begin with, and you don't want to hear any of the explanations I do have. What am I supposed to say, huh?"

"You're supposed to tell me—" Rena began, but whatever else she said I missed.

A brilliant light like a flashbulb from hell went off in front of me, and I ducked away. The streetlights' sensors, fooled into believing it was dawn, snapped off, and in the sudden darkness two people caught me by the arms. "Come on!" Chatterji whispered, and took my stumbling back toward him for assent. By the time I could see again, I was halfway around the block with them.

"What—" I coughed. "What are you doing?"

"Aversion ward, aversion ward, aha!" Chatterji patted his pockets, came up with a paper packet, and scattered the contents ahead of us, muttering as he did so. I held my breath to avoid smelling what I knew would be both magic and various unsavory fluids. "There we go! Keep walking, it'll hold for several more blocks and then we'll be fine."

Wheelwright shifted her arm so that I was no longer leaning on her. "Very nice," she said, scuffing her toe in the dust. "Your own work?"

"Oh, yes." Chatterji beamed. "I liked your trick back there. What invocation did you use?"

"Invocation nothing. Flash powder and a little extra spark, that's all." She sounded inordinately satisfied. "And as for your question, Miss I-can-handle-myself, we are getting you out of a bad situation."

Out of? "No—no, I have to go back, Rena will be furious—"

"The cops won't bother with us," Chatterji said with the confidence of someone who'd gone under the radar for a long time. "And you looked like you needed the help."

"I didn't—" Oh, Christ, even if Rena wanted to believe me before, she'd never believe me now. How was

I going to explain this? "Goddammit, you two, you may have just completely screwed any chance—"

A stink hit me like a board to the face—a smell of rot and excrement and dead things. My knees buckled, and Wheelwright's almost did, and we lurched against the closest wall. I stumbled away and slid to the ground, panting. "Hound, are you all right?" Chatterji asked, in search of the obvious. "Was it the policewoman? My grandfather was always allergic to authority, and I know the debility is possible—"

"No." I pressed both hands against the back of my neck and tried to block out the ugly reek. "No," I said again, partly to myself. "I'm all right. I'll be all right. Just—what the hell did we just walk past?"

Wheelwright glanced over her shoulder. "Broken water main, it looks like. Nothing big; there's a Dig Safe team already working."

"That's not all." I took a deep breath through my mouth, gagged, and tried again. Better, though now I was tasting it. There were a lot of things buried in Boston, I knew. And some of them didn't like being dug up. "I'll be okay. But I'd stay away from here for the time being."

Wheelwright snorted. "Don't have to tell us twice."

Chatterji knelt and offered me his flask. "Here. Drink this."

I think my expression made clear what I thought of that. Wheelwright chuckled and rummaged in her enormous purse. "You might want this instead," she said, handing me a bottle of water.

I took it over Chatterji's protests that really, he thought an infusion of potential loci might actually help more, uncapped it, then turned away, gasping from the stink that rose off it.

"Picky." Wheelwright took a swig of it herself. "Okay, so it's not Monadnock Springs like the label says, but it's good tap water. A little better than your other option."

"Thanks. No." I got to my feet and looked over

my shoulder. No sign of Rena; either she'd decided I wasn't worth following or—more likely—she knew where I lived and would just find me there. "My bike's near here. Look, the two of you ought to get going."

"A thank-you would be nice," Wheelwright began, but Chatterji took her arm and steered her away.

It's shaming to admit it, but I went to Nate's that evening as much because I wanted to stay away from Rena as for any desire to see him again. Which was, it turned out, a good thing.

When I made it up the stairs, I expected to see Nate hunkered over another stack of undergraduate exams. Especially since it was well past eleven. Not Katie by herself, curled up on the sofa. "Katie?" I asked as I dropped my messenger bag by the door. "What are you doing up?"

She looked up from the book (a huge illustrated tome that she'd dragged onto her lap, and even then it still hung off) and her eyes widened. "Evie! I found this book, and—are you still mad?"

"No," I said, and sat down next to her. The book was one of those big pseudo-reference books, the kind named *Witches!* or *Mummies!* in big frightening letters and crammed with pictures to hide how little substance they had. This one had more gory woodcuts than a breathless Victorian's version of the *Malleus Maleficarum*. Good stuff. "No, I'm not. I'm sorry, Katie. I shouldn't have acted like that."

She nodded, eyes wide, then abruptly flung her arms around me, forgetting the book between us. I got a corner in the ribs and another in the thigh, and stifled a grunt of pain. "I'm glad," she mumbled into my arm. "I'm really glad."

"Well, I'm glad you're glad, but Chrissake, Katie, it's nearly midnight! What are you doing awake?"

"It's a Friday," she protested.

"Doesn't explain—" I stopped. "Where's Nate?"

She didn't move, but a creak from the kitchen and

the scent of wolf and worse was enough of an answer: the window was open, and Nate had just gotten in. "Go on to bed, kiddo," I said, closing the book. "Nate'll wonder what you're doing up."

For once, she didn't argue. She too knew what her brother was, what his curse had made him. Though they didn't share a father, the two Hunter siblings were in some ways very alike. Instead she gave me a quick kiss on the cheek—I raised my hand a second later, not quite sure whether to wipe it off—and ran into her room, thumping the door closed so loud it destroyed any hope of stealth.

I got back up, unhooked Nate's bathrobe from the back of the bathroom door, and waited in the doorway to the kitchen. The lights were off, but enough streetlight glow filtered through from the fire escape—and the open window, for God's sake—to glint off a pair of eyes too close to the floor. "You want this?" I said, holding out the robe.

A rumble met my ears, and the scent of hair and sweat and leaf mold sharpened.

"Yeah, I don't think it looks good on you either. But there's walking around in the buff, and there's walking around in the buff with a little kid in the house. I'm pretty sure one's a felony in some states." I paused. "Okay, maybe both are, depending on the state."

The rumble sharpened, and what instincts I had as Hound told me that now would be a good time to take cover, maybe find a weapon. Instead, I leaned back against the doorframe, dangling the bathrobe on one finger. "You left her alone, Nate. I thought you'd never do that."

That did it. A lean, gray shape sidled out from the shadows beyond the window. His skin shivered all over, and with an almost subliminal ripping noise, one skin overtook the other, not growing out of the first but superseding it, bones and sinews rearranging themselves in what Nate had admitted to me was a painful, shivering moment. Forefeet twisted, clenched, became hands in a way that wasn't so much a transformation as the effect of some invisible blender twisting them from one shape to another.

There were things you got used to, in the undercurrent, and then there were things that just seemed wrong every time you saw them. This walked the line between them.

"Evie," Nate said. He rose to his feet and coughed, his human throat still a little unfamiliar. "I'm sorry. I needed to . . . things were rough today."

"Things were rough yesterday too, huh?"

He crimsoned—all the way up from his collarbone, and I had to keep my gaze from going lower—and didn't meet my eyes. Instead he grabbed the robe away from me, turned his back—again with the not looking down, Evie—and slid his arms into it. "She was fine," he said.

"Sure. And you are?"

"I—" He paused, then flicked on the light. In the electric light, we were once again man and woman, nothing more, nothing less, and his excuse was very plainly no more than an excuse. "*Damn.*"

"I'm sorry, Nate." I put a hand on the small of his back, then, slowly, slid my other arm around his waist. He sighed and leaned back against me, but there was still a deep line between his brows. "It's . . . I've got so much to lose, now, and I don't want you to be part of that."

"Glad to see you finally realized that." He turned to face me, running his fingers through his hair. "That you have a lot to lose, I mean."

"Yeah. And I'm working on it." I managed a smile, but it turned sour. "I just need to find . . . I don't know, someone who knows about old Boston. Smugglers' tunnels in the North End. That sort of thing."

"Seriously? Tunnels?"

"Yeah."

"Must be one hell of a lead. I might be able to find someone to help."

"Good luck. Oh, and tell your aunt I found that book for her. She's not going to be happy about it—someone cut it up—but at least I can tell her where to find the remnants."

"She'll manage." He put both arms around me, and I leaned into the hug, then shook my head, coughing. "Hang on," he said. "Let me get you a drink."

He filled a glass of water from the tap, but as soon as he brought it near I winced away. "No good," I said. "Stinks."

Nate eyed the glass. "It's just tap. I don't think we've got a filter, but—hold on." He put down the glass—I dumped it in the sink as soon as I could—and opened the fridge. "I'm sure I saw it in here somewhere . . . Katie fills bottles all during the summer and leaves them in here, I sometimes find them when I'm cleaning out for Christmas . . . ah. Here."

He held out a plastic bottle with a frayed label. I took it, then hesitated. The water inside was strangely cloudy and . . . familiar? "Is this mine?"

Nate frowned. "It might be. Remember, you brought one back after—"

"I remember." I'd filled a bottle at the quarry, before I'd quite realized what was in the water. And then I'd forgotten about it. Well, I'd had a couple other things to think about by that point, not least Nate himself. That it had stayed here this long was troubling, not least because of the way the spirit had attached itself to me. "Nate," I began unsteadily, a sour feeling low in my stomach.

"That's *mine*!"

Nate and I both looked up, and I don't know which of us was redder. Katie, resplendent in My Little Pony pajamas (and oh, she'd be mad that I saw her in something so silly later on), ran forward and grabbed the bottle out of my hand. "Katie!" Nate snapped.

"But I might *need* it!" The words were practically flung over her shoulder as she ran back to her room, and all I was left with was the slightly greasy feel of the bottle on my hand.

Nate sighed. "She does this sometimes. That's why she carries that backpack everywhere—she says she might need all sorts of things, and then she changes them out later on . . . I don't know. Funny thing is, sometimes she's right."

I had a feeling I knew what it was. Katie's Sight wasn't all that predictable, but she might get some idea what might be useful later on. So long as she wasn't turning into some kind of hoarder, she'd probably be okay. "It's okay," I said. "I'm not all that thirsty anyway. But Nate—"

"I know," he said. He turned back to the window, closed it, and latched it. "I know," he said again, more quietly. "I can't keep on like this, Evie. It's . . . it's getting easier for me to make excuses. And if you're gone, if you go—" He caught himself, one hand tight on the window frame.

I joined him at the window, and then, hesitantly, laid my hands over his. This time he relaxed against me, but not so much that I couldn't feel the shivers in him. "I'm here now," I said. "And I won't go. Not if I can help it."

He exhaled a long, ragged breath, then turned and, before I could speak or even draw breath, kissed me so hard our teeth clacked together. I started, then leaned into him, drawing my hands up along his forearms till the pulse in his joints thrummed against my palms. He drew back a second, his eyes dark and hooded, then paused. "What happened to your nose?"

I laughed helplessly. "That's what I need a historian for."

Ten

Whatever they'd dug up in Dorchester, it seemed to be spreading, because the shower in Nate's apartment smelled just as bad as the tap water. Eventually—and to keep from using up all his hot water—I found the stinkiest shampoo in his medicine cabinet, dumped it in my hair, and gritted my teeth through the barrage of both acrid freesia and dead-rat smells. At least the latter went away when I dried off; the freesia, though, would be there for a while.

What research I'd done on line the night before (borrowing Nate's computer) had not filled me with confidence, and another hour's worth at the Boston Public Library confirmed it: I had absolutely nothing to work with. A black woman named Meda, dressed in Colonial-era clothing—and I wasn't nearly enough of an expert to say when that had been based on the cut of her dress—and a tunnel under the North End. The most I could find about tunnels were the breathless reports that you got in books like *Spooky Tales Of Old Beantown!* and other jumped-up pamphlets, and a glance at their bibliographies was enough to tell me that they weren't based on much. I'd probably have better luck with Katie's *Witches!* book. (Though I found a few publications that were entertaining on their own, including the little book that claimed the

T was actually an eldritch symbol of the Elder Gods, though since the author didn't mention the circle under the TD Garden I didn't take it all that seriously.) And the package store was so old that there weren't any ownership records.

Finally I gave up and called Nate. He wasn't answering his phone, but I left a message asking if he'd been serious about finding a historian or someone to help. It wasn't till I finished that I saw he'd already sent the information in a text message: *Talk to V B-P, 17 Gall Ln, Thetford MA*. I smiled and closed the phone.

Trouble was, Thetford was one of those little towns just outside the city, small enough that it hadn't been eaten up by the sprawl past I–95. I thought about biking out there, then discarded it—I'd need more than I had with me, and just now I didn't want to head home in case Rena was there. (Cowardly, but the sentence of midwinter was starting to weigh on me.) But I did know someone with a car.

Sarah hated having a car; she could never figure out the arcane parking laws that governed the traffic cops, and the insurance payments were a lot more than they were worth. And she didn't use it all that often; maybe a few official shop errands, but that was it. Most of the time, if I expressed any interest in the damn car she'd try to sell it to me.

Today was no exception, and after I convinced her both to loan it to me and not to sell it to me, Sarah seemed to relax. Her black eye was looking a little better this morning, but not much, and though she'd dipped into her Halloween supplies for a piratical eyepatch, it was pretty obviously there to hide something. "Plus it itches," she told me, flipping it up to reveal the puffy flesh around her eye. "Everything go okay last night?"

"Not really." I told her about the stunt Wheelwright and Chatterji had pulled. Instead of laughing it off, though, as she usually did with the crap the undercurrent tended to pull, Sarah chewed her lip thoughtfully and opened up one of her notebooks. "That's not good. I'd thought they were some of the saner ones."

"This is the undercurrent we're talking, Sarah."

"I know, it's just . . ." She sighed and flipped the eyepatch back down. "It's a little hard to know who to trust just now. Everything seemed to be going so well, the community watch was actually coming together, and then *wham*. Between the Elect, the Triplets, Tessie, and now these two, I don't even have time to address the fifteen other complaints that came in."

"That bad?"

"You have no idea." She straightened up as the bell rang to announce a customer, and I picked up a Happy Trails Pathfinding Dowser to make it look like I had a reason to be at the counter. "Anything else?" she said, her usual customer demeanor returning.

"Maybe. You remember the, um, the woman you had a discussion with on the docks?" Sarah frowned, then nodded slowly, realization dawning. Yeah, I didn't want to mention trouble with the cops in front of potential customers either. "She's probably pissed with me. Nothing big, but if she stops by looking for me, could you, I don't know, stall a little? This—" I held up Sarah's car keys, "—is important enough that I don't want to be distracted."

Her eyebrows shot up, but she continued nodding. "Sure. If it's that big. Any chance I'll hear about it later?"

I hesitated. I hadn't told Sarah about the use to which I'd put the list she gave me before Halloween, but if it turned out to be nothing . . . if I could find this for Dina and elude the Hunt, why worry her?

Well, one, because she could help. And two, because she deserved to know. "Yes," I said. "But once I get back, okay?"

"Don't bother bringing the car," she said.

Sarah wasn't kidding about how rotten the car was; this little hatchback had probably been through more owners than a dorm sofa, and had seen as much action. The seats exhaled a puff of pot-scented dust when I sat down, and the engine hesitated before starting up, like a skinny woman convincing herself to have a piece of cake.

I know driving's supposed to be second nature to most Americans—the national highway system should be up there with God and apple pie—but it had been years since I'd driven. I rarely needed to leave the city, and where I couldn't get via bike, I could usually either cadge a ride or take the train, slow as it was. Mom's car, the one I'd learned on, had been a tiny two-door with steering that stuck when making left turns. It had also been a stick shift; Sarah's car was automatic, but I kept reaching down for the stick without thinking.

The day was muggy and gross, far too warm for November but certainly damp enough, with a heavy cloud cover that kept the heat in like a stifling coverlet. I managed to get through the maze of Boston streets without causing too many backups and headed out to Thetford.

Out west, past the ring of Route 95 that a lover of mine had once called Taranis' Wheel . . . The trees were just at the far edge of leaf season; most had shed their leaves and were left as a fringe of gray at the edge of the highway. This had been farmland, once, not fantastic ground but sufficient, superseded by the great fields of the Midwest. Now it was overgrown, left to trees and developers and office parks. Thetford had been discovered by the latter two, then forgotten and left to the former.

The address Nate had given me was out past the city center of Thetford, what there was of it. The roads out here closed in tight, winding about in ways that seemed to have no relation to either the cardinal directions or the vague contours of the hills. Bare trees bent in on either side of me, and I remembered why it was that so many slasher movies took place out in the woods.

At last the road petered out into dirt and gravel,

scrabbling under the tires of Sarah's car, and I slowed as a tall gray house loomed up at the end of the road. It looked like the structural equivalent of Frankenstein's monster: a long-preserved central farmhouse with addition after addition tacked on, some starting to sag together.

I shut off the car (it made a coughing, unhappy sound and seemed to slump in place), slung my bag over my shoulder, and got out. The house had a scent of its own, the scent of a building that had been lived in and treated the same way for quite a while, and a plain board over the porch read BROOKS-PARSONS in block capitals that practically announced the name out loud. I tried the doorbell, and, when that produced only a dim coughing noise, knocked.

For a long moment there was nothing, just the faint strain of conversation far within. I knocked a second time, and the voice rose slightly, then dimmed. A door opened and closed, and a light switched on beyond the door, revealing a narrow hallway cluttered with furniture, strange farm implements hanging on the walls, and dozens of pictures tacked up between them. A shadow emerged farther down the hall, and I stepped back, trying to look as if I hadn't been peering through the blinds.

The woman who opened the door was about Sarah's height, but with that shrunken look that some old people get, the kind that implied that she'd once been a good deal taller and hadn't bothered to adjust to the change. Her hair was brilliant white and pulled back in a bun almost as big as my fist, and the glasses she nudged up her nose to get a proper look at me were rimless and thick. She wore a man's denim shirt over a white turtleneck and a skirt that reached to the tops of her boots, and she smelled of thyme, not dry thyme but wild-growing stuff, and of ground-up slate. She gave me a long, silent look as soon as she'd opened the door, and something about those eyes told me not to speak till I was spoken to.

"Hmph," she said at last. "You'd be Nathaniel's friend?"

Nathaniel? "Yes, ma'am. I'm Genevieve Scelan."

"Hmph. He said you'd be along." She opened the screen door, but instead of letting me in, she leaned past me and squinted around at the driveway. "You'd best come in, then. I am Venetia Brooks-Parsons. Take off your shoes."

The statements came one after the other in such declarative tones that for a dizzy moment I assumed that taking off one's shoes was protocol for dealing with a Brooks-Parsons. It might have been, in some proper old-New-England way. I stepped inside, trying not to loom over her—which was surprisingly easy; height or no, I suspected Venetia didn't shrink away from anything—and scuffed off my sneakers, one after the other. Once inside, I could identify the other voice: the moderate tones of some public radio announcer, recounting the events of the week. Venetia circled me, giving me another speculative look, and started down the hall. "You can leave your bag at the door. The parlor is this way."

The parlor smelled of dust and Lemon Pledge, in approximately equal amounts, and more than that, of cramped afternoons. "Actually, there was something I hoped you could help me with. Nate—Nathaniel told me that you were a historian, and—"

"He told you that?" Venetia paused in the door to the parlor and turned to face me, a very thin quirk in the line of her mouth. "Hm."

Oh, boy. I knew it wasn't what the Hounds had meant, but "beware of old women" was really taking on a new resonance. "He did. And that you might be able to help me. I'm looking for information on smugglers' tunnels—"

"Smugglers' tunnels."

"In the North End, specifically. The North End of Boston. Um. Around Haymarket." This wasn't going well, and now Venetia's posture in the doorway indicated that I wasn't even going to make it as far as the parlor. "I'd heard," I tried again, hoping to make this sound a little less crazy, "that there were tunnels leading from the harbor up into the city, used for travel and commerce—"

"Myths and hyperbole. The stuff of Gothic romances and anticlerical potboilers." Her lips twisted, and she folded her hands before her in a gesture as forbidding as Rena with badge in hand. "I am a serious historian, not a conspiracy theorist pretending at historical accuracy. If you want sensationalism, I'm sure I can find you a novel or two."

Great. The kind of historian I needed, and I'd already pissed her off. "Okay, then. Thanks. What about, freedmen and -women in Boston? I mean, how long were there slaves in town?" It was a hell of a leap to make, given that all I had to go on was the color of Meda's skin, but something about how she'd said "the master" had stayed with me. Or maybe I just didn't want her to have been a slave.

Venetia's eyes glinted, but she nodded. "Much more realistic, if unrelated. Officially, slavery ended in 1783, when it ended in Massachusetts, but it was certainly unfashionable for a long time before that. Not that that stopped some families from getting rich off the triangle trade then or for some time to come." I blinked, confused, and her lips quirked again. "It's all right, girl. I'm descended from those same rich scoundrels, I'm allowed to say that my ancestors were terrible people.

"No," she continued, turning back and reaching for a switch on the wall, "slavery wasn't common in Boston for some time before that. Of course there were exceptions, and sub rosa incidents, or idiots like Grauchy and his curio—"

"Grauchy?" *Old Grouchy*, the man had said. "What curio?"

Venetia's lip curled. "*That* story. Hm. Grauchy was a ship captain who wanted to flaunt his riches. He chose the worst possible way . . . he had a personal slave whom he tried to promote as a rarity, an 'intelligent negress.'" She shook her head and turned on the lights in the parlor (which would have been light enough, had she not had the blinds down). "In hindsight, he's possibly related to your other query, since he did have the Townsend house for a time, before his money ran out. The man wasn't even a P. T. Barnum; he didn't have the brains."

"But she did," I said slowly. "Her name was Meda, wasn't it?"

Venetia paused, her hand on the closest chair, then moved back to the light switch and turned it off. "It was," she said, glancing back at me with a furrowed brow.

I held my breath.

Whatever standards Venetia went by, apparently I'd just passed them. "You'd better come into the back, Genevieve," she said finally. "I don't have a kettle, but you're welcome to coffee."

My face lit up before I could help it, and that to, seemed to meet with her approval. "Please," I said.

The kitchen was in the back of the house, a little crowded nook with barely enough room for one person to move, and there were pictures everywhere, crammed in over every shelf and any wall space. Venetia slipped between table and cabinets easily. The coffee was half-caff, brewed up in one of those really old percolators, the kind that splashes the coffee up and around the top of the kettle with a vaguely digestive sound. Venetia set it to brewing again ("to aerate it") and stalked around the kitchen like a lioness checking the boundaries of her territory. I stayed quiet while she searched through bundled books at the back of one shelf.

"There is not much on Grauchy," she said, dragging down a small photo box from a high shelf. (I'd started to get up to help, but the look on her face made me stop right there.) "And there's even less that's reliable.

The good people of Boston have always been horrible gossips, and they cared as little for fact then as now."

She drew a few pasted-together volumes from the box, sniffed at them, and produced a yellowing page from one. It was a copy itself, of a crude drawing in a newspaper or whatever the equivalent had been back then, and showed a clown dressed as a captain—or maybe the other way around—beating a drum and yelling, while a bear balancing on a ball and what could have been a woman followed him. *A certain CAPTAIN wishes to begin CARNAVAL to lighten our spirits*, read the caption, and you wouldn't think sarcasm could translate over centuries, but it came through clearly.

"His girl Andromeda has a little more about her, simply because she was his showpiece. And yes, they probably did call her Meda." She took another book from the box, set it flat on the table, and returned to the coffeemaker. This book wasn't scraps, but notes, closely written, and I didn't need to ask to know it was her own work. "But she's only a different matter because Grauchy made so much of her."

I took a sip of the coffee she slid in front of me: burnt, thick, and tasting very slightly of every other pot that had been brewed. Just the way I liked it. "Go on."

"Well, he tried to promote her. Make a sideshow of her. Keep in mind when this was and how stupid people can be, and I'm sure you can understand why he made such a big fuss over 'an African maid capable of reading both Latin and Greek, who sings both popular and puritanical songs.' One is almost tempted to agree with the locals' assessment of him." She settled into her chair with a sigh, took a long drink of her coffee, and turned the page. "It was a clear case of the servant outthinking the master. He was merely an opportunist; she was a survivor. Quite literally: she was the only one left alive after a wreck on Lovells Island."

"Lovells?" No, we'd been on Georges . . . and I hadn't seen Meda there, I'd seen her later . . .

"Oh yes. Pretty island, but the wrecks on it—the *Magnifique* alone nearly lost us a navy . . ." She started to make a note, then frowned as she realized she didn't have a pen. I took one from my bag and slid it across to her. "Thank you. Reading between the lines, it's clear that she too lost something there; she's listed as 'one, carrying' and then later as just one."

I thought of Meda watching me on the Common. "Does it say where she was from? What she did, where she ended up?"

Venetia cocked a white eyebrow at me. "There isn't an 'it' to say anything. This is sifted from primary sources, gleaned and cast aside. And no, there isn't much else. Andromeda refused to play the talking dog for her master—good for her, and it made him more of a laughingstock—and ran off on the Dark Day."

I was nodding all through "ran off," but the last words caught me up short. "The what?"

"New England's Dark Day. I've got a terrible watercolor of it somewhere . . ." She stood, grimacing, then seemed to think better of it and poured another cup of coffee instead. "May of seventeen eighty. The sun went out for eight hours in the middle of spring. No clouds, no storm, just the light going out. You couldn't even read by sunlight at noon." She took a long sip. "I believe they've linked it to a colossal forest fire, but honestly that's not nearly as interesting as people's reactions to it: it was the end of the world, the sun black as sackcloth made of hair, and so on. Most town councils still met, though, putting 'Judgment Day' at the end of the agenda." She gave a sniff that was almost a laugh. "Practical."

I thought of the sunlight filtering through the grate below the North End, the strange, muted quality of it. What I'd seen—what I was now beginning to suspect Meda had deliberately showed me—might have been the Dark Day. If so, she hadn't wasted any time in leaving. And the sailor whose fingers I still carried in my jacket pocket . . . what had she done with him, once he brought her the sunstone?

It took one hell of a strong magician to set a spell in place that would remain after death. And most of the paths to strength in the undercurrent were puddled with other people's blood.

"So the Dark Day came," I said slowly, then stopped. "Do you know how silly that sounds?"

"Silly now," Venetia pointed out, tipping her coffee mug to me. "When we have all the light we need and can summon more with a switch. But back then? I'd not scoff."

I thought of Dina's pitch-black room in Fort Warren, and nodded. She had a point. "Anyway, Meda took advantage of it to run. Is there any record of where she went?"

Venetia frowned and turned a page in her notebook. "Not quite. Grauchy was said to claim that his greatest treasure had gone to Greenwich, but there's no indication of why he didn't go after her if that's what he meant. Poor roads, I expect, and his fortunes were much depleted by that point. He fades from the record soon after, leaving the whole matter just a footnote to Boston society."

I paused at that. "So how do you know about it?"

A slow smile curved Venetia's lips, like a crack running through frost. "I did say that we were terrible gossips, and I am no less. I simply restrict my gossip to things long past. It's vaguely more respectable this way."

Fair enough. I drank the rest of my coffee, including the sludge at the bottom, and set the mug down. "Thank you very much, Ms. Brooks-Parsons. You've been incredibly helpful." She nodded as if to say *Of course I have.* "Do I owe you anything—a, a consulting fee, or something? At the very least I can leave you my card—"

At that her white brows rose. "You're leaving already?"

"Well, if I'm going to get to Greenwich, I've got some driving to do." Not to mention some thinking up what to do when I got there. Perhaps the scent would be stronger there, maybe I could just go searching for Meda . . . maybe she'd find me, if she'd thought ahead far enough to set a ghost-trap for me earlier . . .

"But Nathaniel said—" A car honked out in the driveway, and she looked up. "Ah. That'd be them now. Come along."

Crap. Had Nate promised something else from me? I followed her back out into the hallway, then stopped as a familiar, lean shape appeared through the window. When Venetia opened the door a familiar sparky blue scent blew into the hall. "Aunt Venice!" Katie yelled, and knocked into the old woman with a hug. Venetia winced a little at the decibels, but her hand on Katie's hair was kind. "We brought cookies from the bakery on Beatton, only they didn't have the kind with the hazelnuts you like, so we had to go with the frosting kind—"

"Good to see you, Katherine." Venetia untangled herself from Katie in time for Nate to give her a kiss on the cheek. "You're late, Nathaniel. Your friend's been here some time already."

"Friend?" He glanced up, and his eyes widened as he saw me. "Evie! I thought—"

"You, uh, sent me the address of a historian," I said weakly.

He shook his head. "Yes, but that was after—I thought you needed Aunt Venice's address for the contract."

I stared at Venetia, then at the picture on the wall next to her: a bright, attractive young woman in a 1970s dress, flanked by three grim middle-aged women. The one on the left, though her hair was iron-gray and shellacked up in a 1970s monstrosity, had to be Venetia Brooks-Parsons. In front of them stood a little boy wearing what looked like the world's most uncomfortable suit and gazing out with a kind of desperation. "Aunt Venice."

"You said you'd found the book for her, remember?"

The book? I cast my memory back, remembering the job I'd taken on, the hunt that hadn't even taken an hour. "Oh yes—the missing pages. I'm sorry, they're currently part of an art installation at BU." I started fishing through my bag for the notes I'd made, my face so hot it must have been fluorescent. What did you say when meeting your lover's family? The closest I'd ever come to that was five years ago, a Memorial Day booze-up out in Southie with the guy I'd been seeing for a couple of weeks—and then it turned out that I'd been invited as the designated driver. Bastard got a ride home all right, but he didn't get anything else out of me after that.

"I suspect there's been a miscommunication somewhere," Venetia remarked dryly, but when I looked up her eyes were sparking. "We'll call it an even trade, then. And you're quite welcome to stay for a while."

"Can't, not if I'm going to make it to Greenwich today." I came up with my notes—I hadn't even had time to write them up into a proper report—and smoothed them out, scanning them to make sure I'd gotten the name of the art installation right. "I'm afraid I haven't written up a formal contract, but I can have it to you by Monday, and here's the name of the artist who used the pages in a collage . . ." I handed her the note, and Venetia took it, her eyes crinkling just slightly at the corners. "I'm sorry I can't stay."

"That's why I made you a snack!" Katie fished in her backpack—now that I knew what kind of a packrat she was, I was a little leery of what else might be in there "just in case"—and came up with a thermos and a squashed peanut-butter sandwich. Without asking to see whether I wanted it, she dropped the sandwich on my bag and unscrewed the top of the thermos. "See? I made Tang, so the water wouldn't taste bad."

Even with the top still partly on, I could smell the chemical orange flavor—and below it, the same stink of the tap water. I turned away, breathing through my mouth. "Thanks," I managed, and picked up the sandwich. "But this'll be fine."

"Of course your water tastes bad, Nathaniel," Venetia said. "It's Swift River runoff, from that mess of a reservoir—I wouldn't drink it myself unless I had to."

I stopped, then took the thermos from Katie's hand. Swift River. The scent of the water. And this scent, the stink of dead things . . .

The water had only started to stink in the last few days. Since the fire. Since Roger and Dina arrived.

"Venetia," I said slowly, still holding the thermos, "did the record say that Meda had actually gone to Connecticut?"

She blinked. "I don't believe so. Only Greenwich."

"There's more than one Greenwich," I said, and closed the thermos. "Or at least there used to be. I've got to go swimming."

Eleven

Let me tell you a story my mother told me.

Once there was a city built on a thin neck of land stretching out into the ocean, and over time more people came to that city than the frail land could hold. So the city cut down its hills to fill in the harbor and dragged up the land from the bottom of the tidal flats. It ate up the sea, and looked around for more, and the land took over where the water had been.

But with so many people in it, the city began to thirst. And the rivers—those poor, polluted things that served as sewers and waterways and everything else—couldn't keep up with the city's demands. The clear springs that had once sufficed for that first, fragile settlement were now gone, built over or dried up or simply lost. The city built reservoir after reservoir, seeking more fresh water—not just for its thirst, but for its fires too, as those consumed neighborhood after neighborhood. But no matter how many reserves the city put in place, they were not enough.

What could you do to quench such a thirst? What would you sacrifice to keep your city from burning?

I took the Pike, got lost a few times, and eventually made it out to what had been the Swift River Valley. The road led me through woods gray with the oncoming winter, and finally to a turnoff with gravel shoulders where hunters or hikers could park. I got out and followed a little dirt path down to a wire fence marked with NO TRESPASSING signs, and there I could see the water.

The Quabbin Reservoir reflected the heavy sky as if it were made of mercury. A flock of geese drifted overhead, honking mournfully.

This is what the people in Boston decided to sacrifice to the city's thirst: a whole valley and the four towns within it. They'd bought up all the land, evacuated everyone—gave them plenty of time, though that doesn't mean there wasn't acrimony on both sides—and dammed one end of the valley. And drop by drop, the Swift River filled up the valley, turning pastures into wetland and then into lake bottom, becoming the Quabbin Reservoir.

When I was a kid, in spite of how carefully Mom had explained everything to me, I still had dreams about the rising water swallowing everything I knew. I'd be trying to put my stuffed animals on a high shelf out of the way of the flood, back in our house in Philly before Mom and Dad split and we moved out here. Doesn't take a psychoanalyst to figure that one out.

But that wasn't the way it had happened. The buildings had all been knocked down; the graveyards had been dug up and moved elsewhere, the remnants of the four towns—Enfield, Prescott, Dana, and Greenwich—had been razed so that they wouldn't interfere with the flow of water. There were no drowned farms, no church towers ringing mournful bells three fathoms down, no sunken cities. Those had only been in my head.

To look at it from an undercurrent point of view, the engineers had gone about it mostly right. Water would carry away any traces of what had been there, and while it would, for a little while, bear some echoes of the towns, eventually any curses, any ill will or even blessings, would wear away under that slow flow.

From another point of view, it was also a good place to hide something. The Quabbin was too large to have a single guardian spirit, and far too young (certain quarries notwithstanding) to make its own, and so it was a sort of null space. In theory, anything tossed into the Quabbin was permanently gone, erased like a footprint in sand.

Unless you had someone like me around. Someone who didn't follow the basic rules of magic in her hunt. Someone whose talent was based on something entirely separate from the run of usual magic, a bastardized hound's power that was entirely misplaced in a human body. And even then, that person would have some difficulty getting to anything that was at the bottom of the Quabbin.

Venetia, when she heard "swimming," had immediately dug out a fifties-era suit from somewhere and handed it to me, insisting that it'd keep me warmer than the "skimpy things they had nowadays." I wasn't entirely enthusiastic about it, but it was a step up from the navy one-piece left over from my college days that was the only suit I owned. Besides, that one rode up in the back. This one qualified more as a unitard than a suit, and honestly I didn't much care. It fit well enough under my clothes, at least.

The sunstone had to be in the reservoir, though. It made sense: I'd only started scenting the water when I'd gotten my full senses back, and that was after the yacht fire. And Roger did say that he occasionally stopped by in Boston for his ally to "recharge." If something had been in the Quabbin that long, it would have lost all individuality—unless it had been protected, or unless it only had any power when its original owner was nearby.

Much of magic is based on the tension of incompleteness. I've even heard a theory that the reason loci are actually useful is not that they're part of someone's soul, but that the person is still tied to them in some way. (Certainly that had been what got me, and what

I had had to sever . . . even if it had left me a little weak.) If the sunstone was here, it was a part of Dina, and that relationship would have been magnified when she was close to the city. Physical closeness would have increased the tension between Dina and her missing stone, in much the same way that magnetic force becomes tangible when you're holding a magnet close to iron.

Hadn't Kassia said that this sort of thing had happened before? I'd wager that Roger's visits to the city matched up with the times she remembered. He might not have known the effects of bringing his ally to Boston, but that didn't entirely excuse him. All the more reason for me to bring this back to Dina, even without my own motives: if by restoring her to wholeness I could stop the bad water and the paranoia, I'd happily do it.

I kicked a drift of fallen leaves out of the way and peered through the fence. The pattern of scents here was no less tangled than in Boston, but there was some differentiation: fewer human scents, more animals, the density increasing as I searched. The miasma of death rose off the water, so strong I could barely find the source. Surely this wasn't all tainted by the stone—but no, it wouldn't matter. It was the contiguous nature of the water, not the specific currents that touched the stone.

I put my hand over the bulge in my jacket, where the fingers rested. There—a trace of tar and salt, further along the shore. North. I opened my eyes, sighed, and got back in the car.

For the next few hours, I repeated the process: drive ten miles, get out, spend half an hour trying to get back in the pattern of the scents, locate the thief's trail and a rough direction, then back into the car. It was the kind of interrupted hunting that I hated, but the Quabbin was large enough that I couldn't just walk around it following my nose. And since the other option I had was to do the same, only swimming, the car was the best bet, even if it meant that this was less a hunt than an act of assembling data points. There wasn't one single road that went entirely around the Quabbin, and so I kept getting lost, turning around once I got to some form of civilization, winding my way down one side of the reservoir and back up the other. The one constant was the scent, and at least that part started to get easier as the day went on.

By the time late afternoon began to slide toward evening, I had it narrowed down to a little layby at the northwest end of the Quabbin, gazing across the road to where a chained-off driveway led down the hill. The closest shore that I could find was off the lawn of what looked like some mogul's summer home: a big, empty mansion with an ATHOL REALTY sign out front. No cars in the drive, no scents of humans around the place (except for me, of course, and the lingering remnant of a few summer parties down the shore plus one or two traces of hunters in the hills). If I was going to do this, I couldn't have picked a better spot.

I locked up the car, then swung my messenger bag over my shoulder and crossed the road. The drive split about twenty yards in, one fork winding about the mansion, one sinking down the hill to the shore of the Quabbin, flat and cold. A flock of starlings chattered overhead as I reached the edge of the water, where a little inlet had once been fenced off. The land here wasn't so much a shore as a mud slick; time and water hadn't yet turned hillside into beach, and wouldn't for decades more. I eyed the sky—still gray, but with the heaviness of rain that would spite everyone by not falling, and unnaturally warm for the season—and tucked my pack under a bush, then stripped down to Venetia's suit. At the very last I picked up Dina's token, the fingers of a thief, and held them like a baton in my left hand.

The water on my toes was warmer than I expected, or maybe that was just the effect of cold air making everything else feel warm by comparison. Up to my knees, now, and the ground underfoot was not just squishy but slimy, crawling with weeds and other underwater things. I shuddered and splashed forward a few more steps, in the hope that getting it over with quickly would help.

Nope. My teeth chattered, but not from the water's temperature. Every time I closed my eyes, even for just a blink, the water shivered around me, becoming icy quarry water, runoff in a great pit, thick with ferns and magic . . . I shuddered as it closed around my calves, my legs, slopping up against the small of my back. My breath was coming in ragged gasps by the time the water reached my breasts. I took a deep breath, then submerged completely—

—and the water around me was only water, only the Quabbin, only the Swift River that had filled a valley. No longer anything to be afraid of. Like a soap bubble popping, like a leash snapping, the chill was gone. Only water.

It was still quite capable of giving me hypothermia, though. I surfaced, scraping hair out of my eyes, and sought for that scent again. Yes. Only a hunt now, and one that was challenging enough in these circumstances. I grinned, spat, and struck out away from shore.

The thief's scent ebbed, but not because I'd gotten away from it. I was on top of it—but diving revealed nothing but a few stones about twenty feet down, and that was as much as I could tell before my lungs tried to escape out my ears. Not that I didn't try several times, finally cursing and rolling onto my back while I rested my arms.

Something twitched against my left hand: the oilcloth, and the fingers in it. I paused a second, my teeth chattering—was this what they meant by the first stages of hypothermia involving bad judgment?—and shifted my grip. The fingers twitched again, then jerked down, a ghostly hand in mine, pulling me under. I caught my breath, kicking to stay afloat.

There were things that could travel outside worlds—the Gabriel Hounds and their silver road, the things that not even the Triplets would dare call up, magicians long severed from their bodies. I didn't know how much I trusted these things, but Meda had found me before. Let her find me now, then. Let her lead me on, and where she was, I might find the sunstone.

The hand tugged again at mine, a gentle pull this time, encouraging. I clasped the hand tighter and dove—

Into clear air, and a town long forgotten.

My feet brushed tall dry grass, waving slightly in a wind that was no longer present. No more than a few feet away that grass turned to pondweed, waving in a current of a different sort. Above, the light fluctuated between the green-gold of dark water and a strange, attenuated glow like sick sunlight. Whatever spell this was, I was carrying it with me.

I let out my breath carefully, and no water rushed in to take its place. Good. Even better, my talent was still present, which put this situation well ahead of the flash in the wine cellar. Following the pattern of scents in this envelope of time was difficult, like reading a page that had most of the ink leached out of it. But there were patterns, nonetheless, and not just ones that my brain had cobbled together to make sense of this place. Hay, apples, cows . . . stone and mortar, freshly laid . . .

I drifted as I walked, the buoyancy of the water not quite gone, so that I skimmed over the ground. The shape of a building loomed out of the murk, first as nothing, then as a spectral, ruined husk, then, as I got right up close to it, as an intact stone wall. I looked from the wall to the edge of the water, where this space ended, and saw the rest of the building blurring in and out of reality. This barn had long been knocked down to make way for the water, but this remnant of magic still preserved it after a fashion.

The thief's scent remained, stretched and faded, no longer tinged with tar but with cow shit, the heavy livestock scent like a skewed filter. I closed my eyes to get a better lead, then gasped as pressure thundered against my ears. When I opened my eyes, the space I walked in had shrunk by half. I yelped, and it bulged out again, restoring the wall to its memory and the sky to its unhealthy light.

Okay. So whatever magic was being done here, it was in some way dependent on attention. Nice to know. I wondered how long I could keep from blinking.

Ahead, past the cows—even they were here, ghostly against the field, memories of memories, and dull in this light. As I reached the edge of town—a few outbuildings, a steeple that flickered in and out of memory—I realized I'd seen light like this before: filtering through a grate set in a Boston street, into a smuggler's tunnel.

"We thought it was the end of the world."

I jumped back, skidding across what felt like both damp hay and lake-bottom muck. A shape flickered back and forth beside me, like a badly damaged film, and one shadow of an arm reached to my own hand. I started to pull away, but paused, trying to focus on him. As I did so, he became clearer, the pressure of attention bringing him forward more clearly.

He was dressed in an old peacoat fastened together with toggles, and the corner of his shirt was homespun, stained from years of use. A gold ring gleamed in his ear, and his hair was slicked back and twisted into a knob at the back of his head. While he wasn't handsome, there was a certain look to the set of his jaw that I thought I recognized.

What was it Nate had once said? Wear the same expression on your own face long enough, you'll learn to recognize it on others. Which meant that here was another stubborn son of a bitch.

"It wasn't the end," he said, his lips curling in remembered amusement. "Even the town council agreed, and they said that the Lord would have to wait for the day's business to end. And Meda knew. For all that her master deemed her a talking dog, Meda knew."

He paused at the edge of a drystone wall. To either side, it stretched out past the envelope of time—one of the few structures that hadn't been knocked down. If I squinted, I could just see the pale line of the stones in the water of the Quabbin, mossy and slick. "Meda knew much."

I followed him over the wall, bouncing a little as I came down. I was no longer cold. Was that a bad sign? Or was that part of this spell, this fragment of unreality that insulated me from the Quabbin?

The man—the thief whose fingers I'd carried—walked on, paying no attention to how I floated beside him. At his feet, the weeds and muck of the Quabbin gave way to flat stones, set in a gently arcing path that unrolled in the dry space below my feet. I squinted ahead to see only the barest ghost of a building. It must have been gone long before the towns were bought, before they were even official towns . . .

"She knew I'd failed," the thief said, and I remembered in time to keep my attention on him. "If I'd brought her with me, maybe . . . but I wouldn't risk her. Not if it meant I'd lose her."

He paused on the path. My feet didn't quite touch the flagstones, but his did, and he scuffed one against the edge of a stone. "I'd never say these things to another were I alive. So I must be dead." He glanced back at me, the first notice he'd really taken of me, and smiled again.

And now I recognized some of what was going on. I was haunted, to put it shortly. This was an imprint, like the ghost rooms left in houses or the emotional remnants left by some great event. But unlike those, this was a purposeful, driven imprint. A skilled magician had constructed this imprint, this haunting, to latch on to whoever came looking.

Meda knew much, all right.

A shadow in the water flexed, then configured itself into a tiny house, its shutters stained red. Someone had painted a set of symbols over the door as well: Greek, I thought, but not the kind that either a modern or ancient Greek would decipher. I took a step closer to the door, then paused. Somewhere within, a woman's voice recited, quiet and steady, without the watery echo that followed every other sound down here.

Careful, Evie, I thought. *You might not have enough breath to get back to the surface if someone yanks the spell away.*

With that in mind—and with a worried glance at the roof of the house; would it disappear in time for me to get out?—I stepped inside.

The house was small, only two rooms, with a swept-dirt floor and furniture dark with age and use. A low fire burned in the hearth, pale against the brightness of the day (and, beyond it, the darkness of the Quabbin loomed), and a rack above it held a small pot that made bubbling noises as it slid further into reality. The smell from it was thin and unappetizing: chicken broth, spiced with onion. Strange fare for this temporary summer day, and stranger for it to be unattended. The whole thing looked a little like an illustration out of my fifth-grade history textbook, or one of the photos our teacher had taken from the class trip out to Old Sturbridge Village. (I'd missed the trip—detention for making Jimmy Parkinson eat the dead caterpillar he'd tried to put in my lunch.)

I turned away from the kitchen (and parlor, and living room, it looked like) to the only other room, from which the woman's voice continued. "Each saw by turns," she read as I entered, her speech broad with an accent I didn't recognize. "And each by turns was blind."

She was in a rocking chair by the window, a book on her lap that was so well-worn it could easily have been mistaken for the Bible in other households. I was pretty sure it wasn't, even though the language sounded about right. And she was definitely the same woman I'd seen under the North End, holding aloft a lantern at the end of a smuggler's tunnel, her dark skin a contrast to the faded pink cotton of her smock. Years had softened the proud line of her chin and bleached her hair to a salt-and-pepper frizz, bound back under a sagging kerchief. For the first time I caught her scent, muted in this envelope of the past: sparks of fireworks, wound about with sage and baking bread. The two latter scents seemed to neutralize the mark of magic on her, not because they were domestic but because they were uncorrupted, benign.

For a moment I thought of Katie, of what I'd told her about inviting magic into one's home. This woman could prove me wrong, I thought, and felt a pang for how much I'd scared Katie. I owed her an apology.

Ignoring the woman, the thief slid his hand out of my grasp. For a second I groped after it, fumbling through air and water both. But he had faded, and a second later I saw why.

Now the man I knew as the thief lay on the bed, tucked under a quilt of faded red cloth. But that epithet no longer quite applied to him: here was a farmer, a worker, a husband or father maybe. He was very old; his hair was gone entirely, the dome of his skull spotted by age, and the collar of his nightshirt revealed a tuft of white hair at his throat. His hands lay folded on his lap, one whole, the other long twisted into a broken, three-fingered claw.

And he was looking straight at me.

I halted in the door, losing my footing slightly and hovering a moment between steps. Hesitantly, I looked behind me on the off chance that I'd timed my visit to coincide with another's. Nothing. I turned back, and he met my eyes, and nodded, smiling. "Eh," he said, his voice creaking but not unhappy, "it's been forty-odd years, and I expected long before now that someone would come looking for it."

The woman glanced up, and her gaze passed over me without the slightest hitch. "Colin?"

"Peace, Meda. It's naught but sight." He smiled at me, and I could see that a cataract glazed one of his eyes. "Go back to your reading, and see it through for me. You will do that, at least?"

She smiled at him, a fond and regretful smile, and leaned over so that she could reach across the counterpane and pat his leg. She had her own pains, though; she grimaced and pressed one hand against the small of her back as she sat up. "That I will," she whispered, and turned the page.

It was a short exchange, but something about it felt terribly private. But the two of them seemed not to care that I watched, and the only effect was to make me supremely uncomfortable about appearing in front of them in a—I checked; the past might hold me, but it had changed nothing about me—red-striped monstrosity of a swimsuit. I started to cover myself, realized how little that would help, and made myself stand like the ghost he thought I was.

Colin saw the movement, and his smile widened briefly, became for a second both wicked and joyous. "Sit," he said, raising one hand to gesture to the bed. "I've visited with angels enough in these last few days, 'twill do me good to know if one has substance more than what's in my mind."

I smiled and shook my head, but came to stand between him and Meda. Meda, not seeing me, kept reading, and continued even when he began to speak over her, perhaps used to it. "We knew," he said slowly, his piebald gaze coming to rest on me, "that it wasn't gone. After the shipwrecks on Lovells, the lovers frozen by the stones, I knew—but I did cripple it, and I did hurt it, and that was enough for these on forty years. No more dead men lingering on Nix's Mate.

No more that claimed more dead. That, at least, we accomplished." He sighed, long and slow. "There was naught we could do but hide, and hide we did, out away from the ocean, where the sun would not go dim and the eyes not find us."

I opened my mouth to try to speak, but for just that fraction of a second the air I tasted was heavy with water and weeds. Meda's magic was weakening under the pressure of water and time.

Colin looked at me, still smiling, then at the woman. "Eh, Meda, and we did have a good run of it, didn't we?" She, either used to these outbursts from him or patiently tolerant, turned the page and didn't look up. "I once thought it could be hidden forever," he went on, not much louder than her recitation. "But Meda knew better, and I'd bled on the eye, after all I'd seen." He brought his mutilated hand up to his face, pointing to his cataract-white eye. "Such sight doesn't go from me, even when I'd have it gone. Meda wove this mantle of dreams for who came seeking, that only one strong enough to do what must be done would find it. And you, now, you know some of that, don't you?"

Not really, I thought. But he was an old man, and dying, and sometimes it was better to comfort than to cajole. "I do," I said, and though the sound never made it past my lips, he understood.

"Then you know as I that some things stay unhidden, if their owners want them back." I nodded, touching the flat, shiny scar at my throat where the Horn had been. "It'd have to come out in time, though we buried it deep. Even if we'd hidden it beneath water—" I looked up involuntarily at that, at where the low roof of their house faded into blackness. "Water, then? How long?"

Another question I couldn't quite answer, partly since I didn't know when this had taken place. "Two centuries," I said, but had to swallow as water trickled in between my lips. I didn't have much time left.

"Hundred years," he said, and I couldn't tell if he was repeating me, or if he'd misheard, or just guessed from reading my lips. "That's worth this loss, then," and he raised his maimed hand. "Worth it and more. Ay, Meda, the world will last another hundred-ought years and more, and we did our part to keep it living. Not what the town council thought, when the sun went out, was it?" He chuckled, and I caught the last flicker of a smile on Meda's face when I glanced over my shoulder.

For a long moment Colin lay silent, slumped back into the pillow. Meda kept reading, and tranquil as the scene was, I still lacked any scent of the sunstone. Was there a trace of Dina in this room, maybe? An echo of its former owner? I'd need to seek it more diligently, and I didn't dare if taking my attention away meant that the water would come back—

"The hearth," Colin said without opening his eyes. "We thought that fire would keep it hidden, and it did, and if you are no phantom then water too has kept it hidden. And now you come seeking it, and if Meda has brought you this far, then she has seen that you are capable of the last step." His eyes flickered open, and he stared unmoving at the ceiling. "Have no fear. It—the gray ones, they love fear, and it is not enough to be a thief. It is not enough."

Valuable advice, maybe, but I was already at the other end of the room, scrabbling at the hearth. This one had no fire, maybe since the quilt kept him already too warm, but when my fingers touched it they didn't touch stone. They sank into muck and weeds, silt drifting up past my face in the negative, grimy twin to fairy dust. The room warped around me, Colin fading and reforming as memory held him in place, but Meda's voice never ceased. "And stole their mutual light," she read, her words holding me in this one place, keeping me in the space where I could breathe.

I dug deeper, yanking fronds out of the way, tearing my nails across stone. The flat stone of the hearth was still intact under water, though slick with slime and lake-bottom muck. I scrabbled around till I found an edge, and pried, my fingernails giving way with a twinge and the muscles of my back echoing them. The hearth-stone—still to my eyes dry and clean, chiseled around the edges with more of the bastard Greek that lined the lintel—creaked and shifted, finally sliding away from me and sinking edge-first into the mud.

My fingers skated over what felt like the skin of a corpse. I steeled myself to look as I got a better grip on it—and saw, lit as if from a stray beam of light that had made it this deep, a greenish pouch, disintegrating from its time under water.

With that, the walls of the house started to fade first into memory, then into the scraps of foundation that were all that remained. Meda's voice continued, a low drone like a guiding thread. "And not one serpent by good chance awake," she said, her voice drawing closer, almost in my ear. "Do what we could not, despite our names and our intent. This I cannot bind you to, this only I beg you—be not thief but murderer."

I turned, but something struck me hard on the right shoulder, digging into my skin. A puff of blood danced up, hovering in the water, and I yelled—but Meda was gone, and now the house was too, and I only had time for a fraction of a breath before the waters of the Quabbin slammed in around me.

I'd say it was like being struck by a bat—the pressure was that strong—but it hit me on every side at once, and so it wasn't so much a slap as a crush, all over me. Had I any room for it, I'd have collapsed. As it was, I didn't even have space enough for any of these thoughts, pushing off the bottom and kicking toward what I hoped was the surface. Green water blurred over my eyes, the dim sky above doing nothing to indicate which direction was up or even if there was an end to this water.

With every stroke, the sunstone got heavier and something jarred against my back. Very faintly, through the water, I caught the scent of my own blood, drifting through the Quabbin. There weren't such things as freshwater sharks, right? Or snapping turtles . . . hell, in another ten seconds I wasn't going to care about either of those, because I was going to drown. I fumbled with the sunstone, trying to keep it from sliding out of my grip and back down to the bottom of the reservoir (and this time I'd have no friendly advice telling me where to look), then gave up the last of my breath in a shout as whatever was stuck in my shoulder dug in deeper.

I burst through the surface in mid-yell, choked, gargled water, and spat. The Quabbin was as it had been when I dove under: still, gray, unchangeable. I took deep, searing breaths, blessing air for its existence and water for its limits and earth for being there for me to swim to in time.

The sunstone's bag, slick and greasy in my hands, rotted away further as I lifted it. I tore the sack off, treading water frantically, letting it sink back to the foundations of the house where it had lain for so long, and raised the stone. "Yes!" I yelled, and a fresh flock of geese startled, honking in reply. "Got it! Hound of Hounds can even hunt under fucking *water*!"

The stone didn't respond, of course, and there was no celestial applause from deities who'd bet on my success or failure. But I knew I'd won, and that was enough. I held the stone up, looking through it at the sky, and sure enough, when I turned it toward the west, it brightened, showing where the fading sunlight was strongest. I drew the stone a little closer, still treading water, then hissed as the pain in my shoulder flared.

It wasn't until I had reached the shore, shivering so violently I could barely see straight, and staggered up onto the bank that I could reach back. Something was jammed between my suit and shoulder, digging in with every movement. I dropped the sunstone onto the grass, where it gleamed an unhealthy gray, and reached back, fumbling like someone trying to get that one itchy spot. My fingers brushed cold metal, cooling faster in this air, and a fresh flow of blood spilled down my back as I withdrew what Meda had used to attack me: a fisherman's hook as long as my hand, cruel and curved, black iron unstained by rust. It was not meant as a weapon, but it settled easily into my hand, the hook emerging between my fingers, the haft cool against my palm.

I turned it back and forth and looked down at the sunstone. "Well," I said through chattering teeth. "Thank you."

Twelve

The heater in Sarah's car only had two settings: off and inferno. The second was just fine for me at the moment, though, and I spent a good twenty minutes huddling in front of the vents, trying to stop shivering. Venetia's suit, still smelling of Quabbin water and leaking little pink bloody tendrils, went in a plastic bag that got tossed in the back; the sunstone went in my messenger bag. If anyone had noticed my quick change on the shore, at least they hadn't called the cops for public indecency.

The long slash down my shoulder blade was a pain, both in how it stung and how hard it was to reach, but Sarah kept a small first-aid kit in the glove compartment, and I managed to staunch the blood with a handful of napkins and slap about six Band-Aids on it. I'd need it looked at—I probably needed a tetanus shot—but it'd hold for a little while.

I thought back to Meda's words—a plea, but not a binding. I'd have been able to tell if she'd enspelled me, and she hadn't. And a little blood in the reservoir wouldn't kill anyone—they'd clean the water, or fluoridate it or something, before it made it to the taps.

Night had fallen pretty solidly by the time I returned to Venetia's house, and both the porch light and a light at the back of the house were on. Venetia leaned out into the hall when I rang the bell and waved me in impatiently, though not so impatiently that she didn't glare until my shoes were off.

She and Katie had staked out the kitchen. A huge, flaking pasteboard box sat at the far end of the table, and I'd barely noticed it before Katie peeked out from behind. "Evie!" she squeaked, and slid out from her chair just as I swung my bag off my shoulder, my fingers grazing the lump where the sunstone bulged out.

For a moment—just a flicker, no more than the fragment of a thought—I saw a flash of silver in her eyes, silver marred by ink and water. I caught my breath, then let go of the bag as Katie reached me. "Good to see you, kiddo." I sat down next to her and pulled her into a hug, ignoring how it strained my shoulder. "You're okay?"

"I'm okay," she returned, or something like that; she'd mashed her face up against my shoulder and as a result wasn't very clear. "Come take a look!" she added, pulling away and dragging the box over to her. "I found this box in the attic and Aunt Venice said I can keep whatever I like from it."

"*One* picture," Venetia said. She didn't turn her voice saccharine, the way some old ladies did when talking to kids. "Have you chosen yet?"

"I haven't even looked at them all yet!"

"Then get looking." She turned to me. "I've put you in the sewing room, with Nathaniel. Will you be staying the night?"

"I—" Oh boy. What was the rule on telling proper New England spinsters that yes, you were sharing a bed with their nephew? Did Miss Manners even cover that? "I don't know yet."

"Hm. Well, there's a place for you, if you like."

"Evie, look." Katie held up a flaking photograph in a gilt-stamped cardboard frame: two stiff-necked men in collars that practically came up to their noses. She imitated one of their expressions—the one on the left looked like he'd just been goosed—and I snickered, then tried to hide it as Venetia gave me the hairy eyeball. Katie giggled and resumed digging through the stack, then stopped. "Oh."

"What've you found, then?" Venetia paused as she put away the last of the dinner dishes. "Oh. Oh, my. How did that end up in . . . never mind. That one's yours, girl."

"What is it?"

Katie held up a round-edged photo of a grinning girl with her hair in pigtails. It could have been Katie herself, save for the carefree smile. "It's my mom. When she was my age."

Venetia had a sad, faraway smile as she gazed down at it. "Angela must have left it with me when she moved out." She set the dishes back in the cupboard and closed the door. "How Charlotte ever managed to raise a girl like that is, well, quite understandable really. Angela Hunter was a darling without the sense God gave a guppy."

I glanced up at that, startled, but Katie didn't even seem to have heard.

"And for all that, she could still charm anyone, including us, when it came down to it. When Charlotte's husband disowned Angela, Charlotte came to me for help. To me, and to Adele—" she gestured to the scrap of wall above the fridge, where several portraits crowded for space, "—and to Millie. We taught Angela enough that she was able to find good work and take care of the boy."

"So you were sort of like surrogate grandparents." I'd had no idea. I'd always just thought that Nate's mother was on her own, since she had been by the time I knew them.

"Aunts, as I said. It was an amicable arrangement; Angela needed someone to act out against, and better us than the boy. And he managed, I think, and for the better. We may not have been his blood relatives, but we are, in many ways, still his family."

I thought of the desperate, uncomfortable kid in the picture, and then of Nate's history. He'd learned repression from the pros; no wonder his father's curse had taken so long to reach him. "It must have been quite a sacrifice for you."

"Oh no." She folded a dish towel, hung it above the sink, then adjusted it slightly. "Charlotte was a friend. There is . . . hm. I don't know if you're quite old enough to understand this. Women did things like that for each other, back then. You take care of your own, as much as you can." She smiled, faintly, looking off into the distance, then gave me an annoyed look. "What is it now?"

"You remind me of someone," I said without thinking.

"Hm. I hardly think so."

I held my tongue, not wanting to tell her who she reminded me of: Meda, and her own magic, her own quiet skill in the face of the Dark Day and Colin's lingering sickness, the determination that drove her magic to linger past death. The bones of New England ran in its old women, and what Venetia and her friends had done together was part of that solidarity. Meda had had something of that as well, despite the differences in time and race and magic.

Maybe Sarah and Katie would have it too, in time. But I wouldn't get a chance to see it unless I got the sunstone back to Dina. "Where's Nate? I saw his car out front—he didn't go looking for me, did he?"

Katie bit her lip and glanced at Venetia, but the old woman frowned as she turned to face me.

"You are *bleeding*, Genevieve."

"I—what?" I turned, and unfortunately, she was right: the patch-up job I'd done on my shoulder had given out. "Um. I had a bit of an accident earlier."

"Then come this way. I won't have anyone bleeding on the kitchen table. That," she added with a thin half smile, "is for the dining-room table, and only when an emergency appendectomy is called for."

"Are you going to tell the Uncle Tadworthy story again?" Katie called as we left the kitchen.

"No, I am not. Pick out your picture, Katherine, and get to bed."

She herded me into the next room—her own room, apparently—and immediately I could see where Nate's habit of having far too many medical supplies on hand had come from. "Shirt, off," she ordered, taking down a large brown bottle that I could only hope was peroxide.

"Um—"

"Oh, don't start getting embarrassed on me. I've seen three generations through more scrapes than you could possibly imagine, and I haven't blinked at one."

Jesus. I was starting to think that no experience with meeting family could have prepared me for Venetia. "All right." I yanked off my sweater and the shirt under it, aware that this was probably not what Nate had in mind when he'd given me her address. She poked at the edges of the scrape, made a disapproving noise, and then set it on fire. At least that's what it felt like; after the first screaming shock of it I could recognize the scent as really strong rubbing alcohol.

"Stop whining." She did something else with what felt like hot irons (tweezers, I saw when I glanced back). "In all honesty, Genevieve," she continued as she added a bandage, "you are not what I expected Nathaniel to bring by when he said he wanted me to meet someone important."

I nearly choked as she smeared what felt like a dollop of chili paste on the scratch. I couldn't identify the actual product; the pain was dulling my senses, and there was a basic awful old-first-aid scent to all of it that eclipsed everything else. "And what did you expect?" I managed through gritted teeth.

"Someone more like his mother, honestly. A flake, but an endearing flake." She swatted the bandage in place, which hurt—actually, a good deal less now, but it still was a nasty thing to do—and handed me my shirt. "You, however, are neither blithe nor anything that could possibly be called a 'free spirit,' and you're not in the least pretty."

I could feel the blood rushing to my face about as fast as the retort rushing to my lips. *Don't cuss her out*, I thought, *don't cuss her out, and don't deck this cranky old bitch—*

"You'll do nicely," she added, and shook out my sweater.

I must have looked like a fish on the block, because Venetia gave another of those faint smiles. "There's a reason Nathaniel doesn't bring people to meet me often. Not even Angela liked me very much, and I don't blame her for it. I'm not friendly. But I'm useful and—"

"—And that's enough for you." I smiled, recognizing some of the philosophy that had gotten me through the last few years. Whatever changes I'd gone through since then, because of the Fiana or the Hunt or Nate himself, I still held on to some of that belief. "But it's still nice to have one or two friends who understand that."

The lines around her eyes softened a moment. "Oh yes," she said. "So you see my point," she went on, packing away the medical supplies with a brisk efficiency. "Even if you've got the poor sense to go getting scratched up like that—I won't ask how you managed it, I'll just say that you must have some talent for self-injury—you've got the sense I recognize."

I took my sweater and pulled it over my head, wincing a little less as the bandages stretched. She'd done a good job, even if she had used pure pain to do it. "Thanks," I said, and turned around, fumbling in my bag to make sure I still had the stone (with so much riding on it, I sure as hell wasn't losing track of it). "So," I added, lowering my voice, "where *is* Nate?"

My fingers brushed the greasy smooth surface of the sunstone, and for just a fraction of a second Venetia seemed to shrink, wizen in on herself. Stranger still, the photos on the wall behind her were blank.

But when I blinked and looked again, she was herself again, the old matriarch with a soul of iron.

"He's gone out," she said. "He went out a little while ago, for a walk around the back twenty. I thought he'd be back by now."

Oh, crap. "How long ago?"

"Just after dinner." She paused a moment, one hand on the door to the hall. "So some time ago, yes."

I ran my hand through my hair, tugging at the ends of it, and let out a long breath. "Do you want me to go look for him?"

Venetia's glasses flashed as she opened the door. "I raised that young man to be quite capable of handling himself on a simple walk in the woods," she proclaimed. "But yes, I would like it if you did. Humor an old woman."

"I'll humor us both." I switched the stone into the pocket of my jacket and left my bag by the door.

Outside, the air had turned crystalline and cold, with that tang that reminds you that winter isn't even as far away as the next day; it's already here, and lurking where you can't see it. My feet crunched on the first gleamings of frost behind the house, past the fence that delineated the end of both the driveway and Venetia's out-of-control herb garden (mint, mint everywhere, and you'd think that would be a reassuring scent, wouldn't you? Not when it's this cold). I shivered and sank a little deeper into my coat.

The scrub behind Venetia's house had once been a field, judging by the faint lines in the ground visible in the way the dead grass crumpled. Between the field and the herb garden stood a crumbling drystone wall and a cluster of trees, looking out disapprovingly.

Nate's clothes lay piled on the wall. His scent hung heavy and rank in the air, like the rumble of unsteady snow on a high hillside. I vaulted the wall and followed the scent into the scrub, past the pricker bushes and away from the open spaces. "Nate?"

No answer. But the back of my neck prickled, and I

didn't need to look to know he was watching. I raised my hands to my mouth and blew on them, then lowered them and closed my eyes.

The silence behind me grew deeper, and short, bristly hair brushed the tips of my fingers. Teeth nipped at the back of my leg, not even enough to do more than tug at the cloth. I'd have called it a love bite if it weren't so damn creepy. "Cut the crap, Nate," I snapped. "You know I can't talk to you like this."

There was a long pause marked by only the rattle of wind in the branches above, then a slow sigh. I opened my eyes to see Nate in mid change, only—

Only there was something different this time. A twist around his stomach, a distortion like the shimmer in a deformed mirror. Remembering the flash of silver in Katie's eyes, and the blank photos behind Venetia, I reached into my pocket for the sunstone, and as my fingers touched its greasy surface the distortion became clearer, girding him like a belt. Even when the last of the change faded and Nate stood before me fully human, gaunt and haggard, that coarse, ugly line remained.

"Evie," he murmured, the name a caress, and despite the cold I was suddenly warm, too warm. He met my eyes, then looked away, moving to cover himself. "I'm sorry."

"Venetia was worried," I said inanely.

"She's right to be. I thought . . . thought I could say goodbye to it. Only it's difficult, so difficult to keep coming back to myself." He shuddered all over, and I looked away, both to spare him and embarrassed by my own reaction. "I need your help."

"You have it," I answered without pause. "Always."

He smiled, only a knifelike flicker in the pale light from above. "You may not say that in a moment." Ignoring both the cold and his own nakedness—how was he not getting frostbite already?—he walked to the wall, bent, and drew something from between the stones. "I did some research," he said, not yet looking at me. "Some back when this first happened, then after a while I stopped, and then when you . . . after you gave the Horn back, and I thought about what it would be like without you."

He turned and extended his hand toward me, offering what he held: a long knife with a horn handle, dark with age. The blade had the dull sheen of old silver, but its edge was bright as a star. "It belongs to Aunt Venice," he said after a moment, through my shocked silence. "She keeps her silver in good condition. I thought I'd borrow it, bring it home, and do this there, but I don't think . . . I don't know if I can keep the resolve."

"Nate," I began, my voice far too high, "what are you asking me to do?"

"My father hit me with a wolfskin girdle," he said, and his hand under the knife was steady as stone. "That's one way to pass on the curse, and because he was my father it stuck. I will not pass this on to any child of mine." The corner of his mouth twitched, trying for a smile. "And that's if I have any, mind you. But there is another way."

I waited for him to elaborate, but he didn't. This had happened before, I remembered, or something like it: Nate's exposed throat, a knife offered to me. Then I'd rejected it. Now, though . . .

When I looked at him, when I held the sunstone and really looked, I could see two images, one laid over the other. Not the two shapes he owned. One was the man I knew, with that strange blurring around his middle, the point where skin and reality shifted. The other . . . the other was a monster. And it didn't make it any better that it still looked like Nate.

"What do I have to do?" I asked, and took the knife from his hand. The handle was cool and smooth, not horn but bone, and even the little scrimshaw work along the edges made it no less stark in this light.

Nate exhaled, a great puff of steam that hung between us for a moment. "You have to cut the curse away from me. I don't know—I don't think you'll have to skin me entirely—"

"*Jesus*, Nate—"

"—but yes, I think it's going to get messy."

"Nate, you don't have to do this. You've come this far, you can control it—"

"It's not a matter of controlling it. I know my own anger. I can—" He swallowed. "I may not be the best at handling that, but at least it's my own. This—" He glanced back at the house briefly. "I could easily get used to it. And I'd forget that it was originally meant as a curse. My father got used to his, and I think . . . I think that was part of what made him who he is."

He looked away. "Sometimes I think that I can only let go because I trust you not to let me go mad. And that's not fair to you. And if you're gone—" He stopped, and I touched the back of his hand. He clasped it in return, so hard it almost hurt. "If you're gone, I don't know whether I'd know how to keep myself in check."

I swallowed. "There's no guarantee I'll always be around," I said. "Even without the Hunt, there's always something that could happen—I mean, you could find someone else," I added, knowing I wasn't making much sense. "Someone else to keep you in check."

Nate's teeth flashed in a grin, just for a moment. "Let's pretend we've already had this conversation and I convinced you that I didn't want that. Okay? Because I'm not sure I can convince you right now, and it's too cold to waste time out here."

I was silent a moment. I hadn't realized how much Nate was trusting me not to let him run wild. I wasn't sure how much I liked that. I thought of how my reaction to him just now hadn't been fear but anger—maybe I was suited for it. "Nate," I said slowly, "if I can stay—if I can make it so I won't go, at midwinter, then you don't have to—" He shook his head. "Nate, it won't fix everything. You'll still get angry."

He let go of my hand. "That's another thing. I can't keep believing that the—the angry part of me is just the curse." His skin was very white in the faint starlight above. "Please, Evie. I can't be like this anymore."

If I were a magician, I thought, and if I had the patience and the knowledge to work it out, I could understand the curse based on what I saw, know what bound him to his other shape. And if I were a magician, a really good one, I could probably extricate him from it without even hurting him.

But I wasn't a magician. And this was not the kind of magic that the Elect or Roger or even Maryam dealt in. "All right," I said.

Nate looked at me and shuddered, one skin peeling back to reveal the other, never taking his eyes off me. The hair on the back of my neck rose—even if I knew that I'd never have to run from him, the dumb monkey part of my brain wanted to get away from what registered very clearly as a predator.

With the sunstone in hand, I could see much more clearly the line where his skin didn't quite match. A band all the way around his middle, unbroken . . . "Okay," I said, and knelt next to him. "Hold still."

I jammed the sunstone into my shirt, where I could keep contact with it, and grabbed a handful of rank fur. There wasn't much to go by; in either form, Nate was underfed and far too bony. But there was just enough, and I didn't wait for Nate to brace himself before slicing under the fold of skin I'd pulled up.

The wolf's body bucked against mine, and a high yelp escaped from between its teeth. "Easy," I said. Blood, black in the poor light, surged up around the knife blade, but I shifted my grip and drew the knife further up, along the line of its ribs. Skin parted easily under the blade, far more easily than it should have, so that it seemed as if I were simply prying a ribbon away. And under the skin, instead of peeled flesh, I saw Nate's own pale skin. That meant I must be on the right track. Right?

Right track or no, blood welled up and over my hands, slicking the hilt of the knife. The wolf growled and flailed, trying to get away, and I flung my other arm around its shoulders—then, as that began to slip, wrestled it down to the ground with all of my body weight just to slice up a few more inches. "God," I whispered. "God, Nate, hold still, I'm sorry—"

The wolf whipped around and snarled at me, its teeth clicking together an inch from my face. I jerked the knife further and its snarl turned into something closer to a whimper. The blood on my hands and shirt and jeans was cold, and that made no sense, not in this air. There should have been steam coming up from the blood, steam like the panting gasps the wolf struggled with. But this was a different magic, not spirit or blood or anything else but a horribly embodied magic, one that had knit itself into Nate's bones. From a dispassionate, detached point of view, it made sense that a curse so embodied must have a similarly visceral method of breaking it.

Detachment was not something I was capable of just now. I was mumbling something over and over—I'm pretty sure it was "I'm sorry," but at that point it could have been "hold still" or just plain curses—as I drew the knife over the wolf's spine and down its ribs. The wolf writhed under me, and the cry it gave was neither a howl nor a scream but something between the two. My own voice joined with it, a wordless snarl more suited to a hound than the Hound, and I pushed myself away, flinging the knife to the side.

"No more," I said. "Nate, I'm sorry, no more, I can't *do* this."

Skin beneath me shivered and twisted. Nate's hand closed over my wrist, pale skin over red. "Evie—" he managed through gritted teeth.

"No. No, I'm sorry, but this is killing you." I smeared a hand over my eyes, then blinked away the blood. "I *can't*."

He drew a deep, shuddering breath, and for the first

time I saw what I'd done. Around his back, where I'd cut, a long line of red skin about three fingers wide stretched like a weal. It wasn't bleeding, but it was raw, painful, and it hurt even to look at.

I dropped the knife and sat back on my heels. "I'm sorry," I said again. "If you can—if I can find a way, one that won't do this to you—I'll ask Dina, I'll change our bargain, get her to lift the curse. If anyone can do it, she can, and she'll owe me for this—"

Nate blinked, slowly coming back to himself, and rose to his knees. "Dina?"

"She's this—" Hearing the fracture in my voice, I forced myself to slow down. "Okay. Put on your clothes and I'll tell you. Please."

Nate was silent a moment, but there was no reproof in his eyes when he looked at me. Instead, he winced as the wind touched the long weal across his back, and for the first time the cold seemed to be hurting him. "Tell me," he said, and went to get his clothes.

I summed up the gist of the deal with Dina: the sunstone for a chance at life after midwinter. My hands didn't quite shake, but I smeared them over the grass and hoped that the blood would dry to unrecognizability before anyone came this way in the morning. "She's strong," I said, plucking at my sodden jacket, concentrating on the story to keep myself from really feeling the clamminess of bloody cloth. "She's . . . well, she might be a demigod, from what I can tell. And she'll owe me big for this. If I—if I push, I might be able to get her to lift your curse."

Nate nodded, bending to pick up his socks and shoes. "Evie," he said after a moment, pulling on his shirt and wincing when it touched the line of raw skin at his waist, "don't do it. If you have one sure thing, then that's enough."

"It's not a sure thing by any means." I took out the sunstone, which though I'd groped for it with bloody hands remained unspotted, as if it repelled even the touch of blood. "Besides, I have something she wants."

I thought of Meda's plea to be a murderer, and shook my head. "And given what she offered me before—"

I stopped. Nate shrugged into his jacket and glanced back at me. "What?"

"Nate," I said slowly, "there's something I need to tell you."

We walked back to the front porch, avoiding Venetia's light for now. The nights out here were too quiet; there was no traffic or yelling or even just a siren to break the silence. The shadows of the branches moved over Nate's face, somehow like his transformation and yet much more fragile. After a moment, he cleared a spot on the porch and sat down. "Go ahead."

I sank down beside him. "Okay," I said. "Do you remember at the quarry, when Patrick pushed you off the edge, and you fell into the water?"

"Barely. I remember hitting the water and then you giving me mouth-to-mouth."

"Well. I think—I think you might have hit your head harder than you thought." I took a deep breath. How did you go about telling someone he might have died? "Do you remember, too, why you were drawn to the quarry, but then you didn't go in the water?"

He rubbed at his forehead. "Vaguely. I . . . it felt safe there, like it was meant as a sanctuary, but something about the water felt—I don't know. Felt hungry." He gave me a sheepish look as he said it, as if trying to make it something ridiculous.

It wasn't, though. "That's pretty accurate. The guardian of the quarry—it doesn't know what it can and can't take. It caught you, either when you fell or when you . . . when you hit your head."

Nate's hand reached up to touch the back of his head. I'd had my own hands back there more than once and never found so much as a goose egg, but I knew what he was looking for: some physical trace of what had happened.

"And when I confronted it, it asked what I would give to have you back. Like a bargain. And I wasn't having any of it, I just called it a son of a bitch, and it said something like, 'I accept,' and hit me with this wave . . ." I paused a moment, ready for the shudder and taste of ice water in the back of my throat at the thought of that wave, but nothing came.

Nate was still silent and unmoving. I cleared my throat. "And then it gave you back. Er. To me. I'm still not sure how badly you were hurt, but I didn't have time to think of any other way—"

" 'Son of a bitch,' " he said quietly.

"That's what I said to it. And Dina, she thinks that I was, just barely, um. Pregnant. And that the quarry took it. And that's how it was, was draining me over the last few weeks. It didn't even have to be real; some forms of magic are based on possibility, and I don't think it even matters whether I was or not, but in the symbolic sense—" I was babbling. To make myself stop, I clasped the boards of the porch so hard splinters dug into my fingers.

Nate ran both hands through his hair and pressed them against the back of his neck. "That doesn't make any sense."

"I know, but it's what—"

"No. I mean it doesn't make physical sense. I don't think—I mean, it'd been only a day. Less. I'm pretty sure conception takes a little more time to, you know, take. And it'd be a hell of a crapshoot for everything to line up just after that one time."

I managed a smile. "It wasn't just the one time, you know."

"Okay. That one night. Whatever. But something's still . . . I'm just not sure . . ." He glanced up at me, and whatever he saw made his expression soften. "Is that why you went into the Quabbin? To get our child back?"

"No," I said immediately, then paused, startled by how easy that decision had been. "No. I don't—I'm sorry, Nate, but I don't want a kid. Even yours. Even before I knew about midwinter. And that's the more important thing right now."

He paused, then shook his head. "You're right. We should probably concentrate on the real problem."

"Which real problem? The werewolf thing, the magic rock, or the mythical hounds coming to eat me in six weeks?"

At that he actually laughed, and for a moment I joined in, giggling—it was pretty damn ridiculous, even given my usual flexible relation to reality. I looked up at him, remembered how many times I'd decided that he didn't deserve to get stuck with me, remembered how many times I'd ignored that. His hand was cool against mine.

After a moment, though, he let go and got to his feet. "I don't know, Evie," he said finally. "I don't know how—how to feel about any of this. Especially because I'd always . . . well, I'd thought that what I did was some way of saving you. And now I find it just screwed you over more . . ." He ran both hands through his hair. "There really isn't any way I can rescue you, is there?"

I thought of midwinter, of the ice water, of the way Nate's head felt against the hollow between my shoulder and breast. "I—maybe I should go." I stood up, checking behind me to make sure I hadn't left stains on the porch. That would have taken more explaining than I thought Venetia would have patience for.

"You don't—"

"I'm covered in blood, Nate. Your blood. I wouldn't let me near Katie like this, and Venetia sure as hell shouldn't."

He nodded, absently, his brows furrowed. "Yeah . . . You said the quarry spirit stole a possibility?"

"As close as I can figure. Severed, now. I no longer have any connection to it." Thank God.

"No. You don't." He drummed his fingers against the porch railing in a quick cadence, one-two-three, one-two-three, the same way he did when he was working late at night. "I think . . . I have to think about this for a little." He leaned down and kissed me, one slow solid touch of his lips on mine. "See you."

"See you," I echoed, and before I could change my mind I walked back to Sarah's beat-up car and got in.

Halfway home I realized I'd left my messenger bag in Venetia's parlor. One more thing to write off.

I touched the sunstone. At least I had what I'd come for.

Thirteen

I got in so late that not even the all-night restaurants had customers, late enough that I could find a parking spot close to my office (which never, ever happens). A heavy fog had rolled in off the harbor, and even as far inland as I was, the ends of my street were bright with reflected light from the fog. The little fountain at the door burbled at me as I got in, and I set the sunstone on it before I locked up.

I dumped my clothes, jacket and all, in the sink and ran cold water over them, then let them soak while I stood in the shower under the hottest water my building's aging heater could produce. (Over the din, I could faintly hear Mrs. Heppelwhite banging on the floor above; the woman claimed to be deaf as a post, but her hearing was suspiciously sharp if you were either doing something gossipworthy or running water through the pipes that went past her bedroom at ass o'clock in the morning.) When I got out, I moved the sodden clothes from the sink into a bucket and poured detergent on top of that. I was moving on autopilot, following my mother's reactions, the same clean-up-what-you-can response that she'd had to any crisis. You took care of the mess at hand, and then you faced the worst of it.

The worst of it, from what I could see when I got

out of the bathroom, was the sunstone, still sitting on the brink of the fountain, its greasy gray matching the pseudoconcrete of the basin. It was the sort of thing that blended in with its surroundings; it didn't seem any more out of place here than it had on the banks of the Quabbin or, for that matter, in a rotting leather bag dredged up from the depths.

Deke wasn't answering his phone. I left a message for him to call me as soon as possible, then took a quick assessment of the office. It wasn't warded, not since someone had used those wards to monitor me, but neither was it out in the open. I didn't think anyone would come looking for the sunstone.

Well. No one living, anyway. If Meda wanted me, she could haunt me like any other ghost. And she'd have to wait till I got some sleep.

I unfolded my futon, dragged a couple of blankets onto it, then sat cross-legged in the center, holding the sunstone. It didn't smell of magic, from what I could tell. It didn't really have much of a scent—just the lingering connection to Dina's, like a painting faded in the sun. The waters of the Swift River had worn away most of what made this part of Dina. Only when she was close—only when Roger brought her to Boston—would it even begin to react, making that tension something to sustain her.

The part of the undercurrent that dealt with other spirits, entities that weren't close to human—what Roger called "alliances"—was one I did not like venturing into, and not just because it had bitten me. Some of them, the ones the Fiana had dealt with, or the lingering ghosts, they were fine. Others, though . . . Humanity isn't a monolithic good; we can be very petty and vicious, capable of calculated betrayal or even just ignoring the rules. Bring human and divine together, and sometimes the divine would teach the human to transcend those flaws. And sometimes the divine would latch on to them like a three-year-old psychopath with a flamethrower.

Even when both sides retain their selves, contact changes the spirit. Look at the Morrigan, chained to the Fiana so long that she was reduced to seeking help through me and in the end chose to die instead of rise again. Look at the Gabriel Hounds, who through their association with a dead man had gained a shred of mortality (and what they'd taken from their time with me, I didn't even want to know).

This stone, though . . . I remembered the pictures fading behind Venetia, the silver in Katie's eyes. *Fear*, I thought hazily, *the link is fear.* Venetia was scared of losing those she loved, the way that Angela was lost, the way that her friends had gone on . . . and Katie, she was afraid of what she saw, how she saw . . . and Nate was scared of himself, not just his curse but his own capacity for anger.

There was something in that. Seeing fear. Something about what Dina was, or perhaps what she'd been reduced to by the theft of the stone. Only there had to be more to it, and to Meda's plea: Be not thief but murderer.

I shook my head, and the room seemed to wobble as I did so. I couldn't do that. Not even for the woman who'd led me to the stone. But I could maybe use the stone as leverage, make Dina do more than I'd asked originally. I switched off the light and lay curled up, one hand around the sunstone, trying not to think about anything beyond the noise of the fountain.

When I got up—really late, but this was a Sunday and the chance of Tania calling me in was if not zero then very damn close—the fog hadn't cleared. "What is this," I muttered, staring out at the dimmed view of the street, "San Francisco?" We didn't get fog like this in Boston. Not usually, anyway.

I tried Deke's number without much hope, but he did pick up. "Hello who is this," he said, the words flat and without pause or inflection.

"Deke, this is the Hound. I found what your friend's looking for."

"Already? Oh, that's . . . No, that's good. Yes. Good."

Great. What planet was Deke on today? "You remember, right?"

"Oh yes." A long pause. If I listened close, I thought I could hear a voice on the other end, too low for me to make out much beyond the murmur of speech. "Yes," he said finally. "Yes, we do."

"Where's Roger?"

"No!" Almost a yelp, that. "No, you don't have to worry about him. Please."

"Okay . . ." I took a deep breath. "I want to talk to you both before we go to Dina. I want some assurance that I'll get what was promised me."

"We can talk about this later," Deke said wearily. His voice sounded distant now, as if he was holding the phone away from his ear.

"No, Deke, we need to talk about this now. I'm sorry, but—" I sighed, turning the stone over in my hand, thinking about Deke by the grill, turning the fire back and forth. "I have what you want, and without some kind of guarantee, I can promise you won't get it. Okay? There's—I want to know that you'll hold up your end of the bargain, and then we'll talk about payment."

"Payment?"

"Yes." The stone had warmed in my hand, and I set it back down. "Like I said, I have what you want. We might need to do some renegotiating." *If Dina wants this thing so badly*, I thought, *then she can lift two curses instead of one*. "Now, when can we meet?"

Another long pause with the indistinct murmur of voices, back and forth. One of them was definitely Deke's. The other sounded too light to be Roger. Too soft, as well; I couldn't imagine Roger speaking in anything resembling an inside voice. Dina, maybe? That was worrying. "Two hours," Deke said finally. "Give me two hours. I didn't think you'd be so quick."

I permitted myself a smile at that. "Hey, chalk it up

to my general awesomeness. But I'm not happy about carting this thing around."

"Two hours. Meet me where you met me before. At the house."

"Okay." I paused. "Deke, are you okay? Is there something—" Hell, how do you ask "are you being coerced" without tipping off whoever might be listening?

Deke interrupted me, sounding a little peevish. "All's well. We'll do what you ask, okay? We'll even talk payment. Just—just be there in two hours."

"If you say so." I clicked my phone shut and tucked it away, tossing the sunstone hand to hand. After some thought, I zipped it into the inner pocket of my jacket (the lighter one, less effective for the weather, but since the other was now hanging up and drying I had little choice). Better to keep it with me.

I thought for a moment about just trusting Deke, going out to the house in a show of good intentions. It might earn me some brownie points, and it would have been a more ethical thing to do—I still couldn't believe I was entertaining the thought of extorting anything from such a wet rag as Deke—but this wasn't just about making nice. This was my life at stake, and Nate's sanity. If I could get Dina to lift both curses at once, that'd be worth any number of excuses I had to make later.

Trust was a worthy cause. But it would also get you killed in the undercurrent. I unlocked the second drawer of my desk and took out my gun. Deke would understand, I told myself, checking the ammo. And I'd try not to scare him.

The fog lifted slightly as I drove Sarah's car inland to Allston, my bike bungeed to the back (I had no intention of waiting for the T today). The Goddess Garden had minimal Sunday hours; Sarah had claimed in the past that they were in place just to establish her pagan cred. I parked a block away, dug in the glove compartment until I came up with an out-of-date map of

Boston, then walked my bike over to give her the keys.

I came in just as she was ringing up a stack of books and a pack of Gryphon Blend Incense Sticks for an older woman in a headscarf and black turtleneck, and Sarah immediately turned on her smile to demonstrate her usual charm to any new customer. Her eyes widened as soon as she saw me, and I could see her swallowing her words down. I stopped at the door, the jangling bells right next to my ear, while Sarah hurriedly made change and handed the woman her purchases ("and we'll be having a sale next week, so stop by!") then watched with a frozen smile until her customer left. "What the hell happened to you?" she snapped as soon as the door jangled closed again.

"What do you mean?" I glanced over my shoulder, then down at myself—I hadn't forgotten to put on pants or something like that, had I? And I knew I'd washed all the blood off . . . "I parked the car down on Cambridge Ave.—it's filled up and everything."

"No, you—" She came out from behind the counter and, to my surprise, pulled one of the shop curtains closed. "Screw the car, Evie. You look like the unseelie host itself just dropped by for cocktail hour and you didn't have enough weenies on sticks."

I stared at her for a long moment. "You've been waiting forever to use that expression, haven't you?"

"No. Maybe. It doesn't matter. What does is that you look both like death warmed over and—" She stopped and stood up on tiptoe to look into my face. "Well, like something caught fire in you. What happened?"

"Went swimming." I managed a grin, and Sarah blew a tendril of hair out of her face. "No, seriously, Sarah, I found what I was looking for. Not just the information, but everything. I just need to get it to Deke, and then, well, we'll see from there. That's part of why I'm here."

"Deke, huh." She tweaked the curtain back and

glanced out into the street. "Haven't heard from him lately."

"He's been busy. Sarah, what's up with the curtain and the hush-hush bit? No one's going to care if I'm visiting."

"That's what I thought a week ago. Now, though . . ." She shook her head. "There was another fire, this time at the argentium in Brookline. And a pair of shadowcatchers down by the Charles got their drain raided by someone who knew to smash every locus. Things are getting bad, Evie."

"Shit." Now I could put a name to the feeling I'd had when I entered the city: dread. This wasn't the reasonable fear that the Gabriel Hounds sowed in their wake, nor the anger that plain sparring would produce. This was something else entirely, something paralyzing.

But the water this morning hadn't smelled of corpses, and the sunstone was with me, out of the Quabbin. If the tension between it and Dina was what had been affecting Boston's undercurrent, shivering along their exposed nerves like firedamp affecting a canary, then I'd put a stop to it already. It just needed time to take. "Have the cops been by?" I asked.

"Yeah. And yes, the skinny Latina chick was one of them. You're not going to be able to avoid her forever."

"Goddammit." I ran my fingers through my hair, still damp from the fog. "It'll get better," I said, though I had only hope to base that on. Sarah didn't quite roll her eyes, but it was close. "Look, I need a favor. I have this—this sunstone that I'm returning to someone."

"Part of a job?"

"Sort of. Not really one on the books."

Sarah's eyes narrowed. "How off-the-books are we talking here, Evie."

"Well, this is a little different. And a little more urgent. See, I really—I need Deke's partner to hold up her end of the bargain, and I know she wants this badly."

"Bad enough that she might just forget to pay you?"

"Something like that." I took out Sarah's metro map of Boston and unfolded it, pointing to the harbor bridge. "I'm going to meet Deke here in about an hour. If I don't call you, say, half an hour after that, can you, I don't know, put in a nine-one-one call or something else to get the cops out there? Tell them you saw a drug deal taking place or some terrorists or something."

"You'd sic the cops on Deke? Evil woman."

"He's scared enough of them that I figure he'll deal if he knows there's a time limit. And I can get out of it. Really, don't worry. Just call if I don't, okay?"

Sarah took the map and gave me a sour look. "Like I need to get in trouble for making a false report . . . fine. I'll think of something."

"You're a lifesaver, Sarah. And don't worry about the rest of it; as soon as this is taken care of, we'll be able to fix it together. Working for the community, right?" I took her hand and pressed her keys into it.

Sarah shook her head, but the first stirrings of a smile were there. She retreated to the counter, then paused. "Does Nate have anything to do with this?"

I stopped at the door, not quite turning to face her. "Nate? Shouldn't. Why?"

"He called about twenty minutes ago, wanted to know if I could take care of Katie for a bit. Didn't say why. I figured you were off together or something, but if you're playing harbor patrol with Deke, then that can't be it."

I closed my eyes. Somewhere back in my apartment, his blood was still draining out of my clothes; somewhere in the back twenty behind Venetia's house, the knife I'd failed to use still lay in the grass. But what Nate did now, he had to do on his own. I could trust him to do that. "Doesn't ring any bells."

"You two aren't fighting, are you?"

"Sarah, drop it. Please. It's—" I glanced back over my shoulder at her. "It's a little hard to explain, and I have to be at the harbor in a bit."

"You'll tell me later?"

"I'll tell you everything."

There are parts of the waterfront that are flourishing. Those parts are all well away from Fort Point Channel, and most of them smell a little better. (Boston Harbor's a lot cleaner than it used to be, but there's no amount of cleaning that will make a harbor other than what it is. Fish are fish, and low tide is low tide; you don't get rid of those smells by making the water clean.)

The fog had turned this part of the harbor into a ghost of itself, but the house remained a dull blot on the water. A light moved back and forth in the windows, no more than a stray gleam. Someone was home, all right. I tried to catch a scent, but Deke had set his wards well. I shifted, feeling my shoulder holster settle into place.

There was a walkway out to the house, nothing more than a line of boards that swooped and sagged alarmingly in the middle. I glanced over my shoulder—no cops nearby, and no one out on the bridge—and scrambled over the fence and onto the walkway.

Which was a lot higher up than I'd expected.

Tides, I told myself, staring down at the yawning gap between the rotting boards and the water below, gleaming with oil from the boats further down the channel. That was the problem. It hadn't looked so far before because the tide was in. But now, there had to be at least ten feet between me and the water. And not just the water: pilings and junk and any number of ragged edges.

Well, shit. Time to hope this thing was a lot more steady than it looked.

The boards didn't just creak. They groaned, like a long-suffering parent reminded of the sins of their offspring, and a few of them sagged under my feet. When I looked down, trying to make sense of the gray against gray, the rotting planks versus the slightly less rotten, all I could see were the pilings in the water far, far below, sticking up like carelessly arranged spears, some of them slimy with mold and moss.

A board shifted under my foot, and I stumbled forward, catching my toe against the next one. The walkway screeched and splintered, and I pitched forward onto the little ridge between porch and door. I hung there for a moment, rotting wood jammed between ribs and pelvis, trying to remember how to breathe.

Something shifted inside the house—not the creak of old wood, but the motion of someone changing position, and I thought I heard a chuckle. "Yeah, laugh it up, Deke," I muttered, and pulled myself up, wincing at the bruises.

The door was locked. Of course. But the window next to it had been smashed so thoroughly that not even the frame was left, leaving it a gaping pit in the wall. Gaping pit would do, though. I eased myself around the side of the house, shuffling one foot in front of the other to keep from tipping off the scrap of a porch, and clung to the wall as I swung one leg up and into the window. "Deke," I said, panting a little more than I wanted to admit, "I don't care where you go from here, but you're going to give me a ride to shore, all right? Because I am not going back out that way again."

I swung both feet over the edge and into the house. Deke's smell was so heavy in this room that it might as well have had his name painted outside; he'd made this place his own. More than that, the stink of old oil and tarpaper blotted out even the smell of the harbor.

Too late I recognized the scent that wasn't woodchuck and smoke; too late I heard the click of a gun's safety going off. "Both hands in the air, and no sudden movements, Evie," said Rena.

Fourteen

I spun, flattening myself against the wall. Rena stood by a huge, corroded machine, something that almost looked like a Looney Toons factory second with chains as thick as my legs now lying slack where once they'd passed through the wall. An electric lantern atop it threw acid shadows across the rust and detritus. The daylight didn't seem to want to come past the windows, hovering outside with the fog, and the lantern's light painted Rena's face with a harsh brilliance. She wasn't in uniform—that was something at least—but her gun was out and pointed at me.

At the other side of the room, huddled up against the wall, sat Deke. He didn't even look up, just rocked slightly, staring at a point on the floor where the floorboards ended.

"Rena, what are *you* doing here?"

"I wish I could ask you the same, Evie." She nodded to Deke. "But I got a pretty good idea already."

"What are you—" I stopped. "That was you, on the phone with Deke. This morning."

She nodded.

"Don't you need, I don't know, an actual warrant for a wiretap like that?"

"Not if he's got the phone on loudspeaker and I'm standing right there." She drew a deep breath, not taking her eyes from me. "And you're his contact."

"Contact? Oh, Jesus." I could have laughed, except Rena still had her gun out, and though she knew enough not to put her finger on the trigger unless she wanted to shoot someone, I knew she was fast enough to do so before I could react. "Seriously, Rena—"

" 'I have what you want, and without some kind of guarantee, I can promise you won't get it,' " she quoted. "I thought you didn't much care for extortion, but it's not the first time I've been wrong about you."

"Extortion, my ass!" But I could feel my face reddening, and not just because she'd skirted a little too close to the truth. "This was a legit job, and I just wanted to be sure I was going to get paid."

"Then you won't mind showing me the contract for it." Rena waited, and this time I had to look away. "Thought so."

"It's still not—" I stopped myself. "Okay. Deke probably misunderstood what you were asking. This was just a business meeting, and even if it's technically off the books, there's nothing illegal about it."

"Maybe." She risked a glance at Deke. "I'm not saying I trust his word. But even if you're right about this, I'd like to know what you're doing with a known arsonist."

"Arson—goddammit, Deke." He cringed at that, and the smell in the air turned a little more rank. "Christ. Can I—look, I just want to see if he's all right. Okay?"

Rena hesitated, then nodded. I picked my way across the broken floor to him, very aware of her eyes on me. "Deke, are you okay?" He didn't answer, or even look up. I tried putting a hand on his shoulder—that was usually enough to get him to flinch away—and he only blinked. "Deke, where's Roger? Is he here? For God's sake, what's wrong with you?"

His lips parted, and an unintelligible whisper passed them. I leaned closer, and he shivered. "I'm scared, Hound."

"I don't blame you. Rena, what the hell have you done to him?"

"I didn't do anything. He sat down the minute we got out here and he's been like that since."

I got to my feet. There wasn't much in the way of an intact floor, but there was enough space in front of Deke for me to stand between them. "Then why is Deke so scared he's practically shitting himself?"

"You'd have to ask him that," Rena said levelly.

Like that was going to do much good right now. "Deke's harmless, Rena. Yes, he's kind of a pyro, but he's never started anything big. Worst he's ever done is burn some trash. That's not nearly enough to bring you out here."

"You may want to think about what you're saying," Rena said. "Especially if you're going to defend him."

"Given the choice between the person with a gun and the weak little guy in the corner, yeah, I think I know who I'd defend," I snapped. "Besides, what do you care? You gonna read me my Miranda rights?"

Rena was silent a moment. The lantern flickered, and for a second the white glare of the fog outside seemed to press closer, changing her expression even as she remained still.

An idea started to rise in the back of my mind. "Where's Foster?"

That was it. Rena blinked, and for just a fraction of a second, her scent was no longer the block of blue ice that it was when she put on that badge, but something pricklier, like broken glass. "Does it matter?"

"It should. He's your partner, right? Shouldn't he be your backup in case one skinny bike messenger and a half-baked pyromaniac decide to get violent? Or maybe you didn't want him here." I took a step closer, rethought it as the boards creaked, and moved to my left instead. "Maybe this isn't as official as I thought."

Now Rena's hands shifted—her index finger moving closer to the trigger. Crap. "If I did come alone," she said, "and there's no guarantee that I did, let's say I had a hunch about who'd show up when Deke met with his boss—"

"Boss? Deke doesn't have a boss. None of us do; you know that, Rena." I pressed one hand to the back of my head, trying to stave off headache and panic both. "I don't have time for this. Look, let me finish this exchange—" let me get out from under the damn death sentence, "—and we'll talk. I'll tell you everything right down to the ground, you want it that way. But not right now."

I held my hands out further, trying to demonstrate that I really had nothing to hide. Unfortunately, that had the wrong effect entirely—my jacket opened a little too far, and I saw Rena's eyes flick to the shoulder holster that wasn't quite out of view. Shit.

"God damn you, Evie," she snapped. Whatever chance I'd had, it was now gone. "I was really, really hoping you wouldn't be part of this. I guess I should have known—"

"No. No, that was—Rena, I swear to God I'm telling the truth."

"There's no way I can believe you," she said, and I knew it was true. I'd left too much out in our dealings in the past, left her in the dark too often. At the time I'd thought it was for her own good, that telling her more about the undercurrent would only drag her into it—it had done that to Nate, hadn't it?—but as it turned out I'd just been laying another stone on the road to hell.

I closed my eyes. "No," I said. "There isn't any way I can convince you either. But I'll tell you the truth anyway, and then you can tell me whether I'm under arrest. Okay? If so, I'll go quietly. Just—can we not go back along the boardwalk? I hated walking over that."

The corner of Rena's lips turned up just slightly, but she nodded—then shifted the gun to point at Deke as he got to his feet, wringing his hands. "No," he stage-whispered. "No, she won't understand."

"Goddammit, Deke, I'm in it and I don't understand." I lowered my hands. "Okay, Rena. What happened is this: I got myself in some trouble. *Bruja* trouble, and big. Enough that I got scared." *Blood in the water*, I thought, remembering the Hounds' assessment of me. "The short way to put it is that it's a curse. Deke, here, has a friend—the one with the boat, the guy who owned it before it caught fire. And no, I didn't know him when we talked before. But now I do, and he—Roger—knows someone who says she can remove that curse, if I do something for her." I glanced at Deke, ashamed of what else I had to say. "Only I got spooked and thought I could get a little more for the job. I wanted to . . . to see if she'd lift another curse as well. That's why I said all that on the phone. I was, shit, I guess it *was* extortion after all."

Deke's hands twisted as if he was trying to scrub something off them. "You didn't have to. She said, she said she'd get it back for you. From the quarry. Roger told me, he told me about the child—"

"There was no child, Deke, okay? And Roger had no business telling you that." I sighed and glanced back at Rena, whose expression had gone from stoic disbelief to outright shock. "That was Dina's first offer," I told her. "She—she told me I'd been pregnant. And that a, an embodiment of the . . . Goddammit. A nixie, call it that. It had stolen the child." Christ, it sounded even worse telling Rena like this. At any moment I expected her to point and laugh, or at the very least give up on me entirely.

Instead she blinked and lowered the gun. "You're kidding." I shook my head. "You're not kidding."

"No. And look, that whole part doesn't matter, okay? What matters is that I said yes, and I found this for her."

I reached into my coat for the sunstone, too late remembering the gun, but Rena didn't move. My fingers slid over the sunstone, and for a moment I could barely see—Deke's fear, so huge and shapeless, loomed up like a tumor on an X-ray, and all I could perceive was that miasma of dread. He hadn't been kidding about being scared.

But more than that, I saw Rena, grayed out, her face made of stone, her hands perpetually frozen around the gun. Which made it even stranger when she snapped the safety back on and holstered it. "Okay. Okay, Evie, you can shut up now."

I started to protest, then stopped as the words became clear. "What?"

"You're an idiot—I'll believe that till the day I die—and you really should have checked with me before carrying a firearm, and I think there's a lot more to this story, but I'll believe you for now." She edged around a gap in the boards and reached forward to clasp my shoulder for balance.

"Seriously?" What had I said? I closed my hand around the sunstone, trying to ignore the stink of abject terror now coming off Deke—what in God's name did he have to be scared of, we were both on his side—and tried to look like I'd expected it.

It didn't work; Rena didn't do anything so obvious as smile, but the corners of her eyes crinkled. "Okay. Here's the situation as I see it. This guy—" a nod toward Deke, who flinched even though she was a yard away, "—got caught setting a fire at a psychic's. Not so different from the other vandalisms lately. So we thought he might have something to do with the rest."

I glanced at Deke. "What the hell were you doing?"

He jammed his hands into the pockets of his dreadful old coat. "I told you," he said, less pleading than peevish now, shuffling his feet against the boards. "I'm scared."

"Yes, but that's no reason—" I sighed. "Okay. Rena, go on."

"That would have just gone under the radar, if Foster hadn't checked out the accelerant he was using, and found a very interesting link." She grinned, a more feral grin than either Nate or I could have managed, even with our canine associations. "And that's not getting into who really owned that boat."

I hesitated—and Deke, who had been standing there forgotten for too long, gave out a shriek like a maimed horse and shoved me aside. I took a step back, my arms pinwheeling as my foot failed to come down on anything, and went sprawling across the floor, boards snapping and creaking under me. Rena turned to Deke, and he slammed his hand against her chest.

No. Not just his hand. I yanked my foot out from the gap in the floorboards and scrambled up in time to see Deke step back, still holding what looked like one of those silver glass balls that people use for Christmas ornaments. Only this one had shattered, and the jagged edges were now the same red as the first few blossoms on Rena's shirt. A murky substance spread out from them, mixing with her blood.

Rena stared at the mark, unable to sense the stink of fireworks that came from it. Her eyes rolled up, and a pinkish froth spilled from the corners of her mouth as she crumpled.

I yelled and struggled to my feet, stumbling over the broken boards. Deke didn't even look at me; he just took a baby food jar from his pocket and tossed it. The lid came off in flight, and the contents—tar, and seawater, and something that smelled like what you'd find at the bottom of a cistern—struck me across the chest.

Gunpowder scent wreathed me like a shroud. I stumbled, the world closing in around me until all I could see was Deke's face.

He was sobbing, and that didn't change even as I blacked out.

Unconsciousness tastes like salt.

I'd just managed that much of a thought before realizing that I shouldn't have even been capable of thought, being, you know, unconscious. But even though the world was still black around me—I wasn't even alert enough to feel pain—there was still some part of me aware of what was going on.

Unfortunately, "what was going on" in this case didn't seem to have much to do with my external surroundings. I saw—or whatever; sight wasn't quite the sense that was being inflicted on me here—Colin as a younger man, stepping out of a boat, both hands whole, a pistol at his belt and a boat hook hanging next to it. The sky above him was the color of brass. He glanced behind him toward the water, and I knew that he was looking back at Boston and the girl he'd left behind, the girl who'd told him what to do in the belief that she'd be with him when the time came . . .

Something was pulling me away from the sight, like a hook in my flesh, like the pressure of the Quabbin. A scent, curling around me but not yet so present as to be identifiable. I shook my head—or whatever—and pushed recognition away for now, because with recognition would come consciousness, and I'd no longer be able to see Colin, now turning his back on the shore and pushing aside waist-high grass, walking with the stride of someone who knows that this is only the first task of many . . .

The scent dragged at me again, pulling me away. I was rising, above a flat lake, gleaming the color of Roger's hair, a lake with an eye at the bottom, a reservoir with a sunstone, flat and greasy-looking and now dissolving into rainbow patterns, unhealthy rainbows like unconsciousness or . . .

I drew a breath and choked on the heavy air.

. . . or gasoline.

My eyes snapped open, and the rainbows stayed a moment longer, flickering off the surface of a slick pool not so very far away. I was flat on my face, one arm wedged under me, the other flung out and stinking of tar from where Deke's locus had hit me. The arm that was free felt wrenched, as if someone had dragged me in the wrong direction, or as if someone had tried to pull my jacket off.

The sunstone. I fumbled in my jacket, but it was gone. The stone was gone, my holster was empty, and the air stank of gasoline. "Deke," I groaned, and pushed myself up to my elbows. "Deke, what—"

I shouldn't have had to ask. This was Deke, after all. A slop of gasoline smeared the floor from end to end of the bridge house, leading to a pair of leaking cans by the great chains of machinery. Not alight yet, but they didn't need to be alight to incapacitate me. There were downsides to having a powerful sense of smell. Deke himself was at the far end of the room, by the last remaining windows. "Oh, God," he muttered, fumbling with a rope bolted to the sill, "oh God, oh God, oh God."

"What the fuck are you doing?"

His head jerked up, and his eyes were wide and weeping. "Hound, I'm sorry," he said, and clasped the sunstone to his breast as if it might protect him. "I'm so sorry. But I'm scared. I've never been so scared." With the hand that wasn't holding the stone, he held up his lighter.

"No!" I struggled to my knees, my limbs like lead ingots tacked on at hip and shoulder. "Deke, you don't have to do this. You don't—"

His face contorted in pity and sorrow and terrible determination. "Sorry," he said again, and dropped the lighter.

The gasoline went up with a *thump*. I fell back and landed against Rena, who groaned weakly. "God damn you, Deke!"

He didn't answer, only swung himself out the window. I didn't hear a splash—of course, over the roaring in my ears, I wouldn't have heard anything. Instead I turned and tried to get an arm under Rena's shoulders. She'd made a noise, that had to mean she was all right, didn't it?

Well, as all right as one could be, stuck in a burning building. Her eyelids flickered, and she managed to focus on me for a second, raising one hand to fumble at her chest. “Evie,” she said, or tried to; the froth at her lips now took on a deeper, red tinge.

“Fuck!” I yelled, and coughed as the smoke dove into my lungs. I got her by one arm—whatever magic had been in the tar, it was burning off, as was most of everything else in the bridge house—and dragged her up, hoping like hell that whatever damage had been done would fade as the locus faded, that I wasn’t just hurting her further. “Stay with me, Rena,” I said, and lurched across the floor, half-dragging her.

I took a moment to glance around and immediately regretted it. The building hadn’t needed the gasoline to get the fire going: it was old, dry, and had been weatherproofed with tarpaper for years. The flames had already seized on the wall where Deke had been, devouring his rope, and they were headed our way. “Rena, did you have a boat? How did you get out here?”

No answer. She slumped against my side, even heavier now. The fire reached the spot where I’d lain just a moment ago, and any minute now, I was going to go up too.

I cursed under my breath, hitched Rena further onto my shoulder, and stumbled to the door, dragging her over the holes in the floor. Her weight nearly overbalanced me as I leaned back to kick the door open, but the force of the kick did enough to keep me upright. And not a moment too soon—the back of my sweater was starting to singe, its acrid scent worse somehow than the gasoline itself, and the backs of my legs went hot, as if I’d been lying in the sun too long.

I reached the porch just in time to see that the fire had outflanked us. The rickety walkway that had brought me here caught, the old wood burning gleefully, as if it’d finally found its purpose in life. “Oh God,” I whispered, knowing I was echoing Deke and not caring.

Someone on shore yelled—finally!—and I raised my head. But any help coming from shore would reach us well after we'd been nicely roasted, and though I could see a few shocked faces watching us from the ferry docks and the waterfront, none seemed to be moving toward rescue.

I looked down, still struggling for breath. Below us were the remnants of the pilings from when this had been a larger house, or from the porch that had long since disappeared into the harbor. Their jagged, mossy ends poked up through the flat water below, now golden with reflected light. Even at low tide, this was still a channel, still had to be deep enough to accommodate ferries, right? Right?

"Sorry about this, Rena," I said, and pulled her with me as I jumped.

The water hit me so hard that at first I thought I'd missed and struck one of the pilings. Rena jerked out of my grasp, but I caught at her and got one arm around her.

That was a mistake; I was still headed down, and the water had gone from a shock to bone-freezing cold. The burns on the backs of my legs tried to lock up, and my shoes—now full of water—were dragging me further down. I got us up to the surface long enough for me to draw a couple of tortured breaths and drag Rena's head above water. The froth at her mouth had been washed away, but she still choked on it, wheezing for breath, and the muck of the locus still clung to her.

Behind and above us, the bridge house was wholly alight. I struck out toward the closest pier, choking on filthy seawater.

The good people of the waterfront had all clustered at the railing to watch the fire and see whether they'd need to worry about their own safety (depending on the wind, even an isolated building could send burning brands into any one of the luxury towers to either side). If one of them was worried about the draggled women clinging to the floating dock, he raised no outcry. "Hey!" I yelled, then broke down coughing. "Hey, we need some help—"

Sooner or later, someone would have to look this way, right? I tried to get one arm under Rena, but either the waters of the Atlantic were a lot worse than the Quabbin or the fire and everything else were worsening incipient hypothermia. My hands didn't seem to want to work right, and though Rena was starting to come around, we didn't really have time to wait. "Someone—" I tried again.

The boards of the dock shuddered, and I clutched at them, trying to hold on to Rena. "This way!" a hoarse voice called.

I stared and squinted. There seemed to be two people heading our way, but I couldn't make sense of their shapes. Finally I settled on the scents instead: something like scraped vellum and sanded-down boards, and paint and rust and—makeup?

"Your timing's wonderful, Hound," the first person rasped as she knelt next to me. "Here I thought I'd have an hour to relax before getting back to work."

I shook wet hair out of my eyes. "Tessie?"

"What is it with you and fire, anyway? Get her arms," she added to the man beside her. For some reason, his arms and face seemed curiously blank—not featureless, but as if I should have seen more, as if they should have been marked up. The two of them pulled Rena up onto the boards, then, as the man helped Rena up, Tessie took my hands. "Come on," she added, helping me out of the water.

Instead of taking us up the steps to the harbor, she turned and staggered up a plank that had been set between the boardwalk and a rusting green boat. "She's here!" she called, and another person emerged from the boat, hurrying up to us.

"Hang on," the man with her added to me, helping Rena over the side and toward the hatch. "It's going to be all right."

"Says you," said another voice—a woman's, an older woman's. For a dizzying moment I thought I'd see either Meda or Venetia when I turned. Instead the dancing light from the burning bridge house fell on a lined, tired face.

"Do you have any idea," Maryam said, "how many people I've put at risk so that I can see you?"

Fifteen

"Maryam." I started to step back, thought better of it as my balance shifted, and followed her down the stairs, leaning on her as much as on the railing. "Maryam, what are you doing here?"

She snorted. "I'm a geomancer, Genevieve, not an erdgeist. There's usually plenty of dirt between me and bedrock; you think I can't take a little water?"

Trust an adept to assume I'm asking an academic question. What was she doing on a boat in the first place? With a few exceptions, magicians didn't like being over water. With a few notable exceptions. "Tessie," I said, trying to think through the frost riming the inside of my skull. "You and Tessie—"

"We got in touch when Sam needed a place to stay."

"Sam?"

"Get inside; you're freezing."

Well, she was right about that. I stumbled down the steps into the boat, blinking in the warm gold light as the space belowdecks opened up into a tiny, messy room with red-upholstered furniture bolted into the floor and walls covered with pictures of Tessie in her better days, before she'd become a magician. I lurched a little and caught myself against the door frame, unsure if the floor was rocking with the waves or just trying to trip me. "Rena—"

"She's going to be fine." The man who'd carried her in stood at the farther door, a blanket in his arms. I managed to make it through the maze of furniture to see him wrap the blanket over Rena's shoulders. Her lips were blue, and her teeth chattered together like nuts in a hull, but her eyes were open and responsive. "Just fine," he repeated, taking a bowl of something from the closest table and cupping it in his hands.

"No. We need to get her to a hospital." I hadn't forgotten that sudden blood on her chest, even if I didn't know how deep the wound was. "Both of us need a hospital, and—"

"No point," he said, and held out the bowl to Rena. She managed to shake her head, and behind me Maryam thumped down the steps and closed the hatch behind her.

No point? I was not going to leave Rena to the mercy of some creepy guy off the street, no matter what Maryam and Tessie said. "Hell with you," I said, and grabbed him by the shoulder.

He turned, and I stared. I knew this face—but the last time I'd seen it, it had been marked by lines of ink, runes and Ogham script and the invocations of a thousand bindings, meant to keep a single entity in place. "Finn . . ." I whispered, then shook my head. "No. What was your name? He told me . . ."

"My name's Sam MacAllister," he said. And yes, it was a voice very similar to that of the man I'd called cousin. The mob calling itself the Fiana had consolidated its power in a number of heinous ways, one of which was to catch the spirits of their old land and imprison them within people, turning both vessel and spirit into nothing more than an ambulatory locus. They'd caught Finn Mac Cool, cousin and master to Sceolang the hound, but Finn had come looking for help . . . and afterward, said that he would leave his vessel, return the man's life to him.

From the looks of this man, he'd had a rough time

since then. "You said—Finn said you had a daughter, that you were going to find her."

"I did." He looked down, away from me, then put on a brave smile. "That's past now. And I can tell you," he continued, "that this woman will be all right. Tess, all good? Mar-bird?"

"I'm fine," she said, though it was with the same tone that someone might use when they really do have someplace to go but know there's no chance they'll be able to get there in time. "Just give me a moment." She settled in at the table, where a shallow tray full of sand took up most of the space. It looked more than a little like a litter box, but it smelled only like the sand and gravel that filled it—a replica in miniature of her usual bed. Absently, she traced a few patterns in the sand.

My sodden clothes abruptly warmed up; not much more than skin heat, but after the chill of the harbor that was a hell of an improvement. Enough that I didn't mind the faint spark of magic rising from Maryam's box. I took a deep breath, and the air seemed to clutch at my chest a little less. "So that's how you kept warm no matter the weather, Maryam," I mumbled. "Always wondered how you managed."

Rena stirred, steam likewise rising from her clothes. She glanced at me, blinking, then at Sam. "Evie, is this—are we safe?"

I nodded and tried to sit next to her, but my balance completely deserted me and I resorted to leaning up against the door frame instead. "Yes. This man, he worked for the Fiana once, but they turned him into a . . . a vessel—"

"More *bruja* shit," Rena muttered, but she clasped the blanket and began to breathe more easily. "Where did the pyro get to? He—my chest—"

"He got out," I said. "Probably heading to Georges now." Rena put her head down and muttered something that I didn't have to hear to understand. "I'm sorry," I said. "I'd thought he was harmless."

"He looks into the future," Tessie said, sinking into

the closest chair. "That's never harmless. Trust me on this."

"Finn is the one who was worried about you," Sam said. "After he—after we released each other, we struck a bargain to still speak, now and then. As much as that's possible," he added with a faint smile. "He may be dreaming beneath the Hill of Allen, but he does stay aware of what his family's doing, and you have been injured."

"What, you noticed?" I snapped, but settled into the chair anyway. As long as I didn't have to get up for a bit, I'd be fine.

Sam chuckled. "No, this was a while ago—he'd only noticed at the turn of the year from light half to dark half." He took the bowl from the table again, whispered over it, and held it out to Rena. "Drink," he said. Rena glanced at me, and I nodded; Finn had healed me and Nate by a similar method once, and Sam might have some residual skill. Shaking her head, she put the bowl to her lips. "You were wounded," he went on, "and while you've been healed since—a soul can be regrown, like the principle of severance and return—it was a wound that nearly killed you. And likely it's what attracted predators."

"Predators?" I shivered, and Maryam made some adjustment to her work. "How'd you knew where to find me?"

"That was me," Maryam said, and for a moment the warmth in my still-drying clothes fluctuated, iron hot and back to normal in the space of a second. Rena hissed, shaking her arms as if trying to get them free of her sleeves. "The stone you carried," Maryam said. "The gray one. It's gone, then?"

"Yes, but—" I shook my head. "Hang on. How did you know? I didn't know it even existed till a few days back."

She shrugged. "A number of things. Mainly, though, it's in my nature to know stone, even when it's free of the earth. I knew when it entered the city."

"Well, it's gone now." Along with any leverage I had against Dina, any chance of getting her to hold up her end of the bargain. "And you told Fi—Sam?"

She nodded, and for just a fragment of a second I caught a look very like one I'd seen on her niece's face, the terrible guilt of something left undone, uncared for. But her scent was unchanged. "I owed him. And we—the three of us got in touch a little while ago."

"That's a very tame way to put it," Tess remarked, and winked at me. "Maryam here had some old skeletons, and Sam knew where they were, and me, well, I just had some convenient connections. Even if I'm in bad shape these days."

The corners of Sam's ears turned pink, and the steam rising off our clothes made him cough. Maryam, though, twisted her hands in her lap. "I—owe you, Genevieve, and I owed them no less. I told you I had some knowledge of stones that pass through the city."

"Yes, but—" I stopped. This wasn't the first time I'd carried a stone linked to power. The Fiana, before they'd moved on to the vessels like Sam, had imprisoned the Morrigan using old magic, binding her with what they called chain stones. I'd always thought of them as pure magic—having a splinter of one in my forearm for a while probably colored my views on them a bit—but they were, ultimately, stones as well. "The chain stones," I said. "The bindings on the Morrigan."

Maryam nodded, haggard with guilt. "I knew they were there. And I did nothing. They paid me to do nothing." She nodded to Sam, who bowed his head (hard to remember that he too had worked for the Fiana before becoming their victim). "But now . . ." She looked away, then back at Sam, and I turned away so as not to see the look that passed between them. Tessie shook her head, smiling faintly.

"You worked for the Fiana," I said, and though I tried to keep the edge out of it, I failed.

For just a fraction of a second I caught the sense of stone from her—not the chain stones or the sunstone, but plain granite. Maryam, Venetia, Meda . . . there was something there, the three gray women arrayed against something else, their human grimness keeping something at bay . . . "I did not work against them, rather. But a sin of omission is still heavy, and I would pay back that debt before I pass on. So when I sensed this new stone in the city, I went to those I knew could help."

"That's also overstating matters. Maybe I could have helped once," Tessie added, "but these days all I can do is be on hand when people tell me to. But," she added, raising one finger, "I figured it out. The fire. It wasn't just an accident."

"No," Rena said, still crouched over the bowl. "No, it wasn't. And it wasn't just arson either, even if they used the same accelerant as your pyro friend did." She sat up, slowly, and put one hand to her chest as if expecting to find glass shards still in it. "It was destruction of evidence."

I turned to look at her. Tessie cocked her head to the side. "Well, I was going to say it was a burnt offering, but yours sounds so much nicer."

That got a chuckle from Rena, even if she still sounded weak. "Neither of those makes any sense," I said. "Why would Deke burn his friend's boat? Besides, Roger said he was with Deke the whole time—"

"It wasn't his," Rena said. She handed the bowl back to Sam, then shook out her shoulders and got to her feet. "That yacht was last registered to an Australian family. They went missing about eight months back."

The smile faded from Tessie's lips, and Sam looked away. "Missing?" I said. "You mean someone stole their boat and kidnapped them—"

"I mean missing at sea, Evie. Most likely they were boarded, the family killed, and the yacht taken."

"You're not serious," I said. "Pirates?"

"Of a sort. Call them marine thieves if you like, if it'll shed the image of someone with a pegleg going 'arr.' Foster and I got stuck with the liaison when harbor patrol noticed the yacht, only it went up in flames before we could find out more." She shrugged and settled in at the table next to Maryam, eyeing the tray of sand warily. "About the sort of thing we get these days."

Jesus. I thought back to Roger carrying Deke out—he may have been saving his friend, but only after placing him in danger in the first place. No wonder he'd been so casual about the loss of his boat.

And I'd let him work magic on me. My skin crawled at the thought of his genial grin. He'd enacted the severance on me, which had been a good deed on its own but, more important, had given him some idea what the quarry spirit had taken. And when Dina had made her first offer, she'd gone straight to what the quarry had taken . . .

"That rotten son of a—" I got to my feet and only then realized I was shaking. Not with terror, or cold, or the backlash of adrenaline, although I could feel all of those things hovering at the top of my spine, ready to settle in as soon as I let them. "I'm going to go kick the living shit out of him." As plans went, it lacked something, but I figured I'd wing it on the rest.

Sam gave me a wary look. "Are you certain?"

"As much as I can be. And—" I paused. Dina was another matter. Roger had used her, as much as he'd used me, but that didn't mean she'd be on my side. Or even that she wasn't part of the whole plan from the beginning . . . but she'd been the one to make the bargain with me, not him. That might be enough to make her keep to it. "And I need to get what I was promised."

"Then I'll help you." He held up both hands. "I owe you, as much as Finn owes you."

"Unless you can take me out to Georges—" I stopped. "Can you?"

He thought about it a moment, gazing at Tessie. Tessie spread her hands. "I have no objections, and it'd pay off my debt to you nicely, Hound. But I'd have to stay below. I can provide limited protection from there, and now that I've spent a night on land, I'd be a liability if I were on deck in sight of the open sea. But Sam can navigate." Sam made an unhappy noise, and she grinned. "I trust you, babe."

Sam exhaled, looking for a moment very like my cousin in one of his dubious moments, then cracked his knuckles. "Ten minutes. And we put Mar-bird ashore."

That sounded about right, at least for Rena and me to finish warming up. I turned and glanced at her. "If you want to come—"

"I've just lost my case," she said, gazing at the sand under Maryam's fingers. "There's no way . . . I hadn't even told Foster that I'd followed this guy, you understand? He's happy handling it as a series of vandalism incidents, and he thought . . . he thought I needed a break when I told him about your undercurrent." She shivered, but it didn't have anything to do with the cold, and put one hand to her chest, where Deke had smashed his glass ball. "He's right. There's no way I can make this look good. But I want to see it through anyway."

"I can't guarantee anything," I said.

"Fuck guarantees. The only guarantee I can come up with is that if I end up dead out there, at least it'll get someone's attention." She folded up the blanket, her clothes still steaming, then settled down across from Maryam and began checking her gun.

I waited while my clothes exhaled their last wisp of steam and Tessie and Sam retreated to the inner workings of the boat. After a moment Rena muttered something and held up a spare clip. "Still good. I can probably account for the water damage to the other."

"That's luck." Especially since mine was somewhere with Deke.

"Not really." Rena glanced at me, and for a moment I thought she might smile.

Maryam cried out, sudden and shocked, as if one of us had stabbed her. The tray of sand teetered, then spilled out across the floor. Sam ran in from the back room, hands full of charts, and dropped them all as he saw her. "That's the stone," she panted. "That's what I feared. Genevieve—" She groaned, the sound rising to a second scream.

And just then someone hammered at the hatch.

Maryam continued to scream. "Sam, shut her up!" I yelled and ran to the stairs. Rena followed me, slamming the clip back into her gun. We paused for a moment on either side of the steps. "You sure you'll need that?"

"After tonight?" Rena shook her head. "I'm not sure of anything."

I nodded, then leaned forward and slid the bolt back. The door slammed back, and for a moment all I could see was brilliant pink, bizarrely out of place in the middle of all this. But the scent—sandalwood incense and funky shampoo—was clearer than any sight. "*Sarah*?"

She practically fell down the steps, stumbling over the hem of her twinkling skirt as she tried to get inside. "Evie? You okay? I called your phone, but got no signal, and I thought Nate—"

I held up my waterlogged phone. "Had a bit of a problem," I said over Maryam's wails. "Did you call?"

"Not when I saw the place was on fire! Katie led me to you, but after what Nate said I figured he'd be here too." She craned around me, and her eyes widened as she saw first Maryam and then Rena. "What's going on here?"

"Negotiations. Hang on." I started up the ladder, squinting a little. The fog had gotten heavier—or no, something else was wrong. And it wasn't just the glow of the dying fire of the bridge house or the glitter of blue and white lights as the fire trucks finally started hosing down what was left of it. "Sorry, Sarah. I kind of had to jump in, and my phone's now shot, and, well, things went kind of wrong—"

"Screw that. You're okay?"

"Parbroiled and frozen, but that seems to be passing now." I managed a smile, first at her, then at Alison and Katie, who stood just at the edge of the pier. Katie clutched a huge bag to her chest—my messenger bag, far too large for her. "What the hell was that about Nate?"

"Said he was going to rescue you." Alison shrugged, an eloquent gesture on her. "That was before he dropped small cute off with us," she added, and put her hand on Katie's shoulder. Katie leaned against her, clutching the bag as if it were a lifejacket.

"Evie! Need you down here!" Rena poked her head out of the hatch. "The crazy rocks lady is doing something weird again."

Shit. I crouched next to the hatch, trying to see down into the room. Sam still held Maryam, putting some of the larger stones in her hand, closing her fingers over them. "Tell me what's wrong," he said, his tone calm and soothing. "Tess is here, and I'm here, and we're not going anywhere. Tell us. Please."

Maryam took a deep breath and shook her head back and forth like a child in a tantrum, then sank her hands into the spilled sand. Slowly, ridges rose in the sand, first shapeless, then twisting into patterns. Even from here, I could see what she was building: the bay, the harbor, Boston with the Wheel of Taranis surrounding it in the shape of Route 128—and a knot in the harbor, slowly spiraling out into the surrounding waters, a spiral twisting everything awry. "The lines," she called, her voice raw. "The lines are shifting. Genevieve, the stone—"

"Babe?" Alison reached past me and tapped Sarah's shoulder. "I think you need to see this."

I glanced at her, but Alison wasn't looking at the harbor fire. Instead, she was looking up, to where the dim white disk of the sun filtered through the fog.

Where it had filtered a moment ago. The fog hadn't gotten heavier, and there weren't any obvious clouds, but the sun's light had dimmed. Just a little. Just enough to turn the air brittle and strange, the color of light glimpsed through a grating, the color of a dark day.

I stretched out my hands and looked at them, at the water past them, at the blank white wall rapidly dimming to gray that was the harbor. *They thought it was the world ending*, Colin had said. I knew it wasn't, but I wasn't sure that knowing what it was made it any better.

Sixteen

Sam refused to let Maryam out of his sight until she'd claimed to be all right at least five times and, for some reason, recited the preamble to the Constitution. Of all the tests for lucidity there were, I'd never considered that one, but then again, there were a lot of things I seemed to have missed lately. "Sarah," I said just as Maryam got to the part about 'protect the general welfare,' "can you take Maryam home, or even just ashore someplace safe—"

"Oh no." Sarah shook her head and planted her feet as if I'd threatened to throw her off the boat. "No, I'm not staying behind to guard the hearthfire this time. Domestic empress I might be"—Alison smiled at what I suspected was an inside joke—"but that's irrelevant right now. You say something's hurting the city. Fine. Then I'm coming with you."

I gaped at her for a moment. "With me? Christ on a cracker, Sarah, you have no idea what sort of thing we might be up against—"

"Do you?" I hesitated, and she nodded. "Didn't think so. This isn't your city to protect, Evie—it's not just yours, it wasn't just the Fiana's, and it's not any one person's or organization's city. You can go off all lone wolf if you like—"

"Wrong canine."

"Whatever. You can do that, and you can get your ass shot off, and the rest of us can each do the same, and we'll still end up with the same problem. I didn't knit together this goddamn neighborhood watch so I could cower inside while you ride the storm."

I was silent a moment. Sarah had me dead to rights. Still, this would be dangerous—Roger alone was not someone to fall afoul of, and Dina—

"First word that something's gone wrong, you head back. Okay?"

"No. But I'll say yes if it'll make you feel better."

I gritted my teeth and nodded. Sarah could be just as stubborn as I am, sometimes. I crouched next to Katie. "You'll have to go with Alison, though. I'll call Nate as soon as we're back." I hesitated a moment. "He'll be okay, right?"

Katie hugged me tight, the top of her head banging into my chin. "Yes," she said, punctuating it with a sharp nod. Still holding on to me with one arm, she unslung my bag and dropped it at my feet. "He said not to worry about him."

Yeah, that wasn't encouraging. But I had to trust him—trust that he knew what he was doing. I gave her a quick kiss on the forehead and stood back up. "Then you make sure you're okay too, all right?"

Alison helped Maryam across the walkway and stood there, one arm around Katie, as Sarah rummaged through the pockets of her coat. "You'll be fine?" Sarah asked. "I don't like leaving you like this—"

"I will," Alison said, and leaned over to give her a peck on the cheek. "Just be back in time for dinner. You know how I get when you're late."

Sarah hugged her, then paused, glancing down at Katie. "Evie," she said over her shoulder, "and you—what's your name again?"

Rena gritted her teeth. "Llerena," she said. "Llerena Santesteban."

"Yeah, you—" Sarah stopped, staring hard at Rena, then started again. "Give us a moment, okay?"

I thumped Rena on the back. "Come on. Sam might need our help." She shook her head, but made her way toward the helm, where Sam was already running through the first checks. I glanced back for a moment, then away, only partly out of a concern for privacy. I still couldn't stop thinking about Nate, headed God knows where—and to rescue me? From what? He didn't know about Roger, or Dina, not enough to worry . . .

Sam didn't need any help, so Rena and I ended up at the back of the boat. (I knew there was a special word for it, but I'd spent too little time around Tessie.) "I owe you thanks," she muttered, not looking at me.

I glanced at her. "For what? Getting you involved in this?"

"I got myself involved, thank you very much. Not everything is because of you, girl." She sighed, the line between her eyebrows reasserting itself, as if bits of the old Rena were only just coming back to the surface. "No. For pulling me out of the burning building, you dumb shit. I owe you thanks—but that's all I owe you, understand?"

"Yeah, I understand." At least she was talking to me. "Thanks."

Rena shot a glance sideways at me, then slouched a little, one hand going to the stained spot on her coat where her blood hadn't quite washed out. "Goddammit, Evie. What is it about me? Why can't I get away from this shit?"

I shrugged. "Hell if I know. I thought—I honestly thought you were doing the right thing, before. At least if you wanted to stay out of all this. And I thought I could keep too much of it from getting to you . . . maybe it's my fault."

"You have no idea how much I'd like to say it was." She closed her jacket and zipped it up. "Foster's going to give me seven kinds of hell if I come in tomorrow like this. And I'll deserve it."

We slid out of the marina, passing warehouses and

docks that ranged from grubby to slightly less grubby. I glanced back at the city as we pulled away. The dull sunlight was barely adequate for January, let alone what had been a relatively bright day in November, and the fog washed everything into forgetfulness. I rarely saw the city as a landscape—well, you don't see it when you're in it, do you? And this was so different from the brilliant, hard view of it I'd seen on the way out here with Deke, different enough that it might have been another city. Or—and a new billow of cloud sank a little lower, obscuring the top of the Customs House—a dream city entirely.

We passed the still smoldering remnants of the bridge house. A few pilings stuck up out of the water like grasping, blackened fingers. A couple of fire trucks were still there, and I could see figures moving, probably trying to figure out what had destroyed it. Rena too watched it as we passed, and though I couldn't read the expression on her face, the cold shell she'd worn in that house had been burned away.

Sarah had joined Sam, muttering on her cell phone, and she wasn't looking at me. In fact, she was being careful not to, seeing as I had moved directly in front of her. "Who were you calling?" I finally asked.

She flicked a glance toward me, and for a moment I could actually see her deciding not to be snarky. "Call tree. You think the watch was just for show?"

"Well, we are talking magicians here," I said.

Rena glanced around. "Watch?"

"Neighborhood watch. Of sorts."

Sam laughed, not taking his eyes from the water. "Good luck with that."

"That's what I told her," I said.

"You interested in joining?" Sarah asked, ignoring me. "You obviously know enough to be part of the undercurrent."

She didn't know the half of it, and I saw Sam's grin turn hard. "No. Swore off it. Too long with other work burned me out." He spun the wheel, bringing us out into the open harbor. "No, I just help a few friends these days."

"That's what we try to do too." She gave Rena a long, hard look, then shrugged. "What I just did was start up the call tree, let everyone know that there's a general threat to the city. Defensive measures, in other words."

"You got them to agree on defensive measures?" In theory, getting adepts to collaborate on a single spell could be incredibly powerful, but in practice it was about as likely as getting a hundred cats to perform a trick.

Sarah laughed, short and derisive. "Hell no! I got them to agree that there *ought* to be defensive measures, though. So when a general alarm goes out, everyone contacts everyone else. Probably ten percent of them will just hole up entirely, ward themselves off until it's clear that everything's safe; the rest will do whatever they think is necessary to guard what they think is important. Which, if I'm right, ought to cover a good deal of the city."

"Sounds pretty piecemeal to me," I muttered.

"It is. But a patchwork quilt can be as warm as a plain coverlet. Although," she added, "a crazy quilt might be a better metaphor."

We were well out in the harbor now. "Okay," Sarah said, visibly pulling herself together. "Tell me everything about what we're up against."

So I did, starting with Deke's plea for aid, moving on through my trip out to Georges and the darkened room, the thief's hand and the Quabbin. Sarah stirred when I mentioned Meda's ghost-trap, but didn't ask any questions, which was good since I couldn't really answer most of them. I glossed over as much of the bridge house as I dared, given that Rena was still smarting from it, and ended up with how Roger scammed me. "Dina's the scary one, but I don't know how much of that is his influence and how much is just her nature." I thought of the Morrigan, of the Gabriel Hounds, how their freedom had changed them both. Could I hope that it would do the same for her? "Either way, I'd watch out for both of them. If we're lucky, she'll still be bound by the bargain I made with her."

"You said Dina was his ally?" Sarah sucked breath through her teeth. "That's not good."

"No," Sam agreed. "There are some things that can't be dealt with on an even basis. They're too strong in some ways, we're too strong in others . . . bring them together and it gets nasty."

"And the stone . . . Evie, what were you thinking?"

"Look, call me stupid if you like—"

Rena, who'd kept a stoic though not disbelieving silence through most of it, finally stirred. "I don't think you're stupid."

"I do," Sarah snapped. "Jesus, Evie, did you really believe that crap about a pregnancy? Did you miss out on all the sex-ed classes or did they switch over to the abstinence-only crap—"

"I didn't say it was reasonable," Rena said. "But she wasn't stupid. I think—look, did your parents give you the talk?"

Sarah looked blank. "Yeah, when I was eight. And every year after that."

"But I'm betting you didn't have any object lessons demonstrating the downsides. There's a sort of . . . of scare about it when you've seen one too many friends get screamed at on the way in to the clinic, or end up washed out and married too young. I had the same goddamn paranoia every time I had a boyfriend up till I was thirty, and I'd bet Evie still gets it." I shrugged; guilty. "That's what this thing played on. The fears that we don't even know we have."

"Thanks," I murmured, and Rena nodded. "And that's what worries me," I went on. "It's a lot of talk to say that you should face your fears, but what about the ones you don't know about? I don't even know what Dina will do."

"I have a guess," Sam said after a moment, and switched gears. The sound of the motor faded to a purr.

I glanced at him. "Something wrong?"

"You tell me." He pointed ahead. "Is it getting lighter out here?"

I squinted. Well, no, it wasn't, not in the sense of actual lights in the distance or anything like that . . . but the fog no longer had any sense of depth to it, and there was no longer a breeze coming off the ocean, nothing to brush away the clinging damp that seemed to ooze up from our feet and swirled around our lights.

Rena leaned forward, and her questing fingers encountered only grayness. The lights of the boat splintered and fragmented, coming up flat. "That's not supposed to happen, is it?" Sarah asked. I couldn't see the skyline anymore when I looked back, or even any trace of the city.

"No idea." The boat rocked a moment.

I don't know how to explain what makes fog so much worse than darkness. For me, I didn't really have too much experience with it—the fog only really rolls in once or twice a year, and where I am, it's usually cleared enough that it's only a little extra dampness in the air. Not out here. Staring at that wall of blankness, your mind starts to react to the total lack of sight, creating images that you can't quite tell are fake, and every now and then the fog will recede just a little, so that what seemed to be just a flicker on your retina is actually a light, farther off, but then the wall rolls back into place and you're left wondering if it was ever there at all . . .

Darkness might be fine for freaking people out, but for wondering what can come next, what's real and what's just your brain inventing fears, there's nothing like fog.

"Can we go around?" Rena asked after a moment.

Sam shook his head. "Around how? I can navigate a

little of the harbor, but get away from the main channels and I'm in trouble. And we're not the only ones out here—I don't just mean your pyro friend, I mean the other ships. They'll be running into the same trouble, and if they run into us as well, we'll have problems. And no Mar-bird to warn us out of them," he added, scratching at the back of his head.

Screw that. I wasn't going to let what I couldn't see keep me from what I could scent. I scrambled over the front of the boat, toward the very tip of it, then closed my eyes and inhaled. "Okay. There's land ahead of us . . . that way."

Sam glanced at me. "You're sure?"

"I can smell grass and scrub trees. Steer the way I'm pointing and keep . . . yes, keep away from that heading," I added, pointing with my left hand to about two o'clock. "Ship that way, leaking diesel. I think that's the only one . . ."

Gradually, moving so slowly the boat's engine groaned, we edged into the fog. I couldn't spare attention for anything beyond the scents, the traces that barely made any sense this far from land. But so long as there weren't too many submerged rocks, far enough from the surface that I couldn't scent them but close enough to drag at the overweighted boat . . . "Steer right here. Starboard. Whatever. There's something close by on our left . . . no greenery, but enough bird shit for twenty statues . . ."

"Evie," Sarah said quietly, "don't stop what you're doing, but would you happen to have any iron on you?"

"Got a pocketknife." I stopped and, foolishly, opened my eyes. The patterns of scent receded, not out of reach—but that wasn't the problem.

I'd been right about the little island, barely a shoulder of land sticking out of the ocean and yes, covered in gull crap. Someone had thoughtfully put a beacon out here, warning ships away, but the light at the top flickered like a guttering green flame. Around it, a scaffold like a shaved-down wooden henge stood. Six dead bodies hung from it, swinging gently in a breeze that had nothing to do with this time and place.

"Nix's Mate," Sam said softly. "Where smugglers were once hanged."

No more dead men lingering at Nix's Mate. Colin had hoped, had maybe lost a friend or two here, and now their—ghosts? imprints?—had been called back. Thieves and smugglers.

Be not thief but murderer. The old women of my past and present, and Meda's plea unmet. I tried to look away from the hanged men and could not.

"They're not real, are they?" Rena asked, and though it'd take a lot to make her actually sound nervous, I thought I heard an edge to it, like an engine starting to overheat. "Tell me they're not real."

"They're illusions," I said. "Nothing more."

One of the dead men creaked around on its rope to face us, mist pouring from its mouth like rain from a gargoyle. I couldn't quite see its face, but something about the dark shadow where eyes had once been made me a little less certain. "Not quite," Sarah said. "Which is why I'm asking about the iron."

I started to shake my head, unable to take my eyes off the dead thing, then stopped. "Yes," I said, fumbling in the bag by my feet. "If I didn't lose it—yes." Rough metal snagged on my fingers, and my shoulder twinged at the touch. "Here," I said, holding out the rough iron hook that Meda had jabbed into my shoulder. I backed up, still watching the men on the gibbet, hoping Sarah could reach me.

She took it without looking—none of us could look away now, and the creaking grew as one by one the hanged men turned to face us. The hull of the boat slapped against the waves, quieter now, drawn unceasingly closer to the rocks. "By iron I charge you," Sarah said, and held up the hook. "By what you were I charge you. By the speech of ravens I charge you. Let us pass."

"That's really going to work?" Rena asked. "Just because we ask nicely?"

"It's all in how you do it," Sarah said, still holding the hook up as if it were a passport.

For a moment the dead men, or their illusions, held still. Then one raised a hand, pointing to the hook, and again the wound in my shoulder twinged. *Iron*, it said, or *I am*, or something that Colin might have understood but I did not. And it closed its mouth and turned away, the motion shifting its fellows enough so that their gaze was broken.

"Now," Sam murmured, able to look away at last, and gunned the engine. We shot across the flat water, back into the fog. I sat back hard on the deck, sliding on the damp planks, and just remembered in time to point away from the nearest scent of land.

The mists receded just enough to let us see more half-imagined shapes, and I saw Rena shudder and look away from one. But at last Georges slid into view, its dock black and slick with moisture. "I'll wait here for you," Sam said. "I'm not—I was never much of a magician, and without my longtime passenger, I have little power in myself."

"Just keep yourself safe." I stepped out of the boat, slipping a little on the boards, and steadied myself against a piling. The faint scent of burnt matchheads curled around the docks, not far from here, and I didn't need to look to know that the little boat Deke had used was tied up close by. "He's been here," I said. "I can scent him."

"Well, that's a relief." Rena accepted my help out of the boat, snagging a flashlight out of Sam's hand on the way. "I'd feel like an idiot if you'd led us the wrong way." She glanced back over her shoulder, and her eyes narrowed as she saw Deke's boat. "I take that back. You've never led me wrong, Evie. You might have refused to lead, but you've usually got the right end in sight."

"Thanks."

She nodded, then thumped me on the shoulder so hard I stumbled forward. "So don't screw up your record this time."

"There's still plenty of time for that," I said. "And there's more. Roger's here, and—" I sniffed. "Gunpowder. Could be magic, could be the gun Deke took."

"You're unarmed?" Sam asked.

"Got my good looks."

Rena snorted. Sam shook his head and reached under the steering. "Take this," he said, and handed me a chipped baseball bat. "Not much, but you can shatter a few kneecaps, right?"

"Jesus." I took it, and Sam grinned—the kind of a grin that reminded you he had once been part of a criminal organization. I glanced back at Sarah, who had started to follow but hesitated, one foot jammed against the heap of tarps and blankets and ropes in the back of the boat. "You said you'd stay back if anything went wrong. I'd say that's already happened."

"I—yes." She paused a moment, one foot nudging the heap, then nodded. "Yeah. I'll stay here."

Rena gaped at her. "Seriously? You made all that fuss, and you're not even going to get out of the boat?"

Sarah looked torn, as if it wasn't her decision to make, but she still sat back down, implacable and unhurried, a strange kind of stability setting over her even as the boat rocked. "I'll do what I can from here."

I'd expected her to argue, too—but if it kept her back here, safe with Sam and Tessie, I wasn't about to ask twice. "Okay. Keep an eye out for anything—and I mean on the island or off. If you have to, stay on the water, but don't go back out into the harbor. I don't trust those things to stay on their gibbet."

Rena shuddered at that, but Sarah only tucked her skirts around her ankles a bit more closely. I nodded to her and turned to the island.

There weren't lights on the path, but the refracted

light through the fog had its own faint glow, enough to tell when a tree was looming out at me. Rena loosed her gun in its holster and followed behind me, undoubtedly taking in a lot more than I was seeing. I had my talent, but she had years of experience, and she knew what to look for.

Deke had been here, but there wasn't much of a fresh scent. He hadn't left, at least not by boat. I didn't have any handle on the stone, nor on Dina's own bloody scent, though I kept expecting the latter to billow out at me from behind the next dark tree. Roger, though . . . he'd been here, had met Deke, and then walked with him . . .

I hefted the bat, silently thanking Sam for it. Behind me, Rena made a disgusted noise, though when I glanced back she was still scanning the mists. "Let's go Red Sox," she murmured. "You're not seriously bringing that, are you?"

"Better than my fists, if it comes to it. Unless you wanna loan me your gun."

"Shit, if I'm in trouble now, I'd be in so much more . . ." She shook her head, but there was a feral, vicious grin tugging at the corners of her mouth.

I returned the grin. "Missed you, Rena."

"Missed you too, bitch." She was silent a moment. "I haven't been clubbing in ages. Missed the Extruded Plastic Dingus show too."

"They were in town?" God, I'd missed a lot.

Rena nodded. "First thing I thought when I saw the ad was, I gotta tell Evie . . . Foster thought I'd run over a puppy, that's how low I was for a while." The road led down, toward the gates of the fort, and Deke's scent did as well, like a line of cigarette smoke. "Guess we can't really go back to doing that again," she added.

"Yeah, probably not." I nodded—she was right—and started forward, to the open gates into the fort. Rena followed, flashlight in hand. "Don't turn that on just yet," I said.

"Why not?"

"Because it'll spoil our night vision." I pointed across the green, to the empty black hole where I'd found Dina before, where Deke's scent led. "And we'll need it more in there."

Rena muttered something under her breath, but followed.

Deke's scent was fading, as if he'd somehow found a way off the island—or Roger had set up multiple wards. I could find my way through them in time, but it'd slow me down. Condensation gathered on the stones and dripped off in steady, almost subaudible beats.

"You know more about this guy than I do," Rena said at last. "Why'd he turn on you like that? I thought you were friends."

"We weren't. But we were allies, of a sort. I think . . . I think something spooked him. You make bad decisions when you're scared." I paused at the edge of the doorway into the fort proper, just where the last of the light made a feeble attempt to reach inside. There was something wrong about the scent within, something like salt rubbed on skin, or bloody shale, organic and stony at the same time.

"Won't argue with you there," she said and switched on the flashlight. I winced, but the beam turned an uneven, impossible floor into mere flagstones with debris caught in their cracks.

The beam swept across empty doorways, graffiti scrawled in black pen, a heap of sticks . . . "Hang on. Go back."

Rena did so, and I knelt next to the heap. It was mostly driftwood, but on top lay a wooden recorder, its mouthpiece stained and grayish. I didn't know much about musical instruments, but I had a guess that this one would sound very like the one I'd heard before. "She was here," I said, dropping my voice down to just above a whisper. "So was Roger. But Deke . . . I don't know; his scent is all garbled up and faded. And there's something else, something I haven't smelled before."

"But he came through here?"

"He did." That much was clear, if cold. The stony scent had turned smoky and metallic both—something like an overcooked sausage, something like charcoal that had gotten dunked in a sewer and then dried out on a stove. If there was magic to it, it wasn't a kind I recognized. And what I'd first registered as gunpowder was no less strong, though it was flattened, as if processed through some kind of filter.

I got to my feet, brushed off my knees with the hand that didn't hold the bat, and used the bat to point at one of the arched doorways. "He went this way. Roger did too, but he's not there now, and he didn't come back . . . I don't understand, the boat was still here, and there's nowhere else for them to go." Rena followed me through the doorway, sweeping the flashlight's beam back and forth as if she were casting a semicircle. I briefly remembered Roger's Gebelin circle, and my skin prickled. "But none of them are here now," I went on, "which is what worries—"

I stopped as Rena cast the light into the center of the room—the room that had been so hollow and empty when I was here before, that had served as nothing more than an echo chamber for Dina's music. It wasn't empty now.

Rena drew a sharp breath as her light revealed the thing hanging from the arched center of the room, picking out every detail of the open mouth, the spike driven through the neck, the chain from which it hung, the coat hanging open to reveal a long slash and the . . . the mess hanging down from that into a grisly, glistening heap on the floor.

I stared, this time not just smelling but tasting the dead-fireworks scent that filled the room. The realization of what it meant hit me, and I turned and retched. Even in the midst of it, I couldn't stop scenting, couldn't push away what my nose was telling me. The stink of gunpowder struck me like a fist to the face, along with the sight of the exploded wounds in Deke's shoulders—one each, and one to each thigh, leisurely potshots meant to hurt rather than kill immediately, and I didn't need to search to know whose gun had been used.

But worse than any of that, worse than the strangeness of Deke's scent that I was only just beginning to understand, was Roger's scent. He'd been here. He'd had the gun. And his scent was utterly unchanged—he hadn't even done so much as broken a sweat while shooting his friend and stringing him up.

Seventeen

Rena carried the light past me, leaving me in darkness. "It's him, all right." She circled the hanging corpse, edging around the spatters on the floor. "Just a guess, but I'd say he hasn't been dead too long."

"No." I wiped my mouth—you'd think that I had nothing left to throw up, considering how long it'd been since I'd eaten, but apparently my body felt otherwise. "No, that's not it." I made myself look at him, at the thing they'd hung up. "He doesn't smell like Deke anymore."

Rena gave me a look that clearly questioned my sanity. "Of course not. He's dead."

"That's not how it works." I walked up to Deke's body, over the blood—and it too lacked the right scent, lacked even the tackiness that drying blood ought to have. "Death changes a scent, but not by this much. He—Roger and Dina did something to him, Rena. They made him not Deke anymore, she changed him so much that he didn't even smell human. And then they left him to die." I rubbed my nose, briefly glad even for the stink of bile on my breath, just because it blocked out what Deke's scent had become. "I don't even sense him as a corpse."

I touched his arm, just below where a shot had ruined the bones. It was hard and glossy, cold as stone.

However you tried to categorize it, you couldn't describe it as human, not in any sense. Deke had been right to be scared. *I see things, sometimes, in the fire,* he had said. *Sometimes they don't go away. That's why I've made preparations.* He'd known. Or he'd guessed. Or feared.

"I am going to find Roger," I said, vowing it to Rena and Deke as much as to myself, "and I am going to put his fucking head on a platter."

"You'll have help," Rena said, but she sounded preoccupied. I turned to see her crouching just where the blood ended, examining it with the tip of her fingernail. "Something's wrong with this."

"Well, yes, I just *said*—"

"No. Wrong in a real way." Just barely audible above the sound of wind outside and the constant drip of condensation came the echo of a faint sizzling—or no, it hadn't just started, it must have been going on for a while and I was only just noticing it now. "There ought to be a lot more blood with these wounds, and it should be splashed around a lot more. This is concentrated, and the edge is regular, like the fringes have been pared away. Foster would know . . . What you said about not making him human—could that have paralyzed him, maybe?"

"Maybe." I didn't quite know what had been done to him, though, and the difference in the scent was all I had to go by. The sizzling intensified, and I looked away, toward the closest patch of blood. Rena held the flashlight so that it cast a shadow both of Deke and of his entrails, long black streaks across the brick floor. I squinted, and for just a second, caught a thin line of smoke rising up at the edge of it, as the blood charred and burned away into powder. The metallic scent sharpened, like the gasoline scent in the bridge house.

I'd want to go out like a Viking, me. I'd go properly.

"Rena—" I backed away from Deke's body, but Rena was too close. She'd gotten closer to the body but hadn't noticed the change at her feet, the line of smoke racing inward and gaining speed. I caught the first spark of gunpowder (faint but real, and the last mark of Deke's burnt magic I'd ever encounter) and took that as my cue to tackle Rena away from the body.

"What the hell—" Rena began. I fumbled for her face and managed to get my hand over her eyes just as the room went incandescent white. I caught my breath and held it, not for the oxygen but to keep the scents away. It didn't work: burnt feathers and cloth and the foully simple scent of what Deke had become all blazed up in one second of cold brilliance. There was no answering *thump* of combustion, no spark catching at me as the bridge house fire had; this was Deke's fire and Deke's alone.

Even with my eyes shut tight, the afterimages still blinded me. Rena groaned and shoved me off her with both hands. "Goddammit," she muttered. "Your magicians and their cavalier attitude toward evidence—" She sat up, blinking, her vision returning at the same slow tempo as mine. After a second, she spat a curse I'd never heard before and snatched up the flashlight, directing its beam to the empty hook. "He was just here, right?" she demanded, the beam shaking so much it practically strobed the room. "I didn't just imagine that—that body—"

"It was how he wanted to go," I said, getting to my feet. "If he couldn't—if he didn't have a better death, then at least he had this." Small comfort; no comfort, really. But I could understand the need for it in that kind of despairing situation.

"Fuck," Rena said in a small voice. "Crazy sand ladies I can take, even the creeps out on the water, but this . . ."

"He was here," I reassured her, and she exhaled and stilled the flashlight with both hands. I bent and touched the ground again. "He was here," I repeated.

Nothing was now left of Deke save a heap of gray ash, slowly sifting down to the spot where his guts had been. Still blinking from the flash, I crouched next to it and sniffed. Tar and the tang of fireworks, magic and, somewhere, Roger. "Here," I said, and reached into the ash, the heat of it sliding over my fingers like Maryam's sand and dissipating much more quickly than real heat would have. "There's a grate here . . . looks like the lock melted, if it was ever there." I put both hands into the ash, shifted my weight, and pulled. A plain iron grate about two feet wide, stained with rust and now shiny patches where the flare of Deke's pyre had burned through, slid free with a ferrous groan.

Rena came to help, and we set the grate down together, wincing in unison at the clang. She shone the flashlight beam into the pit below, revealing a line of rungs stretching down. "Sewers?"

"Doesn't smell like it." Besides, the grate and the rungs themselves didn't quite look like the rest of the fort; not just newer than the 1850s architecture but with an institutional austerity to them. "But Roger's scent leads this way."

For a moment both of us had the same visual image—Roger, leaving Deke to hang, pulling the grate closed behind him along with a few loops of his guts—and though my stomach lurched again, I didn't throw up this time. Rena just nodded; either the dead bodies she'd seen over the course of her career had made this easier, or she was just better at setting it aside. "All right," she said. "I'll bring the light; you follow me."

"You sure?"

"I'm the one with the gun, Evie. I go first. You can, I don't know, do something with that bat."

"Something" turned out to be tucking it halfway under one arm and half into the pocket of my coat, so that I could almost use both arms. Rena just turned off the flashlight entirely and descended in darkness. After a moment, and as I was swinging down onto the first rungs, I heard a quiet "ah," and a thump. "I've hit bottom," she said, and switched the flashlight back on.

I dropped the last few feet when the bat started to slide out from under my arm, and ended up dropping it anyway. The clatter didn't echo, but the sound still seemed to go on a lot longer than it ought to. I picked up the stupid thing, then turned and saw why.

Gray concrete walls, veined with white where salt had begun to seep through, rose up on either side to a flat, low ceiling. The long, lightless space beyond stretched out farther than the beam could reach. "Looks like a tunnel," Rena said, as if it were no more than another address, another crime scene. "Old army or navy work, I'd say."

"You're kidding."

"I'm not." She pointed the beam to what looked like just a niche in the concrete with a shelf halfway up, and it took me a moment to recognize that there were wires coming out of the wall just above the shelf. "See? Phone hookups. It's just a guess, but there were army and navy setups out here, during World War Two and after." She ran a hand over the wall, starting down the tunnel. "That's why Gallop Island's closed off; too much asbestos from the old facilities. Makes sense that they'd add something to Georges as well."

"Weird kind of sense," I said, but I followed, baseball bat in hand. No wonder I'd had no sense of Dina outside the fort; she hadn't needed to leave it in order to come and go.

The tunnel had one advantage over the halls above: no doors opening out onto darkened rooms. And I had the advantage that I could tell no one was behind us, so there wasn't that problem—even if Rena did keep turning back and blinding me with the damn flashlight. We walked, still following the tunnel downward, as the walls got damper and more crusted with salt deposits, and the scent of heavy ocean water sank into my bones. "This doesn't make any sense," I said at last. "There's no way we're still under the island, and it takes heavy magic to cause displacement on this scale—I mean, I've only seen that once and that was the Fiana—"

Rena shook her head. "Who said you needed magic for this? We're under the harbor now, Evie."

"Under—" I admit it; I looked up, as if that'd show me the fish above. The ceiling didn't look any different from the other concrete we'd seen up till now; maybe a little damper, but certainly no more than a plain slab. Not my ideal bulwark against a billion tons of seawater. "Can we maybe start moving faster?"

"What, you claustrophobic?"

I managed a laugh. "No, I just have trouble with enclosed spaces that have an entire fucking ocean outside them."

Rena muttered something under her breath, then stopped, raising the flashlight. I didn't have to immediately look to know something was wrong; the way we suddenly had a bit more ambient light was enough. "Shit," she said, and hurried down the tunnel to where a slump of rock and slabs of concrete blocked most of the passage.

I paused, back where the light didn't yet reflect. Something about the way it glanced off the rock seemed wrong—not seawater damp, but irregular in a way that didn't match fallen rock. And the scent was wrong: not concrete, but a different kind of stone, too close to the thing that had been Deke. "Rena, stop!" I yelled, my voice rattling down the tunnel.

She stopped and turned back to face me—just as a hand shot up from the rubble and seized her wrist. The flashlight dropped and rolled away, sending crazy sparks in every direction, but not before I saw the fragmented rubble crease and shift into a weathered face, a beard no longer gray but stony, keen blue eyes.

"Oh, you're a firecracker, aren't you?" The flashlight was pointed away from Roger, but enough light reflected off the walls to show him ensconced in the broken slabs, not buried but part of them. Whatever had happened to Deke had happened here as well—

but where Deke had been shot and hung up like a hog before it changed him into something inhuman, Roger was still alert and alive.

Dina had turned on him. Or—no, this wasn't the act of an imprisoned spirit against her captor. This had the sense of something done with love, even a kind of twisted, consuming love. I thought back to my assumptions about Dina, what she'd be like if healed, what I could expect from her. I'd been very, very wrong . . . and she and Roger had been well matched.

Roger's other hand, gnarled and knotted like pudding stone on the shore, dropped something that clattered down beside the flashlight, and he reached up to touch Rena's forehead, drawing a symbol I didn't know. "Strong enough to get me out of here, maybe?" he went on.

Rena jerked away, but his grip was tight as a shackle, and her eyes went wide and glassy. The spark of fireworks drifted down the passage to me, sharp as a stiletto.

It wasn't the only gunpowder smell, though. I ran over and scooped up what lay beside the flashlight.

My gun felt as if someone had rubbed cheap alcohol over it and left it in a freezer: cold and stinging. But it was still mine, and I still had decent aim, at least at point-blank range. I put the muzzle of the gun against the mass of rock where Roger's wrist should have been and fired.

The shot rang down both ends of the tunnel, louder than a thunderclap and a lot closer. Worse for me, though, was the sudden stink of hot stone and blood and shattered flesh that rose up from the wound, and though Roger's mouth opened in a roar I couldn't hear a thing. Rena pulled away, crumbled stone falling from her wrist, and the stink of whatever magic he'd tried to work on her faded like mildew in sunlight.

"*Bitch*," Roger said, almost amiably, and though my ears were abused from that shot I still heard him as if we were having a conversation out on the pier. "*And I don't suppose you'd volunteer to give me some of your life either? Figures.*"

Rena, stunned but still herself, caught my shoulder. She pointed to him, mouthing something, but the ringing in my ears was still too much. "I don't know what happened to him," I said, or tried to. Rena shook her head and cursed—I didn't need to be a lip-reader to understand that.

"*What happened to me is that my alliance got a little uneven.*" He chuckled, the sound like stones rattling together, and in the back of my mind I wondered how I could hear him. Was it because he didn't quite have lungs anymore, because in some way this wasn't speech but the words of the stone he had become? "*Perhaps she thought we'd become a little too close—after all, I couldn't expect her to associate with me now that she was whole again. Women,*" he added, grinning like a split boulder, "*always wanting to change you.*"

I raised the gun a second time, but to no effect. He'd used up most of clip taking potshots at Deke. I put the safety back on and tucked the gun away in my salt-stiff holster, then nudged Rena. She hadn't stopped staring, horrified, at Roger, and though I knew she couldn't hear him, I thought the expressions on our faces must have been similar. I pointed down the tunnel—we'd have to climb over what had once been Roger's feet, but there was a way through—and handed her the flashlight.

"*And you thought,*" he went on, the laughter now rattling stones loose above him, "*that it was only wholeness she needed, that she'd be all better and kind and no more a monster if she was all put together again! My Deino, my Enyo, my Persis, my lovely, lovely gray lady . . .*" He shivered, or would have, and even pressing against the wall to get away from him I felt unclean. "*Almost worth it, to have ended like this, touched by her. But kindness? Oh, puppy, it doesn't work that way. My allies are never less than monsters; no one else is worth bothering with.*"

"Except for Deke," I said, and even though I still couldn't hear my own words, I could feel them in my throat.

Roger's head turned with a creak. "*Cam,*" he said, and now I could see that the mess I'd made of his arm was spreading, a stain like dry rot eating away at him. Or perhaps it was just a stain, just blood loss, that made him sound almost dreamy. "*Do you know, he kept coming back to me? Always so scared, always needing a protector . . . and I was his good friend. Just like a puppy, coming back every time . . .*"

"And you killed him," I said, and Rena looked back at me. Her hearing must have started to return.

Roger nodded, and his face creased into something like a landslide, like a scar on the side of a mountain. "*Yes,*" he said, and the last breath passed out of him. I waited a moment, till what was left of him wasn't even anything like a body. Maybe, if I looked long enough and discounted what my talent told me was real, I could find a few rocks that, from a certain angle, looked like a man.

Rena nudged me, then pointed ahead. I shook my head, not understanding. She turned the flashlight off and then back on, and I finally saw what she meant: the passage beyond Roger was not quite pitch-black. Somewhere ahead, a little light had faded the dark. I hurried ahead, clutching the baseball bat.

The tunnel ended in a room little better than the one back in Georges; big, square, and with a step down to another grate, though this one smelled only of water, foul and black with the corrosion of years. A few forlorn wires stuck out of the walls, similar to the phone hookup at the far end of the tunnel. This couldn't have been a radio room; we were too far away from any signal for that to work. But it had been similar. I imagined Cold War troops down here, listening for submarines that never bothered to attack Boston, passing cups of strong coffee . . . okay, maybe the coffee was a stretch. But somehow imagining it helped.

On the opposite side of the room, steps led up to two separate doors, black metal smeared with rust and hanging off their hinges. I started for one, then stopped, cursing, as my jacket caught on an exposed tangle of wires. Rena, though, pushed the closer door open.

Her eyes widened, and she aimed the gun at something beyond the door—something high and to the left. "Stay here!" she yelled, or something like it; her voice still sounded as if it was under water. "There's more than we thought!"

"More? What—"

She shouted something else—could have been an order, could have been a curse—and ran.

I blinked in the sudden darkness and blindly turned toward the faded gray smudge that I hoped led to sunlight. "Rena?" I called. No answer but receding footsteps, and the heavy dampness of fog. I fumbled my way to the door, trying to focus.

A white, faceless figure loomed out of the darkness at me, and I yelped before realizing that it was the other door, now hanging open. Some kids had painted a silhouette on it, doubtless for the purpose of scaring the crap out of people like me. Great; I'd find them and kick their asses for it, but right now I had to follow Rena.

Up that set of stairs, then, baseball bat banging against the wall as I ran. The stairs ended on a landing that split into several different rooms, all dark and featureless as far as my light-deprived eyes could tell. I swore under my breath, searching for Rena's scent. There; mingling with fresh air, through the room on my right, again following that same concrete regularity. Barracks, I thought, or some other army establishment. Only there wasn't room for any of that on Georges Island. We'd made it to another island entirely. For a fraction of a second I remembered that flash of Colin, back when his hand was whole, dragging his boat onto a gravelly shore under a heavy, ugly sky.

I started to follow Rena's scent, then froze as the first real sound made its way through the ringing in my ears: a splintering crack as the flashlight shattered somewhere. "Rena!" I yelled, and Rena answered me with an inarticulate cry—followed by gunshots.

I stumbled, landed on a tangle of bottles, one of which cracked and slid along my calf in a thin line of pain, and clawed my way back up the wall. Fresh air, there was air in front of me, and wasn't it just barely lighter out there?

Another gunshot sounded, followed by a quick succession of them, their echo somehow flatter now. "Rena!" I shouted again, and thought I heard a faint curse in return. I emerged into open air, onto hard-packed earth pocked with stones. Mist curled about me, masking any sight of this new island, revealing shadows of branches, walls, other buildings that might have been wholly nonexistent or might have been part of this army site. Rena's scent was close, but now there was another scent, one I knew too well. Fresh blood.

With the scent came a voice, cool and amused. "Is that her name?" Dina said from somewhere above me, and I could almost see the smile as she spoke.

"Dina!" I turned in place, but she only laughed—above me, on some kind of terrace. I climbed another set of crumbling stairs, then paused, trying to see where she was, where I could go from here. The roar of the ocean was close, and I could see the long branches of dead scrub clinging to the embankment. Below me was an open green, about fifteen feet down, hidden and revealed in turns by the billowing fog. For a second I thought I saw Rena, or at least someone, on the green below, but the mists blew over her, hiding her again. "Dina!" I yelled, and heard a chuckle behind me—no, to my left—

"Call me all you like, you have no claim on me."

"No claim? I brought back your damn sunstone!"

She laughed. "And I should pay *you* for *my* property? My eye, long gone and tainted by time away from the salt? Be glad I don't act as your idiot hunters did and take it out of your hide."

My breath whistled between my teeth. Too trusting, Evie. Too trusting by far.

Some things in the undercurrent are too single-minded to be of much danger. But if they're too human, if they're too close, they get corrupted. I thought of the Morrigan, tainted by the vulnerability she'd used to get close to me, of Patrick and the Horn of the Wild Hunt, and of the sunstone, so long away from Dina, so long in the care of humans . . . Dina had been corrupted long since.

"But I did promise no harm to you or yours," she went on. "So I suggest you leave. I have matters to attend to, and you, you have someone in need of help."

She was ahead of me and to the left. Two steps. "Rena will be all right," I said, tossing the words off as if they were less than the prayer I made them.

"Really? But you should see—"

I whirled and slammed the bat into the mist—too late. A shape, human but shrouded, vanished into an empty arch.

"You should see what she feared," she continued. "Really, I didn't think she had the imagination for it—then again, I didn't think you'd have your particular trigger—"

"Is that what the stone does?" I snapped, and swung again, blindly this time. Something, though, stepped out of the way, drifting closer. "Lets you see people's fears?"

"Hush. Hush. Listen."

I did—but I did more than listen, I scented, and that was worse. At the edge of hearing, just making its way through the ringing that still echoed in my ears, a woman's voice called. Not Rena's, and certainly that thread of incense and greenery wasn't her scent (though the blood, the blood had to be hers, and there was far too much of it).

Sarah's.

I froze, straining for her voice. She couldn't be here. I'd told her to stay behind, and she'd agreed, she'd *agreed.* I backed up a step, trying to hear her, understand why she was calling out, what she was calling for.

But this was Dina before me, and whatever she'd shown Rena had also been bad enough, convincing enough, to draw her out. "No," I said. "No, you can't fool me that way."

A shape emerged from the mist. I couldn't quite get a clear look at her—she spoke with the same voice as in the dark room in Georges, but the mists seemed to hang about her, making what looked first like a winter parka become a denim jacket, what could have been heels become Doc Martens, and back again . . . It wasn't that she was changing shape; there was no external magic to it. I just couldn't focus. Like the forms in fog, she was unreadable. Worst of all was her face: the closest impression I got was a veil like that of a bride, held in place with a ring of dark metal utterly unlike a crown. "No, I suppose not," Dina said.

Her hand snaked out, catching the end of the baseball bat.

"However, it did do one thing," she went on. Her fingers tightened, and ashwood splintered under them, twisting and giving way as if the bat were no more than cardboard. "It did get you closer to the edge." Her other hand struck me on the shoulder, not hard, but enough to make me stumble back onto empty air.

It wasn't very far to fall, but it felt like an age.

Eighteen

I hit the ground hard enough that something went *crunch* along my rib cage, and stars sparked across my vision as my head struck earth. Soft earth, though, close to mud, and instead of knocking me straight out it just stuck to my hair and, as I turned over, to one side of my face.

The remnants of the baseball bat bounced off my leg, the bruise just one more pain among the chorus. I stared up at the blank sky, trying to catch my breath with lungs that felt like they'd been flattened to two dimensions.

Somewhere up on the cliff, Dina paused in mid laugh, as if she'd heard something. "Oh, *that's* tender," she said, or something like it, and her scent faded into the fog.

She might have said more, but just then I'd tried to roll over on the wrong side, and my mind whited out from pain. "Fuck," I mumbled, and heard an answering groan from off to my right. "Rena?"

"Evie?" Now the smell of spilled blood was heavier, tangling with the mists in ways I didn't like. "Get over here, please."

I pushed myself up, gritting my teeth against the pain. I didn't have double vision, though, and nothing beyond a goose egg from what I could tell. But two inches from where my head had hit, a lump of rock poked up out of the ground at the very edge of a campfire pit. I stared at it for a second, aware of the chill of winter behind me and the Hounds' mark on me, then shook myself and headed for Rena's voice.

Rena sat crouched in the door of one of the army buildings, clutching her right leg with both hands. "Take off your belt," she grated as soon as I got close.

"My belt?"

"It's not bad—just a graze—but I want to stop the bleeding." She glanced at me, teeth bared in a vicious, pained smile. "Don't you know any first aid at all?"

"Not enough to deal with you," I said, and handed her the belt.

She laughed through her teeth and shifted position, so that I could now see the dark stain that spread across the back of her calf. "Put your hands here and keep pressing while I tie this."

I did so. The blood was already sticky, and it didn't seem to be coming out in a rush, so it must have missed the arteries. In fact, it seemed like a pretty shallow wound. How she'd gotten it, though—

Something crackled behind me, and the scent of incense curled about us. Dina's illusion—no. No, she might be able to distract Rena, but I'd always trusted my nose and I could do so now. "Sarah?" I called over my shoulder, still holding on to the belt. "That's really you, isn't it?"

There was a long pause—Rena fumbled with the belt, swearing quietly—then, soft and querulous above the drone of the ocean: "Evie?"

"Jesus Christ, Sarah, what are you doing here? I told you to stay on the boat!"

"Evie," Sarah repeated instead of answering me. "Who . . . what was the Sox score tonight?"

What the hell? "What are you talking about? Baseball season's long over—the Sox caved way back in the playoffs. They're not scoring anything for a while. And they won't, not with that offense."

"It *is* you. God, Evie, I thought—" A gust of wind carried a fresh billow of mist into the hollow between the barracks, but it also revealed something fluttering and too pink to be any part of the gray foliage on this island. Sarah, coming up the path, slow and hesitant, fumbling her way from one tree to the next.

"More pressure, Evie," Rena grated. I complied, and she looped the belt just above the wound, yanked it so tight her lips went white, pulled it tighter still, then tied it off. "You can talk baseball later."

"It's not that." I sighed and eased the pressure on the wound, and though the iron seep of blood still stung my nose, it wasn't nearly as bad now. "Sarah, we're over here. What the hell was all that about the Sox?"

"Wanted to make sure you were you."

Rena let go of the belt, sighing. "I don't blame her," she added, and reached for something at her side: her gun, cast aside and still smelling of the shots fired.

"Rena, it's just Sarah—"

"I know. This is useless anyway. I emptied it." She hefted the gun and tried to put it away, hissing as her leg brushed mine. "When I saw what that thing could do—if it made me do that, I didn't want it to have anything else it could turn against me."

"What did it do?"

For a moment Rena met my eyes, then shook her head. "I don't think I want to tell you that, Evie."

Sarah had only gotten as far as the edge of the clearing, and she waved a hand in front of her as if either beckoning or waving us away. "Katie!" she called, and a gull responded mournfully, out somewhere to sea. "Katie!"

"She's back with Alison," I said, getting to my feet. "They're both fine. We'll get you back to them soon enough."

"No, she's not. Evie—" She took another step toward us, close enough that I could finally see her face clearly.

Sarah's eyes were wide and blank, filmed over with a white that wasn't the white of cataracts but of marble. I stifled a curse, and Rena made a gesture that wasn't quite crossing herself. "You don't understand," Sarah whispered, those sightless eyes roving as if to discover my face. "Katie—she said we were in the wrong place, and I poured out the ink—"

"Hang on," I said, and took Sarah by both hands. The touch seemed to calm her, and she drew a shuddering breath. "Dina's run off—I can probably find her, but you two need to get somewhere safe." I guided Sarah to Rena's side, then took off my coat and slung it over Rena's shoulders. "And you, you're going into shock. Keep this."

"Oh, fuck you, Evie." Rena tried to sit up, then slumped against the wall. "There's a ranger cabin nearby—there's gotta be. I'll get there and use their radio to call for backup."

I'd seen better plans in fortune cookies. "No. You stay down—keep the goddamned coat—and I'll go after that thing. You want to get more people shot?"

"That's not the problem," Sarah interrupted, her tone returning to its usual half lecture. "We had a stowaway. Well, you did, I knew she was there—"

I shook my head. "Later. Wait till we can get you to safety—" I paused, her words finally registering. "You're not saying—"

"As a matter of fact, that is exactly what I am saying." She looked around, as if her eyes might spontaneously repair themselves and reveal Katie standing safe and sound nearby. "She talked me into it—said Nate had a plan, and that she had to come with us."

I remembered how careful Sarah had been in the boat, how she'd asked me not to watch her saying goodbye. "Goddammit, Sarah, she's a child! How could you bring her out here!"

"Because she asked," Sarah replied, her chin up and defiant. "And because I'm her teacher. And after I gave you so much crap for trying to get me to stay away, I wasn't about to do the same to her. Besides, it turned out she was right—when you got out onto Georges, she told me to stay. She said we were in the wrong place, that what would happen would be somewhere else. So I got out the ink—"

"Sarah, she's nine goddamn years old! A nine-year-old shouldn't know how to do this sort of thing!"

"She knows it already, it's just a matter of—" Sarah stopped, took a deep breath, and shook her head. "We'll have this conversation another time."

"I sure hope so," I muttered, and the peevish nature of the comment failed to disguise my real misgivings: that there might not be time, later, for us to have this conversation.

Sarah bowed her head a moment, then went on. "I had her look in the ink, and she directed me over here. Sam tied up at the dock, we got out, and that's when I saw you."

"Me? But—"

"I know, Evie, I know, but she looked like you. This woman, I didn't even think to look away, and when she took off her veil she looked like you, and—" She took a deep breath. "Evie, I can't see."

"We guessed," Rena said dryly. "And the girl?"

"I don't know. She bolted as soon as we left the boat; I was following her when I saw you. I think she might have escaped."

"This is an island," Rena said. "Escape isn't really an option. Not unless she's back on the boat."

"Doubt it," Sarah said, and fumbled for my hand. With her other hand she lifted something heavy from her purse: the black iron hook. "Katie said you might need this. I don't know what for, there's nothing magic about it."

I took the hook and, in return, pressed the unsplintered end of the baseball bat into her empty hand. "Here. Trade you."

"What is—" She stopped, running her fingers over it. "Dammit, Evie! Now's not the time for baseball—"

She stopped, fiddling with the splintered end. "Fine. Fine. What kind of wood is it?"

I shrugged, then realized she couldn't see. "Ought to be ash," I said. "Dina smashed it up pretty good, though, so don't put too much faith in it." I shifted the hook to my right hand, where it settled comfortably against my palm. At the very least I'd make a good fake pirate. Better than Roger's real one.

"I got other things to put in it," Sarah muttered. "Go. Go and stop that thing."

I got to my feet. "Sarah?"

She looked up, her blind eyes questing after me.

"How do I kill it?"

"I don't know. I really don't." She huddled a little deeper into her coat. "But I really hope you can."

"And do it fast," Rena added, staring over her shoulder at the empty barracks. For a fraction of a second I had an idea of what face Dina had donned for her. "Not everyone's willing to leave themselves defenseless so that they don't give it a weapon."

I nodded, not quite sure I understood, but the emptied gun spoke for itself. "I'll do what I can." I turned and oriented myself on Dina's scent, out into the skeletal sumac.

The path led out onto a bare spit of land, a skinny length between the rise I'd come out on and a forested lump at the far end of the island. I had a guess where I was now: Lovells, the island that had claimed many ships, where Meda had spent her first night in sight of Boston. Maybe Dina had been here even then; maybe Meda had begun to construct her plan then.

Only she and Colin had partly failed. They'd stolen the sunstone, weakening Dina and keeping her from directly preying on the harbor, but in doing so they'd inextricably tied themselves to her. Too much humanity could taint even a monster.

Shells and tiny stones rattled together underfoot in a treble chorus. I slid and scrambled over them, the wind and fog cutting right through my shirt. Into the trees and down, into a valley cut into the middle of the island. Not a natural one, either; the concrete and stone of Army work was present here, only here it was overgrown and reclaimed by the wild. Blackberry canes, the only trace of their fruit a few wizened pips, dragged at my legs like claws.

A wide plaza opened up on my right: a crumbling concrete structure chiseled out of the hillside. The remnants of a plinth stood in the middle: a gun emplacement, I realized belatedly, set there to watch for incoming enemy aircraft. They'd packed up the gun itself but left the traces of their work.

For a fraction of a second I thought I saw a shadow like a stag's skull, heard an echo like water falling, and something like the memory of pain coiled in the back of my throat, cold and stony. I stumbled over my own feet, but shook my head. No, that was gone and done with. I'd have given more to get Nate back, regardless of where he was now.

I hoped he was out of Dina's grasp.

I emerged onto a flat, swampy spot that must have been inundated twice a year when hurricane season hit. A dull, marshy scent rose up from it, thick with salt and sick fish, magnified by the fog that clustered over the island, wrapping it in a cocoon against the world. A person—or a dead entity—could hide here and never be found. Or make a home here, reaching out through the harbor to the city, feeding on the fear it stoked.

Katie's scent, sparking and electric, clung to a tiny red shed that was the only visible structure on this part of the island—she'd stopped here, but not for long. Across the marsh stood another copse, smaller than the ones I'd come through, clumped and clustered and unwilling to let any light in. She was in there, somewhere.

And so was Dina.

I shifted my grip on the hook. I didn't have many advantages here. Dina had been around since the days when my ancestors were running around hitting each other on the head with rocks (though, granted, we were still up for that these days too) and all I had was scrap iron and hope. Oh yes, and a fragmented, crippled soul, even if Sam claimed I had healed.

Maybe nothing I did would be enough to save me, come midwinter. Maybe everything I did would unravel within a week, and the grand plan of protecting the city would fall back into the Great Unworkable Ideas list of the decade. Maybe all this was just so much screaming at the tide.

Maybe all that was true. But at this point I was slowly realizing that I didn't give a flying fuck. I still needed to try.

Katie's scent led into the trees. I followed it up a steep path, pushing dry branches out of my way with the hook. A deaf stump could have heard me coming up the hill, but I no longer cared. Besides, I knew my relative skill in staying quiet; any attempts to minimize the noise would do nothing but slow me down.

I was just using that to justify my lack of stealth when I remembered that I'd passed a couple of artificial cliffs already, and who was to say those were the only emplacements on the island? How did I know I wasn't about to fall into another?

The realization came a second too late: the leaves under my foot fell away into nothingness. I stumbled back, crashing against a tree. Below me gaped another pocket of crumbling concrete, but this one was rounder, shallower, and more given over to nature. The slabs were broken where saplings had grown up through the cracks, and vines and roots laced down the walls in patterns more suited to temples in the jungle. Here, the fog held back, preferring to coast over this hollow rather than sink in.

In the center of this little amphitheater knelt Katie, bent over a little pool of black rainwater thick with fallen leaves and detritus of the summer. She had to have heard me approach, but instead of looking up or even moving, she held on to the edge of the pool so hard her knuckles had turned white. Her eyes were wide and dark, and an empty paper bag—one with stickers on it, the kind Nate used to pack her lunch—lay at her feet.

Remembering Sarah's eyes, I suddenly wondered if she *could* move. "Katie!" I whispered, then scrambled down the side of the emplacement, skidding on steps that had long since dissolved into sand. "Katie, it's Evie. Are you all right?"

No answer. The surface rippled, stirred by something other than her shallow breaths. I reached for her shoulder, then thought better of it. There was a scent about her—not the gunpowder stink of magic, but something similar, like the residue inside a soaked bullet, like a cracked ballpoint pen, metal and sweet at the same time. "Oh, kid, what did you do?" I whispered, and looked over her shoulder into the water.

Something flickered there, something gray and red and moving too fast for my eye to catch. From the way Katie's shoulders tensed and relaxed and tensed again, I knew she had to be making sense of it, but it meant nothing to me.

Whatever magic she had called on, it was greater than just this pool. I wouldn't interrupt her; though I might not agree with what she was doing, I was not about to break that connection. Not unless I knew something was wrong. Instead, fired by the thought of Deke and of Sarah's stone eyes and Rena's wound, I straightened up and walked to the edge of this little amphitheater. Facing the thicket of woods—the woods that now reeked of stone and blood and everything else I'd come here to find—I drew a deep breath. "Dina!" I yelled. "Gray One! Deino, Enyo, Persis, I name you and call you out!"

For a long moment only Katie's choked breathing answered me, the slow drip of condensation off the withered trees, the roar of the ocean through the arched gate off to my right. The gate, I realized must once have served for jeeps, trucks, and other on-island vehicles. Now it was hung with greenery, an arch beneath which greenmen might live or apprentice trolls practice their skills. I thought I saw a flicker of gray, and moved to see better.

"Hound," Dina said behind me, mimicking my tone, though her voice seemed almost like Roger's now, sliding from his rough tones to hers and back. "Scelan, Genevieve, Bitch. So brave and so wounded, so unaware of the holes in your own soul."

A shadow moved and leaped down into the amphitheater, veils fluttering like Sarah's skirts. That on its own was enough to piss me off even more. She regarded me with a mocking smile, only just visible through the thin gray cloth of her veil.

"Yeah? Mind telling me what good awareness did Roger before you killed him?"

"I haven't killed anyone." She touched her chest, and for a moment the veils rippled, the shape becoming more angular, narrower at hip and breast, broader overall. "What was best of him—" her voice shifted, briefly becoming his, "—is here."

Christ. You found magicians in love with their work, but this was sick. "And Deke?"

She shrugged. "Nothing there worth keeping."

"Picky eater."

Her smile dropped away, one moment visible through the veil, the next no more than a blank. "At least I'm not a gullible little bitch."

I started to bare my teeth, then paused. Entities like her—old as the Hunt, if not older—shouldn't have bothered with sniping like this. She'd learned that from Roger, I realized; she'd been too much immersed in the world of humans. And if she could take pleasure in this sort of taunting, she could be cajoled or distracted or appeased. Possibly fooled. And, maybe, killed.

I shifted my grip on the hook, curling my fingers

over the end. "And you broke our bargain," I said, hoping that at least might distract her.

"I? I seem to remember you hurting me, or at the very least attacking me. I am justified in returning force, if you broke the bargain first." Dina circled the pond, long fingers reaching out to stroke a tree that had grown up through the concrete. "Which is why it amazes me," she went on, musingly, "that you'd call me out here—"

I raised the hook and lunged.

"—with a suitable hostage so close to hand."

Her hand, twisted into a claw, shot for Katie. But I'd guessed right, and I was there in time, grabbing her by the wrist with one hand and, as she brought her other hand down, catching that against the curve of the boathook. Dina hissed, though the hook barely scratched her flesh, and jerked away. Katie didn't move, though she drew a sudden, whistling gasp. "Oh no," I whispered. "No, you don't get to do that. You broke the bargain first, Dina. You hurt Deke, and Rena, and Sarah. You hurt my city."

"Are they yours, then?" She cradled her scratched hand against her chest and briefly caressed my forearm with the other. "That's a lot for you to claim. The whole city, you and yours?"

"Yes." I reversed the hook and punched her in the face. She reeled backward, but my knuckles stung as if I'd dragged them along asphalt. "Yes. The city and everyone in it. Me and mine."

Dina twisted away, successfully this time. "You arrogant bitch!" she spat. "You think that matters? Your bargain meant nothing. You mean nothing."

I stepped back, away from Katie, but my left hand brushed the fluff of the kid's hair. Abruptly, the taste of ice water and ferns filled my mouth, and as if through water a man's face swam in front of me, incandescent with fury: Nate, madder than I'd ever seen him but stripped of the bearshirt rage. Whatever this was, it was purely human, and no less frightening for that. My hand dropped away, and the vision—the fragment of Katie's vision—did so as well, leaving only the lingering taste of ice.

I shook my head and stepped away from Katie, leaving her to her work, to whatever needed to be done. I trusted her, and Nate, too. *You can't save me from this*, I'd told him, and there were some things I couldn't save him from. Nor could I try, without diminishing him.

"No," I said, as much to my own fears as to her. "You don't get it. I don't own them, I don't get to tell everyone what to do. Hell, I don't *want* them to do what I tell them. That's not what it means to be one of mine."

Dina stood with one hand raised again, her scent crackling with something like the air before a storm. I feinted for her head, and when she ducked away, punched her in the stomach. "What it means," I whispered as she doubled over, "is that I am theirs, when I can be, when it counts. That's all. Nothing more."

She caught at my shoulder as if I'd knocked the wind from her, but the blow had done no real damage—the way my fist stung told me that, at least. There was something more than flesh beneath those veils. "Not just nothing more," she murmured back, raising her face to mine as if to draw me into a kiss, "but nothing at all."

Her other hand reached up. I ducked away, but she hadn't been reaching for me. Instead she pulled the veils back, revealing her face.

A blank expanse of gray stone, slick and gleaming, met my gaze. The sunstone from the bottom of the Quabbin, the eye that I'd gone to retrieve, turned into a face.

This was what had turned Sarah's eyes to stone, what had shown Rena something so horrible she'd shot herself in the leg. This was the power that had altered Deke to the point of unrecognizability, that had stolen Roger till he was stone. This was why they were the Gray Ones; the blank dread of not knowing, the fog of real and imagined fears. My limbs went dull and unmoving, struck by the frozen fear of not knowing which way to move. This was the power Dina had siphoned off the paranoia of Boston, the confusion and fear that led to no good result.

Deke had said it himself—there's fear that keeps you safe, and fear that warns you, and then there's fear of another sort. The kind that makes you turn on your friends, that irises the world down to one frightened person. I'd had the world collapse in like that before, and my heart chilled at the thought of it happening again.

The smooth stone turned slightly, light no longer passing through it but reflecting off. There weren't even any features—the smiles I thought I'd seen must have been something she projected, or else I'd just conjured up the expression that went with her tone . . .

I'd followed that thought for a full second before I realized that there was no other effect on me. No blindness, no paralysis—the moment of terror notwithstanding—nothing but the remembered feel of the slick sunstone in my hands as I raised it above the Quabbin, yelling triumph. Nothing but the taste of brassy sunlight, the smell of the hearth where Colin and Meda had lived their lives. I chuckled, and Dina froze, her hand on my shoulder going rigid as a bundle of sticks. "Sorry," I said, and kicked her feet out from under her.

She didn't fall—she and Roger were still magicians, and still stronger than I would ever be—but her posture as she recovered was unsteady and without the liquid grace she'd shown before. "You—" she began, speaking without a mouth.

"I've held the stone. I've carried your damn Eye. Uh-uh." I shifted the hook and lunged again. "You'll have to do better than that, Gray One."

The veils fell across her face again, and for a

moment I caught a glimpse of features that didn't exist, contorted in a snarl. "Oh, I *will*."

I didn't wait for her magic to become manifest. Instead I put my shoulders down and charged, knocking her off the edge of the emplacement. We fell together, onto the hard ground a few feet down.

There is a way for an untrained person to fight a talented magician and have a decent chance of winning: get in close and keep hitting, so that you keep them off balance. I'd used it before, those times when I tangled with the Fiana, and the fact that I was still alive was a point in favor of the theory. However, it presupposed two things: one, that you'd be fighting a normal magician, one who needed time to invoke her loci, to cast her circles. Dina didn't. I was keeping her off balance, unable to summon the power to blast me out of existence, but she didn't need to step back and regroup. Even as I knocked her down, wrestled her to the ground, smeared mud across her stone face, she could still work her magic—freezing my skin, charring the wall behind us, sending electricity through me so that my muscles shivered and spasmed.

The second problem was that fighting assumed I was actually doing some damage. But every blow that landed had as much effect as if I'd swung against a brick wall, and the blood running from my knuckles proved that it wasn't just my imagination. The hook, when it landed, shredded Dina's diaphanous veils like a dragon skinning a princess, but it threw up sparks from the skin that looked so human beneath. If it was hurting her—and I suspected it might be, just a lot less than I'd hoped—it wasn't doing enough damage to stop her.

I swung again, only to catch a blast of something that stank of onions and dead crows. My hair sizzled and crisped, and when I focused on Dina again, the world was red and blurry. A scratch had opened up on my forehead somewhere—okay, deeper than a scratch, judging by the slick feeling running down my cheek—

and the rest of my face felt as if I'd just stuck it in a blast furnace. *Sunburn in November*, I thought fuzzily. *Gonna have fun explaining this one.*

"I always knew I'd have to put you down once this was over, Hound." She darted forward, her hands still glowing white. I ducked out of the way and brought my laced fists down on the back of her neck. She grunted and stumbled, but didn't fall. "I just thought—"

I drove my foot against the inside of her knee, and she fell against the other side of the arch, light splashing up around her like a gout of flaming oil. It didn't stop her, though; a new scent of corroded copper and vomit now rose up around her, and when she turned the smile was clear under her veil.

"—it'd be kinder to do it quickly. But you've convinced me otherwise." She clapped her hands, and the greenery around me withered. "I think I'll enjoy this."

Fuck you, I tried to say, but my throat was too dry. I drew a ragged breath and attacked again—just as Katie cried out. Dina turned slightly, and I jammed the hook into her neck as Katie plunged her hand into the water. She drew something out, something clear and bright, but just then I had other things to worry about.

Dina choked, gurgled, and then gave me a look over her shoulder that, veil or no, was clearly meant to say *You don't seriously mean this, do you?* She knocked my hand away as if it were no more than a spider, then tugged the hook out of her neck—the sound it made was that of a chisel against stone—and dropped it. "Fool," she whispered.

"Evie!" Katie's cry caught me like the call of a horn, and I turned to see her run to the edge of the emplacement. "He's got it!" she yelled, and flung something at me.

I put my hands up to catch what she'd thrown—a water bottle, open at one end, spilling as it tumbled—and missed entirely. The water splashed over me, icy and clear and—

—and I was elsewhere, the world distorted by a lens of water. I stood on the surface of a lake far from here—no, not a lake. A quarry. The place where I'd lost my soul.

I was not alone. I stood within a pillar of water, and above me hung the bleached-white skull of a stag, horns branching like tributaries. The confused shape of a guardian that was too powerful and too young to understand what it was and what it could not do.

Through the water, through the distortion and the haze and the darkness above, a figure on the shore rose up, a pale wisp of a man, the color of bone in the starlight. Nate, as I'd last seen him before I left him on Venetia's porch. No—not just as I'd seen him; he'd left shirt and shoes somewhere else, and though I couldn't see him clearly I could know the gooseflesh that must be rising on him, know it as well as if it were on my own skin.

"Give it back!" he yelled, unknowingly echoing what I'd yelled months ago, when the quarry spirit held his body. "You stole the Hound's soul. Give it back to her!"

The waters around me swirled. *It's mine*, it said. *She gave it to me.*

"Liar!" Nate strode out into the water, ignoring the way it fizzled at his touch, the way the waves ran away from him as if scared. "She gave you nothing!"

The quarry spirit paused, and for a moment I could even feel its wakening apprehension, the worry that maybe it had done something wrong. "*It's mine*," it repeated, defensive and guilty as a child with a stolen toy.

"Then I'll take it back." Nate grinned, and I saw in that grin not just the bearshirt his father had made him but the wicked, dogged, amazing man I had known for a long, long time. "Because if I understand all this right, you stole her soul in a way that didn't just bind you to her. It bound you to me. Me, and my family line."

And with that he charged, shifting as he ran. By all rights he should have gone straight through the water, should have splashed into the depths on the far side, but instead the quarry spirit squealed as his jaws seized just below the stag's skull.

What happened next I could not quite make out, but it involved a lot of snarling, of froth and foam, blood of two kinds swirling like party streamers. At one point I saw Nate again, fully human, grimacing as he tore something from his side. "Here," he said through clenched teeth, seemingly oblivious to the blood, "take this instead, and fucking *choke on it!*"

With that he shoved a strip of coarse, bloody hide into the jaws of the skull. The quarry spirit gagged, water churning through it in frantic, panicky currents. A silvery glow, like an afterthought of the moon, rose through it, up to the surface—

And abruptly I was back where I'd been, drenched in quarry water, the worn and dented bottle at my feet. *Apologies*, the quarry spirit whispered in my ear, *apologies, I did not know, I could not know, make him stop!*

Well, there was only so much I could do from here, and it's not as if I was inclined to make Nate stop. But with the plea came a sudden link, like a cable thrown around me, a conduit to the mainland and the place where a man I loved fought for my soul. Water to water, the link from one to another.

I had just enough time to remember Chatterji's description of severance and return before a flame blossomed in my chest, a mantle of power settling over me like a cloak of gold. *So this is why they do it,* I thought through the haze of sudden power; *this is what all the adepts are trying for.* For a moment I felt a rush of sympathy; for another I was tempted to follow that path, to find ways to sever and steal and claim a soul for my own, if only to keep experiencing this.

This was why Meda had led me to the stone. Not to bring it back to Dina, not to hide it again, but because she knew only someone who'd lost much of her soul would have the chance to regain it, and thus have the strength to do what needed to be done. Even now Dina approached Katie, still seeing her as a so-convenient hostage, raising one hand to her veil; even now I began to understand the pattern Meda had wrought in stone and water and hope.

But more, I could see—scent, even, because here was the point where senses blurred and only magic mattered—the pattern linking me to the Wild Hunt, the chain that bound me as securely as any golden chain of the Fiana, the sentence of midwinter. With this sudden power, I could sever that, cut my ties to the hundred Hunters and their claim on me, walk free of it and live.

Live past midwinter.

I might even be able to save Katie after that. There was so much strength here, so much that had been leached from me day after gray day. I could save myself, save Katie, heal Sarah and Rena, and let Dina run off licking her wounds, never to return to Boston.

I could do all that. No magician could ask for more of a task, and any magician worth her salt would have taken that option. Never mind Meda's pattern, reduced by time to only a plea, a request that I could choose to ignore without consequence. A magician would use this power to claim as much as possible—any adept knew that this was the basis of much of magic, using it to get out of whatever obligations you'd promised.

I wasn't a magician. I closed my eyes, tasting the water that ran down my face, the blood mingled with it, the tang of frost and fog and salt in the air. *It would have been nice to at least see another Sox game*, I thought, and let go of my sense of the Hunt's hold on me, turning instead to the matter at hand.

I stepped in front of Katie—so easy, so quick, with this to draw on!—and knocked Dina aside, backhanding her into the wall of the arch. "Stay here, Katie," I said, and marveled that my voice didn't crack the concrete. She nodded, careful not to look at either of us, and scrambled back to the edge of the pool.

My ears roared with the rush of blood and power; the scent of the island suddenly seemed writ in luminous script before me. With it came a continuous, querulous murmur that was like a welcome pebble in my shoe; something that was not scent nor sound but both.

I smiled, letting my talent recognize that murmur even as conscious thought let it go, then bent and picked up the hook. It seemed soft under my fingers, malleable even, and for a second I was tempted to shape it into something else—I didn't know the magic for such a changing, but brute force could do it. Instead I glanced up at Dina as she backed away, through the arch to the shore.

She seemed to recognize that something had happened—perhaps the backhand had done it. I followed her, but she'd already made it to the edge of the waves, where the damp sand afforded her just enough contact with seawater. She swept the veils back from her face once more, and though the stone did not strike me the same way, it still slowed my steps. "Not what I'd have preferred," she spat. "But I'm whole now, and that's all that matters—even if I leave your rotten city behind, there are cities and coasts and so many haunts—"

She paused, and I did too, one foot on the broken boulders that made up most of the beach here. Off to my left, closer than it had been, the murmur that I'd heard earlier rose, now clear enough that it was sound in truth, separating out into individual voices.

" . . . left! I said left, goddammit, my left, you dumb dyke—" Rena's voice, ragged but clear.

"You keep calling me that, and I'm going to think you don't like me very much." Sarah, out of breath and unfazed.

The pair of them hobbled across the beach toward

us, Rena's arm slung over Sarah's shoulders, Sarah walking for two and Rena seeing for two. Rena raised her head, her expression too far away to make out but clearly seeing us. "I see them," she called. "I—there's something strange about Evie—"

Dina spat again and turned her back on me, raising her hands to the sea. The waves warped and twisted into a funnel that I could tell would carry her wherever she wished, wherever she could plan revenge or simply feast on the fear that we so obligingly provided.

"No!" Sarah raised her hand, and the remnants of the baseball bat caught and shredded the mist like a fan. She'd drawn symbols on it, runes that straggled and strayed but were written in sticky red, powerful for all that. It was, after all, ashwood, and Sarah knew her twice-nine runes and names. No one knew the small magics better than she did. "Forseti and Nerthus and Donbettyr bind you, the net of Kratalis Trienos keep you and reject you."

Ash flared into flame, and Sarah gasped but held on. It wouldn't last long—it was a binding meant for other, homelier things, but it had Dina pinned for now. "Thief!" she screamed. "You, you rotten thief—"

I jumped onto the last rock behind her and caught her by the veils. "Not a thief," I whispered, and brought the hook around to her throat.

For a fraction of a second, it was a cruel, curved knife, a *harpe*, a knife meant for one purpose only. It should not have cut as deeply as it did, but I had the strength of my severed soul, and Meda's help, and Sarah's, and this had been done before, long before.

Dina's body slumped to the sand, and the saltwater shied away from the blood, even as it sank down and was gone. The bloody mess of stone and hair and veils sagged in my hand, and I flung it into the ocean. It hit the water far out—farther out than I should have been able to see, given the mist, and on a flatter ocean than the Atlantic had any right to be—and sank. With the last of the power that the quarry had given back,

I sank the hook into the sand and consigned it to the island.

The sand closed over my hands, and all that was left was seawater, cold and stinging where I'd skinned my knuckles. I let out a long breath, watching as the light from above brightened, becoming once again only the gray light of a cloudy day. The cool light of winter approaching, of days drawing in.

I sat back on my heels and scrubbed my hands over my face, ignoring the salt, ignoring the sting, then stood and turned to Rena and Sarah.

The crumbling bat fell from Sarah's hands. Rena slid off her shoulders to the closest rock, her wounded leg out in front of her. Neither spoke as I approached; Sarah rubbed at her pale eyes, and Rena looked from me to the red sand that was all that remained of Dina. Finally, her lips parted. "This is one of those things," she said as I reached her side, "that I'm just going to have to accept, isn't it?"

I nodded and offered her my hand. "I'm afraid so."

She looked at me for a long moment. "Okay," she said. "Okay." But she didn't take my hand.

Sarah had turned to face the ocean, flexing her burnt and blistered hand. "Don't do that," I said, and turned her toward the west, to the city. "Sarah, the mist is clearing. Can you see it?"

"Of course I can't, I—" She stopped. At the corner of her eyes, there was a gleam that was flesh, not stone, and with every blink the sheen of life returned. "Evie," she said slowly, still staring out at the water.

The mist drifted away as if it had never been, and the skyline of Boston rose up on the horizon, distant and real. "Katie!" I called over my shoulder. "It's okay. You can come out now."

"You found her," Sarah said.

"She led me to Dina." I glanced over my shoulder to see Katie emerge from the arch, squinting to see us better. "She saved my life. She and Nate."

I sank down onto the rock next to Rena as Katie

came up and took Sarah's hand. "We'll get both of you to a hospital," I said softly.

"It feels better already," Rena said.

"Really?"

"No." She tapped the belt ruefully, then froze as the first few notes of music sounded behind us. Flute music, recorder music, the same melancholy air that I'd heard once below Georges.

"Don't," I said as she started to rise. "She's gone . . . it's an echo, of sorts."

"Echo," she said. "I . . . all right." She put her hand on my shoulder and used that to hoist herself up.

"Let's get you home," I said.

Nineteen

By the time we got back to the city, took Rena to a hospital, and had the rest of our wounds seen to, the last of the fog had burned off and night had fallen. I took Sarah home (where Alison had been waiting up, so nervous she'd finished three days' worth of work), then walked with Katie back into Allston. After a couple of blocks, I bent to carry her piggyback, even though it grated the pain in my ribs. But she'd been up all night, and even after all this I had a little more strength left in me.

"I'm sorry," she said as I shifted her weight to compensate. "I should have told you I was coming with you."

"'s all right," I said. "I wouldn't have let you." I tipped my head back so that I could see her clearly. "And where would I be then, huh?"

Katie smiled and hugged me. I stifled a grunt; I wouldn't be able to carry her like this much longer. For now I could, though.

I can't say I didn't know what I'd find. But I still paused when I reached the end of Nate's street. He was sitting on the porch, his elbows resting on his knees, tired but apparently unhurt. He no longer had the burnt-hair, shifter edge to his scent, but the center of it, the sun-warmed-wood scent, was the same, and not even the faint traces of ferns and ice and everything else his battle with the quarry had left could change that. And if the polish of his scent now had something akin to the unridged flesh of a scar, if there was a stiffness in the way he got to his feet, it still suited him, and still left him Nate.

Katie let go and slid to the ground. Nate crossed the street and, without bothering to speak, caught me in a tight embrace.

Too tight. I yelped and moved his hand. "Sorry—ribs. They taped them up at the hospital, but they're still bad."

I shifted my arms around him, trying to find a better way to hold him back, and he hissed as I grazed his waist. "Still raw," he said through his teeth. "Sorry."

"But you're okay?" I leaned back a little to look at him, ignoring the twinge of pain.

"Yeah. You?"

"Yeah."

Carefully, trying to avoid the many little hurts, we shifted into a new configuration, one that ended up with my cheek resting on his collarbone and his hands at the small of my back. "I was wrong," I said into his ear. "You could save me after all."

"Only from this," he said, his breath stirring the hair on the nape of my neck. "And only for a little while. But it worked."

And for now, that was enough.

After a moment, we pulled back enough to remember the rest of the world. Katie stood mutely to the side, smiling what I'd started to think of as a seer's smile, one that responded to something the rest of us weren't aware of. "You did well," Nate said, bending down to scruff his sister's hair. She batted his hand away, her ears turning pink with happy embarrassment. "You're all right?" he added, tilting her chin up.

"Fine," she said, somehow managing to imply that he was silly for even asking. Kid was gonna be a terror when she hit her teens.

"Good. Because tomorrow's a school day, and you've got to get to bed." He ignored her groan and patted her on the back, steering her toward the porch. "As for me," he added as we crossed the street, following Katie's theatrically dejected slump, "I can't seem to remember anything I've got tomorrow that I can't get out of."

I thought a moment about cracked ribs and healing wounds, then shrugged. You could work around anything, with enough forethought. "I'll call in sick."

It took at least three weeks before the emergency call Sarah had put out was finally revoked, due mainly to the paranoid nature of the undercurrent. Not that this had any ill effects for most of the population, or even the undercurrent; the ones who suffered the most were the adepts who refused to come out of their hiding places until they'd gotten repeated assurances of the world's return to normality. The Elect in particular had holed up in the foundations of the Masonic Hall and had to be extracted by Chatterji and Wheelwright working together. (This ultimately resulted in one of the weirder relationships I'd ever encountered, and that was including whatever Tessie and Sam and Maryam had worked out.) If anything, it meant Sarah had a few weeks of rest in which the most annoying parts of the neighborhood watch were out of commission.

She'd taken it upon herself to explain exactly what had happened to anyone who asked, and she hadn't left anything out. I was a little nervous about that, but apparently the message that got out wasn't so much centered on how much the situation had been my fault as on how I had single-handedly taken down the Gray One. Not exactly the message I wanted, but it'd do. So Sarah was building at least some of the watch's reputation on my back. I could deal with that. It wasn't as if it'd have enough time to become a burden.

And though Sarah was working overtime cleaning

up after this, she wasn't as driven as before. I thought Alison had more to do with that than our experiences out on Lovells, but maybe that time she'd spent blind had given Sarah a new appreciation for what she had.

Rena and I were on better terms. We wouldn't be going out clubbing again—that was over, and there was too much space between us now—but we met occasionally for coffee (on my part) and cigarettes (on hers), usually out by the harbor. The cold wind coming off the sea did a lot to clear out the detritus between us, and a lot of those meetings ended up being long stretches of companionable silence.

"I still don't want anything to do with the kind of *bruja* shit you get into," Rena said, one afternoon in early December. The hotel behind us was decked out in twinkly lights and green banners, and the coffee shop had tried to sell me a mocha-ginger-nog latte. I'd glared the barista into silence and gotten something that resembled my usual road tar instead, even if it did have happy reindeer on the cup. Rena just had her cigarettes—I suspected that this was the only time she let herself smoke now. One bad habit to go with a bad influence. "But I like being unprepared even less."

"I can understand that." Even though I was unprepared most of the time, I'd only gotten used to it; I hadn't gotten to like it at all. "I can tell you what I know, if you want."

"You think I want that? Fuck." She took another drag off her cigarette, exhaling smoke and steam and staring out into the harbor. Today the clouds were low and heavy, a flat line of gray hanging overhead, stretching out over the airport and the islands. Neither of us could see the line of Lovells from here, but both of us had our faces turned toward it.

Through the end of November, the snows had held off, giving way to rain or bitter cold or just the endless near-freezing, never-quite-winter days that November was famous for. December hadn't decided to alter that pattern just yet. I was grateful for that, at least; when the snow started in, my days with Mercury would dwindle down to nothing, and though I supposed I didn't need January's rent, the thrift my mother had ground into me meant that I wanted to go as long as I could without losing a source of income.

Rena shook her head and sighed. "Just warn me. When you can."

I took another sip of reindeer coffee and made a face. "I will. But . . ." I glanced down at the marina, the floating platforms, the boats swathed up in plastic for the winter. Tessie had moved hers upriver, and if she'd minded the excursion, I hadn't heard about it yet. "There's something you ought to know."

"You lie to me again and I'll tip you into the goddamn harbor."

I snorted. "And I'd deserve it. No, it's just . . . there are lies you tell by not saying anything, you know? So I . . . I figure you ought to know this. Because while I'll warn you of what I can, I'm only going to be able to do so for a little while."

Rena turned to look at me, but I didn't meet her eyes. Instead I turned toward the scaffolding that had replaced the charred remains of the bridge house, and I told her about midwinter. I sketched in the details of why—the Hunt, the horn that I'd carried, the price to pay. At first she looked like she didn't believe me, then, as I fell silent, her expression turned to outright anger. "Jesus Christ, Evie! That's just a couple of weeks from now!"

"Two and a half." Not that I was counting the days. In fact, I'd made a point of getting rid of the calendars in my office.

"Well, what the—that doesn't make any sense! Why would he punish you, if you're the one who gave it back?"

"Because—" Because gods and demigods didn't follow the same kind of logic that humans did, or when they did, it inevitably had a sting to it. "Because a price has to be paid, and by using the Horn,

I usurped a power that wasn't mine. You don't get to come back from that unscathed. You just don't."

"Bullshit. You could find a way—"

I shook my head. Funny, how much easier it was to take these questions now, now that I'd gotten my own shouting and raging over with. "That's not how it works, Rena. Maybe for magicians like Roger, or Deke—or even the little ones in Sarah's community watch. They're all good at getting out of the consequences. But someone has to take these things seriously. I'm sorry. This is just one of those things."

She stared at me, then cursed and chucked her cigarette into the harbor. "So why aren't you off spending all your cash, going to Vegas, whatever it is people do when they know they've only got a little time left?"

I shrugged. "I don't really want to." Yeah, I wanted to cling to life, hold on to these things with both hands and never let go—but I didn't want to do that by drowning in excess. There was enough joy to be found in making my rounds, in hunting for lost books and missing keys, in coming home to Nate's place to curl up with him, in slow mornings and late nights. Maybe that was setting my sights too low, maybe I was just frittering away my time, but this too felt right.

For the first time I thought I realized why my mother had kept her illness secret for a long time, why she'd kept working, why she'd enjoyed the last few months in her own way. Maybe what I'd done over the last few weeks was a tribute of sorts.

"Shit." Rena shook her head and gave me a quick, one-armed hug. "This doesn't get you out of anything, you realize."

"I know." I punched her in the shoulder. "But thanks."

I'd told Rena. I didn't tell Sarah, because she'd have turned her brain inside out trying to find a loophole. Rena knew there were sometimes things you couldn't do anything about, and even if she didn't like it, she was used to it. Sarah knew a thousand ways of arguing and a thousand ways of searching, and she'd have spent the weeks trying to find a solution and failing, and she'd have taken it on herself when it finally happened.

Besides, if I told Sarah, she'd tell Katie. And I couldn't do that to her. Already, I was wary that she'd see something, that her Sight would catch some of what was headed my way. But it didn't seem to have, yet, at least.

We'd figured out an arrangement with her and Nate and Sarah: no scrying in the house or anywhere that someone could track her to (and that included school, because the one thing her school didn't need was scary adepts waiting outside to see where that last scrying had come from), scrying only with Sarah or Nate on hand, and never on any of her peers. New rules, new approaches to the whole matter. I'd thought the restrictions harsh, but Katie had been spooked by the monsters that had come out of the woodwork, and she didn't question them. I couldn't blame her for turning her Sight elsewhere for now.

I even called up the seer enclave and pretty much leaned on them to find a safe way to teach her, but they stalled, telling me not till the next equinox at least. I didn't ask why—you don't, with seers, unless you want one of the really crazy answers—but marked it down and made sure Nate had the number.

Yes. There was Nate too.

We stayed most nights together, either on the cramped bed in his tiny apartment or, when Katie stayed over with Sarah and Alison, on the lumpy futon in my office, and he didn't mind that I tangled up the sheets when I dreamed of running, or that I woke up muttering about the Red Sox. (I didn't tell him that he did the same on occasion.) We made love, slow and languorous, reveling in the touch of skin and the scent of sweat, or quick and wild, clinging to each other as if we meant to fuse together, or breaking up halfway through to a flood of laughter as one or both of us proved inconveniently ticklish.

The night after the fight on Lovells, I told him about what he'd done, the soul returned to me, and how I'd used it to destroy Dina—and that I hadn't used it to sever the Hunt's hold on me. "So I guess you were right about me having some kind of death wish," I ended, drawing my knees up till I was a little ball sitting on his bed. "I'm sorry, Nate. I had my chance, and I threw it away."

Nate was silent for a long time, but eventually he sat up and put his arm around me. "If you hadn't," he said in my ear, "you wouldn't be Evie. Infuriating as you are." He kissed me, and eventually we lay back down together, but it was still a long time before either of us could relax enough for sleep.

I didn't want to go. But December rolled in, and the carols blared from every store, and the days shortened to thin gray heartbeats. And on Midwinter Eve, I walked out to Boston Common. There were a few holdouts on the Frog Pond, attempting to skate through the first flakes of the first real snow of the season, but picturesque or not, the carolers who'd staked out the best spots had disappeared into the local Dunkin' Donuts for hot chocolate. A giant spruce tree loomed over the square where I'd once met Deke, where I'd begun hunt after hunt.

I put my hands in the pockets of my coat and closed my eyes, turning my face up to the snow. The flakes were so large they thumped softly against my skin, but they didn't muffle scent the way they muffled sound. The pattern of the city spread out around me, intricate at every level and unmappable even to me, brilliant like Celtic knotwork expanded into every dimension and whole, unshadowed, for this moment at least, if not forever. And familiar, close and familiar . . .

I smiled without opening my eyes. "Come to see me off?"

"You could call it that," Nate said. His footsteps creaked on the new snow, and the warm scent of him curled close around me. I opened my eyes and grinned at him. "I'm not yet convinced, you know," he added. "They might still change their minds."

"I knew it. Ditch your curse and immediately you retreat to the world of the rational. Not that I blame you." I nudged him with my elbow, and he nudged back. He'd left his hat at home, and snow caught in his hair, not yet melting. "Katie hasn't guessed, has she?"

He shrugged. "Hard to tell. She's with Aunt Venice for the weekend; I told them I was doing some last-minute shopping. She asked if you'll be joining us for Christmas."

I was silent a moment. That hurt. "I'm not really good at Christmas, Nate. Even without this."

"I wondered. But I don't think she's seen anything."

"That's something, at least. She and Sarah . . . I was most afraid they'd try to stop me. I mean, it's not as if—" I stopped. "I don't *want* to go, you understand."

"But you don't argue with demigods." He shook his head. "Evie, you argue with damn near everyone else."

"I don't!" Nate gave me a look, and I sighed. "Okay. Okay, bad answer. But this is for real, Nate. This is . . . The undercurrent makes such a big deal about being transient. Magic washes so many things away. I think . . . I think that's what turned the Gray Ones into something like Dina. Magic shouldn't be the debased thing we have in the undercurrent. It shouldn't be—shouldn't be the sort of thing you can get out of with some handwaving and a correct sacrifice." I'd told Katie there had been no such thing as a Golden Age of magic. Maybe so. Maybe it was just how you looked at it, or how you used it.

He didn't answer, only put his arm around me. We circled the hill, toward the field where in summer bands played and endless soccer games took place. The trees blocked most sound, and I had to concentrate to hear the traffic close by.

"That's why I gave the Horn back in the first place, Nate. I can't just use magic as a shortcut." That was what Roger did, and Patrick, and the Fiana . . . the magicians who approached it as just another tool, one more trick to get themselves out of trouble, a get-out-of-jail-free card. "I have to accept the consequences. One of them was taking care of the city. The other is this." I stopped and turned to face him. "Do you understand?"

Nate looked at me for a long moment, a strange little smile tugging at the corner of his lips, as if he'd just remembered something funny and couldn't tell me the joke because it would hurt me somehow. "You know," he said, "if we . . . if things had ever settled down to the point where no one was trying to kill either of us, I'd thought about making this a little more official. Between us."

I shook my head. "Going by the last year, 'people trying to kill us' is kind of the default setting. It doesn't get more settled. Not with us."

"Yeah, I should have figured that." He dislodged snow from his hair, shaking it from the tips of his fingers. "Yes. I understand what you mean. More than you know."

"Then do me a favor and kiss me quick, because I can't hear traffic and we should have come around the other side of the hill two minutes ago."

He glanced past me to where the asphalt path we'd followed petered out into dirt and then nothing. The trees above us were still the great oaks of the Common—if I carved an initial into one now, I'd be able to find it the next morning. Well, *I* wouldn't have. But someone else would. But the ground wasn't the ground of the Common anymore, and the only sound was the hush of falling snow. The remaining glow was partly streetlight and partly reflection, that pinkish cast of light that lingers over every hill in this kind of snowfall.

I held out my hand to Nate, and he took it, his fingers cool and human against mine. With the touch came a soft call above us like a flock of geese, distant at first but growing. "There are letters," I said, rushing my words now. "You've got a key to my office; they're on my desk, signed and stamped and everything. For Sarah and Rena and, and my father, and there's one for Katie too—" And there was one for Nate himself, but he wouldn't need to know that till he found it.

"I'll take care of them," he promised.

I nodded and folded my other hand around his. *You should leave,* I wanted to say. But I couldn't make myself let him go.

The cry of the Gabriel Hounds rose to a halloo, and the snow shivered, as if someone had tapped the other side of the sky. The scent of frost rose up around me, heavy with dead leaves and darkness and the end of the year, and with it came the Hunt.

Every Hunt.

The Gabriel Hounds, in their perpetually shifting shapes, crept through the trees to ring me. I'd swear one of them was wagging its tail. *And here you are,* one said.

For our appointment, said another.

We missed you, said a third, and somehow it managed to be both endearing and threatening. I laughed; what else could I do?

Shapes appeared in the snow, manifesting in the spaces between flakes, creating themselves as they approached. A man all in gray with a crown of steel, riding a horse that was barely more real than he, paced out from between the closest trees. Next to him stood another king, though this one went uncrowned and wore a tunic that had no seam. Behind him walked a grizzled man with one eye who seemed to stare at Nate first, though his expression was so stony as to be unreadable. To my left a broad, grinning woman on a huge horse chuckled; to my right walked another woman, glimmering between brilliant white and shadow gray, her face perpetually invisible. And ahead of me, back so far in the trees that he might have been one of their shadows, stood a man half again my height with a profile that was anything but human and a branching rack of horns like the king of stags.

And more, more from between every pair of trees, till even this scrap of otherworld that mirrored the Common groaned with the pressure of so many figures, mythic and folkloric and plain fictional, who claimed a space here. Who claimed a piece of me in return for the power I'd called on.

"You are ready?" one of them, or maybe all of them, said. I drew a deep breath, then started to work my hand free of Nate's.

He let go first. "I fought to get her soul back," he said, and for a moment I thought he was talking to me and referring to someone else. "I gave up my birthright to save her. Does anyone here deny it?"

The assembled Hunters remained silent. I thought I saw the one-eyed one smile for a moment, but it was gone with the swiftness of a falling blade.

Nate took another breath, his word puffing into clouds in the air. "Then that gives me a claim here tonight as well. More, what she did, she did to save me, and so I share in her blame as well. Does anyone here deny it?"

"Nate," I said, "what are you doing? Don't—"

You're the one who was our prey, said one of the Hounds. *The one who escaped. That happens rarely.* It licked its chops with a long, black-spotted tongue.

He has a claim, another said—I thought it might be the one who'd seemed most glad to see me, but it was hard to tell.

"Then listen." Nate looked down at me, and though he swallowed before speaking, his voice was steady. "She had the power to get out of this. And she didn't. Does that count for nothing?"

The assembled Hunters didn't move. The Hounds milled about us, unhappy. *The Hunt must run.*

"But after her?"

You'd offer another quarry? the closest one rumbled.

"That's none of my choice," Nate said evenly, meeting its gaze.

To my shock, the Hound was the first to look away. "Nate, what are you doing?"

"Where she goes, I go," he said simply.

"*What?*" I stumbled away from him, as if insanity might be catching. "Nate, you can't be serious, you can't—" Any other circumstances, and I'd have been touched; there was even a silly, selfish part of me that leaped to its feet and danced. But not here, not now, and not Nate!

"Evie," he said, and the way he said my name made me catch my words short. "Do you trust me?"

Of all the questions to ask me . . . but that was one thing I'd learned. I did trust him. I had to trust him to do what was right for him. But oh, Katie, I couldn't take him away . . . "I do," I said. "But—"

"Then trust me." He held out his hand.

I let out my breath shakily and took his hand. "Okay," I said. "We'll do this the way we did before. I held them off once, I can do it again. You, run."

"You will both run," said one of the Hunters—the hatchet-faced man with a spear, wearing clothes that were one step up from pelts stitched together. "And we will decide." He raised a horn to his lips, a cracked, curled thing the color of sour milk. All around us, the Hunters of the Wild Hunt raised their own horns, steel or jeweled or curved ramshorn, and the air shuddered and turned silver.

"Oh, hell," I said. "It was worth it." Nate nodded.

The call, the Horn's cry, went out in a chorus like the note that summoned Creation, and I took off, Nate's hand in mine. Around us, the Gabriel Hounds milled, charged, ran behind us—

—and around us, and all about us—

—and *with* us.

The Hunt raged about us and swallowed us up, and

though we ran, we did not run as the quarry. We ran as hunters, as hounds and huntsmen among them, as part of the Hunt itself.

It was gift and punishment both; to lose my autonomy in this flight, to be used as I had used the Horn, to be part of the great chaos of which this was only one manifestation.

I raised my hands and let out a yell, and it came out as a halloo of a hound, a cry comparable to any my great ancestor might have made in whatever form. Nate snarled, and the Hounds roared in return, *not bad for once-prey, now part of our timeless company.* Horsemen—or maybe it was one horseman, or maybe we rode horses that were made of nothing but the chill force of the northern wind—charged about us, in silence or clamor, in both, the many Hunts all taking their turn, as they had not for so long. More than the Horn had been freed when I returned it.

There was no time in this Hunt. Only the endless Midwinter night, the sky thick with snow, brilliant with stars, endlessly dark with only the moon to light it. We charged after a stag as pale as a ghost, after a flock of sheep unlucky enough to have found their way out on this of all nights, after a drunken band of students who would find one another huddled in haystacks in the morning and swear never to speak of this, after a golden glowing ball that made the hair on the backs of my arms sizzle.

We were fury and joy and chaos incarnate, and we were none of these. Nate and I ran, humans caught up in the Hunt, and if I had had any space to think I would have thought that yes, he knows this, this is the part of his curse that was no curse at all. This was the joy of letting go.

But I had no word for that. Instead I caught him as we ran and pressed a cold and passionate kiss against his lips, and we were off again, two of us, woman and man, hound and hunter, running through till the end of time.

Dawn came sudden and soon, the first lights of the new half of the year leaking in around the edges of the Hounds' silver road. I barely recognized the trees of the Common till we were in the midst of them, and Nate didn't seem to pay any attention as he slumped against one. I sank to my knees, oblivious to the Gabriel Hounds whispering canine farewells as they nosed about me, and my skin steamed where it touched the fallen snow.

One of the Hunters remained: the great shape back in the trees, the man crowned with a king stag's horns. "*This is what we claim, and what we give,*" he said, the words not so much heard as written into the space behind my eyes. "*For the presumption of using the Horn, and the deed of returning it. That you run with us, once and every Midwinter, from now until the end.*"

I stared at him through the trees, seeing only snow, only winter, exhilarated and terrified. But what had been a shape was now only a shadow, and the Common, and the first noises of early traffic on Beacon Street.

Nate crawled over to me, leaving a long track of dirt smeared against the snow, and sagged at my side. He tried to speak, but shook his head and leaned against me instead. "Nate," I said finally, and saying a human word—saying a name, a name that did not immediately call its bearer—felt unbearably strange. "Nate, did you know? That they would—"

He nodded, then shook his head. "I guessed. And I hoped." He struggled to his feet, snow sliding off him in great damp chunks. "But this—now till the end? What end? What does that—Evie, are we—"

"I don't know." I drew another breath, and it came out in a laugh—a joyous laugh, for the sheer glee of being alive, for the world of wonders. For midwinters to come. "I don't know."

Acknowledgments

Although I'd envisioned it since finishing *Spiral Hunt, Soul Hunt* proved very difficult to write. The very end of the book had always been set in my mind, though it shifted time and place and circumstance, and once I'd set everything up at the end of *Wild Hunt*, in theory all I had to do was write my way there. I'm ashamed to admit that I thought it would be an easy task.

Most of the credit for bringing the reality closer to the idea (or, when the idea was lousy to begin with, scrapping that entirely) can go to the members of BRAWL. The draft they critiqued bore only a superficial resemblance to the novel I'd originally dreamed up, and even then it was still a mess. They saw where I wanted to go, showed me how I'd set my path wrong, and cleared the way for me. Thanks as always to my agent Shana Cohen and my editor Kate Nintzel, both of whom were very patient with the time it took to wrangle this book into shape.

A few notes on sources: Venetia, Meda, and the other "flinty kind of women" as Dar Williams puts it, were inspired in no small part by the New England women I've known over the years.

The Quabbin Reservoir is a beautiful and strange place, particularly when you remember that there are indeed four towns beneath it. There are more stories to be told there, I'm certain.

To my knowledge, there are no tunnels under the harbor from Georges Island. As for the one leading from Lovells Island, it led in a different direction entirely, and it has long since collapsed.

Last of all, I'd like to thank my husband, who encouraged me through the first stages of the book, hiked beside the Quabbin with me, listened to each new plot twist and then each new reason why that wouldn't work, and then patiently sat me down in front of the computer again. Without him, there would be no book, and likely no author either.

If you haven't read the first installment in the Evie Scelan series, turn the page for an excerpt from

SPIRAL HUNT

"I loved, loved, loved this book. I picked it up before bed and couldn't put it down. Fantastic, moving, thrilling—deeply thoughtful—and beautifully crafted . . . [T]his was one of the best books I've read in a long time."

—*New York Times* best-selling author Marjorie M. Liu

"Ronald plays with the supernatural as though it's a variation of the Irish hard men who ran mobs at the turn of the last century in places like Boston and New York City . . . Ronald has done a terrific job with the Celtic mystical matter here, blending folklore with things she's made up so that it all feels whole and complete. Strong characterization combines with a plot that's fast-paced and keeps the reader guessing, and what else do you need for an entertaining summer's read?"

—Charles de Lint, *Fantasy & Science Fiction*

"[A] fun adventure, a promising start to a new series and a solid first novel."

—*Locus*

"I found Margaret Ronald's *Spiral Hunt* refreshing for a number of reasons. [Evie Scelan's supernatural ability is] a great engine for driving a plot, in that it makes Scelan herself the object of desire for many, and it also gives her a good deal of power . . . [Scelan] suffers betrayals and false trails and a great deal of peril with wit and courage, which makes for an engaging narrative. One thing in particular that I found very attractive about this book is that Ronald concentrates entirely on Celtic mythology while building her world. For a book set in Boston, this makes a good deal of sense—obviously, the Fair Folk emigrated at the same time that Boston's other Irish arrived—and it also provides a pleasing sense of cohesiveness to the worldbuilding."

—Elizabeth Bear, *Realms of Fantasy*

One

No one ever calls in the middle of the night if they have good news. You'd think I'd remember that and not answer the phone after, say, midnight. But I'm as trained as any of Pavlov's dogs, and so when the phone shrilled I picked it up before coming fully awake. "This is Scelan," I mumbled into the receiver.

"Evie?" That woke me up. Since high school, only close friends have called me Evie. The man on the other end of the phone cleared his throat. "This is— Okay, you remember Castle Island? I kept branches in my car. Green ones, still living. Organic matter. Right?"

"I don't know what you're—" I stopped, memories of an ill-spent summer in South Boston flooding back around me like smoke from a bonfire. "Jesus. *Frank?*"

"Don't say it! Christ, I forgot how stupid you could be about some things."

Definitely Frank. Jerk. "Thanks very much. What the hell happened to you, Frank? I thought you were—" *Not dead*, I thought; *but as good as, when it came to this town.*

He didn't even hear the question. "I haven't— I'm pretty sure this line is okay, but I can't say the same for yours, and I know they'll be watching; they didn't expect me to get away."

"Frank. Slow down." I reached for the light, flailed a moment, then sat up. My legs had gotten tangled up in a big knot of sheets. "Why are you calling me?" I asked.

"I've got good reason—" The phone line squealed as a booming voice interrupted him, laughing and shouting guttural words that definitely weren't English. I held the phone away from my ear until Frank's voice returned. "Shut up! Look, Evie, I know we didn't part on the best of terms—"

"You called me a stupid bitch and said I deserved whatever *they* had for me. And then you disappeared."

"Yeah, well, I know what I did wrong last time. I'm not staying around here—it's gone too far for that, and I can't . . ." He paused, and the booming voice muttered again, incomprehensibly. "Shut up! I'm getting out. Really getting out this time."

"Yeah. Sure." When half of your business contacts are addicts, it gives you a certain perspective on anyone who says he's quit. Frank had quit before, sure, but he'd been a lot younger and less steeped in the undercurrent of Boston. And I'd helped to bring that crashing down, naive as I was. "Look, Frank, if you're calling me in hopes of a quick screw for old time's sake, forget it. I can't help you get out of the city other than the mundane ways, and you know those are watched."

"I know. Danu's tits, I know." He fell silent, and memory dredged forth an image so strong I could see what he must be doing: rubbing one hand over his face as if to clear the slate of his emotions. Of course, he'd be older now, but the gesture was one I unwillingly knew well. "Look, Evie, I know you probably hate me."

"I don't hate you, Frank." It was more complicated than that, and everything had happened so long ago that it didn't matter now. Which made me wonder why I still mattered to *him*. "I just didn't expect to hear from you again."

He hesitated. "Yeah. Well. I don't need help or anything, but I had to let you know that I was going. I can make it out this time."

"Don't boast about it. Just get out." I tugged the sheets back into some semblance of order, then sighed, remembering bonfires and the smell of crushed greenery. "Good luck."

"Luck has no part in this."

I nearly dropped the phone. It was the booming voice again—but now that I was a little more awake, I recognized it. It was Frank's voice: the same slight lisp from a broken tooth, the same timbre, only pushed down to the bottom of his range—but somehow I knew it was no longer Frank speaking.

"He speaks to you to say farewell. I speak to you to warn you, for I may have damned you with my words." The phone felt unnaturally warm, warmer than my hands could make it. For a second I smelled a trace of something like dust and dry stone, there and gone so fast it left only the memory of recognition.

Impossible. Even I couldn't catch a scent over the tenuous connection a phone provided. But the hairs on the back of my neck tingled, and my breath quickened, as it did when I got the scent before a hunt.

The speaker took a deep, ragged breath. *"But even if I have, I own no shame, for you are needed and by one greater than I."*

"Frank?" I said.

"Hound," said the voice, and ice ran down my back. Frank had never known I was called that. *"Hound, watch for a collar. The hunt comes . . ."*

Nothing more. I held on to the phone long after the dial tone of a broken connection crooned in my ear.

"Frank, you son of a bitch," I said at last. "Couldn't you have stayed dead?"

Two

One of my clients called just as I was on my way out the door the next morning: the little old lady who'd asked me to find her aunt's old recipe book. It had been in a junk store in Jamaica Plain, at the bottom of three cases of similar books, most of which were meant for the Dumpster. I'd taken on the job thinking it could be some quick work to go toward my rent, and forgotten the first rule of bargaining: don't argue with a nice little old lady.

"Yes, I understand your point of view," I said as I unlocked my bike, cell phone jammed between chin and shoulder. "But the fact remains that you did sign the contract for expert retrieval and recovery systems—"

A spate of squawking on the other end managed to convey that I charged too much, was a heartless monster for taking advantage of a senior citizen, and must have had some kickback deal with the junk-store owner in order to find her book so quickly. I rubbed at my temples, thinking that I should have taken my time finding the damn thing after all. "Ma'am, I'm sorry, but I'll have to call you back. I have another client on the line."

It wasn't quite a lie, I told myself as I dialed Mercury Courier; it just left out several major facts, the first being that my business relationship with Mercury was completely unrelated to my other work. "Hi, Tania? This is Genevieve. Where do you need me to go?"

I could hear Tania rustling through the mountain of papers on her desk. I'd only seen it once, but the image had burned itself into my mind. "Genevieve? Honey, you're not on shift just yet."

"I always work the Tuesday morning—"

"Schedule changes. The new system has you for the eleven-to-eight shift today."

"Is this the same new system that wanted me to run a package out to Worcester?"

"There's still a few bugs to work out, honey. Call me at eleven and I'll send you out."

I clicked the phone shut and stuffed it away. So much for getting work done early. On the other hand, that meant I had some time to work for my other job . . . or at least to see what the hell had been up with Frank last night.

There wasn't any address listing for him, which was small surprise. Of the other F. McDermots in the phone book, though, one had an address in Southie that I recognized from way back. I got my courier bag, in case Tania called with yet another schedule change, and headed out.

Rush hour was well under way, with the coffee-propelled masses of commuters already filling the streets. I slid out into traffic, darting between two SUVs and a truck to make it into the far lane. Cars honked, but mostly out of jealousy.

I wasn't the only one zipping through the lanes this morning. The bright weather had brought other cyclists out, and there'd be more as June wore on, until the hot spells descended and commuters could no longer ride to work without arriving soaked in sweat. Today, though, the air was crisp and cool. Perfect hunting weather.

I paused at a light near an orange-fenced yard of cement monoliths: the remnants of the Central Artery highway, now demolished as the Big Dig brought the highways underground. Two high school kids and a woman walking a pair of enthusiastic Labradors stopped at the light as well, next to an old professor-looking guy in a tweed jacket that'd seen better days. One of the Labs lurched toward me, tail whipping back and forth, and the woman hauled on its leash to keep from falling over. The man next to her chuckled, seemingly content to just enjoy the sunlight. He didn't even bother to cross as the light changed, just stood there in the sun, waving what looked like a wide-mouthed pipe made of dull metal.

I'd gotten about twenty yards down the road before I realized he'd been holding a silver sieve.

I yanked the bike into a U-turn, bumping up onto the sidewalk and veering around a stroller full of kids. The man didn't notice me as I hurtled back to his corner, so intent was he on the sharp-edged morning shadows.

The bike stopped at the curb. I didn't; I leaped off, dragged it by its crossbar over the curb, and snatched the sieve from the man's hand. "Did you catch any?" I demanded.

He made a startled, squeaking noise as I took the sieve, like a baby deprived of a toy. "Wha?"

I leaned in close, until the brim of my helmet tapped his forehead. "Did you catch any?" I repeated, waving the sieve under his nose.

A few of the people at the crosswalk gave us baffled looks. He returned them shamefacedly, sinking his hands in his pockets. "No," he whined as the light changed and the tide of pedestrians flowed past us again.

"Good." I smashed the sieve against the handlebars of my bike, tearing the fine mesh. He cried out, as if I'd hit him with it. I glanced up at him, and he fell silent. "This is no good," I said, jamming the broken sieve into a nearby trash bin for emphasis. "Hell, even if it were, this is no way to go about it."

"I needed it," said the shadowcatcher sullenly. "I needed a locus."

"Yeah, well, did you ever happen to think that maybe those people need their shadows too? Maybe more than you need your goddamn locus?" I sniffed the air around him on the off chance that he was lying. There was always a chance that he'd succeeded and some poor bastard had walked away missing part of his shadow, unknowingly fated to go nuts for a while, or be unable to see in color for a few weeks.

The shadowcatcher shoved his hands further into his pockets, hunching over so that his chin disappeared into the folds of his collar. He wasn't that old, I realized; not more than forty. Which meant that he must have fallen very fast.

If it'd been anything else, I'd have tried to send him to detox. But detox is no good when people don't believe what you're addicted to exists.

Still, I couldn't just walk away from him. "Christ. Here." I pulled a scrap of paper from my pocket and scrawled three names on it. "The Buddhist place is downtown. The Carmelites are in Roxbury; even if they can't let you stay in the nunnery they'll have some place for you. Society of St. John is across the river; that's best if you really think you'll relapse. Being across water helps." None of them could cleanse him, not unless he outright asked, but the bindings around each place would keep off the worst of it. There were a few other places that might actively try to wean him off the stuff, but of the people that ran them I only trusted Sarah, and the ambient magic at her shop would be no help to someone still in denial.

"Fuck you," the shadowcatcher said, but he took the paper.

"Get some help. Shadowcatching, man, that's the bottom of the goddamn ladder." I wrangled my bike back into a reasonable position. "This is going to kill you."

The shadowcatcher grinned. He was missing two

front teeth, and one had been replaced with wood—not rowan, of course. Probably something he'd been told was mistletoe. "I'm not sure I care anymore."

As I rode off, a faint reek of overturned trash followed me. I didn't turn back, because I knew I'd see him scraping through the refuse, searching for his sieve.

Aside from when work called me there, I hadn't been back to Southie in years. It had changed, and it was hard to say whether that was for the better. *Different*, I thought, and left it at that.

I made my way to the western end of South Boston and chained my bike to a house railing right in the middle of a changing neighborhood. Across the street, another triple-decker had been torn down, and billboards announced new condos coming to the space in August. August seemed an optimistic date; the house's frame was up but still skeletal, and the carpenters didn't seem in any hurry. A couple of them eyed me warily, but stopped when their boss came over.

Some of the other houses on this side of the street also looked redone; I didn't remember seeing more than a postage stamp of a front yard throughout most of my childhood, but these had enough for a little garden. A mutt was chained up in one yard, and I clucked my tongue at him. He perked up and ambled over to lick my hand, then settled down to some serious napping.

The houses across the way probably hadn't been renovated in years but kept a dignified facade, like a sick man determined to put a good face on everything. Two of them had little gardens out front, one with roses, the other with tomatoes, but the one I went up to remained bare. I glanced down at the gravel, once raked but now in disarray, and decided I'd probably come to the right place.

A woman in her early sixties came to the door when I rang. She gave me a suspicious, pinch-lipped look through the screen door. "Mrs. McDermot?" I said.

"Yes." Her expression didn't change.

"My name's Genevieve Scelan. I used to know your son Frank."

A bewildering range of expressions contorted her face when I said his name: shame, hope, anger, bitterness. She stuck with the last. "He doesn't live here."

"I know that, I—"

"Beth? Who is it?" A tall man emerged into the hall and came to stand beside her. I fought down a wave of déjà vu; the resemblance between Frank and his father was so strong that it could have been an older version of Frank in front of me, minus the junkie hollows. "Who's this, now?"

I steadied myself. "Mr. McDermot, your son called me last night." His eyebrows twitched, and the same mix of emotions raced over his face, settling into uncertain sorrow. "I was a—a friend of his a long time ago. The call I got was—was kind of weird, and so I was wondering if you might know where he is or if he's okay."

"He doesn't live here," Frank's mom repeated angrily, as if that were my fault.

Hell, it might be, I thought.

"We haven't been in contact with him in a long time," Frank's dad said. "You probably know more than we do about whether he's okay."

He isn't okay, I thought. *He's decidedly not okay.*

On a hunch, I sniffed. Most of the smells were plain normal, a sure sign that Frank had not been here: dust, old furniture, sawdust from across the street, and a lingering damp reek. And sweat. Frank's mom glared at me, but she was sweating.

"I'm sorry to bother you," I said over the sound of a car pulling up to the sidewalk behind me, and the nervous scent from her doubled. "Thanks very much."

"Wait," Frank's dad said. Frank's mom glanced from him to the street, then me. She took her husband's arm, but he wasn't paying attention to her. "If you do find anything, please let us know. Please."

"I will," I said, and it wasn't quite a lie. If Frank had gotten further into the undercurrent, it might be kinder not to let them know.

I turned and nearly walked straight into the man coming up the stairs. He stumbled back and caught hold of the railing to keep from losing his balance, and the scent of his cologne hit me like a damp pillow. He was about my height, considerably broader across the shoulders, and bald as an egg, with that prickly look around the edges that suggested he'd shaved it rather than display a changing hairline. It suited him well, though. If he'd looked a little scruffier, I'd have taken him for a bouncer in some high-class club; as it was, it was clear that he was much higher on the social ladder. "Excuse me," he said.

"Excused," I said through the fog of scent. "Sorry."

He gave me a curious look as I slipped past him, but turned back to the McDermots.

I glanced back at their door as I unlocked my bike. The bald man spoke quietly to Frank's parents, who opened the screen door and ushered him in. Frank's mom, no longer smelling nervous (even though the cologne still dulled my nose, I could scent that much) took his arm, and his father closed the door behind them.

Strange. I left my bike where it was for the moment and walked over to the bald man's car. It was expensive, but dirty, and that was the extent of what I could tell about it.

A dog howled nearby as I was writing down the license number. A second later, another followed suit. I looked up to see the mutt in the yard two doors up the street sitting on his haunches and sniffing at the air. He bared his teeth at nothing, then yelped and scrambled away as if he'd been hit, tail between his legs. "What's the matter—" I began, and then it hit me too.

A blast of damp gunpowder scent struck me in the face, and with it came a screeching in my ears like ten subway trains coming to a halt. I threw up my hands in an ineffective guard, but the worst had passed, like a ripple in the air, over me and then gone. As I stood there panting, the howls started up again, this time from behind me as the ripple spread over the city, scaring the hell out of every dog it hit. *Like a dog whistle with a blast radius*, I thought, *or the opposite of a dog whistle.*

The mutt cowered against the closest fence, scraping at it as if to dig his way out. I shushed him and stroked his head, and he calmed down enough to lick my hand a second time. "Okay," I said, more to myself than the dog, "anyone want to tell me what the hell that was?"

"Jesus Christ. Is that Evie Scelan?"

I froze. The voice had come from behind me, and it was loud enough to carry to the next city block. "Who's asking?" I said, and turned.

The boss from the construction site edged around the fence and grinned at me. "Bet you don't recognize me. Hey, I wouldn'ta recognized you either if it wasn't for that black braid you got."

Involuntarily, one hand went to my braid. I was self-conscious about it, but it kept my hair out of my eyes and out from under the bike helmet. Even if it did make me look like I had an electrical cable stapled to the back of my head.

"Yeah. You still got it, huh? Looks like you made up for all the hair I lost." He rubbed one ruddy hand over his thinning hair. "Hey, remember when I played that trick on you in chemistry?"

I remembered an incident with a Bunsen burner and a lab partner who liked laughing at me. I also remembered the six days' detention I got for banging the culprit's head against the lab table. Half of the reason I'd done it was for the stink of burnt hair. I hadn't been able to smell anything for a week. "You'd be . . . Billy?"

"Will," he said, turning slightly redder under his sunburn. He jerked his head back toward the workmen. "Don't let these guys hear you call me Billy, okay?"

"Got it." He hadn't been affected by the ripple, I realized, nor had the workmen. The mutt, though, still cowered in a ball at the end of his chain, and I'd broken out in a sweat just from that sound.

And the scent. The scent was unmistakable.

Will grinned, apparently relieved that I wasn't going to bang his head against anything this time. "So what are you up to these days?"

"Not much." I glanced over my shoulder at the McDermots' door and bit back a curse. The bald man was already on his way out, escorted by Frank's dad.

"Waiting for somebody? . . . Hey, you know, there's a bunch of us all from school who get together at this bar downtown. Everyone'd be thrilled to see you."

"I'm sure they would, but this isn't really a good time—" Too late. The bald man had seen me, and his eyes narrowed. "Maybe later?"

"Later's good. Tonight's better. Here; I'll write down the name of the place for you." Billy—Will—took a pen from his shirt pocket and patted at his other pockets, frowning.

"Excuse me." The bald man had paused at the edge of the street, his hands clasped behind his back. "I can't shake the feeling that I know you from somewhere. Are you a local?"

"Ha!" Will grinned at him. "Always shows in the face, don't it, Evie? Yeah, she used to be a local, same as me, but she sure as hell isn't around here near as often as you. I know everyone around here, Evie," he added as he handed me a folded receipt with a name scratched on the back. "Even know this guy, great guy. Carson, right?"

"Corrigan," the bald man corrected, but absently.

I sighed. "Genevieve Scelan," I said, and shook his hand. His palm was strangely uncalloused, with the exception of rough flesh around the ring on his middle finger. It was a plain gold band like a wedding ring, with a pattern of crude spirals scratched into it, and it was just slightly warmer than his skin.

"Scelan?" he said, one eyebrow raised. "I think I may have heard of you, then. Are you . . ." He paused and glanced at Will, who was happily oblivious to any subtleties in the conversation. "Are you sometimes called Hound?"

I took my hand out of his, too aware of how cold my fingers had gone. "Sometimes," I said, and dragged my bike upright.

"Hound?" Will grinned. "What kind of a name is that?"

I got on my bike. "Better than 'Bitch,' " I said, and left before they could snare me further.